WINTER'S ROSE

For my sister, Marissah.

MARIAH DYER

Check out these other books by Mariah Dyer!
Follow her on Facebook or Instagram @MariahDyerAuthor

The Skin Series

SKIN
SHED
SCRAPE
SCORCH
SCAR

The Powers of Torment

Winter's Solstice

Winter's Rose
6

- Chapter 1: Winter
  7
- Chapter 2: Nolan
  15
- Chapter 3: John
  25
- Chapter 4: Winter
  34
- Chapter 5: Nolan
  43
- Chapter 6: John
  51
- Chapter 7: Winter
  61
- Chapter 8: Nolan
  67
- Chapter 9: John
  78
- Chapter 10: Winter
  86
- Chapter 11: Nolan
  94
- Chapter 12: John
  102
- Part 2
  113
- Chapter 13: Winter
  114
- Chapter 14: Nolan
  121

Chapter 15: John 128

Chapter 16: Winter 134

Chapter 17: Nolan 141

Chapter 18 : John 151

Chapter 19: Winter 163

Chapter 20: Nolan 171

Chapter 21: John 181

Chapter 22: Winter 189

Chapter 23: Nolan 193

Chapter 24: John 202

Chapter 25: Winter 212

Chapter 26: Nolan 214

Chapter 27: John 220

Chapter 28: Winter 228

Chapter 29: Nolan 234

Chapter 30: John 242

Chapter 31: Winter
246

About the Author
254

Winter's Rose

Book 2

Chapter 1: Winter

The trails of the community were dark; the moonlight winking through the dense foliage. Shane's shoulders drooped as he pushed aside overgrown branches. He stumbled over his feet; navigating through the roots that cluttered the path. I made sure to keep a short distance from him. Struggling to keep my balance through the exhaustion.

I yawned; frost coating my hand when I covered my mouth.

It was difficult to remember when I'd last had a full night's sleep. Or a recent evening that Shane didn't have to torture himself by saving children. No matter how much John and Eliza encouraged him to rest, he'd soldiered on. Taking into himself the savage disease that had swept through the Scavenger families.

Shane picked up his pace. Hurrying through the dark streets of the Scavenger community. I'd gotten better at keeping up. The muscles in my legs became much more defined in the months since we drove the Highborns from the community.

The trading lot was vacant, as well as the rest of the rough trails that were referred to as 'streets'. It was late, and John would be wondering where I was. I had only been to the Scavenger community a handful of times over the past months. The people who did know me- what I was capable of- where terrified of me.

Luckily, that was only a handful of people. John and Eliza worked hard to keep me a secret from the Scavengers.

Which was why I shouldn't have been there in the first place, but I wasn't about to let Shane go anywhere alone.

"What are you thinking?"

Shane always did that. I wasn't sure why he wanted to know what was going on inside my messed up head. Not even Nolan would ask me what I was thinking.

He never had to. He could read me like a book.

I immediately pushed him to the back of my mind. Pretended the thought never occurred.

"Nothing," I replied out loud and in sign language.

Signing was still more natural to me. Sometimes I signed without even realizing it. Shane never seemed to mind it though. He'd even picked up some of it since we spent so much time together. We were able to have entire conversations in silence, though Shane wasn't fond of the quiet.

"You seem to be lost in thought." Shane glanced back at me; concern glimmering in his eyes.

"Let's just get to the farm."

Shane nodded and picked up the pace again. We kept to the shadows. Avoiding the Scavenger guards that protected the community at night. Ever since we forced the Highborn Militia to leave the community, John was determined to keep them out. Posting full time guards was a matter of necessity now.

John had proven to be an amazing leader for the community. He was busy everyday; overseeing the Scavengers combat training and the security around the boarders of the community. He had even led missions to steal supplies from the Highborn Union warehouses.

He still managed to keep me a secret from the majority of the community as well. I often wondered if that was wise; considering I could take out an entire warehouse of Highborn guards on my own.

John was like my father in that way. He was very protective of me. I couldn't remember ever having a father. Sometimes it was hard for me to understand what that protectiveness meant.

"You never told me how you found out about the sick children."

"Tamara sent word to Eliza with one of the Scavengers," Shane explained gruffly. "Eliza thinks that it's some type of plague."

I nodded in agreement. The sickness had been spreading through the community for weeks now. It kept Shane so busy that he was constantly drained. His ability to heal sickness and injuries took a toll on him.

Shane needed rest, but he was just as stubborn as Nolan.

I winced; blinking back tears at the intrusive thought. Unfortunately, Shane noticed.

"Okay." He stopped walking and turned to face me. "You need to tell me what's wrong."

I shook my head and walked ahead of him.

"It's him, right? Nolan?"

I tried to ignore him as I kept walking. There were sick children in the house in the meadow ahead of us. We needed to get there instead of talking about things that we couldn't change.

I had refused to talk about Nolan- I didn't want to cry. It would be like I was admitting he was truly gone. That I'd never see him again.

I couldn't do that. Not ever.

"Winter." Shane gently grabbed my arm. He flinched; pulling away from me quickly so we wouldn't end up hurting each other. I didn't stop walking until he hurried in front of me; forcing me to halt.

"Why are you ignoring me?"

Because I miss Nolan like crazy. I signed quickly. My expression hard as stone. *And I don't want to talk to you, or to anyone else, about him. I love him. I'm terrified that he is really gone.*

I stopped signing and clenched my fists at my sides. Shane didn't respond right away. We merely stood in the middle of the trees; staring at each other.

"I don't understand when you sign that quickly, Winter."

Yes, I know. I signed slowly. He rolled his eyes.

"Fine, I give up."

Shane turned toward the meadow. His shoulders slumped more noticeably. I didn't think it was possible for him to heal children in this condition, but I knew there was nothing that would stop him from trying.

I took a shaky breath; mentally preparing myself for what we'd find behind that door.

"You're sure you want to go in with me?"

I nodded.

"I can do this alone."

"Yeah right," I scoffed sarcastically. "Like you did last time?"

Last time, he had to use some of my life force or he would've died. After nearly depleting me, he still had to turn three trees to ash and dust. It took both of us three days to recover from it.

Yeah, I definitely wasn't letting him go in there alone.

Shane glared at me before walking up to the door. I didn't blame him for that look. I had changed a lot when Nolan stopped calling. I was rude and distant. Shane was basically the only friend I had now. He didn't deserve my angst.

"Sorry. I could've said that better."

Shane turned to me before knocking on the door and sighed.

"He'll find a way to contact you when he can, Winter. I know it."

I closed my eyes against the agony for a moment, but I didn't reply. Shane didn't believe what he was saying. He thought Nolan was gone. Just like John and Eliza did.

Shane opened the door, and a gruesome odor hit me. I coughed once before covering my mouth and nose. If Shane was bothered by the smell, he didn't show it. He was stronger than I was in more ways than one.

"Shane?" Tamara called feebly from inside the cabin.

I froze in horror.

Tamara was brave and boisterous. The tone coming from her now was extremely disconcerting.

I pushed passed Shane, who seemed to be frozen at the entrance, and couldn't stifle my gasp.

There were seven children lying on the floor of the room. Too quiet. Too still. The slight tension on their faces echoed how much pain they were in. Tamara and Fredrick were nearly dead on their feet; working to care for them.

They had turned their cabin into a sick room. I had never been to their farm before, but I could tell it used to be a nice place.

Now it smelled like literal death. Decay.

I studied the children's faces; recognizing them despite their gaunt features. Three of them were Tamara and Fredrick's own children. The other four were children that Nolan, Shane, and I rescued from the lab all those months ago.

A trickle of relief settled in my gut that Josh and Ben had been sent away from this place. They'd initially come to live with Tamara and Fredrick-

They were so lucky to avoid getting whatever disease this was.

Shane slumped against the doorframe and closed his eyes. Devastation marred his features. I had never seen him do that before. He never despaired like that.

"It's good to see you." Fredrick clapped a hand on Shane's shoulder. He glanced at me as though I was an afterthought. I didn't take it personally. Fredrick had seen me fight the Highborns when we drove them out of our territory. He never got over his fear of me.

Usually when I saw him I tried to smile, but today I ignored him. I was here to help. Not to cajole a traumatized man.

I knelt next to Alex; his breathing labored and short. This plague was unique, and terrifying. No matter how much medicine the Scavengers stole from the Highborn shipments, none of it helped with this sickness.

All I could do was give them ice.

"Poor Alex's momma passed an hour ago." Tamara's lips quivered as she rested her hand on the boy's forehead.

Fredrick rested his hand on Alex's shoulder; his eyes red with tears and exhaustion.

"We're waiting to bury her in the morning."

"How long has Amelia been sick?" Shane asked gruffly.

"Alex came running here the day before yesterday to tell us she was ill. So, probably two or three days. We brought her here, since our own kiddos were under the weather. Thought it'd be easier to help them all at once. Alex succumbed to the sickness after we got them here."

Tamara stopped talking and sobbed. Fredrick's eyes glazed over as he stared at the sick children.

I pointed my hand at a large wooden bowl that sat next to the fireplace. I felt myself change as the air around me grew cold. My blood chilled and my eyes brightened. Icicles formed at the tips of my fingers as the wooden bowl filled with dozens of tiny ice cubes.

"Which one is the sickest?" Shane pushed himself off of the doorframe; stumbling into the room.

"Alex," Tamara whispered as she helped me pack the ice around the sick children. "I think he'll follow his momma soon."

I couldn't think about that, so I let my mind go blank as I worked with Tamara. Fredrick was frozen in shock; staring at his three sick children. I didn't much care for Fredrick, since he seemed to despise me, but I felt bad for him. I couldn't imagine the pain he felt seeing his children in this condition.

I paused to keep an eye on Shane while he held Alex's pasty hand. The veins in Shane's arm turned black; forcing the sickness from

Alex's body. Shane groaned. His skin morphed into an ashy gray hue. His thick hair turned silver before darkening back to blond again.

I had never seen anything like that happen before. Not even when he'd healed twelve people last week. I hurried over to him; grabbing his shoulders before he could fall over.

He refused to let go of Alex's hand.

So stubborn.

"Shane," I gasped hoarsely. "Take a break."

Shane shook his head and gritted his teeth. Alex's eyes fluttered open. He stared up at us in confusion. Shane quickly let go of his hand and slumped against me. His skin was scorching beneath his shirt; burning my hands and my chest.

"I want my mom."

Shane and I merely stared at the poor, sick boy.

I had met Alex's mother, Amelia Spencer, months ago after we brought Alex home to her. Alex had been kidnapped by the Highborns to be used as Dr. Darkwood's lab rat. His mother had insisted on meeting us; the super-powered-teens that rescued her son.

I couldn't believe that she was dead now.

No matter how much I wanted to comfort Alex- I had no idea what to say to him.

"Shane." Alex weakly pushed himself up on his elbows. "Where is she? Where's my mom?"

"We'll talk in a minute, Alex." Shane sat up fully. Taking his weight off of me.

Alex's eyes widened in shock. My heart broke for him, but I couldn't stop to mourn with him over his mother. It was blatantly obvious that he was still sick, but at least he wasn't in danger of imminent death.

"Who's next?"

Tamara stopped packing ice around her daughter, Lizzy, to point at Reed.

"Reed, he's-"

Tamara froze mid-sentence. Her finger trembled. The exhausted woman needed a break. I was about to suggest she lie down while I tended to the children, but Shane grew very still next to me. I glanced at him-

He was staring at Reed. Desperately.

"Reed!" Shane hurried to the boy's side and took his hand. I watched, expecting to see the black veins appear on Shane's fingers and arms.

Nothing happened.

I choked; struggling to hold back the tears.

"Reed!" Shane exclaimed again, his voice breaking. He pressed his fingers to Reed's neck.

Realizing that Reed was dead snapped Fredrick out of his shocked stupor. He quickly checked every child. Making sure that they were still breathing. Tamara stoically kept packing ice around the sick children. Refusing to allow more tears to fall.

Shane calmly took his fingers away from Reed's neck and covered his face with a blanket. He and Reed where close friends. Bonded by countless weeks of torture and tribulation.

My heart shattered into a million pieces as Shane move away from his friend's body.

"I'm going to start from youngest to oldest." Shane knelt next to Tessa. His voice sounded empty, but he appeared to have gathered some strength. Losing one sick friend was a twisted form of motivation.

Tessa's short black hair clung to her sweaty forehead. At the tender age of three she was so tiny and frail. Even after she was rescued, and brought to live with Tamara and Fredrick, she never seemed to gain much weight. She always held a piece of Shane's heart even before they'd escaped Dr. Darkwood.

If I had let myself get close to the children, she would've held a piece of mine too. Unfortunately for me, the further I stayed away from people the better off they were.

I exhaled in relief when Tessa opened her eyes.

"Hey, baby girl." Shane gently wiped the tears from Tessa's cheeks. "Do you feel a bit better?"

Tessa nodded and threw her tiny arms around his neck. He patted her back for a moment and reluctantly pulled her off of him.

"I gotta help the others now." He rewrapped the blanket around her. "I'll sit with you later, yeah."

Tessa nodded tiredly and closed her eyes. She was asleep almost instantly.

As Shane moved on to the next child, I turned toward Alex. His face was pale, but he was still sitting up. He stared at the blanket that covered Reed's body with hollow eyes. He shifted slightly when he noticed me watching him.

"I want my mom." Tears glistened in his eyes.

Those hollow, mournful eyes knew the truth. He knew his mother was dead. Knew that he'd never see her again. Never hear her voice, or feel her arms wrapped around him.

I swallowed the lump in my throat. Even if I'd lived a thousand lives, I'd never have the emotional experience needed to soothe this poor boy's heartbreak.

"Where is her body?"

I knelt next to him. I didn't touch him since I wasn't in control of myself. The last thing he needed was for me to accidentally frost burn his skin.

"Fredrick has taken good care of her. I'm so sorry, Alex." He didn't respond. He tore his gaze from me and stared at Reed's still form again.

"He was my best friend." Alex's broken voice brought more tears to my eyes. "What is this sickness? Why can't Shane take it away?"

Alex didn't expect me to answer him, so I didn't. It seemed like the plague had a mind of it's own with a vendetta against the children and teenagers. A few of the adults got sick, but only if they had a lot of contact with the kids.

I gave Alex an apologetic look and continued packing ice around the sick children. All while keeping a close eye on Shane.

Hours later, Shane and I walked back to Eliza's cabin through the woods. We were so exhausted and heartsick. It was difficult to continue putting one foot in front of the other. Occasionally, Shane would pause to take the life force from a tree. He tried to only do that to the old trees, but sometimes he had to take young ones. Especially if he kept overtaxing himself like he'd been doing.

"I can't believe Reed's gone," Shane muttered as we walked.

The aching pain in his voice made me glance at him. I had never seen Shane cry before, but a tear dripped from his cheek. He quickly wiped his eyes when he realized that I noticed.

"What am I supposed to do, Winter?" He turned to face me. "I can't save anyone from this plague. It may be tomorrow, or the next day, but at some point they will all be at death's door again."

I didn't say anything. I just wrapped my arms around his waist and rested my head against his chest; making sure my body temperature wasn't too cold. He didn't move for a moment, but he finally wrapped his arms around me.

I don't know how long we stood there in our embrace, but it was long enough for Shane's heartbeat to slow beneath my cheek. I hadn't realized that I was shaking before I hugged him, but my tremors slowed.

"I think the only way to beat this is to find the right medicines." Shane pulled away from me. "When I take the sickness from them, there's a small part of it that remains that I can't get rid of. All I'm doing is alleviating their symptoms. I don't know why."

Even Fredrick and Tamara had the early stages of the disease. Shane had healed them right before we left, but if they were still sick-

Shane grimaced in frustration, and my heart sank.

"They're all going to die if we don't figure something else out."

We continued walking, and my hope for the future of the Scavengers officially faded. Because Shane was right. They *were* all going to die.

When we got to the cabin, we were met by John and Eliza the second we opened the door. They both looked exhausted, but they had stayed up until we got back.

"I was worried." John hugged me tightly. I immediately felt terrible for not leaving a note for him.

His soft beard brushed against my cheek, and I finally felt a small bit of comfort. I leaned into his hug; relishing the strength he offered.

It was short lived.

Comfort was always short lived.

"Amelia Spencer and Reed are both dead."

John stiffened.

"What?" He pulled away from me so he could see my face. Then he stared at Shane who had collapsed on the chair in the kitchen. Shane nodded dejectedly.

"The sickness." Eliza's face paled. "Was it too much for you to handle?"

She pressed her hand to Shane's forehead and winced.

"Bed." She gestured urgently to his cot. "Now."

Eliza could get Shane to take breaks better than anyone else. There was something about her that made him listen. Which was a good thing. He would've killed himself by now without her.

Shane didn't argue. He just got up from the chair and went to his cot near the fireplace. I think he was asleep before his head hit the pillow.

"Are you okay?"

John studied my face for any sign that I wasn't. I kept the stony expression that I'd permanently worn since Nolan stopped calling. John couldn't read my mood like he used to.

I nodded the lie. He frowned at me, but I didn't care.

I'm going to bed, I signed. I turned toward the corner that I slept in. It was the one furthest away from the fireplace.

"Winter," John called before I could reach my corner. I turned and looked at him as emotionlessly as I could.

I love you, he signed.

I usually responded that I loved him too, but I just couldn't do it tonight. There was an incurable plague sweeping through the Scavenger community. Nolan was-

No. Stop it.

I nodded at John and laid down on my pillow. I blinked back the tears, and tried not to think about the boy that had my heart.

The boy that broke it when he stopped calling.

Chapter 2: Nolan

Four weeks earlier

I glanced at the tablet on my lap while I drove the Jeep through the bumpy trail. It was difficult; stopping the tablet from falling to the floor as we bounced over the terrain. It slid toward my knee; forcing me to take my hand off the wheel.

"Let me navigate." Phoenix sighed in exasperation. Her fingers brushed my thigh as she grabbed the tablet. "You don't have to be such a control freak."

I didn't reply as I took the tablet out of her hands; placing it back on my lap where it belonged.

Okay, yeah, I was a bit of a control freak.

But I couldn't let Phoenix mess around with my tablet. If she did, then Willow would think she could too. I couldn't allow that. Willow's affinity for hacking electronics was my worst nightmare.

Outside communications with the tablets were strictly forbidden in the League of Vigilance.

It was a good thing I was a quick study at computer sciences. I hadn't been caught contacting John, Eliza, and Winter yet. But Willow's skills greatly surpassed mine. She could easily catch me if she knew what to look for.

"Okay, fine." Phoenix slumped back in the passenger's seat. "But if we crash it'll be completely your fault."

"I won't crash."

I was also a quick learner when it came to driving. John would've been surprised by that.

I glanced at the map on my tablet, and turned the corner that went north toward the ocean. Our mission was to stop a shipment of medical supplies to the Highborn coast in the old Washington DC area. We had done a mission like this a few times before, but we'd always had Willow with us.

I honestly felt a little out of sorts without her here.

"Do you think Willow will be able to finish what Cade started with the data you guys stole?" Phoenix asked.

"Definitely. I don't know why Kain had Cade mess with it in the first place. Willow is clearly the better hacker."

Phoenix let out a humorless chuckle.

"It's because Willow is a girl. That automatically makes her lesser than Cade in Kain's eyes."

I nodded in agreement, but didn't otherwise respond.

"If Kain would've let her hack into the data we wouldn't be stealing from shipments right now."

I nodded again.

We would've been going after President Lynch's other underground labs instead. That information was in the data that Willow had recovered from the underground lab. The same one I saved Winter from.

"Did you find out how many teams are stopping shipments today?" Phoenix asked.

"Just us and one other team. They're taking weapons."

With the exception of Phoenix, Willow, and I; all of the other Vigilante teams consisted of one boy and one girl. All the rest of the Vigilantes, the singles, where reserved for the more dangerous jobs and suicide missions.

I still hadn't figured out a way to stop that from happening. Every day at least one of 'the singles' got injured, or killed, doing Kain's dirty work. Taking down Kain from the inside had proven to be impossible so far.

I knew it would be difficult, but I hadn't expected to be up against such dire situations.

I'd made a few friends among the Vigilantes. I wouldn't say they were loyal to me, or my two partners, but they agreed to at least train with me. My notoriety as a reckless martial arts expert had spread quickly through the league.

I had been with the Vigilantes for months now and I still wasn't close to dismantling Kain. Willow and Phoenix were the only ones on my side so far. The rest of the Vigilantes were too enthralled with their cult leader.

I'd told John, a few days ago, that if I didn't make some headway soon I would pull out. We'd be on the run from Kain for the rest of our lives, but it would be better than being stuck in the bunker with them.

In fact, if Willow were with us on this mission, I would've been tempted to just drive back to the Scavenger community. It was safer there now that John had become the Scavenger's official leader. Winter had told me that the Feral Morons had either left the community or were driven out. It was finally a safer place for the Scavengers to raise their families and work the land.

I stopped the Jeep a mile away from our target. We'd be hiking from here, but the terrain was pretty smooth the closer we got to the coast.

"Which shipment are we taking?" Phoenix lowered her voice as she kept pace with me.

Phoenix was quick, which was nice, but it also made me miss Winter. She had been slow to hike with, but she always seemed to make me happier. She had such a child-like wonder about everything she saw. Everything she did was incredible. Mesmerizing.

I quickly pushed Winter from my mind; concentrating on the mission ahead.

"Medical."

Phoenix nodded in understanding.

"We aren't going silent on this one. I want stats from you the entire time."

Phoenix gestured in understanding, and I shut up.

That was one thing that was nice about Phoenix. I didn't need to talk at her all the time. Willow, on the other hand, was a different story. That girl lived to converse.

We picked up our speed; dashing through the woods as though we'd spent our entire lives running through them.

Phoenix didn't make a sound as she hurdled over brush and broken off tree branches. She was even quieter than I was. Her long black braids that fell down her shoulders flew behind her in the breeze. Her Native American heritage was her most dominate trait, but she still refused to tell anyone about her ancestry.

She was afraid that Kain would use it against her. He'd proven himself to be an exceptional ignoramus in that regard.

We stopped behind a boulder that overlooked the ocean. A cargo ship that carried the Highborn medical supplies to their hospitals was anchored at the dock.

I glanced at my wristwatch and smirked.

"Right on time." Phoenix tapped her wristwatch triumphantly. "Scenario two?"

I nodded at the code word and she grinned. I didn't necessarily like the idea of splitting up, but it would be faster that way. Since we weren't going silent on this mission I was reluctantly satisfied with the plan.

Phoenix held out her hand for a fist bump. I rolled my eyes, but raised my own fist in camaraderie. Once the fist bumping nonsense was over, her grin widened.

Her personality was so freaking infectious.

"See you at six. Don't die."

Then she disappeared.

It always amazed me how easily she could do that. She was even better at sneaking around than John was, which was saying something.

I waited for a count of ten before splitting off in the opposite direction toward the barge. It didn't take me long to get there even though I kept at a snail's pace. This was a stealth mission, like they all were, and I was an expert at being a ghost.

I put my tablet in its waterproof case and, quietly, lowered myself into the cold ocean. I silently thanked my dead parents for making me take swimming lessons. They'd signed me up because I was such a handful to raise that they did whatever they could to keep me busy. A lot of the stuff I learned helped me survive the Mother Nature Apocalypse.

Now it would help me destroy this cargo ship.

I took a deep breath and ducked under the waves. Even through my drysuit, the water was so cold that it zapped a lot of my energy. The waves pounded against me; fighting to push me back toward shore.

"Checkpoint one." Phoenix's voice in my ear broke through the sound of the waves. "Charges set. I'm assuming you're still underwater, so don't drown."

Apparently, I needed to have a talk with her about conversing too much out in the field. If anyone overheard her they'd know exactly where I was.

"I'm alone," Phoenix continued as though she could read my mind. "So don't get your panties in a knot."

Okay. I was definitely going to talk with her for that last comment.

After a few more strokes, I finally broke through the surface next to the cargo ship. I grabbed the metal maintenance ladder and took a few breaths before pulling myself upward.

"Checkpoint two," Phoenix whispered in my ear. "Charges set. Status?"

"I'm in." I lowered myself onto the dock. "Checkpoint three. Charges set."

I placed the explosive from my waterproof pack to the side of the cargo ship. I waited for the soft beep that indicated that it was stuck tight before stripping out of my drysuit.

"Are you naked yet?" I could hear the smirk in her voice.

"Shut up." I pulled the dry clothes out of my pack.

"So that's a yes?"

What was up with her?

"I just need to know for the time-"

She abruptly stopped talking, and I froze. This was why I hated keeping the comms on during missions. People started to get too chatty.

"Phoenix, have you been detected?"

Silence extended for an uncomfortable amount of time.

I quickly pulled on my clothes and checked my handguns. My waterproof pack generally protected everything, but it was a good idea to make sure the guns stayed dry.

I secured the handguns in the holsters that were strapped to my shoulders, and rapidly stuffed the drysuit into my pack.

"I'm clear." Relief walloped me at the sound of her voice. "Close call though. Heading to checkpoint four."

"See you at six."

I kept to the shadows on the deck; heading for the engine room. I took my remaining explosive and stuck it to the wall next to the engine.

"Checkpoint five," I whispered to Phoenix. "Charges set."

Footsteps sounded on the deck, and a flashlight beam cut across the ship in front of me. I crouched next to the fuel barrels; waiting for the Highborn Militia guards to pass.

As the enemy made their rounds, I kept my eye on where Phoenix was supposed to meet me.

The other side of the deck was where the storage compartments were. One alone was large enough to supply the entire Scavenger community with medicines and equipment. Anger surged through me at the thought. Not a single Highborn cared enough about humanity to soothe their suffering. To relieve their struggles.

At least the Scavengers had people like John and Eliza.

And Winter.

I closed my eyes briefly at the thought of her.

I missed her more than I ever thought possible. It had been nearly a week since I'd last called her. I was planning on calling her after I got back to the League of Vigilance's underground bunker. All I had to do was get through the rest of this mission.

"I see you, Nolan," Phoenix whispered. "You've got four guards in front of you and two behind you. They're close, so don't risk responding. I'll get you out of there. Just follow my directions."

I didn't know how well she could see me, but I nodded anyway to let her know I understood. She must've been on top of one to the storage containers if she was able to see me behind the barrels.

"There's one about five feet to your right. She's alone."

I nodded again, and took a silent step sideways. I couldn't see the guard, but I could hear her. She was on the other side of the stack of fuel barrels, so I silently pulled myself on top of them.

The scent of motor oil hit me as I crouched above my target.

"If you had a cape you'd look like a superhero," Phoenix mocked sarcastically. "Just take her out already. We're on a time limit."

I rolled my eyes.

Completely oblivious to the danger right above her, the guard stood beneath me. I almost felt sorry for her, but she was a Highborn Militia soldier.

I hated all of them for what they did to the street orphans.

Especially to Winter.

I steadied myself on the edge of the barrel.

Three, two, one...

I swiftly dropped on top of the guard. She collapsed underneath me, and her weapon slid a few feet away. My fist crashed into her nose; knocking her out instantly.

I winced at the noise, but no other guard seemed to hear it.

I glanced at the girl's bloody face without an ounce of regret. She was young, like all the guards were, but that didn't matter to me. I was young too, and so was Winter.

We didn't decided to join sadistic psychopaths that hurt children.

Okay, maybe I *did*, but I was working to take Kain out of the picture. I doubted this unconscious girl beneath me had plans to take out Amanda Lynch.

"Nice moves," Phoenix commented dryly. "Now you have a clear shot to me. I'm on top of the second container."

I signaled the 'okay' sign so that she could see I was on my way.

"I'll stay in position until you're in the clear."

It wasn't long before I made it to the second storage container. It took me a moment to spot Phoenix when I got there. Her brown skin and dark hair blended into her black clothing so seamlessly she was practically invisible.

"I'm coming up behind you." The warning wasn't a courtesy. I just didn't want her to accidentally stab me.

Once was already too many times.

"I almost have the door unlocked. Willow would've had it done by now, but we can't all be genius hackers."

I waited patiently; watching her punch the code into the lock on the storage container door. Her tablet was hooked up by wires to the bottom of the lock, and its slight glow made me nervous.

The door lock finally clicked when Phoenix pressed the 'enter' button on the keypad. I grabbed the handle and pulled it open as slowly as I could. I didn't open it wide since it would draw attention if I did.

"The tablet didn't detect any traps or security inside the container."

I nodded, and cautiously stepped inside. Phoenix followed me so closely she was practically pressed up against my back. She turned on the flashlight function on her tablet; flooding the dark container with light.

Dozens of crates filled with medicines, first aid equipment, and every medical instrument imaginable were stacked in the container.

"We could open an entire medical center with all of this," Phoenix whispered in awe.

She was right, but we didn't have the manpower to steal all of it. Besides, all the Scavengers had was Eliza. There were no actual doctors in the Scavenger community or in the League of Vigilance. All of the doctors that survived the Mother Nature Apocalypse lived in the Highborn communities.

There really was no point in attempting to steal things that Eliza wouldn't be able to use. The first aid supplies and medicines were what we'd concentrate on.

Phoenix seemed to have the same idea because she went to the crate closest to her that was labeled 'immunizations'. I rummaged around a crate filled with fever reducers, antibiotic sprays, and pain killers. I was taking the drysuit out of my pack so I could fill it with the medicines when Phoenix gasped.

My hand went to my gun.

"You better come look at this."

She stared at the crate; fear dulling her wide eyes. I studied the tiny bottles that were organized in protective plastic containers. Boxes of unused needles stacked next to them. I must not have been seeing what she was; nothing to cause the terror in her posture.

Then my eyes fell on the label. My blood immediately ran cold.

Sleeping Ache Cure.

"Please tell me this isn't what I think it is," Phoenix's broken voice sent a shiver down my spine.

The Sleeping Ache Plague had run rampant through Asia over a hundred years ago. I'd learned all about it in my eighth grade history class. A plague so terrible, it killed millions of people in the span of a few weeks before a cure could be created. The plague had been expunged and never spread through humanity again.

President Lynch's psychotic scientists brought back the Sleeping Ache Plague.

"Fill your entire bag." The urgency coursing though me made my voice tremble. "Don't grab anything else. We need to take as much of the cure as possible. Needles too."

We worked frantically; knowing what we'd discovered was dangerous enough to end human existence. Forever.

"Exit at the docks?" Phoenix asked shakily.

I nodded; heading toward the door of the container. The docks were the only safe way to get the cure off of the cargo ship. We couldn't swim and risk ruining the life saving vaccinations.

It didn't take us long to get to the off ramp. The guards were still making their rounds. Obviously, they hadn't discovered the girl I'd taken out. Still, we had to hurry. Even though making a run for it on the beach was risky.

Unfortunately, it was our only option.

Phoenix ran in front of me; hurrying silently down the ramp. The air rushed out of my lungs; fogging the cold air in front of me.

I waited for the Highborn guards to see us, but it seemed like we made a clean escape.

It was too bad for them that they were so terrible at their jobs. Now they were about to be blown sky-high.

I didn't feel bad for them at all.

I activated the detonator.

The blast sent a heat wave racing towards us, but I barely felt it. Shouts from a warehouse on the other side of the bay echoed with the sound of the waves. We ran; keeping ahead of the powerful lights that scanned the beach behind us.

We made it to our Jeep shortly after; driving through the woods with the headlights off for the first few miles. I slowed our progress on the trials. I *was* in a hurry to get back to the underground bunker, but I also didn't want to get caught by the Highborns that would be looking for us now.

But honestly, that was the least of my worries.

I had no idea if the Sleeping Ache Plague had been released to the Scavengers yet, but I was willing to bet that it had.

I needed to get the cure to John.

Phoenix scanned the information chip that we'd taken from the crate with her tablet. She studied the instructions, and prepared the syringes while I drove.

Luckily, a healthy person would be immune after just one dose. If they were already sick, it might take more than one.

She stabbed the large needle into her leg; depressing the plunger. She grunted in pain as the liquid rushed through her bloodstream.

"Yeah, I'm gonna insist that you stop driving for this," she muttered through a shaky exhale. "I suck at giving shots."

I wanted to argue with her, but it would be a waste of time. Once I pulled over she stuck the needle in my thigh. I wince when the cure hit my veins; the thick liquid pulsing through me.

"Did we make the right decision, Nolan?"

I started driving again; flipping my headlights on this time.

"About what?"

"Blowing up the rest of the cure? What if our two bags are all that's left now."

I glanced over at her; seeing the deep terror she was spiraling into. That wasn't okay with me, so I took a second to think about how I should respond.

"I highly doubt that the Highborns only had that one crate full of the cure. They probably have factories that are creating more. We only destroyed one shipment."

"Do you think Kain will send us out to find more of the cure?"

"Probably not. He'll think that your pack will be enough for the Vigilantes."

Phoenix glanced at me in confusion.

"We have two packs."

"Nope. I lost my pack on the cargo ship. One of the guards spotted me, and my pack got thrown into the ocean during the fight. That's the official story. Got it?"

Phoenix stared at me for a moment before nodding.

"How are you going to get the *missing pack* to the Scavenger community?"

I hadn't figured that out yet, so I didn't respond. Phoenix sighed; slumping tiredly in her seat.

"You know that Kain isn't going to be happy that you *lost* your pack. I'm terrified that he's going to beat you senseless."

My gut clenched; my palms growing moist.

I'd been beaten by Kain a few times, and it always took a few days to recover from it. Every time something went wrong, I took a beating. The last one was over Willow spilling tea on Kain's desk by accident. I'd been there to stop him from hurting her instead, but I couldn't walk to two days afterwards.

The man was the epitome of a psychopath. I was surprised I hadn't murdered him in his sleep yet.

"Go straight to our room when we get back. You don't have to watch it. I don't want you near him anyway."

Pain lashed across her face as she stared at me.

"You don't have to take beatings for everyone, Nolan. I'll say I lost the pack. Give you a break."

"That's not happening." I gave her a stern glare.

Phoenix looked away from me to stare out her window.

"I don't know why we're still doing this," she whispered.

I knew why I was, but I honestly didn't know if Phoenix was safe anymore. Kain had wanted her dead ever since I stood up to her partner, Brian. The Viking had a very mixed up view of how the League of Vigilance should operate. I was only there to protect the ones that couldn't protect themselves.

It also gave me the opportunity to go out on missions, and slowly take down the Highborn Union.

One of these days we were going to find out where President Lynch was hiding. I was going to be there to stop her. To see her world shatter as her life ended.

That was *my* crusade. It didn't have to be Phoenix's. Maybe her purpose could be greater than mine.

"What would you say if I offered to kill you?"

Phoenix's eyes shot toward me in surprise.

"Are you crazy, Nolan?"

"You could get the cure to John and Eliza Marlo. They would make sure that the Scavengers got the immunizations. I'll tell Kain that you died on the mission. He wouldn't be coming after you."

Phoenix shook her head with wide eyes.

"He would kill you."

I knew there was a chance of that, but I was hoping that the cure would make Kain less murderously angry. He'd been looking for an excuse to kill me, so the cure might not matter.

"It's a risk, but we need to think about the greater good. The Scavengers need the cure. We both know that Kain isn't just going to give it to them. Not without a price."

Phoenix shook her head. "Why don't *you* go to the Scavenger community? I'll tell Kain that *you* died."

"Kain would kill Willow. Then he'd kill you. Without me, the two of you are considered worthless. You know that."

The Vigilantes would turn on the girls so brutally; their deaths wouldn't be easy. I'd never be able to live with myself if that happened.

Phoenix sighed in frustration and closed her eyes. The exhaustion absorbing what little energy she had left.

"We need to do something, Phoenix. What if the Sleeping Ache is already killing people? What if it's killing kids?"

Phoenix opened her eyes and looked at me, considering-

She nodded, and I took a shaky breath.

Glancing at the map on my tablet; I located a cave a few miles from our location. I changed direction, and Phoenix raised an eyebrow at me.

"I'll drop you off at this cave so you can sleep for a few hours. It'll be a couple of days before you get to the community, but I'll give you the rest of my rations."

Phoenix nodded grimly, and pulled up the map on her tablet. We sat in silence for the rest of the trip. When I stopped the Jeep at the cave, Phoenix let out another nervous sigh.

I glanced at her; realizing how intently she was staring at me. A spark glimmered in her eyes, softening them.

"Nolan, I-"

Her eyelids lowered slightly; gazing at me so desperately my heart pounded in concern. Then, suddenly, her lips crashed into mine in a lingering kiss.

I could do nothing but sit there. Completely frozen in shock.

Her warm mouth moved over mine. A passion that I never knew existed within her. It would've been nice if I didn't have, what felt like, a lead weight in my gut.

When she pulled away, I must've had a horrified look on my face. She glanced away, embarrassed.

I was a complete moron.

"Come on, Nolan. It's no secret that I've had a crush on you for a very long time."

Wasn't it though? Because I had absolutely no idea.

I was at a complete loss for words, so I didn't say anything. It was a jerk move, but I really didn't know what to do here.

"Um, anyway." Phoenix cleared her throat. "You don't have to reciprocate or anything. I know you aren't a demonstrative type of guy, but I needed to do that. Just once. I'm terrified that I'll never see you again."

That snapped me out of it. I gave her a small glare.

"Don't say that, Phoenix. Of course we'll see each other again. And I'm sorry, but I-"

Phoenix held up her hand; shaking her head desperately.

"It's okay, Nolan. " *She smiled.* I wasn't sure how, but she smiled. "I know you don't feel the same way about me. I just needed you to know."

Well, at least I didn't have to tell her about Winter. I didn't think that conversation would go over well at all. Besides, this was the last thing we needed right now.

"Be safe, Phoenix. Call me when you get to John and Eliza. I'll send you the coordinates to their cabin."

Phoenix nodded, and gave my hand a small squeeze. I hadn't even noticed until then that she'd been holding it.

"You be safe too. Make sure to tell Willow that I'm okay."

I gave her a nod, and she jumped out of the Jeep.

I watched her walk to the entrance of the cave. She seemed smaller than she had before. Deflated.

I'd done that to her. I hadn't meant to, but I'd taken something from her. I was so freaking obtuse. So insensitive not to notice that one of my closest friends, an ally, harbored such feelings for me.

How often had I led her on without realizing it?

I resisted the irrational urge to punch the steering wheel.

I took a deep breath; forcing myself to drive away from the cave. It was so difficult to leave Phoenix alone, but it was the only option we had. We couldn't let Kain have control of the cure if the Sleeping Ache Plague really was spreading.

Now, I had to stop Kain from killing me.

Chapter 3: John

Winter curled up into a ball on the sleeping mat in her corner. Tears stung my eyes at the sight of her. I knew that she loved Nolan, but I had no idea how much until now.

I had tried to find Kain, or any other Vigilante, to get information on Nolan. But they had stopped coming to the community shortly after Nolan had joined them. I had no idea where their hideout was. Nolan tried to explain it to me, but it was located in a place that I'd never been before. I had no map. I couldn't wander around for weeks trying to find it when the Scavengers needed me to keep the Highborn Militia out of the community.

I had to choose between looking for my brother, and leading the Scavengers. It was slowly killing me. Taking such an emotional toll it was nearly impossible to keep it hidden anymore.

Now with the devastating disease going around, I definitely couldn't leave. I needed to figure out how to enforce quarantine zones before the sickness wiped out the entire community.

"John." Eliza gently grabbed my arm.

She stopped talking, but gave my arm a gentle squeeze. I knew she wanted me to turn and face her, but I didn't do it. I was so emotionally exhausted. I could barely move.

"John."

She came around in front of me. She reached up and pressed her lips to mine. I pulled her closer. Deepening the kiss. This was all the comfort I had now.

Eliza's kiss. Eliza's touch.

She was literally the only reason I was functioning these days.

"Come to bed. We've got a lot to do tomorrow."

I followed her to the bedroom that we added to the cabin. It wasn't a very large room, but it was nice to have the privacy now that we were 'officially' together.

A few weeks ago, I'd given Eliza a ring that I'd made from scrap metal. I told her that I was hers, and I asked her if she would be mine.

We were married in our hearts. Which was good enough for the both of us.

"I think you need to talk to her." Eliza sat on the bed, looking weary.

I peeled off my dirty clothes; throwing them in the corner of the room so the mud wouldn't get everywhere.

I'd been working in the trenches that surrounded our community all day. My clothes were still disgusting; despite how I'd dumped cold river water over me before I came home.

The trenches were one of our precautions to keep the Highborn Militia out of our territory. I missed the days of bulldozers and dump trucks. We were lucky to have found enough shovels to make it work.

The raids on Highborn shipments helped us get a stash of weapons, medicines, and other supplies. Unfortunately, that also made us a much more threatening target for the Highborns and the Vigilantes. The problems that would cause in the future were daunting to consider.

"Winter?" I didn't need to clarify who Eliza was talking about, but I did anyway.

"She's hurting, John."

I pulled on a pair of wool pants and stared at my wife, incredulous.

"We all are."

"But she doesn't have past experiences of dealing with this kind of loss."

I raised an eyebrow at her, completely confused.

Winter had lost more than anyone I'd ever met. Lost all memory of her life. Dr. Darkwood had messed with her mind so thoroughly that she couldn't remember her family, her disability, or even her own name.

"She has more experience with loss than anyone."

"I'm talking about losing a person like Nolan. This is the first time she can remember losing someone she loves. She loved him."

"I know." My broken whisper was a completely foreign sound.

"No, John." Eliza continued adamantly. "She *loved* Nolan like you loved Kate, like I loved David, and how we love each other now."

Tears fell from her eyes. I took her face in my hands; gently wiping the moisture from her cheeks. She took a shaky breath and closed her eyes; allowing my touch to give her comfort.

I wanted to take the pain from her. The gut wrenching loss that I knew writhed within her. Because it festered within me too.

Losing Nolan had been my worst fear. He was the only biological family I had left. He was my entire world.

And I had only cried once for him. All while I watched Eliza cry everyday. She probably thought I was a heartless heathen. I'd been so cold these past weeks. Refusing to talk about anything other than the security of the Scavengers.

"I know she was in love with him, Eliza.

She pulled away from me; wiping away more tears. "I haven't seen Winter cry yet."

"We just need to give her time. She'll come to us if she needs to talk."

I couldn't take Eliza's incredulous stare anymore, so I laid down on the bed.

She didn't join me right away. She always distanced herself when she was this upset.

"So you're not going to talk to her?"

"About Nolan?"

Eliza folded her arms and gave me a pointed look.

"No, I'm not." I sat up; my stomach rolling with nausea. "He was my *brother*. I can't have that kind of conversation with the girl that loved him. *I am not emotionally equipped for that.*"

Eliza didn't say anything. She just listened. No sign of judgement. She even unfolded her arms and leaned in closer to me.

"I'm a complete mess right now." My gut wrenched inside me. "There's nothing I can say to Winter that will make her feel better. Especially since I-"

I stopped talking when tears welled up in my eyes. A pain formed in my chest, and nothing could make it disappear.

"I should have stopped him from leaving." The tears fell from my eyes in agonizing waves. *"It's all my fault."*

Eliza pulled me into a hug; holding onto me as the pain pummeled me. A crescendo of bitter trauma. A dark abyss of endless guilt that I knew would follow me forever.

Nolan was gone because of me. I was the reason the last member of my family was dead.

"John," Eliza whispered after a long moment of silence. "Whatever happened to Nolan; it wasn't your fault. He left because that was his choice to make."

"He wasn't old enough to make that kind of decision."

Eliza sat up on her elbow and turned to face me.

"Yes, he was. Age doesn't matter in the world we live in now. Only survival does. You wouldn't have been able to stop him from leaving. I honestly think he didn't leave sooner because he respected and loved you so much. He would be very angry if he knew that you were blaming yourself."

An inappropriate chuckle escaped me as I thought about that. Eliza didn't comment on the bad timing of my laugh, but it felt weird all the same.

"Nolan was always angry with me, so that thought doesn't scare me."

Eliza smiled at that.

"I guess that's true, but you still shouldn't blame yourself."

She kissed me on the cheek and rolled over. I wrapped my arm around her waist and buried my face into the back of her neck.

Eventually, I was able to fall asleep.

Eliza jerked next to me; pulling me out of a vivid nightmare. It took me a moment to realize, through the dark visions that swam through my memory, that she was thrashing in my embrace.

I pulled my arms away; heart racing. She must've been having a horrible dream. Much worse than mine was. I placed my hand on her shoulder; intending to gently coax her awake-

Her skin burned through her clothes. Her face was pale with a tint of rosy pink in her cheeks. She inhaled rapidly; panting so quickly I was afraid she'd choke on the air itself.

I pressed my hand to her forehead; panic seizing me.

She had seemed fine just the night before.

"Eliza." I kept my tone calm, but strong. I knew I couldn't let her know how horrified I was. "Eliza, wake up."

Her eyes flew open; an agonizing moan shuttering through her. "John," she panted shakily. "Get away from me. Go."

I wrapped the blanket tightly around her.

"I've got the immunities of a rockstar. You won't get me sick."

"It's a plague."

I ignored her concern and got off the bed. I needed to see if Shane was up for healing her before I *really* freaked out.

"Who have you come in contact with recently?" I smoothed my finger over her feverish cheek. I needed to ask her now. It was a gut wrenching reality, but she wouldn't be lucid enough later if Shane couldn't heal her.

I had to push that possibility from my mind before the rage burning in me took over.

"Brian," she whispered through a labored breath. "I saw him yesterday."

I nodded, pushing a few strands of hair off of her forehead. Brian was the ex-Vigilante that Eliza had helped with a broken arm. He had given her a can of coffee in exchange for the medical aid. He'd been helping the Scavengers protect the borders of the community ever since.

"I'm going to go check on him." The mere thought of leaving her like this was infuriating, but it was something I *had* to do. "I'll take Winter with me. Shane will stay here. I'm sure once he's recovered from yesterday he'll be able to help you."

Tears filled Eliza's eyes as sweat broke out on her forehead.

"The poor kid has been overtasked already."

I kissed her cheek, and got dressed as quickly as I could.

Shane couldn't get sick because of his regenerative abilities, but Winter could. I needed to get her out of the cabin and into the fresh air as soon as possible.

I couldn't believe this was happening. I'd already lost Nolan. I couldn't lose Eliza or Winter.

I hurried out of our room and found Shane in the kitchen with Winter; silently preparing breakfast. Winter saw the expression on my face and froze. The temperature dropped slightly as Shane turned away from the sink to look at her.

What is wrong? Winter signed, urgently.

"It's Eliza." I clenched my hands into fists to stop them from trembling.

Winter's wide eyes flashed with fear.

"*Crap.*" Shane quickly dried his hands on a rag. He threw it down on the table; making his way toward the bedroom door.

"We need to leave, Winter." I pointed to our satchel. "Pack enough food for two days. We're going to check on Brian."

She grabbed the satchel and began gathering supplies.

I grabbed the communicator off of the shelf. We had stolen the communicators from the Highborns that we drove out of our community. Only a handful of our people had communicators, but Brian was one of them.

"Brian, this is John. Do you read me?"

I waited for about ten seconds and tried calling him again. He still didn't answer, so I stuffed the communicator into one of the bags. I signed for Winter to wait in the kitchen as I went to check on Eliza and Shane.

When I pushed open the door relief caught me off guard. I leaned against the wall to stop myself from stumbling.

Eliza was sitting up. A bit of the color had come back to her cheeks. Shane was slouched on my side of the bed; a tight grimace contorting his face.

"I think that's enough." Eliza tried to pull her hand away, but Shane tightened his fingers.

"Just a second. There's something different."

He gasped, gently pulling his hand away a moment later.

"Okay, that's so weird."

"What's weird?" My entire body trembled with pent up adrenaline.

"That wasn't the plague." Shane winced. "It was something completely different. I've felt dozens of different injuries and sicknesses, but never something like that."

"Are you alright?"

"I gotta get outside." He struggled to his feet.

Even though I wanted to, I didn't help him. It was hard to watch him stagger, but he looked like he'd drain my life force completely if I touched him.

After he left, I gave Eliza a tender kiss. Reminding myself with her touch that she was still here with me. She didn't feel so feverish anymore and she was breathing easier.

Miraculously, Shane had managed to heal her completely.

"Shane says I didn't have the plague, but we should find out if Brian has it," Eliza whispered when I ended the kiss.

"Winter and I will go. You stay here with Shane. Both of you need the rest."

Eliza nodded tiredly. Even though she was no longer sick, she looked like she could sleep for a week. I kissed her once more before leaving the room.

I gave Winter a nod, and she strode to the door with the satchel strapped to her shoulder. I grabbed my rifle and canteen before following her.

Shane was sitting on the frozen ground in front of the cabin. His pale face gazing up at the majestic sunrise.

"Are you okay?" Winter placed her hand on his shoulder.

"Yeah, I'll go check on Eliza in a minute. I just needed some fresh air."

I noticed one of the trees next to the cabin had been reduced to a pile of ash. Shane sat grimly; studying the morning sky as though it held the secret to unlock the miracles we desperately needed.

"Both of you take it easy while we're gone." I rested a hand on his shoulder. "Hopefully, we'll be back tomorrow."

"Are you sure you don't want me to come?"

He sounded so tired. The sickness that had been plaguing the Scavengers was so *hard* on this kid. He was operating on sheer instinct at this point. Trying to save people, and watching them die anyway, had a massively negative effect on him.

"No, Shane." I gave his shoulder an encouraging squeeze. "Your wellbeing is important too."

Shane shook his head dejectedly, but didn't reply.

"I'm serious. Take it easy today."

It took him a moment, but Shane finally nodded. I glanced at Winter and her eyes lit up in understanding. It was time to go.

"See you later, Shane."

"Bye, Winter."

I followed her toward the trees; surprised by how far ahead she'd managed to get. She was usually slower and more cautious when she walked through the woods.

It was one of the things that I'd noticed that had changed about her. She used to study the things around her, as though she had never seen them before. A permanent look of wonder used to shine in her blue eyes.

Now, they were hollow. Sorrow and defeat replacing that bright radiance within her.

Eliza was right. I needed to talk to her.

I shuddered when the first thing I should say came to my mind. I didn't want to have to relive this moment, but I had to do something to help this poor girl.

"Winter, I think we should talk."

She stiffened and tried to push ahead of me, but my legs were a lot longer than hers.

"I suppose you don't have to talk, but there's a story I need to tell you."

Winter gave me a sideways glance, but otherwise ignored me.

"You've heard about how Nolan and I survived the great earthquake, but did I ever tell you how we ended up in the same car together?"

Winter stopped dead in her tracks, and I turned to look at her. I almost hugged her when I saw the tortured look on her face, but I refrained.

"Nolan had severe anger issues for most of his childhood. Our parents kept him busy. The community service that he participated in taught him to feel compassion toward others. We never did figure out where his anger stemmed from, but a lot of it was directed at our parents. They were the authority figures in his life, so he targeted them quite often."

I cleared my throat; trying to steady my voice. I rubbed my wet eyes before continuing the story; forcing myself not to glance at Winter.

I wouldn't keep talking if I did.

"By the time Nolan was twelve, he and mom couldn't be alone together sometimes. He took his anger out on her the most. He never physically hurt her, of course, but he could be verbally abusive when he wanted to be. My dad wouldn't stand for it, and neither would I. Our three sisters were off to college, and I was a police officer with a family of my own. We lived just across town, so Nolan would stay the night at my house quite often.

"The night of the great earthquake, I got a call from my mom. She said that my dad was still at work, and Nolan had a terrible day at school. I could hear Nolan yelling at her over the phone, so I told my mom that I would pick him up for the night. I left my pregnant wife and three children to go and get him."

I shuddered, taking a deep breath as I remembered the awful things I heard Nolan say to our mother.

He'd told her that he hated her, and that he never wanted to see her again. It was the last thing he'd ever said to her.

I never told Nolan that I'd heard what he'd said to our mother. It was painful enough for him without me trying to talk to him about it. I couldn't tell Winter now. It didn't matter anymore anyway.

"I picked him up, and when we were almost to my house the ground started moving. Trees swayed; falling all around the car. I was forced off the road. We rode it out inside the car while the ground shook violently.

"I'm still not sure how we got so lucky. Nothing fell on us, and the ground didn't swallow us like it did everything else around us.

"Throughout the entire thing, Nolan didn't scream. No matter how terrifying it was. I used to work with brave men, and women, on the police force everyday. They all paled in comparison to his courage.

"I wanted to leave the car during the earthquake. I thought we'd have a better chance outside. Nolan had been levelheaded enough to talk me out of it. He was only twelve, and he's the one that saved us that day."

I stopped walking then; staring at the trees in front of us. It was difficult to think about the fact that Nolan wasn't there in the woods with us now. It was so peaceful; the slight breeze in the trees and the snow falling lightly on the ground. This was what Nolan and I had done everyday before Winter came into our lives. Spending every waking moment in the woods.

Our woods.

"After the ground stopped rolling, we walked the rest of the way to my house-

"My family was gone, and I just- I just collapsed to my knees. Nolan was by my side in an instant; holding onto me while my entire world shattered."

The cold air radiated around Winter; blowing through my jacket. I shivered a little, but kept my composure.

"There wasn't anything we could do for my family, so we hiked the ten miles back to our parents house. It was completely leveled when we got there. We found our parents' bodies in what used to be the living room. The sight shocked me to the point that I went completely numb. I merely stood there staring. Unable to move. I watched as Nolan closed our father's eyes with steady fingers. I remember wondering how odd it was. He could be so calm while my entire body was trembling."

Winter had tears in her eyes. Her frosted hands covering her mouth and nose. Listening so intently to this horrible story of a boy that she'd never see again.

"Then Nolan did something that I'll never forget. He knelt next to our mother's lifeless body. Gathered her into his arms. He rocked her. Buried his face in her hair. The harsh sobs that escaped him were echoes of such agony. I doubt I'll ever hear a sound like it again. It was so hard to believe before, but it was then that I knew- I knew he loved our mother more than anything else."

Winter sobbed heavily; shaking uncontrollably. I would've hugged her, but the cold coming from her was so intense. I had to take a step away instead.

"We stayed there until I came to my senses and insisted that we find higher ground. The earthquake had been bad enough that I knew water would reach us. So we covered our parents bodies as best we could. We left them there."

I wrapped my coat tighter around me; forcing myself to look at the softhearted girl that caused the terrible freeze.

"Winter, do you remember how Nolan used to treat you after I found you?"

Another sob escaped her, but she didn't reply.

"He tried to keep you at arm's length."

Winter wiped her eyes and shuttered.

"Do you know why?"

She wouldn't meet my gaze.

"Nolan was afraid to care for others because everyone he'd ever loved had been taken away from him during the great earthquake. Nolan wouldn't let anyone in anymore. Not even me. Then he met you and, suddenly, he came out of his shell. He was happier."

Winter's tears turned into icicles when they fell off of her cheeks and hit the cold air.

"He loved you, Winter. He loved you so much. You meant something to him. He was scared to love someone the way he loved you, because I think a part of him knew he wouldn't survive much longer. He was all too willing to sacrifice himself to save others. That heroism was what forged him into the man he was."

Another sob escaped her and she collapsed onto a log. It froze beneath her as I watched her fall apart.

It was horrible, but I knew that she needed to come to terms with this.

Chapter 4: Winter

Nolan had kissed me. Once. I told him that I loved him. Once. He never reciprocated that. Never actually said the words I desperately wished to hear.

I regretted it so much now.

At least he knew that I loved him.

Nolan had kissed me so intensely that there shouldn't have been a doubt in my mind that he loved me. But then he'd left me, twice, to join the League of Vigilance. He may have loved me, but it wasn't enough to keep us together. It wasn't enough to save him from whatever fate that befell him.

I wiped the frozen tears from my face; staring at the splintered ice in my hands.

If this was what happened to people who loved heroes; did I want anything to do with it? Did I want to live with this kind of heartbreak and loss?

I gritted my teeth at my ridiculous thoughts, and took a shaky breath.

Loving Nolan was the one good thing I'd done since Dr. Darkwood turned me into an abomination.

At least I could say that I loved someone. A hero. A man that was able to put a complete stranger's wellbeing above his own.

Nolan had thought that I was inherently good, and he couldn't have been more wrong. I felt so guilty that I never told him about the Vigilantes that I'd killed when I escape the underground lab. Or the Highborn I killed in that cabin-

Deep inside me, I was violent and uncontrolled. I hid that part of myself from Nolan when he never felt the need to hide anything from me.

Nolan was *my person*. He was the one good thing about me. I had been so afraid of losing him that I kept parts of my true self from him.

Now he was gone. I couldn't fix that mistake.

The guilt would eventually eat me alive until I was nothing but an unfeeling frozen abomination.

"Winter." John's deep voice broke through my agony, and I was finally able to take a cleansing breath. "Look at me, sweetheart."

My body, and the atmosphere, warmed when my eyes met John's. His brown eyes were red rimmed and puffy. He had a haunted look that almost made me start crying again.

I didn't want to do this-

Why is John making me do this?

"You barely talk anymore." I flinched at the broken whisper. "Eliza and Shane are concerned. I am absolutely beside myself with worry."

I didn't know why he felt the need to tell me this. I didn't talk much because I had nothing to say. Being locked inside my own head was better than facing a world without Nolan. It was cowardly, but I didn't care.

I was an abomination, so it didn't matter.

"Winter, I need you to say something, please."

I sat there; blinking back a fresh wave of tears. I thought about using sign, but I knew John wanted me to use my voice. He would nag me until I did.

"He's not dead!"

John's head shot back as though I'd slapped him. I'd never used that tone with anyone before. It was shocking, even for myself.

What is going on with me?

"If he's dead, then that means I have to move on somehow." My voice soften, so gentle it was barely a whisper. "I'll never do that without proof. Unless I see a body; I'll never believe that he's really gone. We should stop acting like he's dead. We should be looking for him."

John flinched at my words, and closed his eyes for a moment.

"Sweetheart, I want to believe just as much as you do that he's still alive, but it's been so long without contact. I don't have the man power to go look for him. Especially with this plague outbreak. If he's not dead then he's in an underground lab-"

"No!" I shot to my feet; no longer able to sit still. Panic threatened to grip me in its ugly clutches. I couldn't think about the possibility of Nolan being experimented on- Of him going through the torture that I went through.

The thought alone would bring me to my knees.

"You know I don't like talking about this anymore than you do."

"Then why are we doing this?" I hugged myself to ward off the shakes that suddenly made it hard to stand.

"Because you don't talk to us. That's not okay."

"Fine. I'll talk more if that's what you want."

John sighed; a deep longing in the way he gazed at me. As though he wanted to wrap his arms around me. To stave off the aching grief that constantly consumed me.

"Winter, that's not the only problem here. You're hurting, but you're not letting us help you. We are here for you. Even when you feel like we shouldn't be."

I froze, wondering how he could decipher my innermost thoughts so well.

I was an abomination. I didn't deserve these amazing people that called me their family. I'd killed people.

As far as John was concerned, I hadn't crossed that essential line. He believed a lie. He wanted to save as many people as we could. I always did the exact opposite of that.

"We love you, Winter. Eliza and I love you like a daughter, and Shane is a true friend to you. I don't care if you think you deserve it or not. *You're ours.* We're not letting you go through this alone."

My shoulders slumped as the energy drained from me. I would've collapsed if John hadn't grabbed me in a bear hug. I had no more tears to cry, but he still held me in the silent forest. I forced my body temperature to rise; hoping I didn't frost burn him.

"Brian is probably sick and we've just been standing here talking."

"I will never regret this conversation, Winter." John released me and picked up his rifle. "It needed to happen no matter what other crisis there is to fix."

I merely nodded, and followed John down the game trail that led to Brian's cabin.

He lived the furthest away from the community. It usually took us about four hours to get there from Eliza's cabin. I was expecting the rest of the journey to go by in silence, but John had insisted on making small talk.

When we finally got to the cabin, John told me to wait in the trees.

"I really hope he's not sick." John handed me his rifle and canteen. "If he is, I'll come back out and get some ice from you. I don't want you anywhere near the cabin."

I nodded in understanding, and watched him walk through the front door.

I explored Brian's settlement while I waited; keeping hidden in the trees. There wasn't much farmland yet, but some of the trees had been cleared. A shed sat a few yards away from the cabin. A clothes line hung between two trees, and I heard a creek close by. It was an amazing place, considering he'd only been living here for a few months.

A swift breeze blew through the trees; causing an awful smell to annihilate my senses. My eyes watered. An urgent need to gag consumed me.

I knew that smell. The unmistakable odor of decay. Of death.

Even though John told me to stay put, I went searching. If there was a dead body nearby then I needed to find it. Especially if it was Brian.

I covered my nose; moving through the trees toward the smell that seemed to be coming from the shed.

I held my breath as I pushed the door open; peeking my head in hesitantly. It was dark, so it took a moment for my eyes to adjust.

I resisted the urge to scream in rage when I finally comprehended the horror in front of me.

Mutilated animal carcasses scattered the interior of the shed. Such a horrible waste of life and food. People in the community could've used the meat and pelts, but Brian had left them to rot in his shed.

I exhaled as I shut the door; trying to calm myself down. If Brian had gone hunting and then gotten sick; it would explain the waste. But he shouldn't have been able to tell Eliza about the sick children the other day.

These carcasses were more than a few days ripe.

I forced myself to look in the shed again; my mind not computing the savagery. The animals didn't appear to have had an easy death.

I knew the signs of torture better than most.

There was something sinister about the dead animals. More menacing than merely meat being left to rot.

It was then that I realized John had been inside the cabin for too long. I didn't know if it was the dead animals that made me feel uneasy, but I *needed* to make sure John was okay. The thought of John being alone with Brian-

I sprinted for the cabin, not pausing before bursting through the front door.

I was met with the barrel of John's rifle aimed at my face. I paused; raising my hands just as John lowered the rifle.

"Winter!" John quickly strapped the weapon to his shoulder. "Are you trying to give me a heart attack?"

I didn't really know what a heart attack was, so I didn't answer him. I took a deep breath; glancing around the cabin for Brian. I didn't know what I was going to do when I found him, but I was seriously pissed off.

"Where's Brian?"

There was a bed, and a small kitchen; but no sign that anyone had been there in a while. My gaze fell on a large metal cage in the corner of the cabin, and I paused.

It was completely out of place.

"I don't know." John studied me with concern. "What's going on, Winter?"

"Brian let meat go to rot in his shed." I continued staring at the cage. For some reason, it seemed even more sinister than the mangled animal carcasses.

"Crap." John shook his head. "I thought I smelled something weird."

"What is that?" I gestured to the cage.

John sighed grimly as he studied the cage. "It looks like an old torturing device the American government used on terrorists in the 2100's. The first prototypes ran on electricity, but this one is a newer model. It's solar powered, but it seems like it's been turned off. I have no idea how Brian got a hold of one of these."

I shuddered, tearing my gaze away from the cage.

"What kind of torture?"

John's lips thinned into a grim line.

"The kind that made people talk, Winter. The cages were outlawed in the year 2259. They were supposedly all destroyed. I, honestly, have no idea where Brian would've gotten his hands on one."

I glanced around the cabin again. From what I could see there were no clues as to where Brian went, or what he had the cage for.

Or *who* he had the cage for.

I winced at the thought, and kept searching the dimly lit cabin. John found an oil lamp and lit it with his lighter.

My blood ran cold at what the small flame illuminated.

Streaks of dried blood covered the floor of the torture cage; crusted on the gruesome metal bars. I swallowed bile as I thought of the poor, helpless person Brian had put in there. There was a lot of blood. Enough to wonder if the person survived it.

I glanced at the wall next to the cage; rage finally replacing the imminent shock of what we saw.

Written in blood were two words: Sleeping Ache. It was so small I thought I must've been seeing things, but as I got closer there was no doubt in my mind that it was a message.

"John." I gestured for him to come to me. He was by my side a second later, and I pointed at the two words. "What do you think that means?"

John didn't move, or make a sound, while he stared at the wall. I wasn't sure if he was even breathing. I glanced at him in concern, but he didn't meet my eyes.

"Oh no. No."

John stared in horror at the words before burying his face in his hands. He wiped his face vigorously before running his hands through his unkept hair. For a moment, it looked like all the strength had left him.

Then the next second, he was rummaging through the random items in Brian's cabin.

"John, talk to me." I walked up to him. "What's going on?"

He didn't reply. I grabbed his arm, trying to get him to face me. He still ignored me as he ransacked the kitchen, and tore the bedding off of Brian's bed. I wasn't sure what he was looking for, but he seemed desperate.

I grabbed his arm again, and lowered my body temperature to get him to snap out of it.

"Ouch!" John yanked his arm out of my cold grip.

"Talk to me," I signed quickly when he finally looked at me. *"Please."*

Sign language didn't calm John down like it did me, but he seemed to come to his senses. I didn't know if it was the sign language or the look on my face, but his stony expression softened. I could still see the terror in his eyes, and I had to force myself not to panic.

"Winter," he whispered my name shakily. He cleared his throat and ran a hand through his hair again. "The Sleeping Ache Plague went through Asia over a hundred years ago. Millions, maybe even billions, of people died from it. It was the worse plague ever recorded in world history. It spread through parts of Europe and Central America before scientists were able to find a cure."

I glanced at the words on the wall; flinching when I realized what John was saying. Whoever Brian had in the cage was trying to warn us.

Eliza was right. This *was* a plague.

"I'm not sure how the plague came back. It's been eradicated for over a century. But now that I think about it-"

John exhaled; clearly trying to calm himself.

"Sleeping Ache makes people so sick that they can't keep their eyes open. They can't talk, but they're still fully aware of what's going on around them. There's a terrible ache that comes over the victims muscles. They can't cry out in pain, or tell anyone how they're feeling. A lot of people were presumed dead before they actually were because of the symptoms. Especially in the areas where doctors were scarce."

I closed my eyes; remembering all the children that Shane tried to heal. They had all been asleep, but reported being in constant pain when Shane healed them enough to stay awake.

"There is a cure, right?" I glanced around the cabin. "If we can find it-"

I stopped when I realized what I was saying. Just because the plague came back, it didn't mean that anyone had the cure anymore. It had been over a century since anyone had to worry about the Sleeping Ache Plague. Now that there was hardly anything left of humanity, it was probable that no one knew how to get the cure.

"What are the chances of anyone recovering from the sickness?"

John winced, glancing away from me before answering.

"No one ever has without the cure. There were some people that were immune to it, but once a person contracted the disease they were dead within a few days."

John's head bowed. The weight of an entire community's wellbeing gripped him in its sickly fist.

"Not even Shane can heal the disease completely. He's extended the victims lives, but they will die from this eventually. In the mean time, Shane is just exhausting himself while prolonging the inevitable."

Tears filled my eyes when I thought about the children. I quickly blinked them away; clearing my throat stoically. There was one thing I'd already learned that day; crying didn't help anyone.

We continued searching the cabin; hoping to find anything that would give us a clue as to Brian's whereabouts.

We didn't find anything, so we went to the shed of dead animals. We covered our mouths and noses with clothe before John kicked the door open. He held the oil lamp out in front of him; getting a better look at what was inside.

It was worse than what I'd originally thought.

The animals hadn't just been brutally killed. It was obvious by the various wounds on each carcass that they'd been slowly tortured to death. Rabbits, chickens, squirrels, and even a few raccoons hung from the ceiling by hooks and rope. Maggots were consuming their way through the rotten flesh.

Even though I had my mouth and nose covered, I felt like the stench would contaminate my senses forever.

"That sadistic son-of-a-"

John stopped talking when he noticed a piece of paper pinned to the back of the door with. I tore the paper off of the wall, and John reverently shut the shed door. We walked until we were far enough away that the smell was manageable.

I held the oil lamp for John while he read the letter:

"Dear John Delany,

I'm sure you're wondering what is going on, so let me explain things to you. First of all, my condolences on the loss of your wife. Eliza truly was a gifted healer. I'll never forget her kindness. I wanted to give her a more memorable death than just a simple poisoning. Unfortunately, I ran out of time. I had a prisoner here, and she was getting to be a bit more than my cage could handle. I had to make a few short cuts in my plan. I'll always regret that I couldn't let Eliza go out with a slash and a bang like I'd planned. I'm sure you understand. At least this way I was able to make sure that Shane couldn't work his healing magic on her, since he was busy elsewhere helping the dying children.

Now that Eliza's well-being isn't on your mind anymore, I'm sure you'll be spending the majority of your time trying to keep the peace among the Scavengers. Good luck with that. I sincerely mean it, because you're going to need all the luck you can get. I've been working really hard to discredit you, and your close friends, in the community. I'm sure you'll find out soon enough that they actually don't want you to be their leader. Especially now that Eliza, you're better half, is gone.

Kain is more capable than you are. He's got the military experience to create Marshal Law amongst the Scavengers. That's the only way to defeat the Highborns.

Kain will be visiting you soon. I hope you come to your senses so I don't have to take anyone else you love. I know that Shane has gotten close to you. Nolan isn't around anymore to compete with him for your brotherly affections. Keep that in mind while you determine your next step.

I'm sure we'll see each other again soon, but until then keep your rifle close.

Sincerely, Brian."

My mouth hung open as John read the letter.

Brian tried to kill Eliza?

That was unimaginable. Everyone loved Eliza.

I mentally blocked the part about Nolan. I wouldn't even consider what the letter implicated.

I couldn't.

"I can't believe I didn't realize how psychotic he was." John shoved the letter in his coat pocket; his fingers quivering. "I let him join the community. I trusted him and put everyone in danger."

John wasn't really talking to me. He was just thinking out loud, but I couldn't let him blame himself for Brian's actions. No one could've known this.

"This isn't your fault."

"Stop." John gave me a sharp look. "I'm a detective, Winter. I trained for years to scope out degenerates like him. He's got the psyche of a potential serial killer. Hell, he probably *was* a serial killer before the natural disasters. The way he carved into those animals is sick and demented. People like that are hard to read sometimes, but I should've known. *It's my job to know.*"

I didn't respond. I had no idea what a serial killer was, but it was obviously something horrible. I cursed myself for my lack of knowledge, and it wasn't for the first time. I loathed the fact that I didn't know anything. My memories lost in a wave of torturous destruction.

Every night, I had dreams where I almost remembered something important. It was always taken from me the moment I woke up. There was a dark hollow feeling in my heart. A sense that I was forgetting something important.

I'd never told anyone about it. Not even Nolan when he used to call.

It was so difficult. Not knowing what a serial killer, a heart attack, or the Sleeping Ache was. It made me feel stupid. Inferior.

"I need to get you home. Then I need to figure out how to quarantine the Sleeping Ache before it kills all of us."

"I can help you, John." I followed him toward the trail we were on before. "You shouldn't deal with this plague alone."

John whirled around to face me; his eyes squinting with fury. His jaw clenched; his hands balled into tight fists. I had never seen him this angry before.

I would've been scared if I didn't trust him so much.

"You will stay with Eliza until all of this goes away. I already lost Nolan. I almost lost Eliza. I'm *not* going to lose you too. You're staying as far away from this plague as physically possible."

He spun back around, before I could argue with him, and marched into the trees. I had struck a nerve, but I didn't care. I was just as afraid of losing him too.

"You need someone to help you." I picked up my pace; catching up to him easily.

"That's what Shane is for." John didn't bother to look back at me. "He's immune to sicknesses."

"We don't know that."

"Don't do that." John's shoulders were rigid. The delicately bridled rage threatening to unleash. "You know just as well as I do that Shane is invulnerable. The only thing that'll kill him is overdoing it when saving someone else."

I knew John was right, but I didn't care.

I couldn't be imprisoned in Eliza's cabin when there were things that needed done. I knew that I was particularly vulnerable to sicknesses, since my powers required me to remain colder than the normal body temperature.

But I had already been exposed to the Sleeping Ache when I went with Shane to help the sick children. I realized now that I really shouldn't have gone. There was a big chance that I would get sick, and Shane wouldn't be able to save me. I would die quickly with how drastically the body temperature rises with the fever.

I had to get my mind off of that possibility.

"Maybe I should go after Brian."

John chuckled as though I'd said something funny.

"Why is that so hysterical? It's not like he'd have a chance against me."

John stopped walking and turned to look at me. Even though he'd been laughing his face was still a mask of fury.

"You aren't doing that. Not when you've been exposed to the Sleeping Ache. What if you got sick while you're tracking him? You'd be alone. That's unacceptable to me. Don't ask to leave again."

I stared at him incredulously.

He really did think of me as his daughter; didn't he?

Apparently, fathers freaked out when their girls wanted to do dangerous things. The only problem was; I wasn't really his daughter. I was old enough to make my own decisions.

I would never point that out to him though. I loved him too much for that.

I didn't talk for the rest of the trip home. Despite how angry John was with me for my silence.

Chapter 5: Nolan

Four weeks earlier

I pressed a button on the dashboard of the Jeep. With a low groan, the earth shift in front of me as a metal door appeared beneath the forest floor. I pressed the second button, and the metal door lifted up to reveal the cement driveway that went downward toward the hangar. I waited for the lights to activate in the tunnel before driving onto the underground driveway that led to the large hangar below.

It didn't take me long to get to my parking space. There were half a dozen Jeeps, and a few TNX One Hundreds, that were parked on the other side of the hangar. We only used the TNX's for missions that took us further away from the underground bunker than the coast. They did better in rough terrain than the Jeeps did.

Other than that, the League of Vigilance didn't have much for transportation. Most of the traveling was done by foot, especially for the single Vigilantes that hadn't been assigned a partner yet.

They were the ones that had it the worst within the League of Vigilance. So, naturally, they were the ones I spent the most time with. It was still frowned upon by Kain, and his closest followers, but I didn't care.

One of these days, I was going to fight back harder. Phoenix's *'death'* was just another aspect of my rebellion.

I parked the Jeep and turned off the engine. The lights stayed on in the hangar while I sat in the seat. I didn't like the fact that they were still on, but they were motion censored. They wouldn't turn off until I entered the underground bunker.

I pulled my tablet out and glanced around; making sure I was alone. I placed a call to Willow, and it rang a few times before her face appeared on my screen.

She had long wavy dark hair and almond shaped eyes that almost looked black in the dim lighting of the room she was in. She was a beautiful person, inside and out, and was my original partner before Phoenix joined us. She'd become my best friend over the past months.

If Willow ended up kissing me too- I would, officially, give up on relationships.

I was never really good at being a friend in the first place, and I was an even worse boyfriend. I was pretty sure Winter could attest to that. I'd kept myself emotionally closed off from her ever since she admitted that she loved me.

So stupid. So very stupid.

"Hey, Blue Eyes. Why are you calling me?"

"I just arrived at the hangar."

Over the past few months, we created code words that sounded like casual conversation to those around us. *'I just arrived'* was code for *'we need to talk in private. Meet me in our room in five minutes'*.

Kain could listen to all of our calls, so code was necessary for our survival in the bunker. It was painstaking; making sure that he didn't know about the calls I made to John and Winter. I had never thought of myself as a hacker before, but now I knew that I could pull it off when I needed to.

"Awesome!" Willow smiled, emotion vacant in her eyes. "I'm glad you made it back safely."

I got out of the Jeep as we continued talking. I could see that Willow was walking out of the room she was in. I wasn't sure where she was, but I hoped it wasn't too far from the room that we shared.

It was weird, but partners were expected to share everything. Including their bed. Which we absolutely refused to do. I always slept on the couch, while Willow took the bed, and Phoenix slept on a cot.

It had been an adjustment in the beginning, but now I couldn't imagine life without my partners. We'd gone on multiple missions together, and we had each others' backs. It had been a long time since I'd been able to trust someone, besides my family, like that.

"Well, I'll see you tonight."

That was code for '*something bad is going on*'. Willow's face paled slightly, but she kept her fake smile plastered to her face.

"Okay. See you later, Blue Eyes."

I hung up on her, and tucked the tablet in my jacket. The pack full of the Sleeping Ache Plague Cure was strapped firmly to my back, but I still clutched the straps tightly in my fists. It felt like I had the fate of the world on my shoulders.

I guess, in a way, I literally did.

I passed a few Vigilantes in the tunnels leading to my room, but I didn't make eye contact with them. I kept my pace steady; forcing my facial expression to appear neutral despite the anxiety coursing through me. Ever since Phoenix found the Sleeping Ache Cure, I seemed to be in a constant state of panic.

I could deal with evil people, but a plague was something else. I couldn't fight a disease the same way I fought the Highborns.

I really hoped that Phoenix would be okay on her own. She was our only hope to save the Scavenger community.

I got to my room and punched in the six digit code to unlock the door. I hurried inside when the door slid open. I slipped my arms out of the straps and set the pack on the floor next to the door.

Willow was sitting on the couch; tears falling from her eyes. She practically lunged at me the second I put the pack down. She gripped me around the shoulders; burying her face in my chest. I brought my hands up to steady her; my heart pounding.

"She's dead; isn't she? I should've been there."

"Whoa." I ran a hand up and down her back soothingly. She was shaking so badly I thought that maybe something else was going on. "Phoenix isn't dead."

Willow pulled back and looked me in the eyes.

"Really?" Her tone was so meek I nearly winced. "Where is she?"

"I'll tell you everything." I yawned, blinking through the fatigue. "Just give me a second to use the bathroom."

Willow nodded in relief, and sat back on the couch.

I pulled the blanket shut that divided the bathroom from the rest of the room before stripping out of my clothes. I was so exhausted. It was a struggle to do something as basic as showering.

I was grateful that Willow didn't try to ask me questions while I was in the bathroom. I needed the time to think about what I should tell her. I didn't want to hold back information from her, but I didn't want to put Willow in danger either.

I doubted that Willow would let me give her half a story though. I was a good liar, but this was about *Phoenix*. Willow cared about Phoenix more than anyone else. Even more than she cared about me. They had become really close during our trio partnership.

Once I was dressed, I stepped around the blanket and sat next to Willow. She had her knees pulled up to her chest; staring blankly at the wall.

"What happened?"

"Phoenix found something really disturbing in one of the medical shipping containers. Do you know what the Sleeping Ache Plague is?"

Willow's head jerked towards me; her eyes wide with horror.

"She found an entire crate full of the Sleeping Ache Plague Cure. We can only assume that the Highborns are planning to weaponize the Sleeping Ache to take us all out. So we filled both of our bags with the cure. We knew that Kain wouldn't give the cure to the Scavengers without them paying for it in some way. We decided that the Scavengers should get if for free. Phoenix is making her way to the Scavenger community to give it to my brother."

Willow hadn't moved the entire time I spoke. She watched me warily, but relaxed when I told her about the cure.

"John, right? The same guy that is creating his own army of Scavengers."

"That's not what he's doing."

We'd had arguments about John in the past. Kain hated my brother and what he was doing with the Scavengers. Which meant that a lot of the Vigilantes hated him too. I wished that Willow wasn't one of them.

"He's arming Scavenger men that-" Willow stopped talking and shook her head. "This isn't important. Let's get back on topic."

"No, you brought us off topic. Now you have to finish that sentence." I clenched my fists; forcing myself to bury the sudden fury that burned through my chest.

"I don't have to finish anything, Blue Eyes. We need to get the cure to Kain before-"

"Willow."

I shot her a look that told her I wasn't dropping the issue. I hated it when she talked negatively about John. We were going to finish this whether she wanted to or not.

Willow stared at me for a moment; blinking back the tears that formed in her eyes.

"You know that my years as a Scavenger sucked. Your brother is arming those men that made my life miserable."

I never knew exactly what Willow had gone through before she joined the Vigilantes, but I did know the only reason she was here was for protection. Whenever Phoenix asked her questions about her past, she gave a watered down version of what happened to her.

Willow went through years of severe abuse. I'd seen the scars she had from it. Her back in particular was pretty bad. She never told me what the scars were from, but it looked to me like she'd been whipped-

Definitely more than just a few times.

"No, Willow." I met her eyes reassuringly. "I've told you many times. John knows who the Feral Morons are. He would never arm them."

"You don't know that for sure."

But I did. I talked to John about what he was up to on a weekly basis. He drove out as many Feral Morons as he could. He had told me that there were a few left, but they'd been behaving so far. He still didn't grant them weapons though. He kept those for the men and women that had children to protect.

I couldn't tell Willow any of this, so she was left in the dark. Phoenix already knew John, and the good he'd done for the Scavenger community, so she didn't share Willow's opinions. No amount of persuasion ever convinced Willow that my brother was a good man. I think the only male she trusted was me. Even that trust was a bit shaky at times.

"John is a good man. I know you won't take my word for it, but maybe someday you'll be able to meet him. Then you'll see for yourself."

Willow didn't reply, so I got up from the couch and unzipped the pack full of the cure. I grabbed a needle and filled it with the cure as the directions indicated.

The sooner I got the cure into Willow, the better I'd feel.

"This isn't exactly pleasant, but you need to be vaccinated."

Willow nodded and started rolling up her sleeve.

"It's gotta go in your leg."

She winced, her face going pale.

"Just get it over with, Blue Eyes."

I gave her the injection quickly, and she grimaced when the cure hit her bloodstream. My thigh was still sore from when Phoenix gave me the shot, so the pain was still fresh in my memory.

"I gotta go give Kain my report." I strapped the pack to my shoulder. "You stay here."

"No. I need to be there for when he beats you to a bloody pulp." Willow's eyes narrowed at me. "Especially since you're planning on telling him Phoenix is dead."

I hadn't told her that was my plan. It was already obvious.

"I need to give him my report too. I have the Highborn Union data chip ready. He'll want to have everyone there to view some of the footage I uncovered. I'd tell you about it, but you'll just have to see it with your own eyes. It's pretty intense."

That was the best news I'd heard in a while. If the data chip had any information on Amanda Lynch's current location, then things could turn around for us.

Maybe if I let Willow give her report first, Kain would be in a better mood. Willow didn't seem to be worried about that possibility, but I sure was. Kain had once told me, if I lost a single member of my team on a mission, that he'd kill me for it.

This was going to be interesting.

An hour later, Kain finally walked into his office.

Willow and I were sitting in front of his desk. I usually preferred to stand when I gave reports, but I was fighting sleep as it was. I was pretty sure I had dozed off because Willow shook my arm when Kain opened the door.

The Viking looked as formidable as always.

We were expected to stand, and salute, when Kain walked into the room; so I struggled to my feet. It got to the point where saluting became second nature for me. It made me feel like a Nazi saluting Hitler, but I did it anyway. Just so he wouldn't have another excuse to kill me.

I had promised my family that I'd make it out of here alive, so this is what I had to do.

"Nolan Delany and Willow Rivers." Kain's deep voice rumbled through the room. He wasn't shouting, but to my tired ears it certainly sounded like it. "You are missing your third partner, Phoenix Rainer."

He smirked slightly. His bulbous tongue shot out; slowly moistening his cracked lips. He grinned; exposing yellowing teeth.

Gross.

"Since she isn't here I assume she is either dead, or has deserted. Care to elaborate, brother?"

Well, here goes nothing.

My legs started to shake with fatigue, so I sat back down. Which would probably help me sell the lie that Phoenix was dead. The more pathetic I was, the happier Kain would be. I told him about the Sleeping Ache Plague Cure and the explosion that we caused. I added in that

Phoenix had been shot while we were escaping the beach. I didn't have time to grab her pack, but I thought there was enough of the cure in mine for the Vigilantes to get their vaccinations.

Kain glanced at the pack that sat next to my chair, but didn't say anything to me. He looked expectantly at Willow, and she launched into her report without skipping a beat.

Apparently, she uncovered an entire year's worth of video feeds. It would be impossible to watch it in a short amount of time. She had managed to find some other locations of underground labs, but she still had more data to go through on the chip before she would know more.

"I assume you have the data with you."

"Yes, sir." Willow pulled her tablet out of her pocket, and Kain handed over his tablet. She connected them both with a cord and began tapping the screen. A few seconds later, she nodded and unplugged Kain's tablet from hers.

"Now you'll be able to see everything that I've found. They had footage of Casey's mission. It's quite disturbing, sir."

Kain nodded as he studied his tablet for a moment.

"We will view this first thing tomorrow morning. Be at the meeting room right after wake up call."

"Yes, sir."

I merely nodded in agreement.

"All the partners need to know about this. Singles don't need to be bothered. Casey's mission was the hardest on them. They don't need to see it."

Willow tensed slightly, but she nodded. I wasn't exactly sure what 'Casey's mission' was, but Willow used to be a single Vigilante before I joined. Whatever was on the footage must've been just as hard for her to see.

"Nolan Delany." Kain glared threateningly. "You lost a valuable member of the League of Vigilance. Phoenix Rainer was your responsibility. *You failed her.* You are lucky you brought back life saving medicine, and that you've got a second partner. Otherwise, you'd be executed."

Willow stiffened in her seat, but I didn't show any sign that Kain was scaring me.

"Her death is on your head. As punishment, I want you on the mats in five minutes. You'll give me four hours training. No meals until breakfast. If I catch you sleeping; I'll kill you with my bare hands."

I stood up and saluted- a little more sarcastically than I should have. Willow saluted too, and we both hurried out of the room.

"I thought he was going to beat you."

"I thought he was going to kill me. He still might. I'm not going to be able to stay awake for another four hours."

Willow chuckled, nervously, as she opened the door to the large training gymnasium. There were a lot of singles training in there at this time of night.

At least ten of them smiled and waved at us. We waved back and they all followed us to the other side of the gym.

"Where's Phoenix?"

Grace and David, two singles that trained with us often, glanced around the training room warily.

"Our last mission didn't go our way. She didn't make it home."

I'd never been a good actor, but it didn't take much convincing to pull the lie off.

Grace hurried away from us; her hand covering her mouth in devastation. David's brow furrowed in rage; his accusing eyes piercing me like a blade.

The singles that usually trained with us, left the mat. Muttering malicious curses at me as they passed.

"That went well." Willow rolled her eyes. "I'm telling you, Blue Eyes, there's no loyalty among the Vigilantes. We're wasting our time with them. We've been nothing but nice to them. Now that Phoenix is gone they blame us."

"No," I objected with a yawn. "They just blame me. You weren't even there."

"I should've been."

I didn't reply. She knew that was ridiculous without me saying so. She'd had more important things to do. Apparently, she uncovered something that made Kain happy enough that he hadn't killed me.

Yet.

"Do you want to talk about the footage you saw?"

We circled each other on the mat; our fists raised.

"It was just footage of one of the missions that went bad." Willow threw a jab at me. I blocked it easily, but didn't take advantage of the opening that she gave me. "It was pretty bad."

I kicked at her and she rolled out of the way. She'd gotten more comfortable with hand to hand scrimmages recently.

"I knew the people that were killed too."

I lowered my fists, studying her in concern. A haunted look in her eyes dimmed their natural light; holding back a torrent of tears. Life had already been excruciating for this woman. Seeing her friends die on a computer screen had seriously messed her up. More than she was letting on.

"Maybe you shouldn't go tomorrow after wake up call."

Willow scoffed at me, and I rolled my eyes. Her stubbornness rivaled mine most of the time.

"I'm serious." I blocked one of her kicks. "You've already seen it. You shouldn't have to watch it a second time."

She shook her head; lowering her fists tiredly.

"This is *my* project. If I'm not there- Kain will take his anger out on you again. I'm not going to let that happen. It gets old watching him beat the crap out of you. Especially since I'm the one that has to fix you up afterwards."

I didn't argue with her. No matter how much I wanted to.

"You think everything will be okay?"

I knew Willow was asking about Phoenix.

"I hope so."

I couldn't think about Phoenix being out there all alone without panic seizing my chest.

We spend the rest of the night sparing. I wasn't sure how I managed to stay on my feet for the whole four hours. By the time we got back to our room, I barely made it to my couch before I collapsed.

I was asleep before Willow turned off the light.

Chapter 6: John

By the time we got back to the cabin, it was very late. Eliza and Shane were both asleep, but they woke up when we opened the door. Shane was on his feet, wielding Winter's bat, before we were even through the door.

It was reassuring that he had such great reflexes.

Eliza came out of our room holding her handgun, but she lowered her aim when she saw me.

Every fiber within me relaxed. The tightness in my chest finally releasing it's grip at the sight of her. During the entire hike back, I couldn't help but imagine the worst. Shane could heal many things, but he'd never healed poison before now.

"Eliza." I pulled her into a tight hug. Her scent. Her small frame melting into me solidified my relief. "How are you feeling?"

"Tired, but I'm not sick anymore."

It took me a long moment to relinquish my tight hold on her. She knew what seeing her sick had done to my soul, and she clung to me. Reassuring me that she was still there. Still with me even when everything else in the world continued to fall apart.

"Brian?" Shane asked grimly, and I turned to look at him.

"Yeah, about that." I kept my arm wrapped around Eliza's waist. "He's been playing us this whole time."

Shane's brow furrowed as I pulled the letter from my pocket. For a brief moment, I thought about shielding Eliza from the horrible words on the paper. Ultimately, I knew that she needed to fully understand what was going on.

She wasn't a coward. I wouldn't treat her like one.

"He's gone now, but he left this behind." I handed Eliza the letter. "He had a torture cage in his cabin. It was obvious that he'd been keeping someone in there. The letter indicates that it was a girl, but there's no other clues as to who she was."

Eliza read the letter; her face void of feeling. The only emotion she showed was the slight tremor in her hand that gripped the paper.

"That deranged maniac poisoned me."

Suddenly, she looked furious enough to rip the letter to shreds.

I gently pried her fingers open and took the paper from her. I knew exactly how she was feeling. I was beyond angry too, but my experience as a police officer helped me deal with situations like this in a more productive way. I planned to memorize every word of the letter. To analyze it like the detective I used to be.

"No wonder it felt so different when I healed you." Shane read the letter over my shoulder. "Honestly, I'm just relieved it wasn't the plague."

I glanced at Winter, but she didn't meet my gaze. She just sat in her corner and closed her eyes. I hadn't been the best traveling companion on the way back home. If anything, I owed her an apology.

I should've forced the anger from my voice when I talked to her, but I couldn't manage it. Brian's letter, and the tortured animals, infuriated me in a way that I hadn't experienced in years.

But still, I'd never done that to Winter before. I couldn't believe that I'd talked to her the way I had.

"I believe it's the Sleeping Ache, Eliza."

Her hand went to her mouth when I told her about the message written in blood on Brian's wall. She looked so shocked that I couldn't resist touching her again. I held her other hand; gripping her fingers reassuringly.

"If it is the Sleeping Ache, then-"

Shane's broken voice trailed off, and he stared at the wall in a complete daze. Eliza, noticing his odd behavior, let go of my hand to touch his arm.

"Shane? Are you okay?"

He took a shaky breath and stared at Eliza; horror clouding his eyes.

"The Sleeping Ache Plague is the only thing I can't cure." Winter opened her eyes and stared at him. "I remember Dr. Darkwood specifically altered me to heal all sicknesses and injuries. But Amanda Lynch was adamant that I shouldn't be able to heal anyone suffering from S.A.P. I never knew what S.A.P. stood for, but this can't be a coincidence. It explains why I can't heal people from this plague."

Shane grew furious. He began pacing; breaking the stillness that had smothered the cabin. Winter closed her eyes again. A tear trickled down her cheek before she wiped it away.

"I'll work on making quarantine zones tomorrow." I turned to Eliza. "Once we determine who is sick, and who isn't, I'll be able to get a team together. I'm sure if we raid some of the Highborn Union medical shipments we'll find the Sleeping Ache Plague Cure. If Shane is right, and I think he is, then that means Amanda Lynch is trying to wipe us out with an epidemic."

Eliza nodded lethargically, and glanced at Winter. She was still just sitting there. The only time I saw her move was when she wiped the tear off her cheek. Eliza's eyes met mine in concern.

I gave her a kiss on the forehead.

"I'm going to talk to Winter for a minute. You go back to bed."

Eliza nodded and pulled away from me. She squeezed Winter's shoulder as she walked passed her.

"Goodnight, Winter."

She didn't reply.

Eliza's lips tightened in a worried line, and she went into our room.

Shane was still pacing.

"It's going to be okay."

Shane stopped pacing to stare at me incredulously. His eyes glistened with unshed tears.

"How can you say that? Every person I've tried to heal is going to die."

I put my hand on his shoulder to steady him.

"Shane, this isn't your fault. You know that, right?"

"Yeah, it's Amanda Lynch's fault."

Without another word, Shane went back to his cot in the corner closest to the fireplace. I decided to leave him alone until morning. We were all tired, scared, and heartsick.

I went to Winter's corner and sat in front of her. She didn't look at me, even though we were sitting so close our legs were touching. I waited a few seconds; hoping that she would eventually look at me.

She remained motionless.

I gently tapped her arm and she glanced up at me.

"I'm sorry," I signed silently. *"I was angry at Brian. I shouldn't have taken it out on you. You didn't deserve that."*

Winter stared at me for a moment in confusion. I worried that she didn't understand what I was trying to say. Then her fingers started flying. So methodically. Such a somber expression in her perfect form.

"You didn't do anything wrong. Brian tried to kill Eliza. It's okay to be angry."

She wouldn't meet my eyes when she signed. I understood the despair she held within her. A frosty chill seeped from her; causing a shiver to go down my spine.

"Then why won't you talk out loud?"

"I'm tired."

She used her exhaustion to mask a more severe issue.

My own exhaustion drained me; urging me toward Eliza and our bed. But I couldn't leave Winter like this. She would either have a nightmare or she wouldn't sleep at all.

"That may be true, but you're using that as an excuse, Winter."

"It's the plague." She spoke tersely; her blue eyes flashing frigidly. "So many people are going to die. I can do nothing to stop it. I can't even touch anyone without risking freezing them to death. I can't just stay here and do nothing, John. I need to go searching for Nolan."

So we were back to this argument. It didn't surprise me since we didn't really solve anything on the way home.

I grimaced, forcing myself to breathe through the immense frustration.

There was no way I was letting Winter go off by herself. She'd already been exposed to the plague. I was terrified that she was going to start having symptoms. When that happened, she was going to be here with us.

Not suffering alone in the forest.

"I know, sweetheart." I forced myself into a comforting tone. "But it won't do us any good if you got sick when you're alone. Shane wouldn't be able to help you."

She rolled her eyes. My heart pounded painfully; the gesture reminding me so much of Nolan I wanted to sob.

"I feel fine."

I nodded, resisting the urge to collapse on the floor next to her. Sleep kept beckoning me.

"I know you do. Hopefully it'll stay that way, but you've been exposed. We need to be cautious."

Winter relaxed against the wall. A gesture of somber resignation. The fight had gone completely out of her and she looked seconds away from passing out.

"I'm gonna let you sleep. I'll see you in the morning."

"Goodnight, John."

I kissed her cheek, and went to the bedroom. Eliza was lying on the bed, but she wasn't asleep yet. She sat up when I shut the door; greeting me with a forlorn look.

"Is Winter okay?"

I peeled off my dirty shirt; tossing it into a wooden bin next to the bed.

"No." I pulled on a pair of sweatpants to sleep in. "I don't think she will be for a while."

"You talked to her about Nolan?"

I nodded and crawled onto the bed. I didn't want to talk about Nolan, so I didn't stop moving until I was practically on top of her. My face hovered above hers; my lips pressing against her forehead.

"I almost lost you, Eliza." My voice trembled in my throat. "I almost lost you."

Her hands threaded through my hair and she lifted her head slightly. She kissed me with such intensity that I couldn't resist closing my eyes. She smelled like the lavender soap she made; her skin silky beneath my fingertips.

"Shh." Her husky tone soothed the raging inside me. "I'm not going anywhere."

I smoothed my thumbs over the soft contours of her cheeks; lowering my lips to hers again. I could think of nothing else but *her*. She was my wonderful distraction from the sorrows of my world. My reason for continuing on. For fighting the battle I faced everyday.

I wouldn't be able to survive losing my wife again. The first time around almost killed me.

Being with Eliza was the best thing I had now- She was the *only* thing I had now. *My lifeline.* When I took on the responsibility as leader of the Scavengers, she had been by my side every step of the way.

I made her Kain's target and gotten Nolan killed. I would never forgive myself for that.

It didn't matter that all I was trying to do was protect the Scavenger families from the Highborn Union. It didn't matter that I had no intention of going to war against the League of Vigilance. Kain saw any armed group as a threat to him.

I'd known this, but I formed and trained a small army anyway.

I did it to protect people.

I did it because I was done sitting on the sidelines.

I just wished I would've been able to pull Nolan out before he went silent. Now I had to live with that guilt. I couldn't screw up when it came to Eliza's safety.

She deepened the kiss and the air punched out of my lungs. Her fingers tightened in my hair before sliding downward; sending a shiver through me.

I lost all train of thought.

Lost all reason.

Forgot the guilt and the fear.

For a moment, nothing in the world mattered but us.

The next morning, Eliza and I stayed in bed later than usual.

After last night, the idea of getting up was unthinkable.

"Do you remember how it happened?"

I held Eliza close to me. She threaded her fingers through mine before answering.

"As ridiculous as it sounds; Brian must've poisoned me with the apple he offered me. I've always been a sucker for apples."

I tightened my arms around her; pulling her even closer. I buried my face in her hair and let out a shuddering breath.

"I'm so sorry, Eliza."

"It's not your fault, John." She shifted to look me in the eye. "You don't have to feel responsible for this."

I kissed her nose; my beard tickling her face. Her reaction was adorable despite our conversation.

"You're my wife. It's my responsibility to protect you."

"Along with the rest of the world?"

"Yep, that sounds about right."

Eliza smirked, relaxing into the pillow. I closed my eyes and took her hand in mine. Feeling her pulse at her wrist beneath my fingertip. More reassurance that she was still here. Alive and with me.

"What is the plan for today?"

"I'll take Shane with me to prepare quarantine zones. I want you and Winter to stay here."

Eliza grumbled, rolling all the way over so she was face to face with me. I raised an eyebrow at her evident exasperation.

"I'm the Scavenger medic. I should be at the quarantine zone."

"Winter is susceptible to sickness more than most people. She's already been exposed to the Sleeping Ache. She also needs to stay away to keep her identity a secret. You know what'll happen if Kain finds out about her."

Eliza was silent for a moment; a thoughtful look in her eyes.

"You're going to hate me for this-"

"That's not possible."

She smiled at that before giving me a quick kiss with her soft lips.

"I overheard your conversation with Winter last night. I think if she wants to go looking for Nolan then you should let her."

I stiffened, my jaw clenching painfully.

The idea of sending a teenage girl, no matter how powerful she was, to look for my brother was infuriating. Especially since I should be the one searching.

I let out a frustrated grunt, and Eliza narrowed her eyes at me.

"I know what you're thinking-"

I grumbled, dreading what would come next.

"You can't leave the community now, but Winter can. She's resourceful and intelligent. You also have to realize that she'll go off on her own eventually. With or without your blessing."

It took me a while to calm down enough to speak rationally. I was so angry, my fingers trembled. Eliza tried to soothe them by rubbing her thumb over my knuckles.

"Why are you playing the devil's advocate, Eliza?"

"If Winter hasn't gotten the plague yet, then I don't think she will. Especially if she goes off looking for Nolan. She'll be away from the community. Is the plague the only reason you want her to stay here?"

Of course the plague wasn't the only reason I wanted Winter to stay. I couldn't get the memory of what happened the last time I'd left her alone out of my mind.

Ember, a girl with fire abilities, had captured her and taken her to another underground lab. She would've died there if it hadn't been for Nolan. Even though Ember was dead now, I still didn't want Winter going off alone. No matter how resourceful she was.

I had no desire to talk about it with Eliza right now though. We needed to get going. I had to find out if anyone else had succumbed to the plague. The community needed to be updated on the information I'd gotten yesterday.

"We'll talk about it later." I kissed the back of her head. "Shane and I need to get going."

Eliza sighed and sat up with me.

"I'm going too."

"Winter needs you to stay here with her."

Eliza pulled her shirt on and glowered at me.

"What makes you think I would stop her if she tried to leave?"

I stared at her; trying very hard not to let the frustration consume me.

"Winter has a right to leave if she wants to." She laid her hand on my arm. I had to resist the urge to pull away from her. "Besides, what if she finds Nolan, or Brian? What if she finds the cure?"

"*I'm* going to find the cure." I glared sternly. "It'll only take me an hour to form a team. Then we'll be on our way to the Highborn Union by tomorrow morning."

Eliza nodded, folding her arms defiantly.

"What about Nolan? Who's going to go looking for him? It's been weeks."

I closed my eyes; the pain assaulting me.

I didn't know why Eliza was doing this. We'd come to the determination weeks ago that Nolan was gone. There was no way to find him. To save him.

He was dead.

No matter how agonizing it was to admit- I knew it was the truth.

"Maybe we gave up on him too easily," she continued in that soft, gentle whisper. "Shouldn't one of us at least attempt to find him?"

Damn it. She was right.

But still-

"Why does that have to be Winter? We'd be handing her over to the wolves if Kain, or the Highborns, found her."

Eliza smiled, and I had no idea why she would. Maybe the poison had altered her brain.

"She is a force of nature. Not even a pack of wolves can survive being turned to ice."

Yeah, but Winter wasn't a killer. Of that I was certain. She didn't have it in her.

As though she could read my mind, Eliza narrowed her eyes at me.

"You know that Winter would do *anything* to get Nolan back."

Eliza left the room; leaving me alone with my thoughts and rage. I grabbed my rifle and marched out of the room. It took me a moment to realize that I was stomping and I forced myself to step lighter.

There was no way I was giving Winter my blessing to leave. If she ended up like Nolan-

The guilt would destroy me.

Winter and Shane were making breakfast in the kitchen while Eliza packed medicines and other supplies into her bag.

It was infuriatingly amusing that she thought she was going with me.

"You're not coming," I whispered as I walked passed her.

"I wasn't waiting for an invitation." Eliza raised an eyebrow at me. A challenge I would gladly contend with.

I wasn't exposing her to the plague. It didn't matter if she was the medic.

"Don't assume I won't tie you to the kitchen chair."

Eliza laughed. She merely thought I was kidding.

At this point, I was fairly certain that I wasn't.

Winter and Shane ignored us as they set breakfast on the table and started eating. Winter had her bag packed as well-

"You're not going either."

Winter didn't respond. She kept eating as though I hadn't said anything to her. I usually let that kind of behavior slide, but I was extremely angry this morning.

Everyone, except Shane, seemed hell-bent on pushing my buttons.

"Can you at least tell me why you packed a bag?"

It took her a moment, but she finally looked at me. I could see the change in her was hovering just below the surface. She was on the verge of using her powers. I didn't know if it was on purpose or if she was struggling for control, but I needed to be more cautious.

"Are you okay?"

"No." Winter stood up from the chair. She hurried outside with her bag.

I stared in shock at the door she'd just slammed.

"She's leaving, John." Shane stood up from the table. "I tried to talk her out of it, but she's determined."

Eliza glared at me urgently, and I finally came to my senses.

I practically ran outside.

I found her standing next to the clothes lines; staring at the woods in the distance.

She wore a tank top and jeans in the middle of the coldest time of year. It always amazed me how she could adapt to the freezing temperatures like that. I pulled my jacket tighter around myself and walked up to her.

I didn't say anything for a while as I stood next to her.

I already knew what was going to happen if I said what I wanted to say. We'd talk in circles like we had before; neither of us agreeing with the other. She wanted to leave. I wanted to hide her away in the cabin. I tried to tell myself it was only because she was a kid, but deep down- I knew what I really wanted.

I wanted her to be safe from the world because of what that world had done to her. I had saved her once from a group of Scavenger men that wanted to brutalize her. I pictured her as I would my daughter, Emily.

But they were two different people. Two girls from two different lives. Two different worlds.

I wasn't seeing Winter for who she really was.

I was trying to shield her from pain, like any overprotective parent would. I had absolutely no right to do that. I was smothering her. It was wrong of me- no matter how much I cared about her.

Eliza had been right about Nolan too. We did give up on him too quickly. I didn't think he was still alive, but maybe we could all get some closure if one of us went looking for him. It sickened me that it had to be Winter, but I needed to try to see her for who she really was.

She wasn't weak. She was more than capable of finding Nolan if he was out there somewhere. I should've let her go looking for him weeks ago.

I put my arm around her shoulders, despite how cold she was, and I pulled her closer to me. She warmed up a little when she hugged me back.

"If you're going to leave I want you to take one of the communicators." She pulled away from me; her face a mask of shock. "Don't get me wrong; I don't want you to do this. But I can see that staying here is doing you more harm than good. Just don't go radio silent on me, okay?"

Winter nodded, pulling a communicator out of her bag with a smirk on her face. I sighed in relief that she had the foresight to grab it before she left.

It was time that I stopped underestimating her.

"If Nolan's out there, then I'm going to find him. If he's not, then I'll at least find Brian. He shouldn't be allowed to hurt anyone else."

I nodded, glancing back at the cabin.

"Were you planning on saying goodbye to Shane and Eliza?"

"I already did. I knew you'd follow me out here, so I figured I'd say goodbye to you without an audience in case you started yelling."

I *did* want to yell.

The last time I let a teenager make a decision to leave I never saw him again. All I could do was hope that Winter didn't end up dead like Nolan.

It didn't matter what I thought though. Winter wasn't even my actual daughter. No matter how much I wished she was.

"This is hard for me, Winter. I can't go through this again."

She wrapped her arms around me once more. I ruffled her short blonde hair before she pulled away.

"I'm going to come back."

"If you start to feel sick, or if you need anything, call me on the communicator. Shane and I will come get you in the Jeep."

The Scavengers had only one Jeep. We used it to patrol our boarders, but if Winter got sick in the woods somewhere I'd use it to get to her.

Winter nodded in understanding; making the sign for 'I love you'. I made the sign back, and she turned toward the trees.

I watched her walk away until she disappeared into the forest.

Chapter 7: Winter

I began my search at the cabin of horrors.

Brian's true purpose was hauntingly disturbing, as well as completely mysterious.

He had come to Eliza with a broken arm right after Nolan left us. It had been while John and I were still trying to rescue street orphans. John hadn't taken position as the Scavenger leader yet.

Why would Kain see the need to send a spy before John had made any moves?

I also didn't understand how Brian broke his arm in the first place. It was obvious that he hadn't defected from the League of Vigilance as he'd claimed.

Had it been purposely broken so that he could meet Eliza in an innocent looking way?

I couldn't help but wonder if Nolan ever met him. He would've seen right through Brian. Would've known how psychotic he was.

I knelt down; examining faded tracks in the snow. A cold breeze blew, but thick shrubs protected the footprints. Two people walking side by side. Colored blotches littered the snow.

Blood. Old blood had stained the area. Freezing the snow into an icy pink hue.

Brian had forced his prisoner to go with him. Despite everything he'd done to them.

I had planned on going through the cabin one more time for clues, but I decided against it. The urgent desire to save another tortured soul consumed me.

If the girl had any chance of survival, I needed to follow the trail. They had a few days head start, but I wasn't dragging an injured person along with me. If they were going to the League of Vigilance underground bunker, that would be even better.

The torrential darkness had completely taken over within me. The frozen abomination that dwelt in the deepest depths of my soul had clawed its way out. Shadowing my thoughts with determined vengeance.

It was one of the reasons I insisted on leaving. I could feel the force of nature that dwelt within my DNA rising to the surface. I was dangerous as it was, but with how thin my control was-

I needed to find him.

I wasn't going to stand by anymore without knowing what happened to Nolan. If he was dead, then heaven help the people that killed him. If he was Kain's prisoner, then I'd get him out-

And kill every last one of the Vigilantes if I had to.

Nolan had told me once that I was inherently good. He had no idea how wrong he'd been.

The moment I was out of sight of Eliza's cabin I'd let the ice overtake me. Now I was the abomination that had been hiding away ever since the night I'd escaped. I'd killed five people that night. I'd been a monster locked inside an underground cage.

In a way, I was still locked in a cage. Fighting and clawing at the chance to end the people that hurt Nolan.

The trees around me turned to solid ice as I ran passed them. I was usually slower than this, but I had so much unspent energy that I couldn't resist sprinting. I would be exhausted in a few hours, but I didn't care.

Maybe I wouldn't have a nightmare if I was tired enough.

I ignored the screech of an owl that I'd disturbed with my intensely cold temperatures. I should be distraught at the idea of hurting animals, but I was beyond that feeling now. Beyond rational thought as I followed Brian's blood trail.

The snow beneath me turned to ice as I ran across it.

Eventually, the ache in my lungs took away the icy fury that gnawed its way through my soul. I slowed to a brisk walk; forcing myself to breathe through the pain.

It took much longer than I wanted, but the ice around me thawed. I took a shuddering breath; blinking back the tears that threatened to fall.

I didn't know if I could do this without Nolan. I could barely control my powers when I knew he *was* alive.

I had been too cowardly to tell that to my family.

I loved them all too much to saddle them with my burdens anymore. I wasn't sure what I would do when I finished killing Brian and the people that hurt Nolan. If John hadn't found the cure by then, maybe I would search for that next.

I wouldn't go back home though. Not until I developed better control over my darkness. The best thing I could do was exile myself to protect what was left of humanity.

I often wondered if Amanda Lynch created me just for that purpose. Would me living with the Scavengers eventually give her exactly what she wanted? That one day I wouldn't be able to control my ice and I'd kill everyone around me.

Yeah, I was never going back. It would be selfish if I did.

By the time I was too exhausted to walk anymore, the sun had been down for hours. I laid out the blanket that I'd strapped to my back and sat on top of it.

WINTER'S ROSE

The cold night air envelop me, and I basked in it's comfort. I didn't feel like this very often anymore, so I took whatever I could get. Sitting in the winter air seemed to energize me more than a full night's sleep could.

I forced myself to lay down, despite the surge of energy. Closing my eyes to the breeze and falling snow-

It didn't take long for my mind to drift away.

I ran up the steps of a long stairway; merging into a dark hall. Lights flickered, causing my heart to thump loudly in my ears.

Once I'd made it to my apartment, a loud rumble moved through the entire complex. I choked on a gasp; opening the door just as the living room started to sway.

I screamed, the floor rolling like the waves of the ocean. Items soared off of the shelves. Furniture flipped around the living room as the world shook around me.

The shelves toppled over as I dove toward the dining room. I held onto the table legs while everything in the room jumped around as though they were possessed.

I thought over and over again about my father. I wanted him. Needed him so badly in that moment, but I couldn't picture his face. In that moment of sheer terror, all I wanted was to feel his strong arms around me. Protecting me from the force of nature that was destroying my world.

The shaking of the earth worsened. Drywall and wood rained down from above. The building collapsed around me. I kept myself plastered to the floor as I fell through the air.

Luck. It was sheer luck that I had survived at all.

The next thing I knew, I was being dug out of the debris that covered me. A deep gash on my head bled freely.

The rescue worker that uncovered me, pulled me out of the small hole I'd been stuck in. I had so many injuries I didn't want to stand, but the man forced me to anyway-

I woke up screaming. The terrifying nightmare fading away from memory and thought.

My blanket was a sheet of ice beneath me. The trees within a ten foot radius glimmered like solid crystal.

I never had nightmares like that at Eliza's cabin anymore. At least, not ones that made me freeze everything around me.

I wondered what it would do to me if I never slept again.

It took a moment to shake off the terror. To focus on the mission and the target of my pursuit.

I rolled up my blanket; strapping it to my back along with my bag. The contents were completely soaked. The food had been frozen and then thawed. Making the fruit leather I had for breakfast taste a little weird. I washed it down with some cold water before following Brian's path.

I started out at a steady run like I had the day before.

After two hours, I finally came across the first place Brian camped. I took a moment to rest while I studied the area. They hadn't left anything behind that I could see. I searched for any sign of blood, but it appeared that Brian's victim had stopped bleeding.

That was a small mercy.

Hopefully she would still be alive when I caught up to them.

Two days later, I finally found him.

Located at the base of a mountain, the neatly peeled logs and trimmed windows were like a beacon in the snow. Icicles clung to the metal roof that angled toward the ground. Smoke bellowed from a large stone chimney. Lamplight flickered in the windows; illuminating the gray snow that surrounded the cabin.

Most dwellings these days were crudely constructed out of materials the Scavengers could find in the wastelands. The only time I'd ever seen a home this nice was when I was living on the streets. Even then, I could never get a close up look at them.

It would've been beautiful if the people surrounding it weren't Vigilantes.

I hid in the trees; observing the activity around the cabin. It didn't take me long to find Brian through the window of the living room. I was too far away to see what he was doing in there, but I didn't really care anyway.

He was a dead man as soon as I busted the door down.

Five Vigilantes dressed in gray combat gear guarded the cabin. I had no interest in killing them, so I had to play this safe. Even though I'd felt murderous while hunting Brian down, that feral need had subsided now that I had him in my sight.

John wouldn't want me to kill everyone I came across if I could help it.

Luckily for the guards, I respected John enough to do what he'd want. Besides, I needed to locate the League of Vigilance underground bunker-

I wondered how quickly I could get the guards to reveal it to me.

I discarded my bag next to a large tree; creeping my way closer to the cabin. I moved slowly; not wanting to alert anyone to my presence.

I picked up a thick stick that was poking out of the snow- wielding it like a bat. I kept my footsteps quiet as I approached one of the Vigilante guards doing a perimeter check.

Unfortunately for him, he was alone.

I aimed at his head; swinging my stick as hard as I could.

With a soft crack, he went down like a sack of potatoes. He wasn't unconscious, but he was dazed enough that he didn't cry out.

I used my ice to cuff his wrists and feet together. He grunted in pain at the cold. I shoved cloth in his mouth before he could scream for help.

I picked up my stick again.

The remaining guards hovered around the front door. There was a window on the east side of the cabin where Brian was stationed. He stood there, gazing out into the dark night.

There was no way of knowing how many people were in the cabin with Brian, but I was willing to bet that he kept his hostage close.

I crouched beneath the window; pressing my hand against the log wall as I let the cold flow through me. The frost burst out of my hand; rapidly covering the wood. I forced the ice to slow; blanketing the wall a bit more gradually. The ice made its way to the window; the thick frost spreading over the glass.

Brian immediately began barking orders to the guards. The urgency, and panic, in his tone brought a smirk to my lips.

The sound of the front door slamming open echoed through the still night. It wasn't long before the Vigilantes made their way around the corner of the house.

Their guns held out in front of them.

I brought up a large wall of ice to shield myself from their bullets. The sound of gunshots was deafening, but I ignored the ringing in my ears. I surrounded myself with hovering ice shields; protecting me completely.

I stalked toward the cabin door; bullets imbedding themselves in my ice shield.

Crack!

Broken ice rapidly surrounded me on all sides like spiderwebs. I exhaled, willing my ice to repair itself.

I stared in horror at the water flowing through the cracks; soaking my legs and the snow under my feet.

The bullets somehow melted my ice!

A sharp pain seared through my right shoulder. The shock vibrated through me- sucking all the air from my lungs in an instant. I couldn't scream. Couldn't even breathe as I collapsed to my knees.

My ice melted away completely. Leaving me, terrifyingly, exposed.

The gunfire ceased. Shouting voices broke through the ringing in my ears. It was when my vision cleared that I realized I'd been momentarily blinded.

Brian stood over me. A demented smirk marred his handsome face. His gun aimed directly at my forehead.

I panicked, desperately trying to shoot a stream of frost at him.

I knew it wouldn't work. The attempt would only show my enemies how desperate I was.

The Vigilantes had somehow gotten their hands on the very bullets that Dr. Darkwood created to subdue me. To kill me when he was done with me.

Too hot.

My skin tingled; the blood in my veins scorching me from the inside. The pain was so intense I had to fight to stay conscious. To struggle to maintain eye contact with the man that held the gun to my head.

I had failed. *Horribly*.

Brian sneered, shifting his aim to my shoulder. I was already bleeding profusely from the previous bullet that was still lodged inside me-

But the look on his maniacal face screamed for more. He chuckled, savoring every moment as he watched me heave for breath.

"Unfortunately, Kain's orders are for me to bring you in alive." He took a step closer to me; snow crunching under his boots. "But who knows how powerful you are? Better to be safe than sorry."

He adjusted his aim slightly and fired. The force of the shot pushed me backwards, violently. My insides were on fire. The invisible heat rushed through my blood as my heart raced. My skin was too cold. The contrasting sensations threatened to, rapidly, break me apart.

The inferno inside me was all consuming.

I barely felt the gunshot wounds that tore my flesh open. Blood gushed out of me in rapid trickles, but I couldn't move my hand to staunch the bleeding.

Brian knelt next to me; his soft fingers tracing down the side of my face. It traveled down my neck; lingering at my carotid artery. My pulse beat rapidly against his skin; fascination brightening those deranged eyes. He grunted in amusement; moving his smooth palm down my bare arm in a gentle caress.

I gritted my teeth; shivering in disgust.

"You have the softest skin I've ever felt." His words laced with lust. "Is that because you're not entirely human? Or did you have good genetics before Darkwood had his way with you?"

I hated his touch. He knew that, so he kept his hand on my arm. He tightened his grip into a bruising hold. I would've flinched if I wasn't already in so much pain.

"We're gonna have fun, aren't we, Winter?"

Brian slid an arm under my legs and wrapped his other arm around my torso. I struggled as hard as I could, but he merely laughed at my feeble attempts at protest.

I was powerless to stop him from holding me against him.

"You'll learn quickly that I don't like it when my women fight me, Winter." His tone darkened cruelly. "Don't think I won't shoot you again."

I redoubled my efforts to free myself from his hold when he lifted me off the ground. My hand fumbled for the knife I kept on my hip, but I wasn't fast enough to pull it out of the sheath.

Brian threw me to the cabin floor. The air rushed out of my lungs from the impact. My bullet wounds pulsed in agony; forcing a scream from me.

Brian shoved my hand away from my knife; pulling it out of the sheath himself.

He held my blade in front of my face. The cold steel glimmered in the light of the fireplace. I went perfectly still as he traced the tip of the blade along every scar on my face and neck.

He analyzed each one. Morbid curiosity burning in his eyes. I tried not to think about the torture I went through to get those scars. Tried to ignore the pressing fear that Brian could end my existence with a mere flick of his wrist. I forced my mind to go blank as he moved the cold blade over the scars on my chest and arms.

"Dr. Darkwood certainly knew how to inflict pain, yeah?" Brian's dark tone morphed into regret. "Too bad Kain couldn't recruit him before Amanda Lynch got a hold of him."

Brian ordered one of the Vigilantes to stop me from bleeding out, but I closed my eyes. I went so deeply into the abyss that I didn't even dream.

Chapter 8: Nolan

Four weeks earlier

Wake up call came way too early.

Usually, Vigilantes were given a few days to recover after a mission. Apparently, that didn't apply to me this time.

Somehow, I managed to roll off my couch before the door opened. I probably looked like a bleary-eyed lunatic, but that was exactly what Kain wanted.

At least one of us would be happy today.

Cade and his partner, Krissy, came into the room as Willow and I stood at attention. I resisted the urge to rub my eyes, but I couldn't prevent the wide yawn that almost dislocated my jaw-

Theoretically.

I was convinced that my entire face would be permanently bruised if I ever survived this place.

Cade hovered in front of me; a small glare darkening his eyes. I still hated the guy, but he was Kain's second in command now. I had to act like I respected him.

"Are we boring you already, Nolan?" Cade's eyes bore into mine; both of us refusing to be the first to look away.

I merely shook my head.

Cade took a step closer to me. He seemed extraordinarily angry, but I wasn't sure why. I hadn't done anything to him. At least, not for a long time. It was possible that he was just upset about Phoenix, but that didn't make sense either.

He'd never liked her, despite how amazing she is. More proof that he was a raging psychopath.

"We're doing a thorough search of your room." Cade smirked as he tried to stare me down.

"Have fun."

I sat back down on the couch, completely unfazed. Willow came over to join me as Krissy began searching the bed. Cade took out his tablet and turned it on. After about a minute of staring at the screen, he nodded to himself and powered it down.

"No bugs or cameras detected."

Krissy finished tearing Willow's bed apart and turned to glare at us.

"Give me your tablets."

Willow and I got up from the couch and went to get our tablets from the table we left them on the night before. Cade quickly tore apart the couch while Krissy searched our tablets' history.

She put my tablet back on the table, and didn't seem to detect anything suspicious. She did the same with Willow's tablet, and Cade came up behind her.

"Find anything interesting?"

Krissy shook her head.

"Nope, just that Nolan called Willow yesterday when he got back, but they erased that conversation."

Willow and I glanced at each other in confusion. It was clear that she was nervous, but probably not nearly as much as I was.

"Do you do that often?" Cade asked me, and I shook my head.

"Not really. I just wanted to give her a heads up about Phoenix, so I asked her to come to our room. They were close, so I thought it would be best if the news came from me."

Krissy gave me a murderous glare that I'd never seen from her before. She became a Vigilante shortly after I did, but I'd never seen her around the Scavenger community before.

She was tall with long dark red hair and bright blue eyes. She was beautiful, and I remember thinking that she was way too good for Cade. But what did I know. I wasn't in charge of Kain's demented genetic matching he forced people into.

"You got one of your partners killed. You thought that telling Willow what you did, in person, would be helpful?" Krissy hissed angrily. "I hope Kain decides to punish you."

I merely smirked at her; rage igniting in her eyes.

"I'm surprised he didn't kill you last night." Cade stepped up to me. A broad smile erupted on his face. "Maybe he'll let me do it for him."

I glared and took a threatening step toward him. He stumbled back a little as though he expected me to throw a punch. I had no intention of doing that, but it felt good to watch him squirm a little.

"I think it's interesting how much you care about Phoenix now that she's gone. Especially since you tried to abandon her in a cave while she was sick."

Cade's face flushed red; his fists clenching threateningly.

"I was following orders. Kain was testing you."

I leveled a severe look at him. The same look that terrified most of the Vigilantes I'd sparred with.

"Because that's what good, little soldiers do. Right?"

Cade smirked at me and gave Krissy a nod. She went to the door and he followed her.

"Report to the meeting room in fifteen minutes."

Once the door was shut, I let out a sigh of relief. Willow slumped a little and folded her arms across her stomach.

"You okay?" I glanced at her as I picked up the discarded couch cushions.

"Yeah." She nodded unconvincingly. "What was that? Room searches are only supposed to happen once a month. We just had one last week. Plus, they never demand to see our tablets."

"Who knows?"

There was a tick in the back of my mind that told me something bigger was going on, but I didn't want Willow to know how concerned I was.

"Do you think we'll get in trouble for the call yesterday?" I heard the distress in her tone- could see the terror in her- as she stoically tried to remake her bed.

"I hope not, but if we do I'll take the blame."

"Why do you always do that, Blue Eyes?" She snorted incredulously. "Sometimes, I think you *enjoy* getting your trash kicked."

I could admit that I *was* an adrenaline junkie-

Still, I didn't think anyone would enjoy getting their ribs bashed in by a Viking.

"I'm the one that called you. Technically, it was my fault."

I strapped my gun holster around my shoulders before putting on my jacket. My bow and quiver of arrows leaned against the wall next to the table. I didn't get to use them very much anymore. I missed using my bow, but Kain had insisted that bullets were faster. He was right, but I'd never been a fan of guns. There was something about a bow and arrow that made me feel at ease when I was out in the field.

I left my archery equipment where it was, and followed Willow out the door.

It didn't take us long to get to the meeting room. All the other Vigilante couples were there. The single Vigilantes were in the mess hall, since Kain didn't want to subject them to what Willow had uncovered. I still didn't quite understand why.

He certainly wasn't doing that out of the goodness of his hideous heart.

I glanced at my partner and gritted my teeth.

Her face was pale; her lips parting slightly as she tried to slow her breathing. Sweat broke out on her forehead; her entire body tensing as though she were in pain.

If I didn't know any better; I would say that my strong willed, hardcore friend was about to have a panic attack.

"What's going on?"

She straightened her shoulders and glanced at me.

"Nothing, Blue Eyes."

"Don't lie."

Her face paled even more; her lips forming into a tight line. She swayed and I grabbed her arm.

I'd be damned if I let her fall to the floor.

"I'm about to watch my best friend die. Again."

Crap.

No wonder she didn't want to tell me what kind of footage she'd uncovered.

She folded her arms and shifted her eyes to the floor. Avoidance. She was trying to avoid the horror of what her friend went through.

Of all the hellish things I'd been through- I knew Willow's trauma far surpassed my own.

"We'll sit in the back." I didn't know what else to say. Didn't know what I could do. "You can slip out the door when you need to."

She nodded and followed me to the back row of seats. We sat in the chairs nearest the door, and stared at the large screen at the front of the room. Kain was sitting in the chair next to the computer while Cade was working on his tablet-

Preparing the horrendous footage for the audience to view. To kindle the hatred of Amanda Lynch, and the Highborns, that dwelt within each of us.

It didn't take long for the rest of the seats to fill up. When everyone was seated, Kain stood up and raised both of his hands over his head. The room quieted down instantly. Everyone was completely transfixed by his very presence. Every eye viewed him in admiration. An unholy worship that made my stomach squirm.

I still couldn't believe I'd been stupid enough to believe that this wasn't a cult; that Kain would save humanity.

I'd been a complete idiot.

"Willow Rivers has uncovered footage of the deaths of our own!" Kain roared, his arms raised above his head as though in triumph. "Cade and I have been up late viewing additional footage from our other missions that the Highborn Union had on file!"

There was more footage?

My stomach dropped; adrenaline pumping through me. I barely heard Kain as his benevolent ranting continued.

"It is necessary for us, as the leaders of the League of Vigilance, to view it! When we are through witnessing these horrors, we will take immediate action to right the wrongs! To avenge our fallen!"

I groaned inwardly at how ominous that sounded. Before I could wonder too much about what we were about to see, the giant screen in front of us turned on. The lights in the room dimmed.

It took my brain a moment to grasp what I was seeing on the screen. When it registered- when what I saw finally broke through the barrier of denial- my stomach revolted.

Bile threatened to spew from my mouth.

Winter was strapped down to an operating table while Dr. Darkwood injected her with a creamy white liquid. It was bubbling, as though it were being boiled in the IV bag. She was bald, pale, and completely anorexic.

A piercing scream came from Winter's raw throat as she shook violently.

The pain in that scream ripped through me like a blade.

My fists clenched when Dr. Darkwood put his gnarly hand on her forehead.

I had to remind myself that this was old footage. There was nothing I could do to help her now. She was safe with John and Eliza.

Dr. Darkwood was already dead.

I took a deep breath; forcing myself to relax.

"Almost there, Subject Thirty-One," Dr. Darkwood declared in a fatherly tone. *"I'm almost done."*

Winter choked and gagged, but Dr. Darkwood didn't seem to care as he inserted another large needle in her arm. Blood pooled beneath the needle.

It was no wonder that Winter had so many scars all over her body. This psychopath had poked, stabbed, and cut her every single day.

I wanted to jump through the screen and strangle him. I wanted to raise him from the dead and kill him all over again.

I stared at the floor to separate myself from it all, but I still heard everything. Every grunt and moan Winter made had me flinching. Every muscle in my body shook furiously.

Willow put a hand on my arm.

"You okay?"

I didn't respond. I didn't want to start shouting. Besides, I didn't think I could lie convincingly right now-

I definitely was not okay.

"How do you feel?"

"Cold." Winter's feeble voice sounded nothing like the girl I knew.

Dr. Darkwood listed off the things that had changed in Winter's appearance, and the modifications he'd given her. I already knew all of this stuff, but it was apparent that the Vigilantes had no idea that Winter existed until now.

That thought almost made me grab Willow and make a run for it. I needed to warn John that Kain knew about Winter. It was a good thing that Kain didn't know where she was.

At least, I hoped he didn't.

Cade forwarded the video to the footage of Winter's cell. The walls were covered in ice and frost as Winter slept on the hard floor.

Shocked gasps echoed in the room.

Willow tensed next to me; her grip tight on my arm.

Cade paused the video.

Kain stood up; raising his arms again. The murmurs in the room quieted, but he kept his arms up.

"I have known, for years now, that Darkwood was working to alter children's DNA. I had no idea, until yesterday, that he was successful. I had thought we destroyed all of his labs along with his test subjects. What you are about to see are the acts of an abomination created by this madman. An unnecessary evil for us to bear witness to."

A seething rage clouded my thoughts as I stared at the Viking.

He called Winter an 'abomination'. She had called herself that before, and I'd always scolded her for it.

I grabbed the seat of my chair to stop myself from jumping up and drawing attention to myself. Willow was still eyeing me with concern.

I need to chill out.

But when Cade hit play- I nearly vomited.

The echo of an explosion forced Winter awake, screaming. A second explosion made the walls of her cell shake. She slipped on the ice beneath her, and she stared down at it in shock. She studied her hands in horror-

My heart broke for her. I couldn't imagine how terrifying her life was back then. Must still be now.

I really hoped that John and Eliza made her feel safe every single day.

Snow began to fall in the room. Winter merely stood in the center of her cell. Clinically in shock.

When the door of her cell burst open, she cowered in fear. A horrific looking Vigilante with a rifle stood in the doorway. The menacing barrel aimed directly at her heaving chest.

My teeth slammed together. My entire body tensed; ready to jump from my seat.

There's nothing you can do. Its in the past. She is safe with John.

The thoughts whispered through my mind over and over again like a mantra.

I took a shaky breath. Forcing myself to relax as much as I could.

"Are you one of them abominations?"

"Cold." Winter whimpered in agony. "Please, cold."

I knew that's not what she wanted to say, because she was signing rapidly.

It took me a moment to interpret what she was trying to say with her hands. I'd never been good with sign language, but I was pretty sure she was asking the grisly man not to shoot her.

"Of course you're cold, girly. You're living in an ice cube."

"No." She shook her head vigorously. "No. Shoot."

The Vigilante cocked his rifle; the bullet sliding into the chamber with an ominous click.

"Did Dr. Darkwood do this to you?"

There was a pause. I couldn't tear my eyes away from the screen no matter how much I wanted to.

"I'm sorry, girly. You're pretty and you'd probably make it just fine on the streets, but you're an abomination. I gotta put you down."

Nausea hit me again when Winter threw a large icicle at the man. It went straight through his chest with an incredible amount of force. He immediately collapsed; blood gushing from his mouth.

Winter's horrific scream sent panic trickling through my entire body. I was so relieved that I hadn't eaten dinner the night before, or breakfast this morning.

Otherwise, I'd be staring at it right now on the floor.

Winter had no choice but to kill that guy. I hadn't been there to stop it from happening. No one had been.

It all made sense now. She thought she was a killer. She carried that crap around with her every second of the day. She never even told me about this-

I should've just known.

I had failed her so badly. I should've made her talk more about the night she escaped the lab. I didn't want to make her relive anything horrible, but this was something she felt like she couldn't tell me. I should've shown her that she could trust me.

I had been in such a dark place when she first came into my life. I couldn't blame her for not confiding in me.

Forget about being an awful boyfriend. I wasn't even worthy enough to be called her *friend*.

The footage jumped to Winter escaping out of an emergency hatch, but she was stopped again by another Vigilante-

A horribly, mutilated girl in her late teens with a rifle aimed at Winter's head.

Willow squeezed my arm and took in a shaky breath. She pressed her face into my shoulder; letting out a small sob.

I watched as Winter killed this girl with another large icicle to the chest. Blood soaked the ground in large pools beneath the dying girl. Tears fell from Winter's eyes. Her sobs matched the ones that Willow made against my shoulder.

Oh, no. No.

Winter killed Willow's best friend.

I was in so much shock. I barely registered the fact that Winter had to kill two more Vigilantes to escape. She eventually ran out of range of the Highborn Union security cameras.

It took me a while to realize that Willow still had her face pressed into my shoulder, but I just sat there. I'd made no effort to comfort her.

I had no idea what to *do* in this situation.

I couldn't condemn Winter for killing Willow's friend. It was obviously self-defense. Kain had no right to order the Vigilantes to kill her.

Willow wouldn't feel the same way though.

"I'm so sorry, Willow," I finally whispered. "I'm so sorry."

For so many things.

Willow eventually sat up straight; wiping her eyes with trembling fingers. The screen in front of us was blank now, and there was a dead silence in the room. Every once in a while someone would sniffle or sob, but everyone was too stunned to say anything.

"Her name was Lexi. We escaped a group of Feral Morons that held us captive. We joined the Vigilantes together. She and I were singles for a few months. She he never came home from her last mission. I never knew what happened to her until now."

Oh crap.

This was not going to end well.

"Nolan Delany and Willow Rivers!" Kain's bellow broke through my shock. "Come to the front!"

I thought for sure that I'd misheard him, but Willow gave me a wide-eyed look that told me I hadn't.

We stood up.

Willow followed close behind me as we made our way to the front of the meeting room. My fight or flight instinct was working in overdrive. I had to stop myself from grabbing Willow's wrist, and pulling her behind me, when she stood in front of Kain.

"For this next viewing, I think it'll be better for you two to remain close to me." Kain's gravelly tone sent a shiver down my spine.

He was up to something, and that was never a good thing.

Willow caught my eye, and all I could do was shrug nonchalantly.

Kain gestured for us to sit in the chairs next to his. Which was odd, considering those chairs were reserved for Kain's second in command and his partner. Cade and Krissy remained standing.

The screen filled with footage of me, Willow, and Cade entering the underground lab that we destroyed on my first mission.

"It took me a few hours last night, but I managed to clear up the video feed that Willow had hacked into during the mission. She didn't delete anything that day. There was no need to. She just made sure that Lynch's security team couldn't see us as we infiltrated the underground lab."

I froze in my chair. Realization finally rearing its devastating head.

"Let's have a look at Nolan's activities during this mission."

Cade pressed play on the video.

I gripped the arms of my chair until my knuckles popped. I was about to look as guilty as sin itself. Willow and I needed to leave-

We needed to leave right now.

I glanced at her, and she was staring at me in shock.

I *needed* to reign in my emotions, but I had a feeling I was about to be executed very shortly in front of an audience.

The video feed showed me breaking into Dr. Darkwood's lab, and I glanced down at the floor. I didn't need to see it. I had been there. I relived this moment in my nightmares every single night.

There was an occasional gasp from someone in the audience, but the thing that concerned me the most was Willow's silent stillness. Usually, I knew what she was thinking just by looking at her. But she sat there, stoically; watching the screen as though she hadn't a care in the world.

"Come on, Winter." The screen showed me performing CPR on her. I still didn't look up at the video. I'd definitely throw up if I saw her

lifeless like that again. *"You're stronger than this. I know you are. Come on!"*

More gasps echoed in the room. I could feel Willow's stare burn into me, but I didn't look at her either. I just kept my eyes on the floor and listened to the video.

"Come back to me. Come back, Winter."

Kain's enormous hands grabbed the back of my neck. Forcing me to stare at the screen. Bile rose up my throat, but I managed to choke it down.

"This is my favorite part," his voice rumbled in my ear. "I'd hate for you to miss it."

I watched as I stabbed a large needle into Winter's chest. Giving her the large dose of adrenaline that saved her life. The video showed me grabbing her by the wrist.

Pressing my forehead against hers.

I didn't even remember doing that. She was dying, and I must've needed to be close to her in that moment.

"Come on, Winter. Please, don't die on me."

That hollow voice shuttered through me. Washing away the tendrils of shock that held me. Fiery rage, and unrelenting agony, coursed through me. Fighting the shadowy hole within me that sucked me down like a nightmare.

The Vigilantes were seeing this.

Winter was dying in my arms on the screen. This intimate moment was out there-

Out there for the whole world to see.

Tears streamed down Willow's face. A tight glare in her eyes held me there in the present. Condemnation shimmered in that beautiful glare. As though my actions on screen condoned what happened to Lexi.

The whole scene played out before us. Then Cade turned off the screen. Conveniently ending before we helped Shane. Leaving out Dr. Darkwood's death.

I was so incredibly furious. I could barely feel Kain's fingers digging into the back of my neck.

I glared at Cade, his smirk kindling the unrelenting rage in my gut.

"Are you not going to show them the rest of the footage? Dr. Darkwood died. Amanda Lynch's daughter died."

Kain's grip on the back of my neck tightened. I blinked as my vision blurred; resisting the urge to grimace.

"You weren't the one that killed Darkwood. Ember Lynch's body was never found. There's no way of knowing if she survived her injuries."

I growled in response. No one could survive a cave-in like that.

"If you insist on me showing more footage, Nolan, I have no problem with that."

Cade turned on the screen again. A still frame of me and Winter standing next to the Jeep appeared. I was saying goodbye to Winter after we escaped the collapsing hangar.

I would've hurled myself at Cade if Kain didn't have such a tight hold on me.

"I wish I could go with you, Winter. I really wish I could."

Winter stepped toward me and hugged me. I remembered how sick she was. How much I had been supporting her weight at that moment. She'd been covered in various wounds; trembling from exhaustion and pain.

I'd been so grateful to hold her. To feel the life within her after enduring so much fear.

Winter's voice echoed through the meeting room.

"If Kain finds out you're planning to spy for John, I have a feeling things will get really bad for you."

Well, I was definitely screwed.

"He won't find out-"

That was certainly a moronic thing for my past self to say.

The instinct to run made it hard to breath. If I tried to stand up; Kain would have me on the ground in no time at all. Cade turned off the screen, and fixed me with a triumphant smile.

"I could show more if you really want me to."

I really didn't. No one in the room needed to see what came next. Watching me kiss Winter wasn't something Willow could handle.

She continued glaring at me like I was Satan himself. The pain in her eyes nearly consumed me.

This was why I didn't do friendships. They hardly ever lasted.

Maybe if she hated me enough, Kain wouldn't kill her. If Willow had a chance of making it out of this room alive, I knew I had to make this the greatest performance of my life.

I sneered at her.

"I really had you going, huh?"

She spit in my face; standing up from her chair to get as far away from me as possible.

Even though it was what I wanted, it still hurt like crazy. Every man she ever knew had hurt her, and now I had too.

"*Too. Bad.* You fell for it."

Willow froze at the code phrase: *'Too. Bad'*.

In one swift movement, she grabbed my gun from its holster; aiming it at my forehead with an incredibly steady hand. I didn't flinch as I stared at the dark end of the barrel.

Krissy was on Willow in two seconds, and had the weapon out of her hand. Willow glared at me murderously.

Still, I didn't miss the fact that she never cocked the gun. Or how her finger never touched the trigger.

"What do you plan on doing to him?" Willow's throat bobbed as she spoke. Tears glistened in those gorgeous, almond eyes.

Kain chuckled in delight. I didn't see how any of this was amusing at all, but I also wasn't a psychopath. Even Cade smiled, maniacally.

"I suggest you take your place among the singles until I find someone better suited to be your partner, Willow."

She stood frozen for a moment. I couldn't tear my gaze away from her face.

I was so lost in my fear for her. I barely noticed it when Kain threw me to the floor. He pinned my arms behind my back and cuffed them together with a metal that burned my skin.

With his knee in my back, he bent down until his nasty breath brushed my cheek.

"Willow found the chemical formula for your girlfriend's weakness. She has the most brilliant mind of your generation. Which is the only reason I won't kill her in front of you. Until I find someone to replace her intellect, I have to keep her alive."

My jaw went slack as I heaved for breath. Kain's knee dug deeper into my spine until I thought it was going to snap.

"I'm going to kill you."

So weak. My voice was so weak I was surprised Kain didn't laugh in my face.

"It'll be amusing to watch you try."

Kain took his knee off of my back, and Cade hauled me to my feet. Willow watched, silently, as they dragged me from the room.

Chapter 9: John

In the past two days, we found two dead plague victims.

Shane had managed to help a few that were near death. It had taken a lot out of him. I had insisted that he take a break for at least a full day in the quarantine zone. Otherwise, he'd kill himself trying in vain to save them.

We were huddled in a makeshift tent that we put together the day before. The rest of the healthy families had done the same thing. No one left quarantine, except for Shane.

He'd buried his friend, Reed, a few days ago.

Alone.

The trauma of that seemed to make his determination more focused. More centered on keeping everyone alive for as long as was necessary.

Until I could find the cure.

I was leaving in the morning for the Highborn Union territory. Hopefully, Shane wouldn't have to do this for much longer.

Eliza stayed in the quarantine zone, despite being essential medical personnel. It was the only way I'd allow her out of the cabin. She didn't fight me on it, which I appreciated. I didn't think I could argue with her anymore. Not without succumbing to the exhaustion that tugged at me ever since Winter left.

It also didn't help that I hadn't slept since she left either. She checked in every night like she promised. It did nothing to ease my worry. I could tell, through the communicator, that she was enduring horrible internal struggles. Things that she refused to talk about.

Leif poked his head in the tent.

"Is there anything else we need for tomorrow, John?"

He was one of the rare single Scavenger men that Nolan hadn't categorized as a Feral Moron. He was in his mid-twenties and absolutely competent in a crisis.

"I think we're all set, Leif. We'll meet at the entrance to the zone at five in the morning. I feel like we should get an early start."

"Yeah, me too. People are dropping like flies around here. It's gotta stop."

With a small wave, Leif headed for his tent on the other side of the quarantine zone. There were about forty of us that passed the health inspection that Eliza gave everyone that entered quarantine.

It was hard for me to even let her do that, but I knew that she didn't enter into a relationship with me so I could smother her.

As though she could read my mind; she snuck her way under my arm. She rested her head against my chest; wrapping her arms tightly around my waist.

Warmth spread through me. A small knot of anxiety dissipated in my chest.

"Do you think four men will be enough?"

"It'll have to be. Everyone else needs to stay here for their families. Leif doesn't have anyone. James's kids are old enough to help their mom. George doesn't have anyone but his wife."

"George's wife is pregnant," Eliza pointed out unhelpfully.

"George is hardcore. If anyone makes it back it'll be him."

"John Delany, if you-"

I kissed her to stop the rant that I knew was coming. She tried to pull away from me at first, but she eventually melted into my kiss.

I always counted it as a personal victory when I could do that to her.

"I plan on *all* of us coming back, Eliza. I would never leave you alone. You know that, right?"

She tried to nod, but I found myself kissing her again before she could. She finally pulled away from me when Shane came into the tent.

"Don't stop because of me." His mouth formed into a rare smirk.

"Well, we aren't exactly going to keep at it while you've got that creepy stare going on."

Eliza chuckled, and Shane's smirk turned into a tired grin.

"This is what I get for moving in with newly weds."

Eliza handed Shane his dinner with a look of mocked horror on her face.

"Eat this before I do it for you, wise guy."

He ate the rabbit meat and potatoes so quickly, I'd be surprised if he didn't have a stomach ache.

"How are you feeling?"

"I'll be able to get back out there tomorrow. I need to check in on Tamara, Fredrick, and the kids again. Make sure no one is worse."

I nodded in agreement. "Just make sure you don't overdo it."

"Has Winter checked in yet?" Shane gestured to the communicator in my hand. I shook my head and resisted the urge to clench my jaw.

I refused to admit that I was worried about her. She should've called an hour ago, but she promised to check in everyday. She was always true to her word.

"She'll check in soon." Eliza took the communicator from me and set it on the wooden box that we used as a table. "In the mean time, we should get some sleep."

That wasn't happening, but I laid down next to her anyway. Shane was already half asleep on the other side of the tent.

Eliza snuggled into me, and soon enough her deep breathing indicated that she was asleep. I kept my eyes on the communicator and waited for a very long time.

Winter never called.

The next morning, I tried to contact Winter on the communicator. I didn't get an answer.

Eliza was still asleep, so I gently shook her awake. She looked at me groggily and sat up when she saw how worried I was.

"She didn't call?"

I shook my head and handed her the communicator.

"I tried contacting her, but there was no answer. Keep this on you until she calls."

Eliza nodded and gave me a hug. Usually her hugs were comforting, but this time I hardly felt anything.

I kissed her and grabbed my bag. I took her handgun and left her with my rifle. I preferred my rifle, but handguns were better for this mission. I checked the bullets in the magazine before tucking the gun into the back of my jeans.

"I love you, Eliza."

"I love you too. Be safe."

I nodded and disappeared into the dark morning.

I met Leif, James, and George in the middle of the woods where we'd planned the day before. We had done a sweep for cameras in this area after the Vigilantes, and the Highborn Militia, had been spotted setting up surveillance in our territory. We hadn't seen anyone for a while, but we were constantly on the lookout for cameras now.

We were at a severe disadvantage when it came to technology. All we had was what we'd managed to steal from the Highborn shipments that we'd intercepted. The Vigilantes had been doing that for a lot longer than we had. If either of them decided to attack us-

We wouldn't stand a chance.

I kept waiting for the day that the Highborn Militia would bomb our community and completely wipe us all out. It was hard to prepare for that kind of scenario when I was just trying to keep my people alive until the next day.

I quickly pushed the thought from my mind and focused my attention on the three men standing in front of me.

They all had the appearance of a typical Scavenger. They each had a beard and their clothes were torn in some places. At least they were cleaner than the average Scavenger male. It even looked like Leif had trimmed his beard. I knew they'd each bathed recently too.

Eliza had ordered everyone to stay as clean as possible to keep diseases away. It wouldn't help with the Sleeping Ache, but it would with other things.

"Are we taking the Jeep, Boss?" George held out the keys to me expectantly.

I nodded and took the keys.

We only used the Jeep to patrol our boarders, but it would take a lot of hours off of our trip if we didn't have to walk. We needed to move as quickly as possible, especially after we got the cure.

"So what's the plan?" Leif asked after we'd all climbed into the Jeep.

"Get in and out undetected."

"What if that's not possible?"

I honestly hadn't thought that far ahead. If that wasn't possible, then we'd have to figure something else out. I had no maps, and no information on the cargo ships. We were just as unprepared as any other mission I'd led.

"If that's not possible, then we'll have to wait for an opportune moment. We don't have the manpower to take on the Highborn Militia."

"Well, obviously." George chuckled. "I was just wondering if you wanted me to blow some stuff up. That's how the Vigilantes do it."

I gritted my teeth and took a deep breath to steady myself.

"We aren't blowing anything up, George. We aren't the Vigilantes. Besides, the Highborns know our location. How do you think they'd retaliate if we blew something up?"

George merely nodded and glanced out the passenger side window.

"We destroyed the Highborn Militia compound and they haven't retaliated," James pointed out.

"That was different," Leif interjected. "That creature with the ice defeated a lot of them. They probably think it's our secret weapon."

James chuckled, sardonically.

"I still don't think that's actually a thing."

Leif shook his head; leaning further into the conversation.

"You believe what Shane can do is real, right? It's not too far off to think that there's someone out there with ice powers."

"I'll only believe what I can see, Leif."

"Well, I saw it," George muttered, gruffly. "It looked like a girl, but her hair was shaved. Her body was covered in frost and ice. You saw it too, didn't you, Boss?"

I shook my head and kept my eyes on the trail.

George wasn't the first Scavenger to ask me that question. There were rumors that a girl with ice powers existed, but I did everything I could to discredit them.

"I was mostly dead, remember? I'm not even sure where Shane came from. He just knelt next to me and brought me back. He's been staying with me and Eliza ever since."

George nodded. "Yeah, he's a good kid. Hopefully the Highborns don't take him from us."

"I'd die before I let that happen."

We drove for a while in silence. Leif fell asleep in the backseat and started snoring. James tried to drown out the annoying sound by asking George how his wife was doing with her pregnancy. I listened to their conversation for a while until my mind started to wander.

I realized that I was gripping the steering wheel too tightly, and I forced myself to breathe.

"You alright, Boss?"

Nothing ever escaped George's observance.

"Sure, just trying to think things through before we get there."

He saw right through that lie, but I didn't attempt to explain things to him. He used to work for the Central Intelligence Agency after serving for a decade in the Special Forces. He never disclosed which branch of the military, even though the government collapsed nearly four years ago.

He was, basically, a human lie detector. I didn't know exactly what it was that he used to do for the CIA, but I had a feeling that he'd assassinated a lot of American enemies in the past. He was my best soldier, and he oversaw most of the combat training in our community.

Sometimes, I felt like he'd be a better leader for the Scavengers than I was. But when I'd told him that, he just laughed as though I'd said something funny. Then he proceeded to inform me that he wasn't dumb enough to lead a group of people to certain death.

I had decided to take that as a weird compliment and never mentioned it again.

"So this has nothing to do with Nolan?" I clenched my jaw so tightly my teeth hurt. "I don't want to bring up anything painful, but if something is on your mind that might mess up the mission-"

"Nothing is on my mind, George."

My tone was harsh, and he stared at me for a moment. Considering.

"Fair enough, Boss. You've got good instincts. I trust you."

Well, that was somehow even more stressful than thinking about Nolan and Winter. I'd much rather have George give me a sarcastic comment about how I was leading a group of people to certain death again.

I eased the death grip I had on the steering wheel.

After a few hours of driving, we made it to a cave. It was the best place to park the Jeep, but we'd still have hours of hiking before we made it to Highborn Union territory. The sun was bright against the snow covered rocks, and I had to shield my eyes when I got out of the Jeep.

"Well, that's interesting." George shut the passenger door and wrinkled his nose.

"What is?"

He gestured toward the mouth of the cave. It took me a moment to realize what he was talking about.

My gut clenched; nausea rolling through me as I hurried toward the cave. I wasn't sure how George noticed it from that far away, but the smell hit me before I saw the body.

It looked like a young female, but acid had been poured over the remains to speed up decomposition. The scraps of clothing that remained were scattered around the body. Most of the flesh was gone, with some evidence of animals trying to eat the remains. They probably didn't take much because of the acidic chemicals.

"What do you think happened here?"

Leif looked a little green as he took a step away from the horrific scene. James wouldn't even come near the mouth of the cave. He just stood back with his hand over his mouth and nose.

I knew exactly how they felt. I'd worked as a homicide detective for four years. I never got used to seeing this. George and I were able to cover up our emotions from years of practice.

It still didn't mean I wasn't heartbroken for this young woman.

I knelt next to the remains and got a closer look at the evidence surrounding it. I was the furthest thing from a medical examiner, but I'd seen enough bodies, and read enough ME reports, that I knew what to look for.

She had shredded ropes around her ankles and wrists.

"Broken ribs." George gestured to the exposed torso.

I nodded in agreement, and pointed to the left forearm that was bent at an odd angle.

"Her wrist was fractured too."

"It's a girl?" Leif growled furiously. A small shiver ran through him periodically; his eyes blazing with fury.

"Probably between the ages of fifteen and twenty." I continued studying the body as I shared the information. "I can't be sure though, because I'm not an ME, but it's an educated guess."

"I agree." George nodded, gravely. "But I have less experience than you do in this department."

I highly doubted that, but I didn't call him on it. George pretended to be ignorant of certain things just to make me look good. I was going to have a talk with him about that one of these days.

James finally came into the cave, but he steered clear of the body like Leif did.

"She must've been here for a long time in order for her to be this decomposed." James sounded muffled with his hand still covering his mouth.

"Not necessarily." I pointed out the evidence of chemicals. "The little flesh that remains has burn marks on it. I don't know what kind of chemicals were used, but someone poured something acidic on this body. There's really no way of knowing how long she's been dead without a medical examiner. My guess; it's been about a month or so."

George nodded in agreement and stood up. I stayed crouched next to the body in hopes of finding more evidence-

I noticed her hair.

Tears stung my eyes.

Two black braids that had been long at one point. I hadn't noticed them before because something had torn out a lot of the hair. I only knew of one person that had braids like that.

If she was dead-

I choked on the bile that raced up my throat. I hurried out of the cave and immediately lost my breakfast. It had been a long time since I'd thrown up from seeing a dead body, but this was different.

This was the first physical evidence I'd found that Nolan was actually dead, and not a prisoner somewhere.

I puked again.

I couldn't go back in that cave. I stood there; gulping down the fresh air like a man that had been buried alive.

George eventually came up to me after I'd stopped gasping for breath. He just stood next to me in silence for a few minutes.

"Never thought of you as the puking type. Are ya sick?"

I shook my head and George seemed to relax a little.

"Who do you think she is?"

I took a shuddering breath; folding my arms across my chest.

"I don't know for sure, but her hair..."

George nodded grimly. "You think it's Phoenix?"

"I really *hope* it's not her."

He grew silent for a moment; grimacing angrily.

"Me too, but I have a feeling- *Damn it*, John. Phoenix ran off with Kain because the Scavenger community did absolutely *nothing* to help her. What kind of sorry excuses for men are we?"

Men that grieved their losses for too long. Men that ignored the horrific things around them because it was easier. Men that were scared of losing their remaining loved ones.

It had made us cowardly. Made *me* cowardly.

"The kind of men that sat on the sidelines for too long."

George nodded in agreement; anger flashing in his eyes.

"The way I see it, whether it is Phoenix or not, that girl's death is on us. *This is our fault.*"

I agreed with him completely. It shouldn't have taken me finding Winter to realize that the street orphans had it worse than the Scavengers did. It shouldn't have taken me losing Nolan to step up as the community's leader. A leader I knew everyone needed me to be from the start of all this.

Now Phoenix was dead.

Nolan was too.

It was obvious that she had been executed. That meant Nolan and the other girl, Willow, were dead as well.

Unless Kain needed them alive for some reason, but I highly doubted it. If he kept Nolan as a hostage to use against me, I would've heard from him by now.

That was why I couldn't go back into the cave. If I found Nolan's body in there somewhere-

I would never recover. It would kill me.

George clapped a hand on my shoulder in a comforting gesture.

"I'm gonna search the rest of the cave, Boss. You stay out here. Plan out our next move."

I already knew what our next move was going to be. We had to find the cure *before* I sought out Kain and murdered him.

Revenge had to be put on the back burner for now.

Chapter 10: Winter

My eyelids were like lead weights when I tried to force them open. Exhaustion pulled at me. Threatening to drag me into unconsciousness again. But the alarm bells ringing in my head drove me to stay awake.

I didn't know how long I'd been conscious, but it was long enough for me to understand that I wasn't alone. I managed to keep my breathing steady, but-

I was strapped down to a bed. The same way Dr. Darkwood used to do to me.

I couldn't prevent the cold sweat that broke out on my forehead.

"Are you going to pretend to be asleep forever?" A feminine voice broke through my rising panic.

Pain exploded in my head when my eyes fluttered open. The heat, and dim light of the fireplace, caused nausea to ripple through me. I was already overheated from the bullets. But, apparently, my captors thought I needed to be closest to the fire.

I was positive that wasn't a coincidence.

"You know they're going to torture you. *Face it.* Stop being a coward."

The girl's voice was ominously familiar.

I groaned at the pounding that went through my skull, but I opened my eyes again. The glow from the fireplace gave the room a homey feeling-

I shuddered at the thought.

"You look like crap," the girl whispered from the other side of the room. "Just so you know."

I finally forced myself to turn my pounding head to look at *her*-

The psychotic fire-girl that I'd hoped was dead.

"Ember."

I was so weak I couldn't even clench my fists. Let alone struggle against the straps that bound me.

The abomination that dwelt within me sparked to life; roaring through my veins like a freezing river. Every part of me. Every fiber that formed me-

Wanted to see her corpse rotting at my feet.

"Don't look so furious to see me."

Ember's black hair was longer than it had been months ago. It had a slight wave to it that gave her an unruly appearance. She would've looked like an innocent teenage girl if it wasn't for the malice in her eyes. They were dark blue like Shane's, but the sinister glare within them hinted at the fury burning inside her.

Similar to the abominable beast that roared within my soul.

Ember was restrained to a chair with a silver brace clamped around her neck.

I blinked, resisting the rage that attempted to consume me. It had been Ember all along. The girl I'd been so determined to rescue.

"Why are you-"

"Just shut up and listen, Winter. I *hate* you, okay? You and your boyfriends left me to die in that explosion. I'll *never* forgive you for that."

The anger blazing in Ember's eyes softened. Stark grief shone in them. Shock gripped me at the devastation there. As though *I'd* been the one to betray *her*.

The delusion must've been a side effect of the torture she'd endured from Brian.

She tried to kill the people I loved. She rounded up street orphans and gave them to her psychotic mother. She helped turn innocent children into lab rats.

Even though I was an abomination; I wasn't the true monster in the room.

"But since we're both prisoners, we need to plan an escape."

I tore my eyes away from her and focused my gaze on the ceiling.

"No."

"What do you mean 'no'? I've been sitting in a freaking torture cage for weeks. Trust me, you do not want to experience that."

My fingers clenched at the thought. The bullet wounds in my shoulder throbbed incessantly. With every sensation of pain, the fury coursed through me. Cooling my blood.

I'd gotten myself shot, and captured, for *Ember*.

"You wrote Sleeping Ache on Brian's wall with your blood. How did you know what the disease was?"

Ember was silent long enough that I turned my head to look at her. Devastation marred her features. My heart rate slowed; the cool anger melting away at the pathetic sight of her.

"I knew about the plague because my- Amanda Lynch- planned to use the plague as a weapon. She succeeded."

I desperately clung to the last whisper of anger within me. I was burning up as agony pounded through me again. The bullet wounds causing the heat to spread through my veins.

Every piece of me wilting away into nothing but pain, and exhaustion, by the second.

"Lynch used you to spread it. Brian caught you when you came to the community to unleash the disease, right?"

Ember shot a heated glare in my direction, but I noticed the shadow of sadness in her eyes.

"Don't act like you still know me, Winter. I didn't bring the Sleeping Ache here."

I didn't know what she meant by that. I had never acted like I knew her. I hardly ever talked to her before.

"If you didn't spread it, then how did it get here?"

"Who knows? After I escaped the underground lab, I never went back to the Highborn Union. If you hadn't noticed, I *hate* my mother. The only reason I came here in the first place was to warn the Scavenger community about the plague."

I sighed tiredly; wincing when the slight movement shot pain through my shoulder.

"Why would you care to warn the Scavengers at all? Why risk getting sick?"

Ember's eyes bore into me, as though she were trying to convey something important. Her stare almost seemed familiar and-

I shivered; nausea making me lightheaded again.

"I was vaccinated against it over a year ago. Amanda Lynch made sure of that. I came to warn the Scavengers because I'm not okay with genocide."

I managed to scoff at her desperate tone.

"I'm supposed to believe that you did this out of the kindness of your heart?"

Ember finally looked away from me. The rage igniting again in her eyes.

"I don't have a heart anymore, Winter. My mother effectively destroyed that part of me. You may have endured the physical torture of the experiments, but you weren't raised by Amanda. *Nothing* can compare to that."

I glared at her; coldness trickling through me.

Ember chuckled cruelly.

"You're so lucky you don't remember your parents. I'd give anything to forget my childhood. The one good thing about it is gone now."

Ember sneered, and fury gripped my chest.

She had fire abilities that she got without the high cost of torture and isolation. She lived in the underground bunkers during the Mother Nature Apocalypse so no one she was close to died. She had plenty of food, water, clothes, and modern conveniences that I didn't even *remember* having before.

Eliza had to explain to me what a toilet was once.

I closed my eyes, and ignored Ember's further attempts to converse.

Next thing I knew, the front door opened.

I couldn't see the person that came into the room. The straps that bound me were restricting. I couldn't turn my head to the left without my bullet wounds pulsing in agony.

"Hello there, cousin." Brian's voice sneered.

I wasn't sure who '*cousin*' was, but there was no one else in the room. I could only assume he was addressing Ember.

"You really think Kain will be happy with what you're doing here?"

Brian chuckled, but I still couldn't see him. I had my eyes fixed on Ember; studying her reactions.

Her eyes widened. Staring ahead with a hint of fear in her posture.

"Brian." Ember's face drained of color. "Put that away."

"Maybe Kain would prefer it if you were dead, cousin," he continued thoughtfully. "I already know he wants the abomination dead. Maybe he'd want me to kill you too."

I wondered how Kain and Brian found out about me in the first place. They even knew about Dr. Darkwood's chemicals that he'd created to subdue me, and the neck braces that negated our powers.

The League of Vigilance must've stolen a lot of Highborn Union secrets.

"Just put the knife down. You don't need it."

"Tell me where your illustrious President Lynch is."

Brian moved closer to Ember, and I could see him now. He held the knife in front of him. An eager smirk contoured his psychotic face.

"If I knew her location I'd tell you. I hate her just as much as you do."

Brian chuckled as he sat down in front of her; holding the knife in a loose grip.

"Amanda ordered Darkwood to give you some pretty incredible fire powers. I think you're so *grateful* to her. You'd do, or say, anything to protect her."

Ember's lips quivered as she stared at the knife in his hand.

"Only so she could use me as her pawn. I didn't want it."

Brian's smile widened into something more deranged- more sinister- as he ran the knife down Ember's arm. He didn't pierce her skin, but she flinched anyway.

"I don't know what to think." Brian's tone became cajoling. "You and your mother have always been hard for me to understand. I never got the whole '*I hate my mom*' and '*I wish I had a better daughter*' thing you two have going on. At least *I* loved my mother, and she loved me. But, then again, we both know how that turned out. I'm sure you remember the blood."

Ember sobbed; rage taking over her fear.

"She was trying to protect me! She caught you hurting me, you psychopath!"

"But it's so fun hurting you, little cousin."

Ember shrieked when Brian pressed the sharp knife into her arm and-

I panicked.

I wasn't sure why, but the urgent need to protect Ember shot through me. It was instinctual; awakening within me so quickly that I didn't have time to think before I started screaming.

"Leave her alone!"

Brian pulled away from Ember. Blood on the tip of the blade.

Ember whimpered, but courageously straightened herself in her chair. Her wide eyes shot toward me. Her brow furrowed in absolute bewilderment.

"Why should I, abomination?"

Brian took a step toward me; wielding the knife menacingly. My vulnerability in that moment churned my stomach. Nearly making me gag.

"Do you want to take her place? It wouldn't surprise me. You two have always been pathetic about each other."

"Just don't hurt her," I whispered tiredly. "I'm the one you want."

"Actually, I want both of you." He positioned himself next to the bed I was strapped to. He grinned down at me. "What is John Delany planning?"

I had to say something so he wouldn't just gut me right here on the bed.

He held his knife over me. It glistened in the light of the fire.

Images of the poor animals he had tortured to death flashed through my mind. I concentrated on taking each breath slowly as I stared at his disconcerting face.

He was handsome and kept himself clean. It only made him scarier.

"He's helping the families suffering from the Sleeping Ache Plague."

Brian nodded, twirling the knife between his fingers. One wrong move and it would impale my stomach.

He was trying to get a reaction from me, so I kept my face neutral. It was easier than it should've been because-

Well, I was completely dead inside.

"Why did he send you after me?" A cruel smile crept across his face.

"Coming here was my choice."

Brian grunted thoughtfully; lowering the knife toward my stomach. I kept perfectly still. Inwardly bracing for whatever was to come.

He lowered his face to mine. Forcing me to stare into his eyes. They were dark brown, but there was something vital missing in them. A completely empty void studied me. Grazed over me like I was nothing more than meat.

All I could do was stare back into nothingness.

He's got the psyche of a potential serial killer.

I didn't know if Brian had actually killed people before. But I knew he wouldn't hesitate to kill me now.

"How long have you known John and Nolan Delany?"

"I haven't known John for very long. I've never even met Nolan before."

Kain obviously knew about me. Knew what I could do. If I admitted that I knew Nolan then they'd kill him if they hadn't already.

If Nolan was still alive I wouldn't put him in anymore danger.

"Well, that's not accurate." Brian chuckled; the knife dangling above me haphazardly. "For a heartless monster, you're not a very good liar."

I quickly pushed away any lingering emotion. If he wanted to deal with a heartless monster-

Then that's what he was going to get.

"Has Nolan been feeding John information behind Kain's back?"

I merely stared, blankly, at the ceiling.

"Answer me, or you'll find out how sharp a steel blade is."

I smiled at that. I granted him a glance; a low chuckle escaping me.

"Do you know what a scalpel is, Brian?"

Anger flashed in his eyes as the knife lowered to my stomach.

"Dr. Darkwood used to cut me open with scalpels. He never used anesthetic. When he saw fit to grant me the numbing agents, it was never enough to touch the pain. His scalpels were most likely sharper than your knife, but the incisions that hurt the worst were always done with a duller blade. If you want to cause maximum damage to your victim, then you should use dull instruments."

Brian merely stared at me with absolutely no expression. His fist clutched the knife so tightly his entire arm shook.

"You obviously need more training in order to perform your assigned roll as torturer. The way you are conducting this interrogation isn't going to get you the results you want."

Brian's face morphed into a dark flurry of rage. The tip of the knife trembled as he moved the blade closer to my neck.

I stiffened when the tip of the blade touched the delicate skin under my jaw. I remained perfectly still as I waited for him to cut me.

Ember whimpered softly, but she said nothing to try to stop Brian from hurting me.

Just as Brian applied a small amount of pressure to my throat, there was a knock at the door.

"Sir, Kain called in. He wants to speak with you."

Brian removed the blade from my skin and ran a finger down the side of my cheek.

"We'll get back to this later. I'm looking forward to making you scream and writhe, abomination."

I grinned back at him. Showing a disconcerting eagerness in an attempt to throw him off. He merely smiled back; winking at me.

This was nothing more than some psychotic game.

Brian left my bedside, and Ember blew out a shaky breath. She struggled against the ropes that bound her to the chair. Somehow managing to slip one of her hands out of the loop.

"Finally." She let out a low chuckle. "I thought the knife I stole from Brian wouldn't be sharp enough to cut through this."

I stared at her in shock as she revealed a small knife in her freed hand.

Ember quickly cut the rope that bound her other hand to the arm of the chair and cut her feet loose. She took a deep breath before struggling to stand. The blood drained from her already pale face as she staggered.

Ember narrowed her eyes at me. "I really don't think we'll get out of here alive if we don't help each other."

I knew she was right. It pained me, but I gave her a sharp nod.

"Once we've escaped we go our separate ways. You stay away from the Scavenger community."

Ember flinched, but didn't reply.

She got to work cutting away the straps that bound me to the bed. When I was free of the bindings, I struggled to sit up. The pain in my shoulder was completely unbearable.

When it became obvious that I wasn't going to be able to sit up on my own, Ember seized my arm. She pulled me up, and I almost tumbled off of the bed.

"You've been stitched up and bandaged, but the bullets are still in your shoulder. You won't be able to use your abilities until they're removed."

I already knew that, but I didn't have the energy to tell her so.

"Where's the key?" I gestured to her neck brace.

"On the necklace Brian has around his neck." She rolled her eyes. "He thinks he's pretty clever."

Bravado. Ember had it in spades.

I wasn't sure how we were going to get out of there without one of us using our powers. If we had a gun we might stand a chance, but there were no weapons in the room. If we could get to the trees where I hid my gear, we'd at least have a communicator-

I doubted we'd get passed the front door.

"Please, tell me you have some sort of a plan?" I asked hoarsely.

"Of course I do, but you're not going to like it."

Ember went to a large cabinet full of medical supplies and ripped the door open. She rummaged around for a few long seconds before pulling out a syringe full of clear liquid.

I cringed; stumbling backward as I fought for control. Fought to stay in the present. To not allow my mind to sabotage me. To suck me into a horrendous memory.

I *hated* the idea of anyone sticking me with a needle ever again.

"The only way to get out of here is if you're able to use your ice powers. I'm cutting those bullets out of you. *Take control and deal with it.*"

Ember stood before me. Wielding the syringe like a weapon.

I struggled. Struggled so fiercely I was surprised to feel the needle stab into my shoulder. I was so weak. I couldn't fight her off, despite the torture she'd been through.

It didn't take long for everything to go numb.

Ember wasted no time pouring iodine over my wound and the dull knife she'd used to free us. I wanted to struggle, but the haunted look in Ember's eyes-

She wasn't enjoying any of this. Her shaking hands revealed that she was just as traumatized as I was.

"I gotta make this quick. The wounds won't look pretty when it's over, but at least you won't feel much."

I decided not to watch the process. I felt the occasional sharp pain, but nothing compared to what I'd felt in the past. When the two bullets were out of my shoulder, Ember grabbed a medical stapler that she found in the cabinet. She poured more iodine on my wounds before using the stapler to close them up.

"We gotta get going." Ember tucked bandages and medicines into a bag that she'd found. "We've probably wasted too much time as it is."

I gritted my teeth and forced myself to stand. Ember eyed me cautiously, but I ignored her as I headed toward the door.

Chapter 11: Nolan

Four weeks earlier

Being dragged further underground wasn't really all that bad.

It was the handcuffs that were the crappy part.

I wasn't sure what it was about them, but they burned so horribly I was surprised I didn't hear my skin sizzling.

The air was getting colder; my chest constricting in protest.

I had no idea where we were going. I had never been this far down in the underground bunker before. I actually had no idea that this tunnel even existed. It hadn't shown up on the map of the underground bunker that I had on my tablet.

I was sure that wasn't a coincidence.

We finally stopped in front of a large vault door that was covered in dust

My heart pounded so hard, I was surprised the sound didn't echo off the steel walls.

Kain wouldn't want to execute me in private. He'd want all of the Vigilantes to see my final moments to prevent further rebellion.

It was exactly what Amanda Lynch would do.

Kain opened the door with a few turns of the wheel before pulling on the lever. It swung inward, and Cade shoved me forward.

He was hoping that I'd lose my balance, but I was determined to stay on my feet for as long as possible. I was resigned to the possibility that I wouldn't live to see the next day. I definitely wouldn't give them the satisfaction of cowering.

Standing tall helped me feel calm. In control.

Kain shut the door and the overhead light came on.

I stared in horror as the light revealed what was in the dungeon. A cell, made of steel, took up half of the space in the room. A smaller cage was positioned next to the cell- A torture cage.

A girl clung to the thin bars.

She was forced to stand since there was no room to sit in the narrow confines of the cage. Her black hair knotted in messy braids.

Her eyes. Her vibrant eyes had been reduced to empty defeat.

"Phoenix." I lowered my tone, though I wanted to scream her name. I choked down bile when I noticed her raw, bleeding hands.

Just when I thought Kain couldn't be more barbaric-

He had to prove me wrong by doing something like this.

"Let her go," I begged hoarsely. "Please. She has nothing to do with this."

Cade punched me in the gut; forcing the air out of me.

It took a moment for my lungs to start working again. Luckily, Cade didn't hit me a second time. I was able to stay on my feet.

"Did I say you could talk?" Cade grabbed my arm; digging his nails into my skin.

I didn't reply. I wasn't sure what I could do, or say, in this situation that didn't get Phoenix killed.

The Scavengers would never get the Sleeping Ache Plague Cure now. There wasn't even a way to warn them. I'd given Kain exactly what he needed to survive an outbreak. I'd given him the ammunition he needed to eliminate a community of people that he now saw as a threat.

I had failed so horrendously. I had been such an idiot to think I could take down Kain from within.

Not only would I die, but Phoenix-

I glanced at her; willing her to meet my eyes. I had to see that she was coherent. That she wasn't in too much pain.

But she wouldn't look at me. She kept her head hung low. Every few seconds her entire body went tense from immense agony.

"You're going to answer my questions, Nolan Delany." Kain smirked, running a black-tipped finger over the torture cage. "If you don't, poor Phoenix won't last the night."

I took a deep breath and tried to swallow. My throat and mouth were so dry I wouldn't be able to sound assertive when I spoke.

"I'll tell you whatever you want. Just- please-"

Kain pushed a button on the side of the cage. The bars automatically glowed a hellish orange.

Phoenix screamed, letting go of the bars she'd been holding onto. An electric current ran through the cage. Forcing Phoenix's body to convulse as the electricity sparked through her.

"Stop!" Cade grabbed me when I lunged for the cage. "Please!"

Kain ignored me; watching dispassionately as Phoenix suffered. I stared in horror as my friend screamed and writhed in agony.

I continued begging, but the more I talked the worse it got for Phoenix. I finally grew silent. Tears wetted my cheeks.

I didn't even care that I couldn't hold them in anymore.

Finally, after what seemed like an eternity, Kain pushed the button again. The orange glow around the bars disappeared.

Phoenix collapsed against the walls of the cage. She gulped air into her lungs so intently that I worried she would pass out. Sweat made the hair that escaped her braids cling to her face.

She wasn't crying like I was.

She'd already been broken long before I got there.

"If you beg for Phoenix's life one more time, I will push the button again. I won't turn the cage off until she's dead. Understood?"

I swallowed hard and nodded.

"Good." Kain leaned his large frame casually against the bars of the cell. "If you tell me what I want to know, then I will take Phoenix out of the cage. Things will be easy for her."

I nodded again, robotically. I couldn't take my eyes off of Phoenix, but she still wouldn't look at me. There was no emotion on her face.

It was that emptiness that finally broke me.

She was such lively, beautiful woman. So friendly, caring, and funny. Such a lovely soul had been reduced to this shell.

And it was all my fault.

"Have you been communicating with your brother, John Delany?"

"Yes," I replied without taking my eyes off of Phoenix.

"What have you been telling him?"

"Just information about the Highborn Union. I've given him coordinates to shipments. Mostly ones that'll give the Scavengers medicines and clothes."

"And weapons." Cade scoffed. "You've been helping John arm the Scavengers."

I took a shaky breath and nodded.

"Amanda Lynch has been trying to eliminate the Scavengers for a while now. They have a right to protect their children."

Kain laughed, and I finally tore my gaze from Phoenix to look at him. The Viking was staring at me as though I was nothing more than a plaything.

"You think the Scavengers have rights? They weren't even supposed to survive the natural disasters. Only the well-bred perfections of humanity were supposed to exist after nature realigned itself. That was why Amanda and I worked so hard to build the underground bunkers."

Shock spread through my limbs as I stared at Kain.

"Nolan Delany." Kain's eyes twinkled in amusement. "You have no idea the history Amanda Lynch and I have together. We wanted to make humanity better. To give the planet a more sophisticated group of people that would take care of it. Not overpopulate and pollute it. Unfortunately, along the way we disagreed about who would run the show from here on out."

I didn't say anything as I stared at the evil man in front of me. He took a few steps closer to me as he spoke, but I didn't cower. My tears had dried on my cheeks, and I was beyond fear now.

"Once I dethrone Amanda, the League of Vigilance will take over the Highborn Union. I will lead this new world to prosperity. We will create the perfect society. The people will be trained to protect humanity and the earth. All diseases and deformities will be eradicated."

The way he said it; it really didn't sound so bad.

But I knew better.

Kain didn't care who he hurt, or killed, in order to gain control over the population. To create the so called 'perfect' society that he would completely dominate over.

It wouldn't surprise me if he planned on enslaving more groups of people on the continent that were just trying to survive. I'd heard of the small communities spotted in the north. The fortunate villages untouched by the Highborn Union and the League of Vigilance.

For now.

"The Scavengers are poor, pathetic excuses for human beings," Kain continued harshly. "They are a blight on this earth. They must be exterminated like the vermin that they are."

His dark eyes narrowed at me. Boring into me with a raging hate that made my knees quake.

"Nolan Delany, vermin are incapable of possessing any rights. Let alone the right to protect their children. Amanda Lynch had the brilliant idea to kill them off with a plague. Anyone that is smart enough to survive will come to me. They will plead to join the League of Vigilance. Only then will they receive the cure that you so kindly retrieved."

Kain grinned at me. A chill raced down my spine so violently I couldn't prevent myself from shivering.

"You are talking about innocent people, Kain. Babies and children are dying because their parents can't protect them from President Lynch's plague. If we don't do something to help them, then your vision of the perfect society won't be possible. Humanity won't be able to continue existing if we just let them die."

I would have done anything in that moment. Said anything. If Cade allowed me to get on my hands and knees to beg I would've done it.

"You have all the power here, Kain. Please, use it to help those that can't help themselves. That's what I thought the League of Vigilance stood for."

Kain's grin morphed into something so cold, so demented, it nearly made my heart stop. The pain in my chest intensified as the Viking's gaze shifted to Phoenix's broken form.

She could barely stand anymore. She leaned so heavily against the bars of the torture cage. Every ounce of strength within her depleted.

My rant had fallen on deaf ears. Kain didn't care about the Scavengers. He never did.

He just wanted blind followers to uphold his warped morals. Pathetic psychopaths to support him in annihilating anyone that posed a threat to him.

"Adam and Eve began humanity on their own. We will do just fine with those that pass the test."

"What test?" I couldn't resist asking.

"The blood test that everyone takes, you moron." Cade tightened his grip on my arms. The bruising hold brought moisture to my eyes.

"The singles will be exterminated like the Scavengers. The perfect society can only be created with perfected individuals. A quintessential genetic match, like you and Willow, is shockingly hard to find. I sincerely hope that we can find another specimen for her. She is an exquisite creature. Her bloodline would contribute greatly to our future."

Kain's dark gaze flitted from Phoenix to me. There was nothing but murder swimming in his eyes. An abyss of the fieriest circle of hell.

"Unfortunately, you are no longer trustworthy, Nolan and Phoenix. I blame John Delany for that. He will suffer greatly in the end."

I had nothing to say to that perverse insanity. I closed my eyes, briefly, allowing myself a moment of blissful imagery.

This was just a nightmare. I'd wake up at any second. Winter snuggled against me. My tender mother's spirit would appear before us, and this deranged scenario would go away.

All I could really do was wish.

"One last question:" Kain's tone was nonchalant. As though he hadn't been talking about human beings like they were test tubes in a lab. "Where is the abomination now?"

I merely stared at him. Not allowing myself to become enraged for Phoenix's sake.

"I don't know who you're referring too."

Kain smirked- his finger moving for the button on the torture cage again. Phoenix stiffened, but didn't utter a sound.

"Stop!"

"Tell me where your girlfriend is. Unless you want Phoenix to die slowly."

"I don't know!"

"You're lying."

I shook my head vigorously; watching helplessly as Kain placed his finger against the button.

I couldn't do it. I couldn't tell him. Kain already knew where Eliza's cabin was located. I couldn't purposely point Kain in her direction.

It would put every single person I loved in danger.

I also couldn't watch Phoenix die in that cage.

"I swear, I'm not. She gave the tablet to John, but that's the last either one of us heard from her. She's a loner. Being around other people makes her nervous."

Kain didn't move his finger from the button, but he didn't press it either. Phoenix let out a steadying breath; eyes downcast in defeat.

"Did you know that the abomination killed Vigilantes?" Kain's voice dropped to a deadly whisper.

My throat went dry again. I shook my head.

"Speak!" Kain barked and Phoenix flinched in terror.

"No, I had no idea. I swear it."

Kain finally removed his finger from the button.

Phoenix slumped against the bars again. Her strength finally failed her.

My mind raced wildly; trying to think of something I could do to save her. I kept coming up with nothing. Terror engulfed me completely.

I blew out a calming breath. Slowing my raging thoughts. Everything my sensei ever taught me about self-control went through my mind like a whirlwind.

"It's unfortunate that you sided with the abomination, Nolan Delany." Kain opened the cell door. "Now your life is forfeit. You'll stay in the dungeon until I come up with a plan to destroy John. I have a feeling I'm going to need you for that."

No!

Cade shoved me inside the cell and shut the door with an echoing click.

"Turn around, and press your hands against the bars."

I obeyed, robotically. Cade removed the scorching handcuffs from my wrists. The burning subsided the moment the metal was removed.

I brought my hands in front of me, but didn't inspect the damage.

Kain opened the torture cage and grabbed Phoenix by her wrist. She shrieked in pain, but did nothing to struggle against his brutality.

I gripped the bars of my cell as he manhandled her. I had expected Kain to throw her in the cell with me-

I knew. I knew now that wouldn't be happening.

Tears filled my eyes; my mind rebelling against it. Against *all* of it.

This couldn't be happening.

"I'm begging you, Kain. Please, don't do this."

The Viking didn't even look at me as he forced Phoenix to her knees. She shook violently, but didn't cry out again. She was in pain, but there was no terror on her face.

That only made one of us.

"Let her go! Don't punish her for something I did! Please!"

Kain glanced at me, sadistic glee in his eyes, relishing the fact that I was helpless to stop this.

"Tell her you're sorry for getting her into this." Kain stared at Phoenix's broken form kneeling in front of him. "It's the least you can do."

My whole body shook as I collapsed to my knees. I was eye level with Phoenix, but she stared at the concrete floor with those horribly vacant eyes.

Resigned. She was completely resigned to her fate. Didn't fear it. Didn't even loathe it. She just waited for it all to end.

"Look at me, Phoenix."

She glanced up, her beautiful brown eyes sparked when they met mine.

"I am so sorry."

"Don't." Her voice was so low. So hoarse I could barely hear her. "I'd do it all again. I knew the risks."

I shook my head in denial. Tears rushed down my face in torrential waves. I leaned my forehead against the bars as all the strength left me.

How could I have let this happen?

I was going to hell for sure.

"You're the best friend I've ever had." Phoenix soft voice made my gut clench. Knowing this was the last time I'd ever hear it.

"I love you, Nolan."

There was only one thing I could say. I didn't hesitate.

"I love you too, Phoenix," I whispered through my tears. "Don't you ever forget that, okay?"

Phoenix smiled brightly. As though those words from me was the last thing she needed to hear before she could be at peace.

Kain grabbed Phoenix by the braids; forcing her to stand. She didn't take her beautiful eyes off me as Cade dragged her to the door.

"No! No! Stop! You don't have to do this!"

"You've made this easy by already telling everyone that Phoenix is dead." Kain opened the vault door. His dark eyes roamed over me sadistically. "My hands are clean. Yours, however, are not."

"I'm going to kill you, Kain!"

The Viking gave me an amused smirk before he disappeared through the door.

Pain ripped through me when the vault door shut with an ominous click. My body shook from the sobs that escaped me. I sank to the floor again and I sat there for a long time.

I hadn't cried like this since I found my mom's corpse buried under rubble more than three years ago.

I wished I could see her now. I needed her. I needed her so very badly.

I collapsed in the cell, completely helpless. Hours went by, maybe even a full day. There was no way of knowing. I eventually shed all the tears I had in me, but the ache in my chest never went away.

I would never see Phoenix again.

I would never see Winter again.

And I desperately hoped I would never see Willow again. That she would get herself out. Somehow.

I'd drifted into an unconscious, dream-like, state. Images danced through my mind: of Winter holding a hand out to me, of John smiling broadly, of Eliza's warm kindness. Memories of my life before-

I only came back to reality because the vault door had been pushed open.

"You look like crap, Blue Eyes."

I turned around at the sound of Willow's voice. I tried to hide the panic from her as I glanced around the room. If Kain was going to drag her away to be executed too, I-

I didn't know what I'd do.

Luckily, it was just Willow and I in the dungeon.

Willow held a tablet in her hands. She stared at it; horror displayed on her face. Without warning, she flipped the tablet around.

I stepped away from the bars, gagging. I struggled for breath; trying to keep myself from vomiting.

I didn't look at Willow again until she turned off the tablet. Phoenix's lifeless face wasn't how I wanted to remember her.

"Interesting reaction. Did you take acting lessons in school? You seem sickened by your own mess."

"Willow."

My pleading voice was raspy, haunted, even to my own ears. I had no more tears left in me to shed, but my eyes still burned with the need to cry.

"You lied to me. You lied about everything. Did you pull the trigger? Or did you abandon her in the cave after the Highborns shot her? At least tell me how she died. I deserve that much."

"Too. Bad."

The words were barely a whisper. I hoped that she understood. I couldn't tell her anything with the cameras on us. I would never make that mistake again.

From here on out everything would be said in code.

"You owe me an explanation, Nolan."

I stared at her for a moment. I didn't think I'd ever heard her call me 'Nolan' before. In this instance, it meant that she understood.

"She was already dead when I left her in the cave. I told Kain and Cade where to find her."

Realization flared in her eyes. Realization that Kain and Cade were the ones that killed Phoenix.

"Why did you lie, Nolan?"

I took a shaky breath as relief hit me. She understood. She understood what I was trying to convey.

"The truth isn't simple, Willow."

"Why did you lie to me about the monster that killed my friend, Blue Eyes?"

A wave of intense emotion spread through me. I didn't think it was possible for me to feel more guilt. Apparently, I had been wrong.

"I didn't know that she killed your friend. You'll never know how sorry I am about that. But Winter is not a monster."

Willow's face paled, and she wiped a tear from her eye.

"How can you say that after what we just saw on the footage? She killed an entire team of Vigilantes."

"Because-" I paused.

I couldn't tell her that I had a close relationship with Winter without giving Kain reason to suspect that she was with John right now. I quickly shook my head and rubbed my eyes.

"Too. Bad. You'll never understand. I don't ever want to see you again."

I stared at Willow intently. I didn't think Kain would kill her. He needed her too much, but that didn't mean she was safe.

"You got it, Nolan. Enjoy what's left of your miserable life. *I'll make sure John gets what's coming to him.*"

I had to stop myself from exhaling, dramatically, in relief.

She was going to find a way to warn John about the Sleeping Ache Plague. The only way she could relay that message to me was if she made it sound like a threat.

I gave her a hard glare to let her know that I understood. She gave me a curt nod before leaving the dungeon.

The vault door closed, and I sat back down on the dirty concrete. It would take Willow a while to be able to escape the underground bunker, especially since Kain would be keeping a close eye on her.

Even though Willow was smart, and more than capable of putting a plan together, I was still terrified.

She had no one now.

All I could do was hope that she'd be able to survive on her own.

Chapter 12: John

I went to the Jeep to retrieve the shovel that we had brought with us, and got as far from the cave as I could. I kept my mind preoccupied by breaking through the frozen ground with the nose of the shovel. The least we could do was give Phoenix a proper burial.

I really hoped that I wouldn't be digging more graves today.

I lost track of time as I dug. The frozen ground got a little softer as I went deeper, but it didn't do much to ease the soreness in my arms. I refused to take a break, since I didn't want my mind to wander. Only bad things would come of that.

I didn't think I could handle anymore emotional torture.

I was merely digging in the dirt, but that simple act calmed me.

Digging by hand was a humbling experience. We generally didn't bury people anymore. We would burn them when we could, or just leave them in the wilderness when we couldn't.

Phoenix deserved better.

I was going to make sure she got a proper burial. It wouldn't be exactly how we used to do them before the natural disasters, but it would be a lot better than what we'd done in this apocalyptic world.

I stopped digging and turned around when footsteps approached.

My heart raced in anticipation as George made his way toward me. James and Leif stayed next to the Jeep, their expressions grim.

I stiffened when George stopped a few feet away from me. He stared at the grave for a moment before glancing at me. He held up a tablet bag in his hand.

A tablet that we didn't have when we arrived here.

"There were no other bodies, Boss." The news should've been a relief, but George's demeanor was grave. "James found this tablet by the mouth of the cave. He gave it to me when he realized what was on it."

I held my hand out expectantly, but George shook his head. He strapped the bag to his shoulder in a not-so-subtle attempt to inform me that I couldn't have it.

I gave him a hard glare, but it didn't seem to faze him.

"Kain knew that we would come here eventually. He left Phoenix, and the tablet, here for us to find. He wants us to know what he's doing to these kids."

A lump formed in my throat.

"What's on the tablet?"

I already knew what was on it, but I couldn't stop myself from asking anyway.

"Nothing good, John." He usually didn't call me by my given name, so that alone wasn't a good sign.

"Give it to me."

George shook his head firmly.

"You've already thrown up once tonight, Boss. You don't need to see what's on this right now."

That was ridiculous and he knew it.

"George, give me the tablet. That's an order."

He squared his shoulders and gave me an incredulous look. I didn't back down.

"I gave you the chance to lead the Scavengers. You refused, so I make the decisions. Give me the freaking tablet. Right now."

George blew out a breath and looked away from me. He didn't lower his gaze or act agreeable in any way. He just blatantly ignored me-

Which *really* pissed me off.

I was beginning to toy with the idea of taking it from him by force, but he sighed and finally held the tablet out to me. It was a good thing too, since the guy could wipe the floor with me if it came to blows.

"Don't say I didn't warn you."

I took the tablet bag from him and pulled out the rectangular device. There was no passcode or eye scanner system in place. Kain had wanted whoever found the tablet to be able to access the data easily. The blank screen filled with video footage of Kain's dark, hairy face. His beard had gotten longer since the last time I'd seen him.

I tapped play on the screen, and noticed that the sound had been turned down. I turned the volume up-

And immediately understood why James had muted the footage.

The echoing sound of a whip. A harsh scream.

Agony and terror broke the silence of the night.

I stood there, frozen, while I held the tablet in a death grip. I still couldn't see anything except Kain's sneer on the screen, but I heard the sound of the whip again. This time, I recognized the scream.

An intense shudder ran through my tired muscles.

"This is a message for John Delany. His brother, Nolan Delany, has been having a rough week. His life depends on John receiving this message."

Kain was cut off by another piercing scream from Nolan.

It was extremely horrific, to hear my baby brother scream in that much agony. I couldn't see what they were doing to him, but it wasn't hard to guess that they were flogging him. It was a medieval technique, but still effective despite the barbaric nature.

In order to keep watching the footage, I had to mentally detach myself from what I was hearing.

I had to think like a cop; not a brother.

I quickly glanced at the time stamp on the video. It had been taken a little more than three weeks ago. Kain continued talking, and I had to rewind the video when I missed what he'd said.

Gritting my teeth, I forced myself to focus.

"I have someone monitoring when this footage will be watched," Kain continued in a deep gravelly tone. "Whoever is watching this: if you are John Delany, our facial recognition system will verify the date you watched this. The date today is December 30, 2249."

Kain paused when Nolan screamed again. My fingers twitched when the Viking chuckled in amusement.

"Three weeks ago." George peeked over my shoulder at the screen. "I really hope the kid hasn't been beaten like that more than once."

I hoped so too, but I wasn't stupid.

Nolan would be lucky to still be alive when I found Kain.

I kept my emotions detached as I stared at the screen. The green light of a scanner erupted from the camera lens on the tablet. The light glided over my face, and I stood still so that the tablet could verify that it was me.

"After the tablet scanned me it went blank a second later. I have no idea what's going to happen after this."

I gave George a nod of understanding, but didn't take my eyes off of the screen.

"I'm sure you want to see your brother to verify that he's alive."

Kain turned the camera until Nolan came into view.

My teeth slammed together so hard, I was lucky I didn't crack my molars. George muttered a string of profanity at the sight of him.

He was suspended by his wrists to the ceiling; his feet barely touching the floor. His head hung over his chest as though he didn't have the strength to keep his neck upright anymore. His dark hair dangled over his eyes. But I could still see the bruises that decorated his cheeks and mouth. All he wore was a pair of ripped and stained jeans. His feet were bare against the cement floor.

Blood dripped from my brother's lacerated back to the dirty ground.

I had to stop myself from dwelling on the disturbing puddle of crimson liquid that Nolan stood in. A blond haired young man was behind him; holding a multi-tailed whip loosely in his hand.

I forced myself to stop staring at Nolan, and memorized his surroundings. I couldn't see much, but it looked like he was in a room made of mostly concrete and steel. I spotted a wall of bars, but the screen cut off the rest of the room.

I assumed this was where Kain kept and tortured his prisoners until he decided to execute them. I didn't know if there were any other people in this room besides Nolan, Kain, and the young man that was whipping him.

The camera shook a little when Kain turned it to face himself again.

"As you can see, John Delany, he's still alive. If you want him to stay that way, you'll do everything you're told in the timeframe that I give you."

I listened intently; ignoring James and Leif as they walked up to us. I didn't even glance at Leif when he let out a horrified gasp.

"Nolan is being punished because of you," Kain continued angrily. "You sent him to spy on me to further your own agenda."

That wasn't true. Nolan had made that decision on his own.

But I had let him, so this *was* all my fault. I should've insisted on Nolan coming home. Sure, I'd tried to convince him many times to escape the League of Vigilance bunker, but he had always insisted on staying.

I should've tried harder.

The gut wrenching guilt made me shake as I stared into Kain's psychotic eyes.

The camera moved again, and Nolan came into view. James and Leif both looked away from the screen, but George and I studied every second of the footage that we could.

Nolan hadn't been whipped for a few minutes, and he seemed to be perking up a bit. He lifted his head slightly, but I couldn't see his eyes. His whole body was wracked with violent shivers; revealing how much pain he was in.

Kain grabbed Nolan by the hair. Black fingernails sank into Nolan's scalp, and he drew in a sharp breath. The camera shook slightly as Kain forced his head upright.

Forcing Nolan to stare at the camera.

I had never seen agony like that in my brother's eyes before. I had to look away for a brief moment, so I wouldn't become nauseous again.

When I glanced back at the screen, I couldn't hide my shock at what else I saw in Nolan's expression. I may have never seen him in that much pain before, but I had *never* seen him look more defiant. I'd witnessed his anger plenty of times, but the murderous fury in those blue eyes was something completely different than what was normal.

He was on the verge of exploding his rage all over Kain.

I had no doubt that if Nolan wasn't chained to the ceiling, he'd have Kain in a chokehold within seconds-

Despite his injuries.

"Give your brother the message," Kain ordered.

It was the wrong way to ask anything of Nolan, especially when he was that pissed off. All it did was trigger the rebellious side of him.

I tried to stop the trembling in my fingers by gripping the tablet even tighter. If my hold got any stronger, I'd probably break the stupid thing.

Nolan's lips twitched slightly as though he were fighting off a defiant smirk. I recognized the reaction. I'd seen it countless times throughout his life.

"No."

Even though Nolan's voice was weak, there was a finality to the word that rippled through the atmosphere.

Kain thought he was breaking Nolan down by having him flogged-

The Viking didn't know my brother at all.

My whole body tensed as I watched the young man raise the multi-tailed whip with a sick glint in his eye. The knotted leather straps hit Nolan's back with a resounding smack. I couldn't see how many tails the flogging whip had, but I knew each one left a bloody mark. I could only imagine that his back looked like shredded meat.

Nolan's face went even paler when the whip hit him. He didn't cry out this time, but his eyes closed as he bit into his bottom lip. He let out a shuddering breath before opening his eyes again. His pupils dilated. His eyes red from unshed tears.

He was trying to show me that he was still strong. By remaining silent. By refusing to cower.

Tears stung my eyes. I didn't want him to have to act strong for me.

"Give him the message!" Kain tightened his grip on Nolan's hair. He winced slightly, but that defiant look on his face hadn't dissolved. If anything, his anger seemed to grow stronger.

"Easy, Nolan," I whispered, even though I knew he couldn't hear me. There was nothing I could do to change what was going on here.

Nolan didn't say anything for a few more seconds. I didn't know if he was trying to choose his words wisely, or if he was having a hard time speaking in general.

"John." Nolan stared into the camera. The angry defiance still burned in his eyes like a violent flame. "He knows everything. He wants *her*. Keep her safe. Please."

Kain roared angrily, and tore the camera away from Nolan's face. I stared in horror as the video wobbled toward the concrete floor. I couldn't see anything but Nolan's bare feet, and large pools of blood on the floor.

Nolan yelled something, but I didn't understand what he said.

"Rewind it," George ordered, needlessly.

I pushed play, and listened intently to what Nolan was trying to tell me.

"Don't let them hurt her, John! Don't do what Kain wants!"

I paused the video; letting out a shuddering exhale.

Nolan was talking about Winter. Somehow, Kain had found out about her. I didn't know why Nolan thought the Vigilantes were capable of hurting her. She was basically untouchable, unless-

I froze when the memory came to me:

Dr. Darkwood's bullets. A steel neck brace that negated Winter's powers.

If Kain had somehow gotten a hold of those things…

I had let her go off on her own. Now she wasn't answering her communicator. Eliza would've contacted me if she had.

I pushed all thoughts of Winter aside. My brain could only handle so much at one time.

I glanced at my comrades, and noticed all three of them staring at me. James and Leif looked like they'd eaten something that didn't agree with them, but George gave nothing away in his expression.

"You alright, Boss?"

His tone reminded me that he was keeping his head, and that I should too. I cleared my throat and pushed play again.

"Have Willow delete this part of the footage," Kain ordered.

The video still showed the concrete floor, but I assumed he was talking to the young man torturing Nolan. It was also possible that there was someone else in the room that had been off screen. Either way, I recognized the name 'Willow'.

"Yes, sir," the reply came through a small grunt that was followed by the resounding smack of the whip again. Nolan gasped in pain. He'd managed to hold in the scream that I knew tried to escape him.

In that moment, I was in complete awe of my brother.

"Continue until he passes out. Just make sure not to kill him."

The footage cut out, and I stared at the screen for a few long seconds until Kain's face popped up again. The time stamp on this video feed was two hours later.

George reached over to press pause on the tablet, and I gave him a sharp look.

"I got a question for ya, Boss. Do you have any idea what that was all about?"

He wasn't referring to Nolan being flogged.

I stared at him; considering what I should say. He wanted to know who Nolan was talking about, and who Willow was.

Willow was still loyal to Nolan. She helped me receive Nolan's warning. He had told me once that Willow was an expert with computers. It was possible that she was still alive because Kain needed her skills.

I really hoped that was true. I didn't want to find another teenage girl's corpse abandoned somewhere. Willow's or Winter's.

"I know exactly what that was about, but I'm going to have to swear the three of you to secrecy. If this gets out, it could put someone I care about in even more danger than she's already in."

I wasn't sure if it was possible for Winter to be in any more danger, but I felt like I needed to say that. I knew some of the Scavengers would react badly to her ice powers. Some would probably try to kill her. Luckily, I didn't think James, Leif, or George would want to hurt her. Especially since she had saved us when we drove the Highborn Union from our territory.

The three of them nodded in unison, and I told them everything about Winter. I didn't give any of them a chance to interrupt me, or ask questions about her. I needed to get this out of the way, so I could find out what message Kain wanted to give me.

George swore under his breath, but didn't say anything to me directly. This wasn't the time to discuss Winter, or the lies I told to keep her a secret.

I ignored the three of them, and resumed the footage from Kain.

"I'm sure you want to see your brother to verify that he's alive."

The camera turned, and I blinked in shock at the sight of Nolan now. I didn't think he could look any worse than he had in the previous video, but I had been wrong.

He was no longer standing on his own. He hung like a limp spaghetti noodle from his wrists. His toes were covered in blood; flecks of it staining his ankles. I couldn't help but wonder how long it took him to pass out. There had been a lapse of two hours since the time of the last footage.

I couldn't imagine the hellish nightmare Nolan went through in those two hours.

All I could think about, in that moment, was the horrible damage flogging did to the human body. Stories ran through my mind of men and women who had been whipped so severely; they either died or were permanently crippled.

Nolan wasn't dead. Kain wanted him alive to get to me-

If my brother was permanently damaged because of this, I would hunt down the sadistic Viking. There was absolutely nowhere that he could hide in this apocalyptic world where I wouldn't find him.

"Revive him, Cade."

The young man with the multi-tailed whip grinned at Kain.

Now I knew the name of the second man I was going to hunt down for this.

I watched, helplessly, as Cade picked up a bucket of dirty water and dumped it over Nolan's head. He jerked slightly and moaned, but that's all he did. There was no defiance, or sign of life, other than that small sound and movement. He didn't even open his eyes to give Kain the hateful look that I was so desperate to see.

"John Delany, you're actions have consequences. Unfortunately, your little brother is being punished in your place."

Kain paused, and turned the camera lens to face himself again.

"If you want to see your brother alive, and spare him from further pain, then I suggest you pay very close attention to my instructions."

I blew out the breath I was holding in as I stared at the monster on the screen between my hands.

"I want you and the abomination you call 'Winter'." He spat coldly. "In exchange for Nolan Delany. I will meet both of you at the coordinates indicated on the tablet that you have. I will give you two days from the time you watch this to meet me there. If you aren't there within that time allotment, then Nolan will be released from his pain."

There was a dramatic pause while Kain stared into the camera. It seemed that the footage had come to an end. I could no longer rewind it, so watching the video again was impossible.

Suddenly, the map application opened. Revealing the coordinates Kain, or Willow, had inserted.

George looked at the tablet, and shook his head in frustration.

"It'll take you two days to get to this location by foot. That's only if you're hurrying."

I sighed grimly; trying to think about what I should do. Even if I could get there within two days, I wouldn't have Winter with me. I doubted Kain would believe me if I told him that Winter was gone. Not that I would ever take her with me in the first place.

I needed to come up with another way to get Nolan back.

"So are we just going to forget about the Sleeping Ache then?" James folded his arms, grimly. "Is saving one life, over the lives of the rest of the community, worth it?"

I glanced at the three men, and what I saw completely humbled me. I could see it in their eyes; the loyalty. They'd follow me anywhere I decided to go. Even if it meant aborting the mission.

"No, it's not. You three will go get the cure. I'm going to talk to Kain."

George blew out a low whistle, Leif shifted uncomfortably, while James just stared at me as though I'd gone crazy.

"And by 'talk to Kain' you really mean-"

"Killing him slowly." I nodded to George. "Yeah."

"Well, I'm going with ya, Boss." He picked up the shovel I had dropped. "I don't believe in leaving anyone behind. Especially a soldier like Nolan Delany."

I stared at George in shock.

Calling Nolan a soldier caught me off guard. In our past society, Nolan wouldn't have been old enough to enlist in the military until he was twenty.

"You can't come with me. We've got a lot of people that need the cure."

George smirked as he dug into the grave.

"Nolan needs medical attention. I would suggest that you don't fight me on this, Boss. I wouldn't want to make you look bad in front of James and Leif."

All the anger was about to spew out of me in a red hot wave of rage. Before I could scream at him, Leif stepped between me and George.

"He's right, John. We need Nolan with us. He's just as important to the community as anyone else."

Something shifted within me. Something more than mere rage. An ugly, smothering coldness swept through my entire being; defiling my very soul.

"You don't think I know that?"

The question was nothing more than a whisper. So dangerously quiet; Leif had the good sense to step away from me.

It all came to the surface then. Exploding out of me so violently; there was nothing I could do to stop it.

"Nolan is my brother! He's the *only* reason we've been able to form a resistance in our community! Without the information he's given us, we would've succumbed to Amanda Lynch weeks ago! We wouldn't have been able to steal weapons and medicines from the Highborns! He's been imprisoned- tortured- because of us! Because of me!"

I took in a ragged breath; my vision going dark. I doubled over; resting my hands on my knees.

I hadn't realized how lightheaded I was until now. I couldn't stop shaking and, for a brief moment, I really wished I had access to alcohol.

I was never much for consuming liquor before the natural disasters, but this situation definitely called for it.

I forced myself to stand upright again.

George handed the shovel to James and stepped toward me. He rested a hand on my shoulder. His warm palm a gesture of solidarity.

"Which is why we are coming with you, Boss. We *need* Nolan. People like him are our future. Shane can handle the Sleeping Ache victims until we get our hands on the cure. In the meantime, let's give Phoenix the burial she deserves. Then we're gonna get our soldier back."

I stared at the three of them- surprised to see James nodding in agreement. I still didn't like the idea of putting our mission on hold, but there really was no choice to make here.

I *had* to save Nolan.

I knew I couldn't do it alone. No matter how much I felt like I should. The Vigilantes needed to be dealt with, and now was the time.

Kain was going to find out what happens when someone imprisons, and tortures, a Scavenger. Especially Nolan Delany.

Part 2

Chapter 13: Winter

The doorknob turned before I could reach it; stopping me mid-stride.

Ember bumped into me from behind; jarring my wounded shoulder. I managed to stifle a gasp, but the pounding pain made me stumble.

The door swung open, and the temperature in the room plummeted. Ember jumped away from me with a startled yelp.

A Vigilante woman, with wide-set brown eyes and dreadlocks that hung to her midsection, stood in the doorway. Her cruel face morphed into horror when she beheld me.

I had never actually seen what I looked like when I used my powers. From what John and Nolan had explained to me, I looked every ounce the abomination that I was. I didn't feel much, besides a small ache in my shoulder, as I raised my hands toward her.

Welcoming the cold as it covered my burning fever like a blanket of snow.

I blasted the woman with a stream of frost that slung her out of the doorway, as though she weighed nothing more than a feather.

I didn't see where she landed, but I heard her screams of terror and agony. Wounding someone so brutally usually grated against my conscious, but I was completely serene as she continued wailing.

I was tired. So tired of being tortured.

A primal instinct took over within me as I stalked toward the chaos I created. I would kill anyone that got in my way.

Without hesitation.

Ember understood, as she kept as far away from me as possible. She had effectively unleashed me upon Brian's band of Vigilantes.

A tall man with a battle axe rushed toward me. I barely paid him a glance as I raised my hand outward. He stopped, his battle axe in mid-swing, as my ice beam slowly engulfed him. The air punched out of his lungs in a guttural *whoosh* sound.

As the man died, it didn't take long for the other Vigilantes to start firing their poisoned bullets.

I didn't bother sending up my ice shields as I took cover behind a pile of firewood. I crouched there; closing my eyes in calm concentration. I visualized the guns in the hands of the Vigilantes; relishing the screams as I turned each weapon into ice.

Once I was no longer being pelted with poisonous bullets, I slowly peeked over the top of the woodpile.

The Vigilantes were all down on their knees; clutching their frozen hands to their chests in agony. Their screams echoing in the stillness of the trees.

I rose from behind the firewood; raising my hands toward the four injured men. The woman with the dreadlocks was sprawled on the ground a few feet away, completely motionless. Whether she was dead, or merely unconscious, I didn't know. Didn't even care.

I had no intention of letting any of them live anyway.

Just as I was about to send a beam of frost at the injured Vigilantes, there was a soft banging sound that came from the cabin.

I glanced over my shoulder; irritation swept through me at the sight of Brian standing in front of the door.

Evidently, he had somehow gotten around me during the shootout.

He had an arm around Ember's waist with a small knife held underneath her jaw. Poking into her skin just above the neck brace they'd forced her into.

"Surrender! Or I will slit her throat! I'll make you watch her bleed out!"

As though I should care about Ember: the girl that turned her flames against the ones I loved most in this world.

I stared at them without saying a word. I hadn't stopped using my powers. Even now, I could feel the waves of cold making their way toward them.

Brian claimed that I was a heartless monster. He had been right.

I ignored him; turning back to face the four men that were still writhing on the ground. They were defenseless and weak.

They thought they could hold me captive and torture me. They thought they could interrogate me about the people I loved.

Now their lives were in *my* hands.

I pointed my icy fingers toward the men, but a voice in my head whispered a memory.

You are inherently good. It's just who you are deep inside.

Nolan's voice.

My eyes stung with tears. I paused. Hesitating.

"If you kill them! I'll kill Ember! I swear it!"

I lowered my hands as the agonizing fever rushed through my veins. I stumbled, the deep muscle aches pounding through me. The sickness intensified as I tucked the remaining kernels of my power away.

Surrendering completely.

As though that inherent goodness that Nolan thought dwelt within me could ever win. Could ever hold sway in this unforgiving world.

I didn't say anything as I turned to face Brian and Ember. Her face had gone a sickly shade of green. I knew that she would be fine immediately after the neck brace was removed. Dr. Darkwood had made her special in that way. She never had to endure discomfort the way Shane and I had.

It was rather difficult not to hold resentment for that. Of course, her kidnapping street orphans for Dr. Darkwood was reason enough to despise her.

Still, I surrendered for her. Despite how foolish it seemed.

"That's what I thought." Brian sneered as he tightened his arm around Ember's waist. "So pathetic."

"Let her go and I'll let you live."

I don't know if it was my exhausted tone, or the fact that I could barely stand upright, but Brian cackled with laughter.

"Perhaps I'll just wait you out. You'll be on your backside soon enough. Then we'll *play*."

Brian's eyes roamed over me, predatorily. An amused smirk marred his lips. But it was the sheer panic in Ember's eyes that drew my attention. She squirmed in his grip, and he merely chuckled. The hand holding the knife lowered away from her jaw slightly.

"This must be torture for you, little cousin. Bearing witness as Winter takes the brunt of the torture. All so you don't have to."

I'd had enough of this nonsense.

Without warning, my countenance changed. I was back to looking like the abomination the Vigilantes feared me to be.

Brian gasped; trying to bring the knife back up under Ember's jaw-

The knife, and Brian's entire hand, formed into a block of solid ice. It took him a moment to register what had happened-

Then the ghastly screams ensued.

Ember stumbled out of his grip; staring at his frozen hand that still clutched the knife.

Then, with speed and finesse that I didn't know she possessed, Ember grabbed a machete that leaned against the log wall. With one smooth motion, she chopped off Brian's frozen hand.

I watched in horror as Brian collapsed from the pain- Unconscious before he hit the ground. I had expected there to be blood, but there was none. I stared at the severed frozen hand that still gripped the iced-covered knife.

Nausea threatened to overcome me. My stomach rumbled-

"Stop gawking at the gross hand and help me."

I tore my gaze away from the hand and glanced at Ember. She was holding a key that was attached to a long chain. She must've taken the key off of Brian while I was occupied with the severed body part in front of my feet.

When I didn't move or say anything, Ember rolled her eyes.

"You're wasting time, Winter." She thrust the key at me. "I can't reach the lock, so hurry."

I reluctantly took the key from her. Dreading that I was about to do something incredibly stupid.

"You're not going to hurt anyone, right? Because if you do-"

"Oh, come on." She sighed; running her hands through her short hair in exhaustion. "Give me some credit."

I would've gaped at that if I wasn't so exhausted.

I shuffled forward and she turned her back to me. She was a few inches taller than me, so I had to stand on my tip toes to find the lock. With trembling fingers, I was able to get the key into the tiny hole. Ember gasped in pain when the neck brace broke open.

I couldn't help the twinge of empathy that tightened my chest.

There was a lot of blood oozing from the tiny wounds that the needles made in her neck. I didn't remember there being that much blood when Nolan had taken the brace off of me, but he had been holding me against his chest at the time.

Ember didn't seem to care about the blood as she let out a deep sigh. She radiated so much heat that I had to step away from her; nearly tripping over Brian's motionless body-

It took me longer than it should've to realize that Ember's hands were on fire.

"No! Don't!"

Ember ignored me; throwing her flames at the injured Vigilantes. They were engulfed in the scorching fire before any of them had a chance to run.

Their screams filled the night. The glow from their melting flesh shined like a beacon in the dark. The nausea finally overcame me as the stench of burning meat filled my nostrils. Annihilating my sense.

I heaved in the snow. Knowing I'd see all of this again; haunting my nightmares.

Ember let out a fierce battlecry before she finally extinguished her flames. I finally looked away from the Vigilantes that Ember had murdered-

The Vigilantes that allowed her to be tortured for weeks.

Ember turned around slowly; raising her hands toward Brian's unconscious body. Her face contorted in a jumble of pain and rage. Her blue eyes widened; swimming with cold fear.

Her hands hadn't turned to flames yet, but I could tell it was coming.

I should've blasted her with a stream of frost, but the fear in her eyes stopped me. I grabbed her by both wrists and held on. My hands blistered from the heat, but I refused to show anymore signs of pain tonight.

I gritted my teeth; staring into her fear stricken eyes.

"Ember, it's okay. You don't need to kill your cousin. We are safe. *You are safe.*"

Ember glared at me. The heat flared in her arms. I gasped in pain, and immediately released her. I could feel the blisters forming on my hands, but I didn't look at them.

I couldn't take my eyes off the dangerous girl in front of me.

"I'm not going to kill him!"

Her glare deepened and she took another step toward me.

I retreated until I was inside the cabin again. It wasn't ideal to let her corner me, but I had to get her away from Brian. I wouldn't trust her not to kill him, or make his injuries worse.

I needed to distract her somehow.

"What is a cousin?"

Ember paused, staring at me blankly.

Then she laughed. The sound so joyous- It was disconcerting after all the people she'd just burned alive.

I stared at her until she finally calmed down enough to speak.

"Woah!" She wiped her watery eyes. "I haven't laughed like that in years."

I shrugged, trying to remain calm.

"Um, okay."

"You really don't remember anything, do you?" She huffed out a small chuckle that sounded more uncomfortable than humorous.

I didn't reply.

When it became apparent that she wasn't going to answer my question, I went back to eyeing her warily. I couldn't help but think that she had become unhinged. That this whole situation had left her insane. Being able to laugh, after cutting off someone's hand and killing five people, was not normal behavior.

Not that I could blame her. Being held captive did things to a person's mind.

"You don't have to watch me like some rabid animal. I'm not going to hurt you."

I glanced down pointedly at my blistered hands to inspect the damage.

"Well, obviously you shouldn't touch me when I'm upset. That was your own fault."

Okay, I could agree with her on that point.

I stumbled to the cabinet full of first aid supplies. I applied ointment to the burns and, awkwardly, wrapped them myself. Ember didn't offer to help me, but I was okay with that.

I didn't want her to touch me ever again.

"I found Brian's tablet." Ember waved the rectangular device in the air. "I don't know what your plans are, but I've got a score to settle with Kain."

I just wanted to see if Nolan was still alive.

Now that Brian was no longer a threat, I felt like I could move on with my plans. I glanced at the porch to make sure that he-

My thoughts sputtered as I stared at an empty porch in shock.
Brian was gone.
Ember swore loudly; rushing to the door.
"Why weren't you watching him?"
She rounded on me as though this was all my fault. I was too tired to care.

I merely shrugged and brushed by her. I didn't think it would be hard to find Brian, since his hand had been brutally frozen and amputated.

"I need his fingerprint, or his eyeball, to open this thing. Otherwise we will never find the bunker."

I ignored her as I stumbled off the porch.

Ember liked to talk a lot. I now understood why Nolan called me annoying all the time. I had talked to him almost constantly throughout the day when we first met. Granted, I was just trying to learn how to talk verbally at the time.

Had I really been this annoying?

Just as I was about to step off the porch, an engine echoed in the still forest.

Brian must've had a vehicle hidden in the trees somewhere. We'd never be able to catch up to him now. Unless, I froze the entire forest or Ember set fire to it.

I didn't like either option.

"Crap!" Ember's heat ignited around her furiously.

"Don't burn the trees just to get at him."

"Why not?" She rounded on me, incredulously. "We need his fingerprint-"

I stared pointedly at Brian's hand that was still lying on the porch next to the door frame. If Ember really thought we didn't have Brian's fingerprints, then she need a lot more help than I was willing to give her.

It was disgusting, but there was nothing else we could do at this point. Luckily, Ember's fires had negated my ice and the hand was completely thawed out.

Ember stared at it for a moment, and visibly cringed.

"Well that doesn't solve the problem of him warning Kain about me coming."

I sighed and blinked a few times. I *really* needed sleep, but first I had to find my pack and the communicator. John and Eliza were probably worried sick.

"Could you at least act like you care?"

I shrugged, wrapping my sore arms around myself. A dull ache gathered in my upper back and spread downward.

"Let Kain know we're coming. There's not a thing he can do to stop us. Especially if we work together."

Ember folded her arms and scowled at me.

"What makes you think I want to work with you?" Her eyes roamed over me in disgust.

"Um, you told me you did."

"That was just to get out of this mess."

Ember gestured toward the cabin in emphasis.

"I'm going after Kain too, so we might as well do it together."

"No, you're not. He's *my* problem to take care of. Besides, you don't know him at all. You've never actually met him."

It was true. I'd never even seen Kain before. I had no idea how Ember could possibly know that.

"He took someone from me. Someone that I love."

Ember merely stared at me. I held her gaze; refusing to be the first one to look away.

I needed to show her that I wasn't as weak as she thought I was. Yeah, I was sick from the poisonous bullets, but I could still use my abilities. Nothing would stop me from getting to Kain.

To Nolan.

"Fine, you can come with me. But you can't kill Kain."

Ember's hands burst into flame. Her eyes glimmered in the sparks of the fire. I took a step back from the heat, but I didn't show her any sign that I was scared of her.

"He's *my* problem to deal with. Do you understand?"

"Fine, but we *are* going to work together." Ember narrowed her eyes at me. "If you want to take out Kain alone, when we get there, then be my guest. I'll be too busy looking for Nolan anyway."

Ember extinguished her flames and gaped at me.

"Nolan shot me with an *arrow*."

I stared at her incredulously. She couldn't be serious.

"Yeah, and you threw a *fireball* at him. He's not like you, me, or Shane. He would've died from that."

I turned away from her before she had a chance to reply, and walked toward the trees where I'd hidden my bag. My heart sank when I saw my bag was ripped to shreds; my communicator smashed to bits.

I closed my eyes; trying to stop the tears that burned them.

There was nothing I could do to spare my family of their worries. Of the fear that would keep them awake at night.

I dragged myself back to the cabin; forcing myself to regain control. To hide from Ember all the dread that threatened to consume me.

She was still on the porch with the tablet in her hands. She rapidly tapped the screen with her fingers.

"I found the coordinates to the underground bunker. It'll be a two day hike. Maybe three." She gestured to the rolled up blanket and my extra tank top that hadn't been torn to pieces by the Vigilantes. "That's all you brought?"

Ember eyed the items in my arms incredulously.

"The Vigilantes destroyed the rest of my supplies. Let's see what Brian's got stored in the cabin."

I didn't wait for her response as I stumbled into the room.

I still felt the sickness spreading through me, but the cold night air had helped. I could only hope that I'd continue recovering in the cold weather.

Worry tugged in the back of my mind, but I ignored it.

I just needed to keep some distance from Ember's scorching body heat.

There wasn't very much food in the cabin. Most of the food I didn't recognize since they were all in cans. The labels were peeling off and some of the cans were rusty.

I grabbed a backpack hanging from the log wall and began filling it with canned food and medical supplies. Ember stared at me as though I'd gone insane while I worked.

"I'm surprised you're not grabbing the pop tarts." She pointed at the colorful boxes sitting on the shelf. "Brian's been eating those in front of me for weeks."

I grabbed a few of the boxes and shoved them into the backpack.

"You don't even know what pop tarts are, do you?"

I merely shrugged as I started zipping up the backpack. Ember held out a metal device toward me.

I stepped away from her, cautiously.

"It's a can opener, Winter." She gently placed it in my hand. "We're not going to be able to open any of the canned food without it."

Without another word, Ember walked out the door. I carefully strapped the backpack to my shoulders, despite my protesting bullet wounds.

I followed Ember at a slow pace. I knew I should try to keep up with her longer strides, but I simply didn't have the stamina that she did. Hopefully, the distance would be a good thing.

I still wasn't sure what Ember had planned.

She wasn't pretending to be nice, but the trusting act was entirely suspicious.

Chapter 14: Nolan

Present day

Every muscle, every joint, throbbed as I leaned against the wall of my cell. I kept myself as still as possible; knowing that the slightest of movements could reopen the festering gashes on my back.

There were moments I thought I'd bleed out during my imprisonment. I still couldn't comprehend how I'd managed to survive without first aid supplies. Each session on the flogging post left me nearly dead.

Intense cramping ripped through my gut, but I forced myself to press my lips to the concrete wall anyway. Nausea gripped me as I lapped the trickle of water that descended from the broken pipe above me.

The gnawing hunger was all consuming. Rusty water didn't make it better, but it was the only thing keeping me alive. Water, and the heat vent on the other side of the dungeon.

The Viking finally understood what a waste of time it was interrogating me. And feeding me, apparently.

I kept waiting for Cade to come and repair the broken pipe. To turn off the vent that kept me from freezing to death.

Perhaps they wanted to see how long it would take for me to finally clock out. It wouldn't be long either way. I could feel myself beginning to shut down completely.

They hadn't broken me. My anger kept me sharp. Kept my will strong enough to fight against every lashing, every punch, and every torture serum they injected me with.

All Kain's questions about John and Winter went unanswered.

I wasn't someone that could be broken. It was a pride that I'd take to my grave.

Every time I fell asleep, my last thought was whether or not I'd wake up again. I was at a point where I didn't really care anymore. Even if John saw that damned footage Kain took of my torture sessions; I hoped he wouldn't come for me.

I didn't need my brother's death on my conscious.

Then there was *Winter*.

I didn't want her anywhere near this place. Kain kept bragging that he was onto her- that he'd developed the weapons he needed to stop her.

It made me sick to imagine what he'd do to her. How he would study her and tear her apart piece by piece in front of me.

Winter had this childlike hope that most people didn't have. If anyone thought that I was still alive, it would be her-

I was thoroughly terrified that she would come here to try to save me. The very thought made me break into a cold sweat.

I heard the vault door open, but I didn't bother to open my eyes. Two sets of footsteps entered the dungeon, but I still didn't look up. I already knew who it was.

"Put the cuffs on him." Cade's gruff voice echoed through the concrete room. The hinges squeaked on the cell door. "He's still dangerous."

I would've smirked if I wasn't so tired. Cade was terrified of me, and he *should* be.

I *was* going to take him out-

When I found an ounce of energy I'd get right on that.

Kristy's soft fingers gripped my raw wrists, but her touch didn't hurt. It never really did. Of all the people that tormented me, she was the only one that didn't want to cause me more pain. She was merely complacent toward what Kain and Cade were doing to me.

Not that I blamed her. There was no telling what Kain would do to her if she didn't follow his every order perfectly.

Krissy locked the cuffs on my wrists. I schooled my expression; refusing to flinch at the agonizing burn on my raw skin.

My eyes flew open when Cade shoved a needle in my neck.

A violent rush of energy flooded my veins, and my heartbeat thudded in my ears. I used to groan in agony when they injected me with whatever serum it was they used to torture me with. I quickly learned to suppress that weakness. To deprive them the satisfaction of seeing me writhe in agony.

I'd be in severe pain in a few hours from the serum. Hopefully, I'd be alone by then.

"Rise and shine, Nolan." Cade sneered in delight at the sight of my bare torso. Bruises and dried blood covered nearly every inch of my exposed skin. "Eat this."

Cade held an apple in front of me, but I didn't move to take it.

"Eat it, or I'll shove a feeding tube down your throat."

The adrenaline from whatever Cade injected me with was the only thing that helped me eat the apple. By the time I finished the fruit, my jaw was seizing up.

The nausea intensified.

Cade shoved a bottle of water at me. I gulped it down, greedily, despite the cramping in my gut.

"Brian's back." Cade forced me to my feet. "He wants to talk to you."

I refused to move.

Cade and Krissy smirked, but I merely stared at them. Even though I was handcuffed, and ridiculously weak, I thought of moves I could use against them to get out of this mess.

I did *not* want to see Brian ever again.

He'd come back to the bunker to interrogated me a few times in the past month. The first two interrogations he used his torture cage, but he took it with him the last time he'd left the bunker.

I was happy to see it go, because that thing sucked-

Literally, it sucked the life out of me.

The last time he'd interrogated me, he told me things about the Scavengers that I hoped were lies. He reveled in the fact that they were plagued by the Sleeping Ache.

Brian did his best to break me every time he came here.

It was unfortunate that Kain hadn't actually kicked him out when I'd beaten him in that fight. Instead, I'd given them the perfect opening for Brian to spy on the Scavengers.

To threaten my family.

Ultimately, I knew resisting was stupid. Fighting Cade and Krissy would do nothing but weaken me further.

I reluctantly followed Cade out of the cell.

Walking was no easy task for me now, but I managed to make it to the interrogation room without any help. Even in my weakened state, I made Cade and Krissy nervous enough that they had no desire to be close to me. That desire was mutual, so I made it a point to act stronger than I was.

Weeks without proper food made me sluggish, but I was just as stubborn as ever.

Cade opened the door to the interrogation room, and panic wrapped itself around me like a snake.

The room was equipped with oneway mirrors. Cameras were mounted on every corner of the room with one located above the door. A white machine that resembled an old printer, used centuries ago when paper was still used regularly, sat next to the interrogation table.

My first thought was that Brian had found another demented torture device. But when I fully entered the room, I noticed that Brian's arm was attached to it at the wrist. Blood dripped from his arm; spilling onto a plastic tarp on the floor.

The machine wasn't here to torture me.

It was a medical device that performed lifesaving operations. A small window on the machine showed the stub that used to be Brian's hand.

He'd gone through something extraordinarily traumatic. I glanced at his face; relishing how pale he was.

I had to fight hard not to grin like an idiot.

Cade shoved me down into the chair on the opposite side of the table from Brian. He chained me to the metal bar that was bolted into the table.

I sat there patiently; waiting for whatever would come next.

"Krissy, Kain wants you in the observation room with him."

She nodded at Cade before leaving the interrogation room.

"Do you want me to stay, Brian?" Cade asked, eagerly.

"That's not necessary." Brian's tone was weak, but fury burned in his eyes. Cade was about to walk out the door, but the intercom crackled in the room.

"Cade stays in the room at all times." Kain's voice boomed. "As a precaution."

I snorted in amusement.

"Apparently, I'm still a threat."

"Shut up, you moron," Cade snarled.

I merely chuckled; leaning forward slightly. I forced myself to smirk through the agony. I refused to give these sadists any satisfaction at seeing my pain. Especially before the torture even started.

The medical machine made a clicking noise, and Brian pulled his arm out of it. The appendage ended with a stump covered in bloodstained bandages.

He trembled slightly; staring at me with furious eyes. I didn't know if his shaking was from pain or anger, but I hoped he was as uncomfortable as he looked.

"Hey, Brian." My smirk morphed into a delighted smile. "Not to point out the obvious, but you're missing a hand."

Brian's pale face darkened with anger. He gritted his teeth; taking a ragged breath as pure loathing contorted his features. I half expected him to hit me, but he didn't move an inch. I must've looked just as horrible as I felt. No one had assaulted me yet.

They were probably afraid that one punch would kill me.

"Your monstrous girlfriend froze my hand. It had to be amputated."

I stared at him, blankly. My bruised abdomen clenched, and I formed my ruined hands into fists. If he even touched Winter, I wouldn't leave this room until one of us was dead.

I narrowed my eyes at him; daring him to say that he'd hurt her. "Where is she?"

Brian laughed hysterically. It was unnerving- watching him laugh while clutching his handless arm to his chest.

"I'm sure she's dead by now. The person I left her with wouldn't have tolerated her for very long."

The pain threatened to swallow me whole, but I managed to smirk.

Winter was intelligent and resourceful. A survivor. But I wasn't there for her. I'd left her to face Brian and his psychopathy alone.

I'd *never* forgive myself for that.

"But that's not really what I came here to tell you." Brian's maniacal grin deepened. "I wanted to offer my condolences for the passing of one of your close friends."

I continued staring at him; exuding complete serenity. I must've heard him wrong because I didn't have any close friends. They thought Willow despised me. If John was dead, then we wouldn't be having this conversation since they would've just executed me. He didn't know if Winter was dead or alive. So the only other person he could be talking about was-

Eliza.

"Poison does agonizing things to a human being. I'm sure Eliza Marlo's suffering was terrible before the end."

He was messing with me. He *had* to be.

If Eliza was dead- I would know it, wouldn't I? I couldn't imagine that the world would continue spinning if Eliza was no longer in it. Life everywhere would just end, right?

At least mine would. There was no way I could live in a world where Eliza was gone.

"You're either lying, or you've been extremely misinformed."

Brian leaned closer to me, smirking gleefully. I searched his dead eyes for something- anything- to show the deception I longed to find.

He was cold. Collected. Completely unrepentant.

"You missed many brutal things while wasting away in the dungeon, Nolan Delany. I assure you, Eliza Marlo *is* dead."

I *smiled*. I don't know how I managed it, but I let the satisfaction shine through my eyes. That they hadn't beaten me. That this lie was a last ditch effort to crumble me at last.

I'd survived it. Survived every bit of torture that they threw at me and came out the other end.

Unbreakable. I was unbreakable despite the wounds. Despite the torture serum. Despite the sight of Phoenix's lifeless body that haunted my every moment.

My grin turned feral as I met Brian's evil gaze.

"If Eliza is dead as you claim; then surly you have evidence to show me. Surely you wouldn't be stupid enough to come here without proof. Unless, of course, you're out of ideas to torment me. It's pathetic that you've had to resort to lies in an attempt to break me."

I kept staring into the dark pits of his eyes. For some reason, I just couldn't look away. There was so much evil staring back at me-

I was wary to turn my back on it.

Brian's attitude morphed from mocking to complete fury. He clenched his teeth; seething angrily. He leaned forward; his nose practically touching mine as he fumed like the animal he was.

"I poisoned her myself. She couldn't have survived it without Shane to heal her. He was gone; healing little kids from the Sleeping Ache. I made sure of it."

He hadn't even seen her dead body, or else he'd be bragging about that.

I grinned triumphantly. He was rattled. Completely afraid that he failed to kill Eliza. Failed to capture Winter. Failed to break me over the past weeks.

Undoubtedly, Kain was furious with him.

"I hope you set your affairs in order. The Viking won't tolerate your incompetence for much longer."

Without warning, Brian pulled out an enormous knife. He stabbed it into the table merely half an inch from my hand.

I didn't even flinch.

"If you make one more snarky comment- You'll find out what it feels like to lose an appendage."

I glanced at the knife that was imbedded into the wooden table. It took a lot of force to make it go in that deep.

I lifted my gaze to Brian.

"How are you going to remove the knife? You'll need to use two hands. I suppose its just another thing you'll fail at."

Brian merely stared at me. As though he couldn't believe I'd made that comment after threatening to cut off my hand. I knew it was stupid too, but all the bottled up rage inside me kept spewing out into sarcastic comments.

If I couldn't punch Brian in the face, then I had no other choice but to mock him. It wasn't my fault he'd been idiotic enough to confront me while recovering from a severe injury-

Winter had taken on Brian, and won.

I didn't think it was possible to love her more than I did at that moment. I should've told her how I felt when I'd had the chance. She had no idea how much she really meant to me. There was no hope that she ever would-

Since I was fairly certain that Brian was going to kill me now.

He drew a gun from the holster on his hip, and aimed it at my head.

Cade jumped into action a second before Brian had the chance to pull the trigger. The gun still went off; the bullet embedding itself in the cement wall next to my head. The ringing in my ears gave me an insane migraine, but that was the least of my problems now.

Because Kain was in the room.

"I'm done observing this nonsense!"

I traded a minor problem for a major one.

Fantastic.

Cade escorted a fuming Brian out of the room, and Kain sat in the empty chair. I met his gaze, unflinchingly, like I always did.

There was a short time, after they killed Phoenix, that I felt like I didn't need to meet Kain's eyes. I learned quickly that I'd been wrong. I *needed* to stare him down. To let him know that no matter how hard he pushed me, he'd always lose. Even if I was the one that was abused. Even if I was the one that ended up dead.

He would always be the one to lose.

"I assume it comes as no surprise to you that Willow Rivers disappeared earlier today."

I continued to stare at him, even though my insides were jumping around like crazy.

I knew Kain was terrified. Willow was extremely intelligent, and enraged by Phoenix's murder. She probably started plotting vengeance the second she left me in the dungeon four weeks ago.

She had been too timid to move against Kain before she met me. Before she formed a bond with Phoenix. But now-

She had a reason to stand up to the Viking.

"You will tell me, right now, where Willow Rivers went." Kain's deep voice vibrated through me. "If you don't, you'll be back on the flogging post."

I shrugged nonchalantly.

"I thought she was your loyal hacker, Kain."

He narrowed his eyes at me.

"Winter killed her best friend. I'll always stand by my girlfriend. Willow knows that. She no longer trusts me."

The Viking sneered angrily; baring his grotesque teeth behind blackened lips.

"You ruined her, Nolan Delany. I made a mistake in letting her live. I made a mistake in letting *you* live for this long."

My heart raced at the ominous statement.

"I've scheduled your execution for two days from now. This warning is not a courtesy I normally grant my enemies. I suggest you make peace with your demons before then."

Giving me two days to freak out over my own execution was not a courtesy. It was more psychological torture. A last ditch effort to get me to loosen my tongue. To plead for my life while offering all the secrets I harbored about the Scavengers.

I wouldn't give him the benefit of watching me squirm.

Kain stood up from the table; placing his imposing hand on my shoulder.

"I hope you find forgiveness before the end, Nolan Delany." His touch made my skin crawl. His breath was as rank as ever. "But you will find no mercy from me."

With that cryptic comment, he left the room. I blinked the tears from my eyes; waiting for Cade and Krissy to take me back to the dungeon.

Chapter 15: John

"The whole point of me driving was so you could sleep, Boss." George eyed me from the driver's seat with a crooked glare.

It was interesting that he'd say that, considering I didn't want him to drive in the first place.

He had, quite literally, shoved me out of the drivers seat. To be fair, I'd been navigating through the rough terrain for over twenty-four hours.

I was beyond exhausted.

Still, I couldn't silence my worries long enough to fall asleep. Driving had been a necessary distraction. Unfortunately, I was so deliriously tired that I nearly drove us into a deep ravine shrouded by incredibly dense vegetation.

It had been the last straw for George, apparently.

He was probably right to take over. I would be hallucinating dancing clowns and prancing unicorns any minute now.

"We'll be at our destination in about two more hours." George glanced at the tablet displaying the map. "We have sixteen hours before Kain is supposed to meet us there. We don't want to be burned out when the time comes."

I closed my eyes, taking the hint. My brain was still in overdrive, but I didn't want George nagging me anymore.

Leif's loud snoring didn't help the situation either, but there wasn't anything I could do about it. At least, not without smothering him with my bare hands.

I opened my eyes again.

"If you aren't going to sleep then you might as well be honest with me." George's eyes flicked to me again. "About the ice girl."

I sighed, suppressing a grimace. I knew this would come up eventually.

"I found her on the Highborn Union streets. Nolan was dying from an infected knife wound. I was on my way to get him medicine when I happened to run into her. She was being chased by a group of Feral Morons."

George raised an eyebrow in confusion.

"'*Feral Morons*' is a nickname that Nolan came up with for the Scavengers who prey on the weak."

George smirked and nodded his approval.

"Anyway, I helped Winter get away from them. She agreed to help me get medicine for Nolan. She's been living with me ever since."

"How did she get those powers?"

I grimaced; thinking of the horrendous scars that covered Winter's porcelain skin. She had thick hair that had grown out over her ears now. It covered the scars on her scalp, but there was nothing that could hide the rest of them.

She wore the marks of her suffering like a morbid badge of honor. She endured torture over and over again. She had earn her powers and scars. She deserved to be respected for them.

Unfortunately, people would fear and hate her instead. I hoped that George wouldn't be one of them.

"She was captured by a man named Dr. Darkwood. He used her as a lab rat to experiment on. Same thing happened with Shane."

George's face paled significantly, but he didn't take his eyes off of the trail he maneuvered the Jeep through.

"In my time with the CIA, there were whispers about top secret government programs that tested theories of creating human weapons. They dabbled with experimentation in the most inhumane of ways. Most of the agents just shrugged the rumors off, but I never did. I knew something was going on. I could never prove it, despite the efforts of me and my superior. The man I worked for was named Simon Keller. You know him as '*Kain*'."

I froze, staring at George with hard eyes. My fingers twitched to grab for my gun, but I satisfied myself by resting my hand against the cold metal.

George glanced at me, sorrow darkening his eyes.

"I know what you're thinking, Boss, but I am not sympathetic to Simon Keller. He's a barbarian, a cult leader, and an opportunist. I knew before the natural disasters that he was a narcissistic psychopath. When he asked me to be his second in command in the League of Vigilance, I told him where to shove his offer."

We fell silent for a moment; listening to the two men snoring in the backseat.

"I've been hiding from Simon Keller ever since."

Panic fluttered in my gut as I kept my hand on my gun.

"How did you survive the natural disasters, George?"

"I was in one of those underground bunkers that the government made. I was ordered by Amanda Lynch herself to stay in one of them. It flooded during the tsunamis. Most of the people drowned, or got trapped. It was a miracle I escaped the bunker. When I did, I knew it was my chance to oppose Amanda Lynch's tyranny."

George was a Highborn by breeding, and a Scavenger by choice?

I shook my head in disbelief.

"What person, in their right mind, would want to slum it with the rest of us?"

"I'm with you because I wanna be, Boss. I didn't survive because I was lucky enough not to get swallowed up by the earth, crushed by a tsunami, or caught in an ash storm. I'm only alive because Simon Keller and Amanda Lynch hand selected me to survive. That's the reason I turned down your offer to lead the Scavengers. Our enemies know me personally. They know the actions I would take. They don't know you, so you're unpredictable."

I merely stared at him silently. He clenched his jaw at my scrutiny, but otherwise showed no emotion. He stopped the Jeep next to a large boulder that concealed us from the dense forest.

"I met the woman I love after escaping the flooded bunker. She is a Scavenger. I'm a Highborn. I don't care, and neither does she. Now she's pregnant with my baby- a child that is tainted in the eyes of Simon Keller and Amanda Lynch. Impure breeding is a criminal offense to them. My family is worth nothing more than a speck of dirt to those people. I *hate* them for that. My loyalty is to my wife and my unborn child. My loyalty is to the Scavenger community. To you as our leader... I hope you can believe me."

I took a deep breath and removed my hand from my holster.

George was a good man. Of that I was certain. He'd never given me a reason not to trust him like many of the other Scavengers had.

"Do you have anything else you want to get off your chest?"

"Nope." He grinned. "You know all my secrets now, Boss."

"You were a SEAL and worked for the CIA," I snorted. "I highly doubt that."

George chuckled and started driving again.

We traveled silently as George turned a sharp corner through the trees. The terrain was nearly impossible to navigate in some places. I often wondered if walking would be just as fast, but it was nice not to have sore feet.

"You don't have to tell me where you've hidden Winter. Just for my peace of mind; you've got her safe, right?

I gritted my teeth; knowing what my silence would indicate.

"*Damn it*, John!"

Leif snorted in the backseat, but didn't wake up.

"She went looking for Brian. He's a Vigilante that was posing as a Scavenger. We think he took a girl captive. Winter wanted to do something productive. She took a communicator with her, but she's missed her last two check-ins."

George swore again; his tone lower. "Brian was a Vigilante? Why am I hearing about this now?"

"I didn't have a chance to tell you before. I didn't really want anyone knowing about Winter. Brian somehow knew about her. I didn't want any Scavengers to go hunting for him so he could start blabbing what he knows."

George glared furiously at me.

"So you sent Winter after him alone?"

I had to stop myself from shouting; my mindless worry morphing into anger.

"She didn't give me a choice. I didn't want her to go, but she's a teenager with the power to control the temperature. She's not my prisoner."

George let out a mumbled string of swearwords that would've made a sailor blush.

"Nolan seemed really worried about her on the video. Dr. Darkwood invented some kind of chemical that negates Winter's powers. It makes her very sick. I think Nolan was trying to warn me that Kain has Dr. Darkwood's formulas."

George glanced at me urgently.

"Kain is a very skilled scientist. If Brian leads her to the League of Vigilance underground bunker, and if they're armed with that chemical-"

I closed my eyes; wishing I could stop imagining the horrors Kain could do to her. To stop seeing the image of Nolan hanging by his wrists. Of the blood.

"She wants to save Nolan more than anything. Even when I thought he was dead, she was still confident that he was alive. She wouldn't think twice about going there."

"It's a good thing we're meeting with Kain then," George replied. "Do you have a plan, Boss?"

"I'll go alone. You guys cover me from the woods."

He grimaced at my response.

"Kain will have Vigilantes in the woods too. You'll be surrounded."

I nodded in agreement. "I'm hoping that your skills aren't rusty. You're going to need them to make sure the Vigilantes don't take me out."

George smirk, but didn't say anything.

"Kain will take me. He'll want to torture me, and Nolan, to make an example out of us. You'll follow him to his bunker."

George's expression was unreadable as he processed my plan.

"Its risky to use you as bait. Kain will know that you've got Scavengers in the woods. He'll try to take us out first."

I knew George was right, but there really wasn't anything else I could think to do. Kain had Nolan and, possibly, Winter.

I needed to think of something else before I lost my mind.

"You've been training Leif and James for a few months now. Do you think they'd be up for a stealth mission in the woods?"

By 'stealth mission in the woods' I meant eliminating the Vigilantes that would be trying to surround me.

"Absolutely. They're two of my top recruits."

I already knew that. Both of them had killed before- were certainly capable of it.

But I was still nervous. I didn't like the idea of handing myself over to Kain. It went against every survival instinct that I had.

"We're here, Boss."

George's deep voice jerked me awake.

I wasn't sure how long I slept, but a quick look at the tablet told me that we were two hours early. There was a chance that Kain was at the location already, so we needed to be careful.

"I parked us about a quarter of a mile away." George pocketed the keys. "I figured we should scope the place out before we separate."

I nodded in agreement, stifling a yawn.

James and Leif were already out of the Jeep-

Thwack.

A long slender piece of wood stuck out of the glass directly in front of my face.

George drew his pistol. "Is that an arrow?"

I nodded, taking my own gun out of the holster. I knew immediately that it wasn't Kain or the Vigilantes. They wouldn't use such a primal weapon, but that didn't give me any comfort-

It was disconcerting, not knowing who our new adversary was.

James and Leif had taken cover outside of the Jeep, and I couldn't envy them more. There wasn't enough room, and my legs were already cramping up.

I rolled down the window; trying to listen for anything that might give away the hostile's position. So far, they'd only shot at us once, but that didn't mean there wasn't more than one of them out there.

"Could be some Feral Morons trying to relieve us of our Jeep."

I was about to agree when a feminine voice echoed through the trees-

It came from all directions, like a surround sound system in the foliage. I glanced at the branches around us, but couldn't spot the speakers that had been set up.

The woman didn't want us to hear where she was. It was a clever way to put us at a disadvantage.

"Get out of the vehicle with your hands up."

I nodded at George, who merely shrugged.

I kept my handgun at my side, clicking the safety off. George and I slid out of the jeep, cautiously. Leif and James shifted toward us, using the vehicle as a shield.

"Put your weapons down." The voice echoed around us. "Place your hands on your head."

My gut clenched in frustration; knowing that we had to comply if we were ever going to get a chance to see this woman. She probably had cameras surrounding the area too. She'd see our every move.

I set my gun on the ground in front of me; making sure it was within easy reach. George, James, and Leif did the same.

Once I put my hands on my head, footsteps rustled in the bushes a few yards away from me. I turned slightly, my glare narrowing on a set of brown, almond shaped eyes.

Great, another teenager.

Chapter 16: Winter

Following Ember through the woods wasn't conducive to recovery from bullet wounds.

She never slowed her pace.

The fever settled itself into my muscles, my body shaking with every step. The staples holding the bullet holes together had fallen out miles ago, soaking the backpack strap in blood. I'd refused to cry out. Refused to even wince as the sharp pain intensified with each mile.

I wouldn't give Ember the satisfaction of seeing me broken; physically or mentally.

I'd lost sight of her a mile ago, but I knew she'd never truly leave me behind. Not when I held the backpack that contained all of our supplies.

Eventually, I turned a corner in the trail and found Ember standing impatiently in the darkness. She held a flame in her palm, illuminating the shadowy trees that surrounded us. Through the receding light from her flame, I noticed a dark ravine. I couldn't see how deep it was from here, but it was sure to be a deadly fall.

"It's about time you caught up." A disgusted glare darkened her hollow eyes. "I've been waiting here for ages. I thought I'd have to go back and find you."

I was in too much pain, and too sick, to explain myself. I merely ignored her; mustering up the courage to remove the backpack from my damaged shoulder.

The pain was going to be excruciating.

"We should stop here for the night. I can't have you tripping and falling down a cliff with my backpack."

I stared at her incredulously.

"What?" She snorted with laughter. "You think the backpack is yours? Think again, Winter. You're a useful pack mule. It's the only reason I'm keeping you around. Seems like you're slowing down though."

I kept the agony from my expression as I lowered myself to the cold ground. I had planned on re-dressing my wounds, but there was no way I was taking the backpack off now.

I couldn't risk her stealing it and abandoning me in the middle of nowhere.

"So, you have nothing to say to that?" Ember growled angrily. "I thought we could at least keep some conversation going, but I guess that's too much to ask."

Her constant talking was starting to make my head spin. The dizziness was so intense I nearly vomited.

I swallowed, breathing deeply to calm myself.

"I'm not sure what you want me to say, Ember."

She raised her hand and threw a hot flame in the center of the game trail. I flinched when the heat engulfed me, but I didn't have the energy to move away from it.

The campfire burned without any kindling; staying in the same place without spreading to the rest of the forest. If I hadn't despised Ember so much, I would've been impressed.

"Just say *something*. Why do you think I keep trying to get you angry?"

I met her eyes; forcing my voice to be strong. "Because you're a horrible person."

Ember laughed, which only confused me more.

"You look like you've been about to collapse ever since we left the cabin." Her voice gentled, and she couldn't conceal the worry that flashed in her eyes. "I've been trying to bring out your competitive spirit. You know, giving you a purpose by carrying *our* backpack. Hiking faster than you so you'd feel the need to keep going. Mocking you to piss you off. I knew you would need that fury inside you. You already hate me, so I figured it didn't matter anyway."

She smirked triumphantly, but her features grew solemn as her eyes fell on my shoulder.

"You should let me take a look at your wounds."

All I could do was stare at her. I must've heard her wrong. There was no way she was treating me so badly just to bring out my competitive spirit. Sure, I *was* competitive. I wouldn't have survived as long as I had if I wasn't.

"You're saying that you've been a horrible traveling companion because you thought it would help me?"

Ember laughed again, but I didn't join in. She was either crazy or extremely stupid.

"Yep." She grinned nastily. "And it worked. We'll probably make it to the bunker tomorrow evening if we keep the same pace we did today. Take off the backpack and let me look at your wounds."

There was no way that was happening.

"Stay away from me."

Ember rolled her eyes. "I'm going to look at your wounds whether you want me to or not. I can wait until you pass out if I have to."

I absolutely did not want her touching me when I was unconscious, so I reluctantly took off the backpack. It was torture; trying to remove the strap from my wounded shoulder. Blood crusted to my skin; fusing the material to my wound.

Ember ended up helping me. More gently than I thought imaginable, she peeled the strap away slowly. I couldn't help but wince at each movement, so I turned my face away from hers. I kept my eyes closed and held back the tears of pain.

Finally, she set the backpack down next to me.

"Making you carry the backpack wasn't such a good idea. I should've known you wouldn't say anything about the staples ripping out. It's probably going to get infected."

I already knew that, but I didn't let myself worry about it. It wouldn't be the first time I'd gotten an infection. One of Dr. Darkwood's experiments got so infected that I'd almost died. But that had been the worst case. There were a few other infections I'd had that made me sick, but I was able to recover quickly from those.

Ember dug into the backpack; pulling out sterile sprays and a bottle of fever reducers.

"The fever reducer won't do much to help me," I told her dryly. "And I can patch up myself."

Ember shrugged nonchalantly.

She put the bottle of fever reducers back into the bag and handed me the sterile spray. I took it from her; grimacing as I applied it to my wounds. I picked out the two staples that had come lose during the day and covered it with a clean bandage.

She tried to offer me food, but I just shook my head and sipped some water. I couldn't eat without being sick, and I didn't want to waste the food.

"Amanda Lynch forced me to do it."

Startled by how forlorn she sounded, I glanced at her. She stared at her fire with cloudy eyes.

"She didn't give me a choice. Those orphans- I destroyed their lives. I was too weak to stand up to her. To stop her from using me."

I had no idea why she was telling me this, and I really didn't want to know her reasoning.

This was all a ruse. A way to get me to see her as human, and not the evil flamethrower that she'd proven herself to be.

She also seemed so sincere. So heartbroken.

Ember's toned muscles had withered to mere skin and bone. The weeks she'd spent with Brian had obviously been physically devastating. Exhaustion clouded her eyes, the dark circles around them conveying a skeletal resemblance. My gaze lowered to her hands that rested on her knees. Her sleeves were pulled up to her elbows, and I noticed something that I hadn't before.

On her wrist was a design. A tattoo.

I studied it closer; struggling to catch my breath. Something tugged at the back of my mind as I stared at the tattoo. Causing a new wave of nausea to plague my aching stomach.

The tattoo. It was the most beautiful thing I had ever seen. I wasn't even sure why I thought that, but every part of my being was drawn to it. The ink was shaded in simple colors, but that only made it more alluring. The art really wasn't anything special. It was beautiful, but small and tasteful.

A red rose engulfed in yellow and orange flames.

"Why do you have a tattoo?" I couldn't stop myself from asking. Completely ignoring her attempt to talk about the street orphans.

Ember stared at me in surprise before her brow furrowed in disdain. She grabbed her sleeve and yanked it down over the tattoo. Concealing it from me.

I sighed and stared at the fire in front of us. I knew she was still glaring at me, but I tried to ignore her sudden shift in mood.

"I take it you regret getting the tattoo. I have one too, but I'm sure you know that."

I glanced over at Ember. Her hands were fisted in her lap. She tore her glare away from me and shuddered. It surprised me that she was displaying any kind of vulnerability, but I ignored it.

"Mine is on my collarbone. I've never actually seen it for myself, but John told me about it when I first met him. It just says 'Winter' so that's where I got my name. Weirdly, I don't regret having it because it gave me an identity when I wouldn't have one otherwise."

Ember relaxed slightly at my explanation, but she didn't contribute to the conversation. I let the silence linger, but it was awkward.

I didn't like Ember. But perhaps I'd been too quick to judge her, despite what she'd done in the past. She was rude, heartless, and destructive. But she had motivated me to keep going today. Even if her methods were questionable.

"I'm sorry your mom made you do such awful things. I can't imagine-"

"Don't apologize, Winter," Ember snarled. "I only told you that so you'd know that I don't want to be a monster. Besides, you've done terrible things yourself. You killed all of the men in my command. Every single one of those men had families. Wives. Children. They're Highborns, but they are just like me. Not everyone is lucky enough to be free like you and the Scavengers. At least you have choices."

Ember was totally delusional. My actions had been made in self-defense.

"As for my tattoo," Ember carried on gruffly. "I got it when I was eleven years old. It was totally illegal to get it so young, but my sister found a tattoo artist who would do it for us despite our age-"

Ember paused suddenly, and stared at me with wide eyes. Some of the life seemed to drain out of her. I didn't know why, but a part of me wanted to soothe the pain in her eyes.

"We snuck out one night and got matching ones," Ember explained. "Fire for 'Ember'. A flower because my sister's name was 'Rose'. She was a year and a half older than me. We didn't have the privilege of growing up together. We had different dads. Amanda Lynch didn't want anything to do with Rose. She had a disability. Amanda didn't want Rose to tarnish her image of the perfect family. She lived with her dad and I lived with my parents."

I had so many questions, but I refrained. Ember didn't seem inclined to stop talking long enough for me to ask them anyway.

"We never would've met if it wasn't for her dad. He insisted that we got to know each other through video chats. I never would've even known about my half sister if her dad hadn't sought me out and introduced us.

"We spent years getting to know each other over video chats. The first time we ever met in person was when we got our tattoos. We didn't know what the future would hold for us. We wanted to have something to remember each other by. I got mine on my wrist because I wanted to be able to see it whenever I felt alone. Rose got hers on her stomach so that her dad wouldn't notice. He would've been upset with us if he found out. I didn't have to worry about that though. Amanda took one look at my tattoo and told me I was childish. She never said another word about it."

Ember smiled slightly; unconsciously rubbing her hand over the sleeve that covered the tattoo.

It was disconcerting to see this side of Ember. She acted like a completely different person from the girl that tried to kill Shane and Nolan with her flames mere months before.

Could someone really change that drastically?

"I tried to convince Amanda Lynch to put Rose and her father in one of the underground bunkers with us. She refused; saying they were the imperfections in society that she wished to purge from the earth."

I winced in an attempt to suppress my rage. Ember merely nodded, as though she knew what I was feeling. That she mirrored my opinion about her mother.

"Her words, not mine." She clarified unnecessarily. "I made plans to smuggle Rose into the bunker, but she wouldn't come with me. She refused to go anywhere without her dad. We both knew he would never go along with the plan. He never believed that the natural disasters were going to happen in the first place."

Ember stopped talking as her fingers dug into her wrist where the tattoo was. I stopped staring at her hands and glanced at her face. Tears glistened in her eyes, but she blinked them away.

"Your sister died. I'm so sorry, Ember."

Finally, a tear fell from her eye. She pierced me with a look that held so much anger-

I would've backed away from her if I wasn't so exhausted.

"She was the best part of my childhood, and now she's gone." Her voice rose with each word she spit out. "She wouldn't come to the bunker with me even after I begged her to! She didn't want to leave her father- An idiot that refused to believe the world was ending! She abandoned me to a life of hell with our sadistic mother!"

My heart raced as she stared at me. Anger, a rage I would never be able to comprehend, dwelt in her eyes. I tore my gaze from hers; staring into the dancing flames between us.

There was nothing I could say, or do, to relieve her suffering.

After what she'd done to the people I loved-

I still wasn't sure that I wanted to bond with her.

"I didn't plan on sharing any of this with you. Don't ask me any questions about my past. Don't ask to see my tattoo."

I gave her a curt nod, but she rolled her eyes. Annoyance masking the fury that burned within her.

"Figures you'd give in so easily to my demands. You're weak and cowardly. It's a complete mystery that you've managed to survive this long."

I glared at her; my fingers signing rapidly.

I don't trust you.

Ember chuckled, mirthlessly.

"I don't trust you either, Winter."

I ignored her, not caring that she could interpret sign language. I laid down gingerly on my back; coaxing myself into breathing slowly.

I shivered, despite the hot fire. I knew it wasn't a good sign that I could be so close to flames and not overheat. There was nothing I could do about my sickness.

My whole body seized and ached. Every muscle seemed to be at war with each other.

Fever reducers wouldn't work, because I already knew what this was. My mind rebelled at the thought, but I knew I'd die soon without the appropriate treatment.

The cure. If such a thing truly did exist.

Eventually, Ember started snoring lightly. I couldn't sleep, no matter how motionless I remained. Whenever I drifted off, I was roused from intense muscle aches.

For hours I laid there in misery, until-

I fell unconscious. So deeply that I didn't even dream.

"Wake up."

Ember nudged me with the toe of her boot. I bit back a groan from the impact. She didn't kick me, but it sure felt like it.

I couldn't move no matter how hard I tried.

Ember knelt down; resting her hand against my forehead. Her touch was so cold, I would've shrieked if I could.

My fever must've been horrible if the fire girl's hand was colder than my clammy skin.

"Are you trying to die on me, Winter?"

She rummaged through the backpack. I was surprised that she didn't just pick it up and leave me there.

The next thing I knew, she was shoving a pill in my mouth- Forcing water to my lips.

"You need to get up." Ember's hands shook as she helped me drink. "I'm not letting you go this easily. You didn't survive Darkwood only to let a flu kill you."

She said that last part with a touch of sarcasm.

She gripped me under the arms, and pulled me to my feet as though I weighed nothing. My legs wouldn't hold my weight, so she threw my arm over her shoulders.

"You'll feel better once you get something in your stomach." She shoved a piece of fruit leather into my trembling hand. "I should've made you eat more yesterday."

I took small bites as we walked along the game trail. Ember managed to keep me upright while navigating with the tablet.

She had been right about the food. I started feeling a bit stronger as the day went on. Despite the agony I was in, I eventually stopped allowing Ember to help me walk.

I still didn't know what her plan was when we got to the bunker, but I didn't really care anymore. As long as I got to find out what happened to Nolan, everything would be worth it.

I wouldn't be able to rescue him in my condition.

I'd steal a communicator and contact John.

Deciding that would be my endgame; I quit thinking so much about what would happen to me. Or how long I'd be able to endure this sickness.

Each step I took through the forest was agonizing, but I kept up with Ember better than I had the day before.

Finally, after hours of hiking, Ember held up her hand. I stumbled to a halt behind her.

"We're at the back entrance to the bunker," Ember whispered. "You still plan on killing Kain?"

I merely stared at her when she turned around to face me.

I honestly didn't know what my plan was anymore. My sporadic, fevered thoughts sifted through my mind like falling snow. I could barely recall what I was doing here in the first place, despite the adrenaline coursing though me.

I took a shaky breath and shrugged my shoulders.

Ember eyed me warily. "Do you think you can use your ice?"

I shook my head. There was no way I'd be able to do that in my current condition.

"I could use my fire, but I don't want to burn the place down. I guess this means we are going with plan B."

I stared at her, trying to recall what plan B was. My head throbbed; blood rushing through my skull like a river.

Ember rummaged through the backpack and pulled out a large syringe. I recoiled instinctively at the sight of the needle.

A trap. This whole journey had been a trap.

Ember sank the tip into my neck, despite my weak resistance. Panic gripped me as the serum rushed through my veins.

I couldn't draw oxygen into my lungs. I trembled so violently, I couldn't stand upright anymore. The world spun around me, and I slammed my eyes shut.

Consciousness drifted away.

"Sorry, Winter. You're plan B."

Chapter 17: Nolan

I gasped, the bucket of water raining down upon me.

"Wash him." Kain's order rumbled through the freezing room. "He must be thoroughly cleansed for the proceedings."

Krissy, followed by two other girls, came toward me with washcloths and bars of soap.

The ropes attaching me to the flogging post dug into my bloody wrists; my feet barely touching the ground. My clothes had been cut off of me. Except for my underwear, thankfully.

I wasn't sure why Kain wouldn't allow me to take a shower by myself. I mean, I was weak, and it would probably be a struggle to get myself clean, but at least I'd have some dignity left.

Which was probably why he was doing this to me. He wanted me at my lowest before he paraded me around the underground bunker and executed me.

The joke was on him though. I was trapped so far inside my head. I barely registered what was going on around me.

Images of Winter, Willow, John, and Eliza flashed through my mind in a constant loop. Just knowing that they were alive, and not here in the dungeon with me, was invigorating.

I was torn from my thoughts when Krissy ran a washcloth over the lacerations on my back. I groaned, the intense pain making my stomach clench with nausea.

My obvious discomfort did nothing to stop her from scrubbing my wounds.

"It's done." Warm blood dripped down my back when she removed the washcloth. "No one will touch your back ever again."

Krissy moved away from me and picked up the bucket of ice water.

"Brace yourself," she warned, right before the chilled water cascaded down my head and back.

Krissy immediately rubbed soap into my hair, and I closed my eyes again.

Her fingernails gently massaged my scalp as she worked the soap into my matted hair. My headache from the icy water gradually went away as her warm fingers speared through the thick strands.

It was the first time I'd been touched with gentleness since I'd been thrown into Kain's dungeon.

A lump suddenly formed in my throat, making it hard to swallow.

The other two girls threw more water at me to rinse the soap off of my shaking body. I wasn't sure if I could take much more of that without passing out, so I was happy to notice that there were no more buckets of water left.

After the girls dried me off, Cade untied me from the flogging post. I stumbled, but managed to keep my balance before I face planted on the concrete floor.

"Put these on."

He thrust a white shirt and black sweat pants into my arms. I gripped the clothes tightly to my chest, so I wouldn't fumble them with my clumsy fingers.

The white shirt was spotless, and smelled like it'd been washed with laundry detergent. I was convinced that it was the cleanest thing I'd ever smelled in my life-

The temptation to inhale deeply was overwhelming.

By the time I was dressed, Krissy and the girls had left.

Unfortunately, Brian decided to chose that moment to enter the dungeon. He had a smug smile on his face that made me want to knock him unconscious, but I refrained. Barely.

I knew, if I lunged myself at Brian, I could probably take him down. But I wouldn't be able to get back up again.

Cade placed the burning hot handcuffs around my wrists, taking the violent temptation away.

"Nolan Delany," Kain stated formally. "You are hereby sentenced to death for crimes against the League of Vigilance. Those crimes include; traitorous activity, stealing, subterfuge, withholding important information, and frolicking with the enemy."

I snorted.

"Did he say something funny?" Cade glared at me.

"I'm fairly certain I've never frolicked in my entire life. But, if that's what you think rescuing innocent children from horrific experimentation was, then more power to you."

Brian rammed his fist into my stomach. I would've collapsed on the concrete floor if Cade didn't have a tight grip on my arms.

"Most prisoners are smart enough to stay silent."

Brian's stump of an arm was wrapped snuggly against his chest. Despite being unable to take a normal breath, I grinned. Maybe it was primal of me, but I *loved* seeing the evidence that Winter got the best of him.

That she permanently crippled him.

"You still think this is funny?" Cade asked incredulously. "You're gonna be a dead man in two hours."

He held up the appropriate amount of fingers as if to prove his point.

I wouldn't let that thought sink in as I continued grinning like an idiot.

I had made the decision to go down my way, not theirs.

I would *smile*. I would *smirk*. I would *laugh*.

"Kain, I've got the torture cage back in my room." Brian sneered angrily.

I stopped myself from flinching by laughing in Brian's face.

I knew I wouldn't be able to survive another round in the torture cage. I was shaking from sheer weakness. I couldn't feel my hands because the cuffs had severely injured my wrists. I had a pounding headache that never stopped. I couldn't even stand up straight anymore.

Maybe the torture cage would be a fitting end. A better way to go than the public execution they had planned.

"Absolutely not," Kain growled angrily.

The Viking pulled out a video camera, seemingly out of nowhere, and held it up to my face.

The last time he'd filmed me was during one of my flogging sessions. I wasn't sure what Kain wanted me to say this time, but I continued smiling.

"State your full name."

I smirked.

I didn't want to do this. I didn't want to cause John anymore pain. Not to mention Winter and Eliza. I just hoped that they didn't end up seeing my final moments.

But Kain had his ways of making all his enemies suffer.

"Nolan Jensen Delany."

"Do you have any last words for your loved ones?"

I laughed, and Cade tightened his grip on my upper arms. I merely stared at the camera with defiant eyes.

"I don't normally do this for my prisoners, Nolan Delany. It is a true sign of respect that I offer you the chance to say goodbye to your brother and friends."

Kain was trying to rub it into John's face that he'd won this sick game he'd been playing.

It pissed me off to no end.

"Willow, if you're seeing this, which you probably are since you've got eyes everywhere-" I smirked when Kain's face turned beet red. "Make sure John doesn't see this footage. He's going to try to insist on it, but Kain just wants to cause him more pain. Don't let him. Please."

I paused and took a shaky breath before I continued. If, by some miracle, Willow was with John; I needed to give her time to get away from him.

I swallowed the lump in my throat, and let my smile shine through my eyes.

"I just wanted to let you know that you did good, Willow. You should've seen the look on Kain's face when he told me that you ran off after wiping out his entire system. It was the best news I've heard in a long time. I can't tell you how proud I am of you.

"I'm really sorry about what happened to Lexi and Phoenix." My voice broke and I blinked the tears from my eyes. "I hope you'll stay safe. I hope you find happiness. You deserve that. After all you've been through; you deserve all of the safety, happiness, and comfort you can find.

"You're one of the best friends I've ever had. My life was better because you were in it, even if it was for just a few months. I'm so relieved that you got out of here. The fact that you caused Kain a lot of problems when you left just makes it all the better."

I was mildly surprised that Kain didn't shut me up. It was clear that the Viking was extremely angry, but I didn't care. It didn't matter.

"I know how you feel about Winter," I continued in a broken whisper. "But if Kain gets his hands on her it wouldn't be good for anyone. If you could find it in your heart to help her, I would really appreciate it. I know I don't have a right to ask that of you- but I love her. I love her so much. I'm not gonna be around to protect her. Please, Willow-"

Tears were falling down my cheeks now, but I didn't try to stop them. I knew talking about Winter would make me cry, but I couldn't die without at least asking Willow to help her.

Besides, someone had to know how I truly felt about Winter. That I loved her. I'd never said the words out loud, but now that I had-

It felt like a burden had been lifted off of me.

"Winter is just a kid. Just like you and me. Like Phoenix was, and the street orphans that Amanda Lynch rounded up to experiment on. We say that our age doesn't matter, but it does. We should be going to school, getting mad at our parents over dumb crap that doesn't matter, and dreaming about who we're going to be when we grow up.

"Instead, we are fighting for our lives. We're trying to prevent people like Kain and Amanda Lynch from destroying what's left of humanity. We can't let them win. The fact that you're still out there fighting is a huge relief to me. I love you, Willow. I love John and I love Eliza. I'll be cheering you guys on from the other side when you take Kain and Amanda down."

Kain turned off the camera and glared. I smirked at him, and Cade shoved me so hard I couldn't keep myself upright.

I hit the concrete floor, and the air was knocked from my lungs. I tensed for more abuse, but someone opened the vault door before anyone could beat me.

I was surprised to see that it was Grace, one of the singles I used to train, and she was holding a bowl of what smelled like soup.

"Krissy told me to bring Nolan his last meal."

Kain grunted, and brushed by the young woman. He went out the door with thundering strides that echoed through the dungeon. Cade followed without giving Grace a second glance.

Brian stepped to the side, and indicated for Grace to walk toward me. She cast her eyes to the floor, but obediently stepped around him. At the last moment, Brian stuck out his foot-

The bowl fumbled from Grace's hands and the contents went flying. Broth and chunks of vegetables covered her clothes as the rest of my last meal hit the concrete floor.

I didn't really care about the food, so I kept my eyes pinned to Grace's face. Tears spilled from her eyes and a choked sob escaped her throat.

"Too bad the kitchen is closed." Brian smiled, wickedly. "I guess you'll have to die on an empty stomach."

He rounded on Grace, and she flinched when he raised his hand as if to slap her. I wanted to stop him, but my body wasn't cooperating. Even if I did managed to get to my feet, I wouldn't be able reach him before he hit her.

Luckily, he stopped before making contact with her face.

"Clean your mess up," he growled. "Then come to the meeting room."

Grace sobbed again, but nodded vigorously. Brian eyed her as though she were a disobedient dog before stalking out of the dungeon.

"I-I'm so sorry, Nolan," Grace whispered shakily. "I really wanted you to be able to eat this."

Tears were coursing down her cheeks. I wanted to take her hand in mine, but the burning cuffs around my wrists were unbearable.

"It's fine, Grace." I tried to sound reassuring, but my voice was weak. I wouldn't have been able to eat much of the soup anyway. I was too anxious, and it had been too long since I'd had a real meal. I would've thrown up if I tried to put anything in my stomach.

"No, it's not. None of this is fine."

My eyes automatically went to the cameras mounted in the corners of the dungeon. Willow had fried the security system, but I had no idea if Cade had managed to get the cameras working again.

If anyone overheard Grace talking against Kain, things wouldn't go well for her.

"Grace-"

"I was made Brian's new partner today."

She met my eyes, and I finally noticed the bruises that covered her face. Her throat-

I didn't know what to say. The helplessness consumed me.

"What you taught me will be the only thing that keeps me alive until I can escape."

Without another word, she cleaned up the mess and left the dungeon.

I tried to wiggle my numb hands through the handcuffs around my wrists. I knew it probably wouldn't work, but I had to fight until I drew my last breath.

All too soon, the vault door opened again.

I took a fortifying breath as Cade and Brian walked up to me. They unchained my feet, but kept the handcuffs around my bleeding wrists. I barely felt them yank me to my feet and drag me toward the hallway.

I took another breath; keeping the rising panic at bay.

I couldn't stop shaking-

Kain met us in the hallway; his camera focusing on me.

"Say hello to Willow Rivers. Since you were so thoughtful to send her that message, I'm sure she will appreciate the opportunity to bear witness to your demise."

My stomach rolled. If I had eaten anything in the past two days, I would've vomited.

I would much rather be tied to the flogging post, and beaten within an inch of my life, than have Willow see me like this- to watch my execution.

"Lead the way to the meeting room, Brian."

Kain kept the camera focused on my face. I refused to look at the red light that blinked at me.

I took another deep breath. Inhaling the musky odor of the bunker tunnels.

It didn't take long to get to the meeting room, but the minutes felt like hours.

The room was packed full of Vigilantes. All of them anxiously waiting to witness my impending death.

"I'll give you one last chance to say goodbye to your family."

My muscles tensed at the arrogance in Kain's tone.

I ignored the camera completely; fury bubbling up in my chest.

I discreetly worked at freeing my hands from the cuffs, even though blood was dripping down my fingers now.

"No."

Kain chuckled, but kept the camera pointed at my face.

I didn't lower my gaze from Kain as I took in his obvious excitement.

This man was a complete psychopath. I considered making a quick speech about how crazy the Viking was, but I refrained. If the Vigilantes were too stupid to see how insane this was, then there was no hope for them.

Cade hit me in the back of the knees; forcing me to kneel in front of Kain. Brian stood to the side and brandished a pistol-

He cocked the weapon; sneering triumphantly.

"For crimes against the League of Vig-"

Kain's speech was cut off by the door swinging open; the groan echoing off the metal walls.

I stared at the girl in the entryway; shock finally coursing its way through my entire body.

Her hair was a bit longer now, and unruly with curls. Her blue eyes pierced through the dimly lit room as she glared at the Viking.

"Hello, Kain." Ember put her hands on her hips. "You really should upgrade your security around here. I got in way too easily."

Brian spun toward Ember; his finger gripping the trigger. Kain was on him in a second; his hand wrapping around Brian's wrist.

The gun still went off.

The bullet ricocheted off the concrete floor right next to my knee. Adrenaline washed away the lingering shock; forcing my mind to focus.

I kept working my wrists through the cuffs.

"Don't shoot her," Kain breathed violently. "Not yet."

"She killed all my men!" Brian yelled back.

Ember rolled her eyes as she sauntered closer to Brian.

"You kept me in a torture cage for weeks," she replied vehemently. "But I still spared your life, cousin."

Random gasps echoed in the room from spectators.

"I'll deal with you later, Flamethrower," Kain growled. "Carry on with the execution."

Brian lifted the gun again, but Ember put a hand on his wrist. He yelped as though she burned him.

"Before you do that, Kain." Ember smiled, almost sweetly. "I have a surprise for you. I know you want to study Dr. Darkwood's work, so I brought you the perfect specimen. In hopes that you'll spare me from further experimentation."

I froze; glaring at Ember so violently she attempted to avoid my gaze.

If she brought Winter into this hellhole, I *would* find a way to kill her.

"Subject Thirty-One is unconscious just outside the door. I carried her right into your bunker. It wasn't even hard to get her here. She's so naive. I'm sure she'll be cooperative during any studies you wish to perform."

Yeah, Ember was a dead girl walking.

She met my gaze with hatred simmering in her eyes. I knew she was remembering the arrow I shot at her-

Next time, that arrow would go straight through her heart.

My hands kept working to free themselves from the handcuffs. The blood was like a lubricant, and I slowly slipped my hand through the hole.

With one hand finally free of the burning cuffs, I relaxed my shoulders slightly.

"Carry out the execution," Kain ordered.

Brian took a step toward me; the gun mere inches from my head-

I moved so quickly, Cade wasn't able to finish yelling a warning before I disarmed Brian.

The gun slipped through my numb, bloody fingers and clattered to the floor between my feet. I ignored it for the time being; concentrating on subduing the piece of garbage in front of me.

Brian tried to punch me, but I clumsily dodged his blow. Grabbing his bloody stump of an arm as I moved.

He shrieked so loudly, it made my ears ring. I spun him around; wrenching the stump behind his back. I pushed upwards as hard as I could.

The sound of his bones breaking echoed through the stunned silence in the room.

Brian dropped to the ground in a dead faint; mere seconds after I disarmed him.

I spun around to face Cade. He'd pulled his own gun out and tried to squeeze the trigger. I disarmed him so quickly, his eyes widened before I wrenched his arm behind his back-

Sparks filled my vision as pain exploded from a blow to the back of my head.

I didn't lose consciousness, but my vision went black for a split second. Then the pounding headache started, accompanied by debilitating dizziness.

I tried to stay on my feet, but my body failed me again. I fell back to my knees; using my forearms to stop myself from falling flat on my face.

A split second later, I noticed Brian's gun on the ground next to me. Adrenaline coursed through me as I gripped the cold steel as hard as I could. I couldn't lift my arm very high, but I didn't need to in order to hit my intended target.

I squeezed the trigger, and Kain grunted in pain.

Cade swore furiously and pinned me to the ground.

The gun in my hand accidentally went off a second time. The echoing crack hurt my already ringing ears and I bellowed in pain. Someone screamed, but I couldn't see who it was that I'd accidentally shot.

Krissy stood over us with a wooden club in her fist. Apparently, she had been the one that hit me when I attacked Cade.

Figures.

Kain staggered a bit as he clamped a hand on his bloody leg. I grunted in frustration, and pain, as Cade pressed me into the floor with all of his weight.

I swore angrily at the Viking's superficial wound.

I'd intended on shooting him in the head. If Krissy hadn't dazed me with the club I would've had better aim-

I'd failed Winter.

The thought sickened me.

I still had the gun in my hand, but Krissy hit my knuckles with the club. It barely hurt, but I reflexively let go of the weapon.

"He shot Brian!" Krissy exclaimed in disbelief.

Kain swore furiously; grabbing my hair in his meaty fist. Strands pulled out of my scalp, but I refused to cry out in pain again.

"I will hunt down every person you've ever met and torture them until they beg for death."

He gripped my hair harder. My eyes watered as his knuckles dug into my scalp.

"Congratulations, Nolan Delany," he continued bitterly. "You've successfully extended your life. But I promise, you're going to *wish* you were executed today."

Relief walloped me out of nowhere, but I tried not to let it take root in my soul.

The torture would last for weeks, months, years-

With Winter as Kain's new toy.

Cade and Krissy escorted me back to my cell. I tried to get a glimpse of Winter in the hallway, but they forced a hood over my head.

I struggled against Cade's iron grip on my arms, but Krissy hit me in the abdomen with her stupid club. It was so painful, I almost fainted.

She ripped the hood off of me, and I got a glimpse of her face.

Terror marred her delicate features.

I grinned at her, teeth bared. Meeting her eyes with such animalistic hunger that she flinched.

"It's okay, Krissy." Cade grunted as he hauled me toward the vault door. "I can handle him."

Krissy was white as a sheet, but she nodded slightly. She opened the vault door and Cade pushed me through it into the familiar dungeon.

Something had been tossed into my cell that hadn't been there before.

All the fight went out of me when my vision cleared, and I realized that it was a person.

My person.

Winter was unconscious; her shoulder covered by bloody bandages.

Bile rose up my throat and I gagged. Kain hadn't been lying. He would torture her until I begged him to stop. He'd make me wish, every second, that I'd died in the conference room.

The moment Cade shoved me into the cell, I went to Winter's side. I ignored them as they shut the door and locked us in.

Even though we were in a dungeon, even though she was covered in blood, she was still the most beautiful thing I'd ever seen.

Her various scars were more prominent than usual; contrasting against her porcelain skin. Her hair had grown out over her ears now, and I couldn't help but touch her soft strands.

I gasped when my fingers touched her brow. She was so feverish.

The bandages on her shoulder weren't covering her wounds completely, and I could see two bullet holes oozing blood. I swallowed hard; forcing my numb fingers to fix the bandages. If I ever found out who shot her-

I pushed back the thoughts of revenge and focused on her. I hadn't talked to her in over a month. I hadn't been close enough to touch her since the day of my fateful first mission. I'd been so stupid to kiss her, and abandon her immediately afterward.

She should've hated me, but instead she'd told me she loved me-

My fingers shook as I tried to check her vitals.

It was hard to continue using my hands, especially the one Krissy smashed. It was already bruising and swelling to twice its normal size. My wrists were so damaged, and infected, that I didn't know if I'd be able to keep my hands.

That's if we were ever rescued before we died.

Winter stirred slightly under my touch, and I froze. She opened her eyes into slits, but closed them again almost immediately. She was completely limp, but obviously she wasn't totally unconscious.

Her brow furrowed, and her breathing was terrifyingly erratic.

"Winter, if you can hear me, just open your eyes one more time."

I stared at her closed eyelids intently, but they didn't open. Her brow furrowed a bit more, and her breathing hitched slightly.

Panic seized me as everything I'd learned about Sleeping Ache victims flashed through my mind.

Tears filled my eyes, and I didn't stop them from running down my cheeks in salty waves. I didn't want to let her know that I was crying, so I kept as quiet as I could while I laid next to her.

"I'm right here, Winter." I kissed her forehead and pulled her as close to me as I could. I rested my cheek against hers. Failing to ignore the heat coming off of her skin. "I know you're in a lot of pain, but I'm right here. I've got you."

Her breathing slowed a little, and I rubbed her head with my damaged fingers. I closed my eyes; trying to commit to memory how good it felt having her next me after all this time.

Chapter 18 : John

"Why are you here?"

The girl's voice was softer now and didn't echo through the trees around us like it had before.

"We are supposed to meet someone. Who are you?"

She ignored my question, and stepped away from the bushes that concealed her. She had a bow with an arrow aimed directly at my chest.

"Where's the abomination? The one you call 'Winter'."

I didn't reply. Agitation burned in the girl's almond eyes. Her fingers twitched slightly. The tip of her arrow trembling.

There was something familiar about the weapon, and my eyes suddenly burned with tears. The intricate designs on the wooden bow, and the slender sticks with the triangular arrowheads, had once hung above the door of Eliza's cabin.

I remembered my brother carving the designs; talking with Winter while he did it. It had been the first time I'd seen him joke in years.

I had no idea what this girl was doing with Nolan's bow and arrows. But I knew exactly who she was. Her fingers twitched again, a violent tremor shot through her arms.

Willow was absolutely terrified.

"It's okay." I kept my hands firmly on my head as I met her eyes. "We aren't going to hurt you."

"Answer my question. Where is the abomination?"

I took a deep breath and shifted my feet so I was practically standing in front of her.

"I don't know an abomination. But if you're asking about Winter, then I'll happily answer your question."

She stared at me incredulously before tightening the string on the bow. The tip of the arrow was merely a foot away from my chest. If she let that thing loose, I'd most likely die. It wouldn't be a quick death either.

"Where is Winter?"

"I don't know." I smiled nonchalantly.

She balked and took a step away from me. Her grip on the bow and string never wavered, but I was still nervous about her moving around with that thing aimed at me.

I didn't want to think what would happen if she tripped.

"All of you stand in a straight line. I want to see your faces."

When my men didn't move, I quickly told them to do what she said. George and James angled themselves so that they stood shoulder to shoulder with me. Leif slowly turned around to stand next to George, but he froze before he could get in line.

His face went completely white, as though he was about to be sick. He dropped his hands from his head and took an involuntary step forward.

I was so preoccupied by Leif's reaction. It took me a moment to notice that she was no longer pointing the arrow at me. The weapon hung loosely in her hands as she lowered her arms.

She focused on Leif with murderous rage burning in her eyes. Yet, she seemed just as frozen as he was.

"Willow?" Leif whispered timidly.

She didn't move, or respond.

"Willow." Leif took another step toward her.

She raised her bow and pointed the arrow straight at his face.

"Don't take another step, Leif."

Her whole body was racked with violent shivers, and I was terrified that she was going to kill Leif. I was about to tackle her down, but Leif stared directly at me.

"Don't. She's not going to kill me."

Willow bared her teeth in a silent snarl as her body stilled. The arrow trained on the space between Leif's eyes.

"It seems like she hates you, man." George stiffened next to me. "What did you do to her?"

Leif let out a sigh. An expression of intense shame flitted across his face.

"Nothing."

Willow kept her aim steady; rage still simmering in her eyes.

"That's why she's so angry. Because I did nothing when she needed me the most."

Suddenly, Willow took a step back and aimed her arrow at me again.

"Nolan said you weren't arming Feral Morons." She spat on the ground at Leif's feet. "Either he lied to me or you lied to him. I *knew* this was a bad idea."

Yeah, she was definitely Nolan's friend.

"Willow, we aren't here to hurt you. We are supposed to meet Kain. Do you know where he is?"

Willow kept the arrow tight against the string, but she stopped aiming it at my chest.

"He's back at the bunker." She clenched her jaw, as though she was contemplating aiming the arrow at me again. "I'm the one that sent you here. I was expecting you to bring men with you, but I thought Winter would be here too. I definitely didn't expect my so- called *brother* to be part of your little crusade."

Wait, what?

"You're related to her?" James asked, giving Leif a sideways glance.

Leif nodded, tears glistening in his eyes as he spoke. "I thought she was dead."

Willow's eyes flashed back to her brother.

"Quit acting like you care, Leif."

I quickly brought her attention back to me. No matter how shocking this turn of events was, we didn't have time for it.

"Willow, I know this is difficult for you. I promise, I'm going to listen to your story, but I need some information from you first. Is Nolan alive?"

Finally, Willow looked at me and nodded. The relief hit me so hard that my knees shook.

"Does Kain know that you're here?"

She shook her head.

"Kain has no idea that I sent you the entire footage of Nolan's torture. I tried to warn you that Kain knows about Winter. That's why I want to know where she is."

Willow's eyes flashed toward Leif for a moment.

"I told you the truth." She looked back at me, trying to ignore her brother. "I don't know where Winter is. I hope she's out of Kain's reach, but there's a strong possibility that she's not. Especially if she went looking for Nolan."

Willow's jaw clenched, but she didn't make another comment about Winter.

"I've heard that Scavengers are sick." Willow finally relaxed her grip on the bow and slid the arrow into the quiver on her back. "Nolan and Phoenix tried to warn you about the plague, but-"

She stopped talking, abruptly, and cleared her throat.

"I can guess what happened." I kept my tone gentle; implying that I didn't need her to explain further.

"I have the cure with me. Nolan and Phoenix stole it during their last mission together. Kain was able to replicate it in his lab, and I escaped with a cooler full of it. I don't know if it'll be enough to vaccinate everyone, but you can save some people."

Well, at least I knew for sure that Willow was on our side. Despite how scared and angry she was.

"I really appreciate that, Willow. I'm sure that wasn't easy for you."

"It's in the cooler behind those trees." Willow pointed to our left, and I nodded in understanding.

Then she turned to leave.

Before I could stop her, Leif strode forward. He didn't touch her or talk to her. He just followed her through the trees for a few paces.

I was about to follow them, but George placed a hand on my shoulder.

"I think you should let them have a minute, Boss."

I knew he was right, but I didn't have time for this. I needed Willow to show me where the bunker was, and I needed to get the cure to the community.

I shook off George's hand and hurried over to the estranged siblings.

"Get away from me," Willow demanded tersely.

Leif took a step away from her, but he didn't go much further away than that.

I'd never seen Leif look so forlorn before. He was usually upbeat and energetic. It was hard to imagine that anything could beat him down, but when he looked at Willow-

There was so much guilt in his eyes.

I ignored it. I had to.

"Willow, I can't let you leave until you tell me where the underground bunker is and how to get inside. I have to save Nolan."

Willow flinched slightly and walked toward me. It seemed like she was trying to distance herself more from Leif, since she didn't exactly want to talk to me either.

It was obvious that she had a deep fear of men.

I briefly wondered how Nolan dealt with that.

"I'm sorry," Willow whispered in a broken voice. "I wasn't exactly truthful when I said Nolan was still alive. I mean, he *is* still alive, but not for long. Kain scheduled his execution when he realized I had escaped."

Frantic. That was the only way to describe the rush of adrenaline that flood my veins.

"I have to get there before that happens, Willow."

Tears filled her eyes, but she quickly blinked them away.

"It'll take too long to get there. Nolan will be dead by then."

George and James came to stand behind me, listening intently.

"How do you know this, girly?" George asked.

Willow pulled a tablet out of her bag and showed us what was on the screen.

She had hacked into the surveillance cameras in Kain's underground bunker. Dozens of tiny squares filled up the rectangular screen. They all showed the different rooms in the underground bunker. She flipped it back around before I could get a closer look.

"I overheard Kain scheduling it the other day. I swear, if I had known that Kain would kill Nolan when I left- I wouldn't have escaped. He's my only family. It'll destroy me when he's gone. But I promised him that I'd get you the cure for the Scavengers."

I studied her face and saw no sign that she was lying.

Nolan had managed to find a true friend within the League of Vigilance.

"Please, tell me where the bunker is? I need to at least try to save him. If I can't, then I'll kill Kain. Either way, we'll be done with this."

Willow thought about it for a moment before she nodded.

"I'll do better than tell you where it is. I'm coming with you."

Leif stepped forward and crossed his arms over his chest.

I had a feeling that he did it to prevent himself from touching his long lost sister.

"Like hell you are, Willow. Just tell John where to go. I don't want-"

"I don't care what you want," Willow hissed furiously.

I stepped between them before a fight could ensue. George put a hand on Leif's shoulder and steered him away from us.

James stood next to me now, and resumed his formidable looking pose. He scanned the trees; keeping watch to make sure none of the Vigilantes followed Willow here.

"You're not going to get inside the bunker without my skills." Willow held up the tablet in her hand. "Kain will have stepped up his security after I left. Cade is the head tech for Kain's team, but I'm better than he is with the tech.

"I stole one of Kain's Jeeps. The tracking system was fried and it was the only thing I could steel. I only managed to escape with the cure and Nolan's bow and arrows. He trained me to use them. I'm useful in a fight too."

I believed her. She had been able to make four fully trained men take cover with one arrow, and she seemed exceptionally intelligent.

"Alright." I turned to James. "You and Leif will take the cure to the community. George, Willow, and I will go to the bunker."

"No," Leif walked up to us. George was close behind him; carrying the cooler that Willow had left in the trees. "She's not going anywhere without me. Never again."

Willow flinched slightly, and wrapped her arms around her midsection. A breeze blew through the trees and she shivered. Even though it was chilly, she wasn't merely shivering from the cold.

Yeah, she didn't just hate Leif. She was terrified of him too.

"James, George; take Willow to the Jeep and form a plan to get into the bunker. Leif and I are going to talk."

Willow gave Leif a wide berth as she followed James. When they were out of earshot, I gave Leif a stern look.

"She called you a Feral Moron."

Leif nodded in bewilderment.

"Some sort of insult, I guess? She's always been prone to creative nicknames."

He *really* wasn't understanding my point.

"It's a nickname my brother gave to the men that rob, torture, and murder the innocent. I make it a point not to have them in the Scavenger community. I already let Brian sneak in. *I'm not letting it happen again.*"

Leif paled slightly, but he looked me in the eye. His stare didn't waver as sadness swam in those almond shaped eyes that matched his sister's.

"I know why she called me that, but that's not me, John."

I certainly hoped not.

"Explain."

"Have you heard of the Green Northern Clan? They migrated to the other side of the mountains after the natural disasters."

I shook my head, and Leif seemed to deflate even more.

"Yeah, not many have. My father was their leader. He established his position by torturing, and killing, the people that wouldn't submit to his leadership. He was an abusive and neglectful parent before the natural disasters, especially to Willow. But after the whole world went down the drain, he got worse. Probably because our mother died. I think she reigned him in a little. Put herself between us and him."

Leif quickly wiped a tear from his eye and cleared his throat.

"People say that Winter is a monster, but they've never met my father. He kept Willow, and a girl named Lexi, as slaves. He hurt them, badly. Over and over again. I never participated, but I never stopped it either. I don't know if I could have, but I never even tried. He had me so conditioned, and beaten down, that I believed any type of rebellion would be useless.

"Lexi was my girlfriend before the natural disasters, but my dad had effectively pitted us against each other. He took her for himself. A year later, it got so bad that I finally felt like I had to do something. One night, I caught Willow and Lexi sneaking out. They had somehow freed themselves from their chains and were running through the woods. I was my father's guard. It was my duty to bring them in, but I didn't. I let them escape."

Another tear fell from Leif's eye, but he didn't wipe it away.

"You did the right thing in letting them go, Leif."

He snorted sarcastically. "I thought they would die in the mountains, but I knew it would be better than what they were going through in the Green Northern Clan. I should've gone with them, but I was a coward."

"That's not who you are."

"Are you sure about that?" Leif looked me directly in the eyes. Nothing but emptiness dwelt there. "I eventually poisoned my dad after Willow and Lexi escaped. I couldn't even look him in the eye when I killed him because I was already running. There's nothing more cowardly than that."

Leif didn't take his eyes off of me while he awaited my decision regarding him.

"I need you to go with James and get the cure to Eliza. She'll know what to do with it."

He was about to protest, and I didn't blame him. He thought his sister was dead and, now that he knew she was alive, he didn't want to let her out of his sight.

Willow didn't understand that, but I did.

"I'll protect her with my life, Leif. I need you to do this."

He closed his eyes, but finally nodded.

"She wouldn't function at her best if I was with you anyway."

I had to resist nodding in agreement, because it was true. At least Leif wasn't oblivious to how much Willow feared him.

It didn't take us long after that to get into the two Jeeps and go our separate ways.

George sat in the passenger seat while I took a turn driving. Willow had her tablet on her lap, in the backseat, so she could watch Kain's every move while she navigated us to the underground bunker.

The desperate silence was unbearable.

A few hours into the trip, Willow let out a horrified gasp from the backseat.

I turned to glance at her and watched as her face slowly drained of all color. She swayed slightly as though she was about to faint. Her fingers gripped the tablet so hard they were completely white.

I stopped the Jeep and turned around fully in my seat.

"Willow?"

I didn't know what else to say. I didn't know this girl very well, but I had a feeling she wouldn't react like that to something on the screen if it didn't have to do with Nolan.

"What have they done to you, Blue Eyes?" Her entire body tensed as horror darkened her eyes.

"Willow, if you don't tell me what's going on right now-"

"I'll need to set you up with another tablet," Willow muttered quickly, pulling herself out of her shock. "I can't give you my tablet since Kain's tech team is constantly trying to kick me out of their system. But I'll set it up so that you're seeing what I'm seeing."

I gave George a quick glance and he nodded. We got out of the Jeep to switch seats. I was going to be useless after watching whatever it was that Willow was seeing.

If it was Nolan's execution, I wasn't exactly sure how I was going to react.

"Kain is giving him a chance to say goodbye." Willow handed me her extra tablet. "I'm not sure if Blue Eyes will say anything or not. He's pretty stubborn."

I stared at my brother's emaciated form in complete shock. His ankles were restrained to the floor with a thick chain and bolts.

He was wearing a special type of handcuffs that had been illegal for police officers to use, since they were incredibly inhumane. They caused blisters on the skin from chemical reactions in the metal itself. They were only used for terrorists or dangerous prisoners that were prone to escaping.

A torture device that was unthinkable to put on a teenager.

Nolan truly looked awful. He was skin and bones with hardly any muscle left. His usual tanned skin was pasty, and even his hair looked dull. It was usually thick and lush like our mother's had been, but now it looked stringy and was in need of a cut.

I couldn't even look at his hands, since they were easily the worst of his ailments. It was obvious that he had no more circulation in them from the damaging handcuffs he'd been forced to wear.

He addressed Willow in a weak voice, and asked her to stop me from seeing the footage.

A split second later, my screen went blank. Willow muted her audio. I turned in my seat and fixed her with a stern look.

"Turn it back on, Willow," I ordered firmly. "Right. Now."

She freaking ignored me-

And proceeded to put an ear bud in her ear so she could listen to what Nolan was saying. I reached out to grab her arm, but she flinched away from me before I could touch her.

"Willow, I know you're trying to honor Nolan's wishes, but that's not a good idea right now. I need to see and hear what is going on so that we can all try to find a way to help him."

George agreed as he continued navigating through the dense forest. "Withholding footage is never a good idea."

Willow continued ignoring us as she listened to Nolan. Tears filled her eyes at whatever she was seeing and hearing. My gut clenched when she smiled sadly at something Nolan said.

She finally glanced up at me after a few minutes. I knew I needed to tread carefully with this girl. She didn't seem to take orders well, and she was, obviously, completely terrified of men.

From what Leif told me about what happened to her, that was totally understandable.

"You're not missing much. He's mostly just trying to piss Kain off. He asked me to keep Winter away from Kain, and he said that he loves you and Eliza. Seriously, you didn't miss much."

I knew that couldn't be true.

"Did you record it?" I asked tersely.

"Yeah, of course," she replied indignantly. "But I'm not going to let you see it. He's got two hours left before they'll execute him. We are at least another six hours away from the bunker going at the rate we are."

I immediately felt nauseas at hearing that, but I refused to throw up.

"Can you do anything to their system to prevent that from happening?" George asked; driving a bit faster through the rough terrain. "Or at least delay it?"

"I've had my hands full just trying to remain locked into the system. They've been trying to kick me out since I escaped. I have to keep on top of it or else I'll lose video and audio access to the bunker. The only way I know how Blue Eyes is doing is from what Kain and the others say about him. They keep him away from the cameras on purpose, so I was surprised that Kain filmed him again. Blue Eyes was right. Kain was doing it to mess with you. That's why he didn't want you to see it, John. I'm going to respect his wishes."

I had to resist the urge to scream at her and, by the defiance in her eyes, she fully expected me to.

I closed my eyes and took a deep breath.

"When was the last time you slept, Willow?" George asked. "If you've been fighting to keep in the system that doesn't leave much time for anything else."

Willow let out a shaky sigh, and ignored George's question. I took another look at her eyes and saw that George was right. They were bloodshot and she had dark circles under them.

"I don't know much about computers, but could you walk me through what to do so you can take a nap?"

Terror flashed across her face as she shook her head.

"They'd eat you alive. They aren't as good as me, but there's a whole team of them. You wouldn't be able to keep up with it all."

"How much longer can you do this?"

She merely shrugged.

"As long as it takes to break in and kill Kain. I'll try to cause as many distractions as possible to delay the execution, but-"

Her voice trailed off and her eyes grew wide.

"Holy crap." She ran her fingers over her screen before glancing up at me. "Look at your screen."

I stared down at my tablet, and pressed my fist to my mouth as I stared at the image in front of me.

It was Ember, with an unconscious Winter slung over her shoulders in a fireman's carry. She had accessed the vault door to the underground bunker. Carrying Winter right through it-

Into the horrific depths of Kain's cult.

I had no idea how Winter ended up being Ember's prisoner again, but it didn't matter. The fire girl was going to turn her over to Kain.

I swore furiously under my breath. Closing my eyes, I leaned into my seat.

The desperation. The helplessness. It was eating me alive.

Two hours went by in silence as we waited for Nolan's execution. The only sound came from Willow's tablet as she constantly worked to remain locked into Kain's system.

Then, without warning, another video popped up on my screen.

Nolan was being dragged through the hallways while Kain filmed him. All for Willow's benefit.

"No," Willow whispered in horror. "Please, no."

"Just focus and ignored it, Willow," I murmured as soothingly as I could. Watching my baby brother on the tablet was just as horrifying for me, but I tried to keep my voice calm. "Can you trip the alarms to cause a distraction?"

Willow shook her head dejectedly as she stared at her screen.

"Don't watch it, sweetheart. Concentrate on what you were doing before. Kain is trying to distract you so his team can kick you out of his system. Can you lock the doors to the rooms?"

She shook her head again, letting out a small sob.

"Can you find Winter?"

Willow nodded and clicked a few buttons on her screen.

"Ember has set explosives all over the bunker." Willow's voice shook in stark terror. "She broke into Kain's armory and destroyed most of their weapons with her fire."

I took a shaky breath and nodded in understanding.

"Is Winter with her?"

Willow nodded. "She's still unconscious. Ember is dragging her down the hallway toward the meeting room they just took Nolan to."

George had stopped driving; parking in the middle of the game trail.

There was no way we'd get there in time. We all knew that.

George didn't try to stop me from watching the footage of Nolan's execution.

I was stuck in a tunnel.

The blood pounding in my ears seemed to echo as I watched Brian pull the gun out of the holster. I barely noticed the fact that he only had one hand now. When Ember opened the door, interrupting the execution, the nausea finally overcame me.

I thrust the tablet at George, and opened the door just seconds before I vomited.

When I was finished being sick, I sat back in my seat. I could hardly breathe. I was shaking so badly. I didn't even try to take the tablet back from George.

I could still hear the commotion coming from the footage through the blood pounding in my ears.

"Whoa, Blue Eyes," Willow whispered breathlessly.

"Damn." George shook his head as he glanced at me. "You're baby brother is a freaking machine, Boss."

I stared at him in shock. He held the tablet in front of me.

Nolan had somehow gotten himself free of the torturous handcuffs; which was supposed to be impossible. He'd disarmed both Brian and Cade. Even after a woman hit him over the head with a club, he still managed to shoot both Kain and Brian.

He'd fought back. Just like he'd been born to do.

The screen suddenly went blank. The panic seized my chest; stealing the air from my lungs.

"Just a second, John." Willow concentrated on the tablet in her lap. "They are trying to boot me out of the system. I'll get into the feed again soon."

A few moments later, the footage appeared on my screen again. Nolan was still alive, and being dragged back down the hallway.

"We're going to lose footage of Nolan after they get him through that door," Willow warned, grimly. "There's cameras in the dungeon, but they aren't hooked up. There's nothing for me to access in there to see how he's doing. They took Winter down there too."

"Well," I whispered under my breath. "At least they're both in the same place."

"Brian and Kain are in the infirmary," Willow explained clinically. "Kain has announced that he won't be executing Nolan at this time. He plans on studying the specimen. I'm not completely certain, but I think that means he wants to study Winter. Ember is with him in the infirmary. I don't have audio, so I have no idea what she's saying to him."

With each word Willow rambled, it was apparent she was in shock. She sounded calm, but she swayed in her seat. Her face was completely drained of all color; making her look extremely ill.

I grabbed hold of her wrist, and she looked up at me in confusion. Her pulse pounded rapidly against my finger. Her chest heaved; indicating that she was on the verge of collapsing.

She didn't even react when I pulled the tablet from her hands.

"I need you to sleep for the rest of the trip," I told her gently. "We're four hours out. If you get booted out of the security system, it won't matter now. We'll figure out how to get in the bunker when we arrive. Alright?"

Willow nodded robotically. I, gently, coaxed her into sprawling across the backseat. She tucked up her legs and rested her head in the crook of her elbow. I grabbed a wool blanket off of the floor and covered her with it.

I couldn't help but be amazed by her. Without her, I never would've gotten this far in finding Nolan. She did it all without any backup.

It didn't escape my notice that we were very fortunate to have her on our side.

Chapter 19: Winter

Scorching blood burned through my veins like boiling water.

The pain paralyzed me in a way I'd never experienced before. I couldn't open my eyes. I couldn't even moan.

It was terrifying.

Now I understood just how awful the Sleeping Ache was for the people that Shane attempted to heal. How painful it was for him to absorb their ailments into himself.

I was vaguely aware of Ember carrying me through the tunnels of Kain's underground bunker. I wondered how long I had been unconscious, but it didn't really matter.

I must've slipped into unconsciousness again.

The next thing I knew, I was being locked in a prison cell.

Nothing like the sanitized one I'd been locked in at Dr. Darkwood's lab. This cell smelled strongly of body odor, urine, blood and pain.

Not long after I was locked in the cell, another person was thrown in with me.

I tried to shift away when they touched my hair, but all I could manage was a slight grimace. I didn't know who it was-

I had no desire to be locked away with a touchy stranger.

Then the person touching my hair made a small noise that sounded like a gasp.

A spark of recognition helped me open my eyes slightly. My vision was blurred, but I caught a glimpse of the one person that I'd been so desperate to see. The dark hair, the permanent scowl on his lips, and the beautiful blue eyes.

Nolan.

I wanted to open my mouth. To tell him how much I missed him. That I loved him-

But all I could do was furrow my eyebrows again.

Nolan whispered to me in such a weak voice, I wanted to wrap my arms around him. After a few minutes, the low rumble of his words seeped into my soul. A peaceful warmth enveloping me.

When his fingers started softly rubbing my head, tears stung my closed eyes.

His whispered words of reassurance calmed me as he rubbed my aching head. Then he slowly moved down to rub my neck and my upper back.

He was aware of the parts of my body that hurt the most from the Sleeping Ache. I didn't know how he knew, but his touch helped ease the burn.

He was probably in as much pain as I was.

But he was still trying to ease my discomfort.

His selflessness never ceased to amaze me. I would've told him to stop using his injured hands but, since I couldn't speak, I just laid there. Concentrating on his light touches.

Each soft caress sent warmth through me that contrasted with the burning pain.

"Winter." Nolan's voice rumbled in my ear. My name on his lips was so tired and weak. It broke my heart all over again. "I know you're exhausted and in pain, but I need you to do something for me."

Was he crazy?

I couldn't even open my eyes.

"You probably think I'm insane," he continued, proving that he could always read my mind. "But you need to try to lower your temperature."

I had tried that when I was with Ember. I hadn't been successful.

My fever was so high that I was surprised I wasn't dead yet. Since my body needed a lower temperature, it was dangerous for me to have even a slight fever. Let alone the Sleeping Ache Plague.

"Your fever is too high, Love," he whispered tiredly. "And it's scaring me."

My heart almost stopped at the endearment. He'd never called me anything but '*Winter*' before. He sounded so vulnerable when he said it.

I would've thought he was begging if I didn't know any better.

So I did the only thing I could do; I tried to lower my temperature.

After a while, sweat broke out on my fevered skin. Nolan had long since grown quiet, and had stopped rubbing my aching muscles. I had assumed he fell asleep, but then his arms tightened around me.

"Your fever is breaking. That's good. Just keep doing what you're doing."

I had succeeded in lowering my body temperature by at least a few degrees. The aches didn't go away, or even lessen, but I felt a spark of energy that I hadn't felt since Ember sedated me.

I gingerly opened my eyes, and was relieved by the dim lighting in the dungeon. There was just enough light that I could see Nolan's face mere inches from mine.

He took short and frequent breaths, like he couldn't physically take a full inhale. His face was covered in bluish-yellow bruises. There was a deep cut above his eyebrow that was only slightly scabbed over.

Despite his physical condition, he seemed to be fairly clean. I could smell the soap on his skin, and I couldn't help but feel self-conscious. It had been a week since I had the opportunity to bathe.

Still, I couldn't resist the urge to touch him.

I raised my arm weakly and brushed my fingertips across the awful bruise on his cheek.

He drew in a quick breath as his eyelids flew open. His blue eyes dilated at my touch and he shuddered slightly. I didn't want to cause him more pain, so I eased my hand away.

He slowly shifted closer to me; pressing my fingers against his bruised cheek again. He didn't move his fingers when he brought my hand back to his face. But he didn't seem to be worried about his damaged hands.

He was staring into my eyes with such intensity, my heart pounded.

If I needed a reminder of how fierce Nolan was, the look in his eyes did a decent job of it. Even injured, and malnourished, he looked like he would defeat the world to protect me.

"It's so amazing to see those beautiful eyes again." His voice sounded more husky than weak this time. "And you moved your arm. That's good."

He tested the temperature of my forehead with the back of his hand. Relief replaced the pain in his eyes.

"You did it." He pressed his forehead against mine. "You lowered your temperature. It's annoying how awesome you are."

There was so much love in that sentence; I smiled slightly despite our situation. I knew I'd probably sound pathetic if I tried to talk, but I didn't care.

"Grumpy."

Nolan pulled back slightly and kissed my forehead.

"Just keep your temperature down, and I won't be grumpy anymore." I could see the smirk on his lips when he rested his head on the dirty floor again.

"You're hurt."

Nolan turned his head, slightly, to look at me.

"And you were shot. Which completely pisses me off, by the way."

"Sorry."

My eyes drooped from exhaustion, but Nolan tucked a swollen finger under my chin. I forced myself to meet his eyes.

"Not at you, Love." He spoke firmly despite his condition. "I'm pissed at the person who shot you."

Whatever had happened to him in this bunker had changed him. I could tell by the fierce intent in his eyes. He'd always been quick to defend, but now-

Sheer violence thrummed through him.

"Was it Ember?" he asked gently, despite the savagery in his eyes.

"Brian."

It was getting harder to talk. My temperature was trying to spike again, and I concentrated on keeping it lower. Using the ice within me caused the blood to rush to my head. My temples pounded in agony.

Nolan kissed my forehead again.

"You're doing great, Love. Just keep your temperature low. I know it hurts, but it's helping you."

He grabbed my wrist and rested my hand on his chest. I could feel his bones protruding through his skin and baggy shirt. It broke my heart how thin he was. I remembered how it felt to be starved, and it *killed* me that he was experiencing it.

But that wasn't the biggest issue he had. His hands looked horrific. I doubted he'd be able to make a fist if I asked him to.

"Hands."

I whispered the word so quietly I was surprised he heard me.

"Don't worry about it."

I appreciated the fact that he didn't try to tell me he was '*fine*'. We both knew he wasn't. He needed Shane to help him, but that wasn't going to happen.

We were going to die here. It was only a matter of time.

I was about to close my eyes when the vault door in the dungeon swung open.

Nolan tensed next to me. I used the last of my strength to tighten my hand around his shirt. He glanced down at me as I blinked a few times; trying to keep my eyes open.

"I can't let him near you," he whispered tersely. "Let go of my shirt, Love."

I kept the tight grip on his clothes.

I didn't want him to get hurt anymore. Not for me.

Another Vigilante entered the dungeon; pushing a gurney-

A violent shiver went through me at the sight of the medical bag that was strapped to the Vigilante's shoulder.

"Please," I whispered to Nolan. "Don't."

He gently, but firmly, pried my fingers from his shirt with his one working hand. He slowly got to his feet; staring at the man and woman on the other side of the cell door. His entire body tensed savagely.

"Step away from the abomination, Nolan. She belongs to Kain now."

Nolan stood protectively in front of me. A wall of brutal fragility.

My heart lodged itself in my throat when the man pull out a gun and aimed it at him.

"You finally gonna do it, Cade?"

"Only if you don't stand down. I won't let you hurt Krissy."

Nolan chuckled, but didn't move.

"Krissy isn't the one you should be concerned about."

Cade cocked the gun.

I tried to use my powers to freeze the weapon. It didn't surprise me when it didn't work, but I had to try.

My vision went dark for a moment from the loss of energy. When I could see again, I watched Nolan lunge himself at Cade.

Luckily, the gun didn't go off when Nolan tackled him to the ground.

They wrestled on the concrete floor until Nolan's strength gave out. Even though he wasn't in any shape to fight, Nolan still managed to give him a bloody lip and a nasty cut over his eyebrow.

Cade cuffed one of Nolan's wrists to the bars of the cell and spat blood on the floor next to him.

Nolan gasped heavily; his arm pinned at an uncomfortable angle against the bars. Despite his agonized wheezing, his lips were tinted with blue.

Terror wrapped itself around me. Lack of oxygen would kill him if he didn't stop exerting himself.

"Nice try, Nolan," the girl, Krissy, mocked as she approached me.

She pulled out a syringe full of clear liquid.

"No." I tried to shriek, but it only came out as a pitiful whisper.

I wanted to lash out with my ice. To freeze the very blood in their veins.

All I could do was twitch my fingers.

Cade gripped my hair while Krissy inserted the needle in my neck. I felt the injection, but the rest of my body went numb from shock. Whatever it was that Krissy injected me with; it sent a shot of adrenaline through me.

I finally found the energy to scream. Cade covered my body with his; trying to keep me down. He grunted when I managed to buck my hips.

"Hold still, Subject Thirty-One-"

"Subject Thirty-One, you must hold still," Dr. Darkwood whispered; his breath caressing my ear. "I have other subjects that could replace you, but then all of our hard work would be for nothing. All your pain would be worthless if you die."

Winter's Rose

 My whole body immediately went limp at Dr. Darkwood's cruel words. It was difficult not to thrash around when I was in so much agony, but I forced myself to remain completely relaxed through the rest of the morbid process.
 Dr. Darkwood chuckled when I let out a small whimper of pain.
 "You've gotten better at holding in your screams. Perhaps, if you're not nauseas tonight, I'll let you eat something. I hear the cook is making beef stew."
 The thought of food made me both hungry and sick.
 Dr. Darkwood inserted another needle into my arm, and I moaned in pain.
 He smiled, blood staining his rotting teeth. His mouth formed the word "Winter", but all I heard was moaning.
 Blood burst from Dr. Darkwood's mouth. His eyes formed into black endless pits-

---

 "I'm here, Love. I'm with you."
 My eyes flung open.
 I tried to sit up, but I was being held down by a thick strap across my chest.
 I realized then that they'd secured me to the gurney during my flashback. The cold hard leather of the straps around my hips, wrists, and ankles dug into my skin.
 I shuddered; concentrating on breathing through the panic. Having flashbacks always drained me, but this was worse than usual.
 My eyes found Nolan's furious stare.
 He was no longer trying to free himself from his bindings. Instead, he just held my gaze. Even with the tears stinging my eyes, I refused to blink. I couldn't lose eye contact with him-
 I'd be stuck in a hellish nightmare if I did.
 "She went from having a fever to being cold as ice within seconds." Krissy's fingers flew over the screen on her tablet. "It'll be interesting to see what Kain discovers about her anatomy and physiology. I doubt she can even be categorized as human anymore."
 Cade chuckled at Krissy's hypothesis. He ran a hand down my bare arm.
 "Let's get Subject-"
 "Shut up, you idiot," Nolan growled. Interrupting Cade before he could finish calling me by the name Dr. Darkwood had given me.
 I drew in a small breath; keeping my eyes on Nolan's as I tried to stay in the present.
 Cade took a step toward Nolan, but Krissy laid her hand on his arm.

"I'll deal with him. You need to get the abomination out of the cell."

"Be careful," Cade ordered sternly. "Make sure he's firmly restrained."

Then he turned and fixed Nolan with a hard glare.

"If you touch her, I don't care what Kain wants, I'll end you here and now."

Nolan didn't even acknowledge Cade's threat with a glance. He kept his eyes on me the entire time. His gaze was hard and angry, but extremely desperate.

Cade pushed the gurney out of the cell.

The gurney that would be my last resting place.

I hoped Kain wouldn't keep me alive like Dr. Darkwood did. I hoped I wouldn't fight for my life as hard as I did last time.

Cade wheeled the gurney closer to the bars that Nolan was cuffed to. Close enough that Nolan could touch my arm if he wanted.

Cade secured a strap over my forehead; forcing me to stare at the cold metallic ceiling.

Suddenly, he shoved a needle into my brachial artery.

The scream ripped through my throat the second the needle entered my flesh. My back arched as I tried to get away from a second needle that he shoved into my hand with rough fingers.

Cade swore angrily, tightening the strap across my chest so I was completely immobile. My inhales came in sharp gasps as I was forced to slow my breathing. The leather strap was so constricting-

I was going to suffocate.

Cade lowered his face toward mine. His breath hot on my skin.

"If you ever scream like that again, I'll-"

"You don't want to finish that sentence, Cade." Nolan warned. "You have no idea who you're dealing with."

Cade chuckled humorlessly.

"This monster killed Casey's entire team. I know exactly what I'm dealing with: An abomination. It's capable of killing multiple people without blinking an eye. Without remorse."

He chuckled as his face drew closer to mine. His lips nearly touching me.

"I may have psychotic tendencies, but I don't hold a candle to a monster like you."

A tear rolled out of my eye.

If Cade knew what I'd done, then so did Nolan.

He'd never see me the same way. He'd never say that I was inherently good.

He'd finally see what I really was.

"Nolan knows." Cade smiled; reading my every emotion. "He watched the entire thing on the footage that we stole from the Highborn Union. I remember the look on his face when he watched you attack the Vigilantes with your ice powers. I thought he was going to be sick. Imagine how hurt he must've been. The person that he loved had lied to him. She's really just a murderous abomination. Worse than the rest of us."

Cade licked his lips. His crazed eyes roaming over my face.

"Don't listen to him, Love." Nolan's voice rumbled soothingly.

Cade chuckled and turned to his companion.

"Does the abomination need anymore medication before we leave? I got blood samples and the IV is in place."

"It'll need the Sleeping Ache Cure before too long. The cocktail of meds I gave it should postpone the inevitable. Unless it can somehow cure itself from the plague. It might be interesting to see if it can recover."

"We'll see what Kain says," Cade replied nonchalantly. "No need to waste the cure if we don't have to."

Cade and Krissy left us alone without another word. The IV needle was still in my hand; making me lightheaded from the medications being forced into me.

I closed my eyes. Stepping toward oblivion.

"I need you to stay awake, Love."

I wished I could turn my head to face him. If only to see the reaction that he'd had to Cade's words. I couldn't believe that Nolan knew my darkest secret.

I wasn't inherently good.

I swallowed hard, but didn't open my eyes.

"I know you think I care about what happened to you, but I don't."

Weak. He sounded so weak.

"I've killed more people than just the Vigilantes when I escaped, Nolan. None of them stood a chance against me. Once they were unlucky enough to cross my path, they were done."

My voice broke and a fresh wave of tears fell down my cheeks. I choked back a sob and closed my eyes. It was easier to continue talking if I didn't have to stare at the dungeon ceiling anymore.

"I hear their screams in my sleep sometimes."

Nolan's warm fingers caressed my arm through the bars. I clenched my jaw; fully expecting him to tell me off for being too hard on myself.

"I have a story I want to tell you." Nolan rubbed his thumb soothingly over my skin. "You know I've had to kill people before, but I need to tell you about what happened the first time. I won't give you the horrific details. You don't need to hear it, and I don't need to relive it:

"John was being beaten to death by a Feral Moron, so I intervened. Eliza decided it would be best to try to save the Feral Moron's life instead of helping John. My brother was bleeding like crazy. I had no idea what to do for him. Still, Eliza worked really hard to save that scumbag's life. I was furious with her. It wasn't until recently that I fully understood why she tried to save the Feral Moron.

"She was trying to protect me from the guilt of what I'd done. I didn't understand that because I didn't *feel* guilty. I was just angry like I always am. But the anger got worse after that. I withdrew from Eliza and John. I put myself in danger to protect others.

"I didn't think I deserved anything good in my life. I thought if I helped other people it would, sort of, make up for not feeling guilty in the first place."

More tears fell down the sides of my face. Nolan continued stroking my arm with his fingers; trying to comfort me.

"That is how I deal with it all. It may not be the best way. It's definitely not safe, but it's what I feel like I need to do.

"I don't think you've been dealing with it, Love. I think you hid it from me, John, and Eliza because we think you're amazing. And you are. But that doesn't mean you have to live up to this insane notion that we think you're perfect. No one can live up to that."

He wiped the tears from the side of my face that he could reach.

"I'm so sorry. I should've talked to you about this a long time ago. I should've known that you didn't escape Dr. Darkwood's lab unscathed. When I was forced to watch the footage of you escaping the lab, I felt so incredibly guilty that I wasn't there for you. I swear I'm not going to leave you again. I'm not going to let you go through this alone, Love."

His warm voice soothed me as I succumbed to the medication coursing through my veins.

Chapter 20: Nolan

It was shocking.

So shocking, that I could rest my hand on Winter's arm without squeezing the hell out of her. I probably shouldn't have been touching her at all with how angry I was. But she was on the verge of having another flashback.

Cade was an absolute moron. He had a death wish; provoking Winter like that.

If she hadn't been so sick, we all would've been frozen solid when Cade called her 'Subject Thirty-One'.

Even in her condition, the cold rushed out of her like a gust of arctic wind.

Merely hearing 'Subject Thirty-One' was a trigger for her. It was solid proof that she had major psychological issues, and rightly so.

She'd been through hell.

At least the flashback had forced her ice powers to come to the surface. She got to have a reprieve from the raging fever that plagued her. I knew it wouldn't last long though. I could already feel her skin warming under my palm.

Her breathing gradually evened out as she lost consciousness. I loathed seeing her unconscious on the freaking gurney. Being strapped down was an absolute nightmare for her. Every fiber of my being wanted to tear the damn thing apart.

Unfortunately, I had to get out of the handcuffs first and figure a way out of the cell.

I shifted my legs and felt something wedged underneath my thigh. I scooted over, with more effort than it should've taken, and found a small leather pouch. It was a struggle, but I managed to pick it up with my swollen fingers.

The fold flopped open on my lap. Two silver keys and a syringe fell out. A small note was folded neatly in the pouch. I struggled to slide it out of the sleeve and unfolded it.

You have a key to your cuffs and a key to the cell. It should also work on the vault door. Get the abomination away from Kain. If he figures out how to create more like her, we are doomed.

You're on your own now. Please, destroy this note.

I took a shuddering breath; processing the words on the paper.

Krissy just gave us a chance.

I had been so focused on Winter- and the horrible things Cade was saying to her- I hadn't even realize that she had tucked the leather pouch under my leg.

I managed to tear up the paper into tiny bits; shredding it beyond repair. I studied the syringe, and stared at the label taped to it.

Adrenaline.

It had to be a trick.

If I injected myself, would I be in a tremendous amount of pain and wished I'd died earlier in the meeting room?

That very experience happened to me a couple of weeks ago when they'd injected me with a serum. They led me to believe it was medicine. It had hurt so badly that I'd thought they'd poisoned me.

But if there was even a remote chance that this was adrenaline, I needed to use it. I was going to die soon anyway.

Taking a deep breath, I plunged the needle into my leg and injected the serum. I gritted my teeth; my heart pounding so hard my ears rang. I shook uncontrollably as a surge of energy rushed through my veins.

I fumbled around for the keys and managed to pick one of them up between my fingers. It hurt, severely, to use my hands. They were no longer numb like they had been before.

It took a few tries, but I finally inserted the key into the lock on the handcuffs. I nearly moaned in relief when the key turned without difficulty.

It had been a long time since I didn't have the burning agony wrapped around my wrists. I refused to glance down at the damage the cuffs had done.

I grasped the last key in my fingers, and went to the cell door. My legs wobbled feebly, but the extra adrenaline gave me a boost. I pushed my hand through the gap in the bars. My fingers shook, but I managed to inserted the key into the lock.

The lock clicked open, just as the vault door groaned on its hinges-

I sat down next to Winter with the bars still between us; securing the leather pouch under my thigh. My heart pounded so hard, I was worried I would have a heart attack. I probably gave myself too much adrenaline.

Or maybe Krissy lied, and what I'd injected into my veins wasn't adrenaline at all.

The vault door swung open slowly-

Ember stepped into the dungeon.

Burning rage stole what little air I had in my lungs. The sight of the fire girl sparked such aggression within me; my hands ached to grip her throat. To strangle the life out of her.

Her eyes roamed over Winter's frail body. Her lips formed into a grim line as she gestured to the needle in her wrist.

"Do you know what they're giving her?"

I didn't reply.

I wanted to scream at her for bringing Winter into the Vigilantes bunker.

I gritted my teeth instead.

"How did you get out of those cuffs?" Ember's eyes narrowed at me.

Again, I didn't reply.

Ember sighed heavily, and approached the gurney Winter was sleeping on.

Every muscle in my body tensed; vibrating with fury. I would give anything to have a gun right now. Even a knife would do.

"How am I supposed to help if you don't talk to me, Nolan?"

I blinked, my entire body going numb from shock-

From how delusional Ember was.

"I didn't bring Winter here so that Kain could kill her." Her eyes bore into mine. Pleadingly. "I was trying to get her medicine. Kain has the cure under guard."

I still didn't say anything. If I did, I knew my voice would tremble.

"I needed to get Kain to trust me for what I have planned for him."

I scoffed and glared at her, viscously.

"Wow, I can see why Winter likes you." Ember smirked sarcastically. "You're incredibly hot when you glare like that."

I rolled my eyes, and looked away from her again.

"Anyway." She carried on as though she fully expected me to respond to her. "I brought you food. I found a key that can unlock the cell door too. Don't ask how I got it though. The details are unpleasant."

My eyes shifted to her again; my entire body tensing-

But she was already at the cell door with the key. It swung open the second she put her hand on it.

She stared at me, incredulously.

I didn't respond verbally. I held up the key I'd stowed underneath my thigh.

"Wow, I'm impressed. Here's some food and medical supplies." She tossed a backpack at me and turned to walk out of the cell. "By the way, the whole bunker is rigged to explode. Get Winter out of here before that happens."

She paused for a moment, a solemn expression rippled over her face.

"She is a special person, Nolan. Make sure she gets out of here alive, yeah?"

"What?" I croaked in confusion.

Ember cleared her throat; tearing her gaze away from me.

"You shot me with an arrow. You and Winter left me to die in the underground lab. The only reason I survived was because I managed to crawl out from under the rubble. It was an absolute miracle. I'm still not sure how I managed it. Then I was kidnapped by Brian, almost immediately after surviving. I was his prisoner for weeks in his hellish torture cage."

I simply stared at her. If Brian had tortured her, then I completely understood why she killed all of his men.

"Amanda Lynch may be my mother, but her sadistic agenda sickens me. She *forced* me to do all those terrible things I did. So take the food and water. Get Winter out of here. Giving you both a chance is the least I can do."

I stood up now; ignoring how fast my heart was racing.

"Ember," I whispered. "You can't blow the bunker."

She stared at me for a moment. Her mouth hung opened like I'd said something shockingly offensive.

"Kain wants to *study* Winter. He plans to open her up and sew her shut. Just like Dr. Darkwood did over and over again. I saw everything that psycho did to her. I know for a fact that she'd rather be dead than go through it again."

I had to swallow down bile before I replied. I couldn't think about what Kain planned on doing to Winter.

Not right now at least.

"This bunker is a refuge that the Scavengers could use. Amanda Lynch doesn't know about this place. You know as well as I do that she could wipe out the entire Scavenger community with a snap of her fingers. This bunker is the only option. *Don't destroy it-*"

I stopped talking when I realized I was shaking with rage.

Despite the fact that Ember gave me a backpack full of food and medical supplies- I still wanted to wring her neck. For all I knew, Kain had put her up to this.

"Fine, but how are you going to do this? Kain is too powerful for the Scavengers to take over the bunker."

I chuckled darkly. "I'm not a complete moron, Ember. Even if I did trust you, which is still in question, giving you vital information would endanger Winter and the Scavengers. If you truly did care about us, you'd want me to keep my mouth shut. You wouldn't want to know anything. Especially if our enemies decide to torture you for information."

Ember flinched, and took a step away from me.

"Fine, I won't blow the place. Just get Winter out of here. I'll try to hold off Kain for as long as I can. I assume you can find a place to hide, right?"

I didn't reply. I was taking up too much energy listening to her nonsense as it was.

Luckily, she didn't say anything else. She turned around and stalked out of the dungeon. She left the vault door open, and I knew I had to hurry if we were going to get out of there before someone noticed it.

I didn't know if the cameras in the dungeon were working, but I assumed they weren't. There was no way Kain's security team would allow Krissy and Ember to help me.

Unless this whole thing was a trap-

Which was probably the case.

I took a deep breath, and strapped the backpack on. It wasn't very heavy, but the straps dug into my bony shoulders. I already knew I was dangerously thin, but I was surprised by how much the added weight affected me.

I suddenly wondered if I'd be able to carry Winter out of this place-

Even with the adrenaline boost, I was still ridiculously weak.

I studied Winter's wrist; trying to concentrate through the fog settling over my mind. Her skin was bruised around the needle that connected to the IV fluids. I glanced at the bag full of whatever medicines and chemicals Krissy saw fit to give her.

The mere thought of Winter being filled with whatever concoction-

I shook my head when my vision went fuzzy. I had to stop thinking about things that made me lightheaded. Otherwise, I wasn't going to get Winter out of there.

I decided to leave the needle in her wrist, for now. She might need to be hooked up to another IV later. I doubted she wanted to go through being poked again.

I unhooked her from the bag of fluids, and the leather straps that bound her to the gurney. I took a deep breath before scooping her up in my trembling arms.

She was incredibly light, but my muscles had atrophied.

I could barely lift her.

Once I had her in my arms, I staggered. The backpack straps seemed to cut into my shoulders even more as I took a step forward.

When I made it to the vault door, I took a fortifying breath and stumbled down the tunnel-

Leaving the dungeon behind me. Forever.

I would die before I'd allow anyone to drag me back there.

My original plan had been to get to the hangar and steal a Jeep. But I knew that wasn't an option the moment I lifted Winter off of the gurney. I was lucky that I even made it out of the dungeon without needing to take a break. The extra adrenaline had helped a bit, but the little strength I had was fading fast.

I quickly considered all the places we could hide, but the safest place was my old room. Willow would've done everything she could to keep Kain, and his tech team, out of the place she'd done all of her planning. There were no cameras in our room- Willow made sure of it- so Kain wouldn't be able to see us in there.

If Willow still managed to keep the cameras in the bunker offline, that would be extremely helpful.

I was realistic enough to realize that probably wasn't the case.

But, if I could get to our room, I'd be able to barricade us in. At least for a short time. Until Willow could bring John and the Scavengers here. They'd take over the bunker, just like they'd fought the Highborns out of their territory.

I *had* to believe that, or I would just give up. I would collapse, with Winter, in the middle of the underground bunker.

I held onto her as tightly as I could; stumbling through the vaguely familiar tunnels. It took a long time to get to the main corridor that led to the countless rooms.

I had been amazed by how large the bunker was when I first joined the League of Vigilance. I remembered thinking how wonderful it was to have such a large sanctuary that Amanda Lynch had no idea existed.

I had been such an idiot back then; to believe that Kain even wanted to give sanctuary to the Scavengers.

And now, I was mentally cursing how large the freaking bunker was.

My muscles screamed; demanding to rest.

But I couldn't stop. If sat down, I wouldn't get back up again.

I stumbled, and almost dropped to my knees. I gritted my teeth; blinking through the cloudy haze that crossed my vision. It was sheer power of will that kept me upright.

My arms shook as I clutched Winter's limp body to me. I didn't really have all that far to go now, since the door to my room was just at the end of this tunnel, but it might as well have been a hundred miles.

"Nolan."

The gruff voice forced me to a halt.

Terror shook me, and I buried my face in Winter's soft hair.

This was it. We'd finally been caught.

I was rather surprised that we made it as far as we did without anyone noticing.

"Come on."

The person behind me grabbed my arm, and I flinched. I turned to face him, and was surprised to see David standing next to me. His eyes were wide with abject horror as he stared at me.

I wasn't sure what that look was for. I was fairly certain this guy hated me.

"You'll be safe in your room. Willow made it impregnable. No one has been able to get into it after she ran off, but I'm sure you can figure out how to get in there."

David tried to usher me forward, but I jerked out of his grip as best I could.

"I'm trying to help you before the wrong person finds you. Word is; Brian didn't survive the bullet wound. You killed him. Kain is going to torture Winter in front of you, and then kill you slowly. He's been making plans for it with Cade, and that fire breathing weirdo that crashed your execution."

If Ember was making plans with Kain then why did she purposely try to thwart him?

This whole thing had to be a trap. There was no way that it wasn't.

"Let me carry her."

David tried to slip his arm under Winter's legs. A new surge of fury went through me, and I ripped Winter away from him.

There was no way that was happening.

"No one touches her." I summoned a glare that made David flinch. "Not ever."

"You look like you're about to collapse, man." His face was a mask of concern. "I promise, I won't hurt her."

He tried to take Winter from me again, but we were interrupted by footsteps in the hallway behind me.

David glanced over my shoulder and winced. I didn't want to look, but I turned my head anyway.

Grace was hurrying toward us; her delicate features marked with bruises. The last remnants of Brian's psychopathy.

"Nolan, how did you get out of there?"

Grace stared at me in horror. When her gaze drifted to Winter, I gritted my teeth.

David abandoned his effort to take her from my arms and rounded on Grace.

"Your partner just died," he growled tersely. "You shouldn't be here."

"I was told to leave the viewing room." Her face paled, the bruises becoming more prominent. "They just wanted family there to cremate Brian's body. I'm not considered family. Thank heavens."

I was so tired, I really didn't know what they were talking about anymore. I got the gist that Brian was dead, and that I had killed him-

I didn't have the mental capacity to dwell on that at the moment.

I continued walking down the hallway; ignoring David and Grace as I went.

I was surprised that they didn't stop us. They followed closely; each placing a hand on my arms to help me along. I didn't even try to shake them off.

I was just so *tired*.

"We're almost there, Nolan," Grace murmured when I stumbled again.

"You sure you don't want me to carry her?" David asked uncertainly. I merely ignored him.

I hadn't been kidding when I said no one would touch her.

I kept putting one foot in front of the other until I got to my door. It was apparent that the Vigilantes had tried to knock the door down.

Countless times.

It was dented on every inch of the surface. Scorch marks and debris surrounded the area from their attempt to remove the door.

Willow must've really ticked Kain off. If I wasn't so tired, I would've smiled.

I was so thankful that Willow had the foresight to make her room impregnable in case of emergencies. With her brilliance, and understanding of technology, she had done it before I even joined the League of Vigilance. After she learned that she could trust me, she included my handprint on the secret scanner that she installed next to the door.

Luckily, Kain hadn't done any damage to the scanner.

I glanced around to make sure that no cameras were in view and tapped the keypad next to the door with my elbow. The scanner slid out of the secret compartment with a soft *'click'*.

Grace gaped in shock. David merely stared at the hidden scanner, completely dumbfounded.

"How did Willow install that without anyone knowing?"

I merely shrugged, and situated Winter in my arms so I could press my palm to the scanner's screen. Within seconds, the damaged door slid open.

I stumbled through it, acutely aware of David and Grace closing in behind me.

I automatically angled Winter toward Willow's bed. The blanket was spread, and the pillows sat perfectly where they always were. The sight was so familiar, I nearly collapsed in relief.

It felt like home. Like Willow would saunter out from behind the blanket that concealed the bathroom-

As though she never left.

I set Winter's still form on top of the blankets. I didn't know if she was awake or not, but her body was uncomfortably cold against mine. There was no way I'd risk her temperature rising by throwing blankets on top of her.

I turned to the bedside table and, nonchalantly, rested my hand on top of it. I glanced at Grace and David. Both were staring at me with completely different expressions:

Grace; concern. David; severely pissed off.

"Are you going to let us help you? Or are you going to shoot us with the gun that you're reaching for?"

Grace stared at me in astonishment. David's questions obviously caught her off guard.

"Depends." I grabbed the handgun that Willow always kept hidden behind the bedside table. "Are you going to tell Kain about the hidden scanner and help him break in here?"

I knew Kain could do it too. He had plenty of copies of my handprint. He'd be able to get in easily once his tech team figured out the code to open the scanner's hidden compartment.

David raised his hands in surrender. "You were right about Kain. I know it. Grace knows it. A few other people do too. You helped a lot of the singles even though you didn't have to. You trained us to defend ourselves when Kain didn't care enough to teach us basic gun safety rules. You gave us a chance. I'm not here to turn you in. I'm actually relieved that I found you and made sure you got in here. You look like you're about to drop-"

Grace punched David's arm. He flinched; taking a step away from her in surprise.

"Ouch."

"Stop pointing out how tired he is." She glared sternly, the bruises contributing to the severity in her tone. "You're making him nervous."

I rolled my eyes, and set the gun on the bedside table within easy reach.

"We don't want to see you hurt. We don't want to see Winter get tortured by Kain either. I have a feeling she's had enough of that in her life."

I studied Grace and David; attempting to ascertain their true motives. I was so exhausted, I didn't trust myself to make competent decisions. For now though, trusting the two Vigilantes that stood in Willow's doorway was the only option.

"You both need to leave. Not just this room, but the bunker. Grace, if Brian is dead, that means your life is in danger." I met the man's eyes that stood protectively next to the abused young woman. "David, you gotta get her out of here. If there's anymore singles that need to get out, then take them with you. I don't know if Willow still has the security system offline, but getting out now is your best chance. Kain is injured, and grieving over his nephew. If you don't leave now then you won't get another chance."

Grace balked at me as though I'd gone crazy. David's glare deepened as he took a step toward me.

His gravely voice lowered to a growl. "We aren't leaving you here."

"Yes, you are." My voice was pathetically squeaky. Despite my best efforts to sound firm. "You're going to get Grace as far away from Kain as you can. Brian was her partner, and he's dead. Her life is, basically, forfeit now. After what happened with me, Willow, and Phoenix- I doubt Kain will take any chances by keeping Grace alive."

Moisture filled Grace's eyes, but she blinked it away. She squared her shoulders; trying to act courageous even when terror dulled her eyes.

"What about you?" By this point I was pretty sure Grace wasn't faking her concern.

I tried to stop myself from swaying. I *really* needed to lay down.

"Go without us. We'd only slow you down. We'll be fine. I've got a plan."

"You've got a plan?" David raised his eyebrows suspiciously. "I don't know if I buy that."

If Ember decided to blow the bunker then none of it would matter anyway.

"We'll be fine." I had to believe that. Willow wouldn't let me down, and neither would John. They would come for us. "Just go, before I decide that you're working for Kain and shoot you."

I didn't know if threatening them would work, but they seriously needed to leave.

David merely rolled his eyes and crossed his arms.

"Okay." Grace laid a hand on David's arm. "We'll go. I hope we see you again, Nolan. Thank you for all you've taught us."

I watched them leave; the door sliding shut behind them.

I sank down on the bed next to Winter's feet, and shrugged off the backpack. I ignored the burning pain in my back as the fabric slid down the infected lacerations.

I needed food and water. Then I'd see what I could do to get Winter's temperature down. If I could keep us alive long enough-

John would come for us.

He *had* to.

Chapter 21: John

The cacophony of crickets echoed through the dense foliage. Masking the sound of our shallow breathing. I cautiously followed Willow to the entrance of the underground bunker, dreading every unavoidable sound we made. Within seconds, we were leaning against the boulders that surrounded the entrance to the Vigilantes bunker. The vault door was large enough for vehicles to exit, but somehow the entrance managed to blend in with the natural surroundings.

The camouflage made it nearly invisible.

George was hiding somewhere in the surrounding forest; keeping watch from a distance. It made me feel a bit better having him at my back, but I was still uneasy.

After waking up from her long nap, Willow managed to hack into the security system again. I'm glad I insisted on making her sleep during the rest of the trip. We did lose some footage- I couldn't keep hacked into the system without her- but she managed to take over the bunker's security system a second time.

"I think something is wrong." Willow winced as she glanced at the door." It all feels too easy."

"Then it probably is. George? Status."

"All clear out here, Boss." George's voice echoed from the comm in my ear.

Apparently, Willow had stolen more than just a Jeep and a few tablets when she fled from Kain and the Vigilantes. She took comms, speakers, and even a few laptops with internet access. She told me we had to be careful using them since they could be traced.

So far, the teenager hadn't ceased to amaze me.

"Willow's got a bad feeling." She glanced at me sharply. I would've thought she was annoyed with me if I didn't see the surprise in her eyes-

Surprise that I even took her seriously at all.

"Never ignore a bad feeling." George's gruff tone rumbled. "Stay cautious. I'm on high alert."

"Will do. Thanks George."

Willow entered in the door code. A soft click joined the cacophony of crickets before the door slid open.

"I'll go first. Stay right behind me."

Willow nodded and adjusted Nolan's quiver on her back.

The dark tunnel expanded into a vast emptiness that caused my heart to pound. It was unsettling that there were no lights, but it didn't really surprise me. Willow had wiped out their entire system, and I figured the electricity must've taken a hit too.

I had to make sure Kain didn't get his hands on her. He would torture her for her defiance, just like he did to Nolan-

"Do you have any updates on Nolan and Winter?"

"Not yet." Willow's tone was so low that I could only hear her through the comm. "It's like the past eight hours never happened. The cameras must've been malfunctioning, or Kain's tech team deleted all of the footage. I don't know how serious Kain's bullet wound is, or if Brian survived. I shouldn't have slept."

I stopped when we reached a corner and glanced at her.

"You wouldn't be useful right now if you were exhausted."

I peered around the corner and nodded; indicating that we were clear. Willow raised three fingers; telling me to go passed two more tunnels before turning down the third.

Our first stop would be the dungeon, where I hoped we would find some good news. Even if Nolan was beaten within an inch of his life, I could deal with that.

I could handle anything as long as he wasn't dead.

We came across a giant vault door, and Willow surprised me again by using her tablet to open it. A gust of stale air hit me, and my eyes watered at the stench.

Ignoring the churning in my gut, I took a step toward the dark room-

"Well, well, if it isn't John Delany."

I spun around, but wasn't surprised to see Ember standing in the darkness; an orange flame dancing in her hand. I stepped in front of Willow; putting myself between her and Ember's fire.

"How have you been?" The fire girl smirked, but no humor reached her eyes.

I aimed my pistol at her and she chuckled. Her orange flame raced up her arm with a soft hiss.

"Kain will have to interrogate you. Figure out how you managed to find this place, and break in, *all on your own.* I'm sure he'll enjoy torturing Nolan with you as his new toy."

I stared at the Ember in confusion. Willow was literally standing right behind me. Her tablet in one hand and her pistol in the other. It was obvious that I wasn't alone-

Footsteps echoed in the dark hallway, and Ember glared at me urgently.

What in the actual hell was going on?

Ember rolled her eyes, and gestured for Willow to hide behind the vault door. Willow hesitated and glanced at me.

"Don't be too stupid to live." Ember's tone was so low I could barely hear her.

I nodded, and Willow disappeared into the dark dungeon.

I took a shaky breath; staring at Ember's relieved expression. I was so confused, but I knew better than to ask questions when five Vigilantes appeared behind Ember.

I gritted my teeth, and raised my hands in the air with my handgun turned upside down; dangling on my finger-

Thundering footsteps came up behind the group of Vigilantes, and Kain appeared around the corner.

I kept my face neutral as a surge of complete loathing assaulted my emotions-

This monster had tortured my teenage brother, and the vision of that wouldn't leave my head.

I spotted the young man that had flogged Nolan standing next to Kain. I'd only heard his name once, but I would never forget it.

Cade.

I hated him nearly as much as I hated Kain.

"John Delany." Kain's psychotic eyes narrowed at me.

"I came for Nolan. Where is he?"

"How did you find this place?" My fists clenched as Kain completely ignoring my question. "Especially my dungeon. You couldn't have hacked into my system. My tech team's skills are unrivaled. Especially compared to a traffic cop like you."

I was never a traffic cop. I was a detective. But I wasn't about to get into that with Kain.

I took one step toward the Viking, and all the Vigilantes pointed their weapons at me.

I ignored them. They wouldn't shoot me until Kain gave the order.

"Where is Nolan?"

Kain's deep chuckle echoed through the dark hallway. He closed the distance between us, limping severely. Nolan got him good. I had to resist the urge to smile.

Kain ripped the gun out of my hand and handed it to Cade without a word. I glared at Kain as we stood eye to eye. He was slightly taller than me. He had a lot more muscle, but none of that concerned me.

All I wanted was to know if Nolan was still alive.

"Your brother took his last breath just moments ago." That declaration ripped through me like a red hot knife. "Would you like to hear his last words?"

I head-butted Kain right in the nose. The satisfaction of hearing Kain's bones crunch, and seeing the blood squirt from his nostrils, was well worth the ghastly headache.

The butt of Cade's rifle swung toward me, but I managed to shift away from the blow. Forcing me closer to the bleeding Viking-

I rammed both fists into Kain's gut. He doubled over with a grunt and I brought my elbow down onto his bandaged leg.

Kain howled in pain; the sound invigorating me. I briefly wondered how many times he made Nolan scream. My lips formed into a snarl.

I was going to make him scream as much as I could before I killed him.

Kain's legs buckled under him, and he went down on his knees. An easier position for me to bash his skull in with my bare hands-

Cade charged toward me with the rifle; raising it like a bat.

I ducked under the butt of the rifle again, and buried my shoulder into Cade's stomach. Tackling him to the concrete. The air wheezed out of Cade's lungs, and I frantically punched him in the face with every ounce of my adrenaline fueled strength.

His jawbone crunched under my knuckles.

Most people would've screamed from having their jaw dislocated, but Cade merely went limp.

"Cade!" A young woman gaped in horror.

Sensing that I was about to be attacked from all sides; I grabbed Cade's rifle from where he'd dropped it. The next second, I had the butt of the rifle to my shoulder and the barrel aimed at Kain's bloody face.

"If a single one of you moves, I'll put a bullet in your cult leader," I growled angrily. "Everyone drop your weapons. *Now!*"

All of the Vigilantes glanced at Kain for approval before doing what I'd ordered them to do.

I really didn't want to have to kill Kain now. I had plans for him. Maybe it was maniacal, but I needed him to be punished for what he'd done to Nolan. And no doubt countless others.

I kept a steady finger on the trigger as I slid a bullet into the chamber.

I met Kain's eyes and gave him a hard glare.

"Do as he says."

The clatter of guns falling to the floor left a sick twist in my gut. Just knowing that these maniacs had access to so many weapons was completely daunting.

"Kick your weapons toward me. Then lie face down with your hands on your head."

It felt like I was getting into a familiar routine at this point. I'd made countless arrests as a homicide detective. Unfortunately, most of them had involved lethal weapons. Criminals didn't like the idea of being disarmed and sent to prison.

Regrettably, the only backup I had was a teenage girl who was hiding in the dungeon behind me.

"Do as he says," Kain ordered again.

The Vigilantes obeyed, except for Ember-

"Krissy! No!"

I glanced at the fire girl; her eyes wide with helpless urgency.

Something crashed into the back of my skull. Hard. My vision blurred, and I stumbled. My knees buckled out from under me.

Crap, that hurt.

Adrenaline spiking; I quickly spun around on one knee. My finger held steady on the trigger as I aimed at a dark haired girl standing there; holding a wooden club-

The same girl that hit Nolan when he'd fought back at his execution.

She didn't have time to react as I squeezed the trigger. The shot echoed in the tunnel as the bullet buried itself into her thigh. She fell backwards without a sound, but she screamed in agony when she hit the floor.

It took me a moment to get my bearings before I noticed all the Vigilantes were standing again.

"All of you, down!"

The Vigilantes were no longer looking at me. They were staring at their leader with calm expressions. Even as the girl I shot lay crumpled on the ground. No one even looked concerned for her.

Kain got to his feet. I slid another bullet into the chamber, but I didn't hear the click that I expected. Kain smiled at me. And I knew, instantly, that I'd made a terrible mistake-

I was out of bullets.

Kain gestured toward two Vigilantes, and they stepped toward me.

I swung the rifle like a bat. I hit one of them in the head, but the second one managed to punch me in the face. A second later, I was surrounded by Vigilantes.

They forced me to my knees, and one of them held a gun to my head. Ember glared at me in annoyance, which I thought was odd, and Kain kept glancing down at the bloody bandage on his leg. At least he was still distracted for the moment.

"That isn't necessary." Ember stepped toward the man that held the gun to my head. "Lower the gun."

"You aren't the one giving orders! Stand down!"

Fire erupted from her fingertips as she sneered at the large Viking. "It's time that you two talked without the threat of violence."

Kain stepped toward Ember, completely ignoring the fire that engulfed her hands, and loomed over her.

"You do not get to come here and order me around," Kain whispered dangerously. "The only reason I haven't killed you, yet, is because you brought me the abomination. I still haven't decided what I'm going to do with you. So far, your future wellbeing isn't looking very optimistic. You betrayed me once already."

Ember flinched and her flames extinguished in a plume of smoke.

I couldn't help but stare at her in shock. From the one interaction I'd had with Ember, and the stories I'd heard from Nolan and Winter, I would've thought she'd burn Kain alive for threatening her like that.

What was she up to?

"I want to take down Amanda Lynch. Just like you do. Just like John Delany does. I don't understand why the two of you are fighting. You should be working together and-"

Ember's voice broke when Kain clasped his beefy hand around her throat. She wheezed, clutching his hand with her fingers. She still wasn't trying to burn him, and I had no idea why.

It was then that I saw Kain drop a syringe. It clattered to the floor at his feet as he lifted Ember into the air by her neck. She kicked her legs; gasping for air. But Kain barely noticed her attempts to break free of him.

He dampened her fire abilities with whatever he'd injected her with.

Ember's face morphed into a terrifying shade of blue-

"Hey, I'll do what ever you want. Just let the girl go."

Kain glanced at me, and released Ember.

She fell to the floor, coughing violently. Even in the dim light I could see the red mark on her neck from Kain's grip. It would be a nasty bruise in the morning.

"Bring him," Kain ordered. "And the girl. Take Cade and his partner to the infirmary."

"Nolan isn't dead, John." Ember's voice cracked through a harsh gasp. "He's hiding somewhere in the bunker with Winter-"

One of the Vigilantes picked up the wooden club and struck Ember's face with a sickening crack. She slumped to the ground, completely motionless.

Kain growled furiously, and seized me by the throat. Fortunately for me, the Vigilantes holding me hostage were stupid enough to let go of my arms.

And, unfortunately for Kain, I wasn't a terrified teenage girl.

I raised my foot and stomp kicked him in his wounded leg. Before he had a chance to release me, I kneed him in the groin. He heaved in agony and collapsed to his knees.

Choking at the pain in my throat, I turned to face the threat I knew was behind me.

Three Vigilantes were aiming guns directly at my chest.

They all squeezed their triggers simultaneously.

Without forethought, I threw myself into a body roll. One of the bullets ripped through my shoulder. I barely felt the pain as shock replace my adrenaline. I ignored how much I was shaking and jumped to my feet as quickly as I could.

I was trying to take cover around the corner in the tunnel when an arrow flew over my head. I was too slow at dodging it, but luckily the arrow wasn't meant for me.

A second arrow soared passed me-

Two of the armed Vigilantes were on the ground with arrows sticking out of their chests. Blood already pooled on the cement floor beneath them.

The third Vigilante was lying face down on the ground with his hands on the back of his head.

"Please, don't shoot," the Vigilante gasped in terror.

Kain was just getting to his feet again; snarling at the dead and wounded Vigilantes that littered the tunnel.

Ember had backed away during the fight; slowly making her way down the tunnel. I decided to let her go. I doubted she was going for backup after what Kain did to her.

The Viking's bearded face turned a light shade of red as he glared at me.

I smiled back with the widest grin I could muster.

"Willow?" I held Kain's stare as I spoke. "Do you think you can get the cell door open in the dungeon?"

"Yeah," she responded from the concrete pillar she was crouched behind. She had an arrow aimed at Kain, and a feral look in her eyes. An animalistic urge to kill that I completely related to.

But destroying Kain would have to wait until we found Nolan and Winter.

Running footsteps echoed down the dark tunnels. Shouts and urgent voices sounded through the walls, and I stiffened. Willow glanced at me with wide eyes before glaring at Kain.

She let the arrow loose, and it embedded itself in Kain's uninjured leg. He cursed furiously as he fell to the ground again.

"You're going to regret betraying me, Willow Rivers!" Kain bellowed angrily. "I will kill everyone you've ever cared about! I will make sure that you are left alone, and helpless, before I gut you like a-"

I kicked Kain as hard as I could in the face. He slumped back to the ground without so much as a squeal.

He was, finally, unconscious.

"I think Kain's having a bad day." Willow smirked, despite how pale she was.

I picked up the wooden club and hit the remaining conscious Vigilante in the back of the head. His limbs went limp, instantly.

"How many do you think are coming?"

The sound of footsteps was getting closer as Kain's backup closed in on us.

"I can't say for certain. There could be five of them, or twenty-five."

"Do you know where Nolan would've gone?"

We hurried through the dark tunnel, leaving the dungeon behind us, as we spoke.

"He would've gone to our room." She winced. "Well, if he could make it there... He was pretty beat up."

"He made it." I wasn't sure how I knew that, but I just did. "Is he safe there?"

"We are the only two that have access to the room. I made sure of that a long time ago."

I nodded and took a second to catch my breath. Once I met up with George, we'd be able to come up with a plan to get them out of that room. In the meantime, Nolan and Winter both needed medical attention.

"I need you to get to Nolan," I whispered.

Willow nodded, but eyed me worriedly.

"We need an exit strategy. I don't want to go to my room if I'm not gonna be able to get Nolan out of there. What's the plan?"

"I've got one, but I can't tell you." I gestured to the walls around us. "They could be listening. Please, Willow, just trust me."

She hesitated a moment before nodding slowly. I gave her an incredulous look, and she smiled wanly.

"Don't be so surprised. I don't trust easily, but I trusted Nolan with my life after the first day I met him. You and him are a lot alike in that way. You're just a lot nicer than he is."

I grinned, and she held her hand up for a fist bump. I hesitated for a split second before participating in the gesture. My kids and I used to fist bump each other all the time before the great earthquake took them away from me.

Willow was the first person I'd done it with in over three years.

"George and I will come for you guys," I whispered to her. "I promise."

She nodded, and darted around a corner without saying another word.

I pulled the tablet out of my pocket and followed the blueprint of the bunker that Willow downloaded for me.

As I hurried through the dark passages of the underground bunker toward the exit, an invisible weight lifted off of me.

Nolan and Winter were alive. Kain was injured.

The situation was manageable. At least for now.

Chapter 22: Winter

I slowly opened my eyes; ignoring the stabbing pain in my head. I gritted my teeth; moaning at the burning aches surging through my muscles. I *needed* to move, but it was hard to even keep my eyes open. Gasping from the sheer agony, I forced my arms to shift. The motion was slight, but I nearly passed out from the exertion.

I was in the most comfortable bed I had ever been in, and all I could do at the moment was stare at the pillows that surrounded me. Foggy memories of what had happened in the past couple hours stole my focus.

Nolan was safe now.

I tore my gaze away from the pillows when the sound of someone vomiting echoed through the room.

I don't know where I found the energy, but I swung my legs over the side of the bed. My feet didn't touch the floor, so I had to find the strength to hop off of it.

I took a moment to catch my breath before attempting such a feat. The last thing Nolan needed was for me to fall flat on my face while he was dealing with an upset stomach.

There was a blanket hanging from the ceiling; concealing part of my view of Nolan as he knelt in front of the toilet.

He retched again, and I gritted my teeth:

Determination overriding the debilitating fatigue.

I didn't care how sick I was with the Sleeping Ache Plague. He had helped me in the dungeon, and now he needed me-

The second my feet hit the floor I did, in fact, fall on my face.

I was so lightheaded that my vision went completely black for a moment. It had been a long time since I'd been this weak.

"Are you okay?" Nolan's voice was raw and painful, but there was worry in his tone.

Before he could reach me, I forced myself to sit up. The room spun, and a wave of severe pain shuddered through my torso. Nolan squatted in front of me; placing a cool hand on my shoulder.

"The meds that Krissy gave you were pretty strong, I think." He stared at me in surprise. "You shouldn't even be able to open your eyes right now. Did you fall out of bed?"

I shook my head, and immediately regretted it when the room spun on me again.

"No?" Nolan asked in concern.

"No," I whispered weakly. "You. Sick."

"I'm not sick, Love. Don't worry about me, okay?"

I almost shook my head again, but thought better of it. What little energy I had was slipping away.

"You. Sick."

I was reverting back to the way I used to talk when John had found me on the streets. By the concerned look on Nolan's face; he'd noticed it too.

"I just ate something that didn't agree with me." Nolan reassured me in a low tone. "Or, maybe, I ate too much."

I knew exactly how that felt. I'd thrown up many times from eating the wrong thing, or eating too much, when I was on the streets.

I stared at Nolan in concern, but he ignored my expression and just kissed my forehead.

It was so comforting.

I almost closed my eyes, but I kept them open. I didn't want to fall asleep again. The idea was suddenly quite terrifying. There was no way of knowing if I'd ever wake up again.

"If you didn't fall off the bed then how'd you end up on the floor?"

Nolan grabbed a backpack that was leaning against a couch that was covered in blankets and pillows.

It was the same backpack that Ember and I had packed at Brian's cabin. It must've been where Nolan had gotten the food from.

He noticed me eyeing the supplies.

"I have no idea why, but Ember gave it to me. There's fever reducers in here. I want you to take two of them since you're awake. Do you think you can swallow them?"

It took me a moment to realize that Nolan had asked me a question.

"Yes," I croaked.

Nolan took out the pill bottle and grabbed water from a box in the corner of the room.

I stared at the blood seeping through the back of his shirt. I desperately wanted to know what happened to him, but I didn't ask. I knew I needed to save my strength. Especially if I had to swallow medicine.

Nolan came back to my side and fished two pills out of the bottle.

"We'll try it one at a time, yeah?"

He gently urged me to open my mouth. It was surprisingly hard to move my jaw. It felt like I was swallowing knives. He pressed the bottle of water to my lips. I forced the water and pill down my throat, but couldn't stop myself from whimpering.

"Good job, Love."

I didn't respond. Every move I made nearly drove me to tears. I knew I was dying, and it pissed me off.

I'd been through hell in Dr. Darkwood's lab. He tortured me. He starved me. He put me through medical procedures that brought me to the brink of death. He performed operations that permanently altered my body. None of those things killed me. Yet, here I was-

Dying from a stupid plague.

At some point, Nolan had scooted himself behind me and rested his back against the bed frame. Leaning against the bed had to be excruciating, but he didn't seem to care. He spread his legs behind me and pulled me against him with my back to his front.

I immediately sank into him and rested my head under his chin. I tried to keep my eyes open, but I was just so tired.

"Would you be more comfortable on the bed?"

I barely heard the question.

So tired. So much pain.

"Winter, please." Nolan's arms tightened around me desperately. "There's a cure, okay. You just have to hold out a little longer. Please-"

I didn't hear the rest of what he said. My mind went blank as I drifted off-

My eyes flew open again when something rough jarred my body. I wasn't sure what it was at first, but it felt like I was floating-

Nolan had somehow managed to pick me up.

It hurt to be moved, but it was a small mercy to be on the soft bed again.

"Sorry, Love." Nolan kissed my forehead. "Didn't mean to make it worse."

He tucked the blankets around my shivering form, but it did little to relieve the shakes. I would've given anything to be next to one of Ember's hot fires.

Nolan crawled into the bed next to me. He snaked his arm around my waist and gently pulled me to him. His warmth spread through me and into my shivering limbs. I rested my head on his chest and took a shallow breath.

"The fever reducers will help you. I also cleaned your bullet wounds with sterile sprays while you were sleeping. You're going to be okay."

I listened to him with everything I had. His breath felt warm against my cheek; his gravely voice so comforting. If I could snuggle deeper into his embrace, I would've. But given our proximity that would've been impossible.

"I love you."

Nolan stiffened and glanced down at me. His blue eyes shimmering with rage.

"I spent five months spying on Kain. Then I spent a month being tortured for it, and somehow avoided being executed. I had to watch Cade manhandle you, and strap you down to a gurney. I somehow carried you through the bunker to get us here. *I* didn't go through all of that- *you* didn't go through all of that- just so you could give up now that we are safe."

I ignored him; using what little strength I had to look him in the eyes. His fierce blue irises pierced through me. A warmth I hadn't felt in months made itself home again within me.

At least, this would be a peaceful way to go.

"I love you," I whispered again. "I love you, Nolan."

His jaw clenched; his bottom lip trembling slightly. It was such a subtle movement. I wouldn't have noticed at all if I hadn't been studying his face so closely. Tears clouded his eyes, and his voice wobbled when he spoke.

"Don't do this to me. Don't say goodbye. Not like that-"

"Say it back."

He shook his head, and pressed his lips to my forehead in a light touch.

"Say it back."

I needed to hear him say the words. I needed him to do it now before I fell asleep.

What if I never woke up again?

My throat clogged. I fought back the panic that gripped my chest.

Nolan's weak fingers tilted my chin up and his lips brushed mine. I caught a mild taste of mint before he pulled away.

It wasn't a real kiss, not like the first one he'd given me. This was a gesture of comfort and peace. Just a slight caress to let me know he cared.

Nolan pulled me closer so my head rested on his chest again.

"I won't say something like that when you think you're dying. You'll have to wait until you're better for me to tell you what you already know."

My mind slowly drifted away as I slipped into a dreamless sleep.

Chapter 23: Nolan

Not again.

I would not break down again.

Winter was still breathing for now. All I needed to do was monitor each inhale and exhale. Each time the air filled her lungs, I was able to breathe too.

But if she died on me-

I wouldn't recover from that.

As it was, I wasn't sure if I'd recover from Kain's torture techniques. My back was bleeding again. My wrists were giving off a foul odor. I couldn't even look at them without feeling queazy.

I was lying on my back, which was extraordinarily painful, but I ignored it.

If I moved, it would jostle Winter too much. Motion was the very last thing she needed.

Luckily, we had food and water. Not to mention the antiseptic sprays and fever reducers in Ember's backpack. I didn't know if the fever reducers would help Winter at all, but all I could do was hope.

Now I just needed to get my hands on a syringe of the cure. In order to do that I had to leave the safety of the room-

Leaving Winter sick and alone-

No, I couldn't do that. It was frustrating, but we were stuck here for now. I was betting our lives on John finding us. That was the only way Winter had a chance at surviving this plague. Her fever needed to break soon, but I didn't ask her to lower her temperature again. It was obvious she wouldn't be able to do it anymore.

She tried to say goodbye to me.

I already knew she loved me, but the way she said it sounded too final. Too desperate.

She nearly broke me when she demanded that I say it back.

I leaned toward her ear even though I knew she probably couldn't hear me. I was about to say the words, but something stopped me. I really didn't need to say the words right now. There would be time later-

There *had* to be time later, or none of this was worth it anyway.

"You know how I feel about you." I pressed my lips to her feverish temple as she slept. "There's no way that you don't."

Stupid. So very stupid.

I jerked when a fist pounded on the door.

I froze for a split second before moving Winter off of me.

Her breathing hitched as I slid out from under her. Even in her sleep, she couldn't hide her discomfort.

At least not from me.

Most people probably wouldn't notice the slight quiver in her lips when she breathed. Or the subtle moan she made with each exhale.

I didn't have time to try to be more gentle though.

I rolled off the bed and picked up Willow's handgun-

I'm not safe with this thing.

I couldn't move my fingers properly. It sent a burning pain through my wrist and palm when I tried. The other hand was broken; thanks to Krissy's wooden club.

I had no idea what I was going to do if that door opened. I was too weak to fight. I doubted I'd be able to do something as simple as a stomp kick.

I grunted; forcing my fingers to close around the handle of the weapon. It wasn't that heavy, but it might as well have weighed a hundred pounds when I lifted it.

The door opened with an ominous slam.

Shock made my blood run cold.

Willow!

She looked horrific. As though someone had taken a club and beaten her senseless with it.

Blood coated her hair. Her face was bruised with blood trailing down the sides of her cheeks. Her shirt was torn; revealing the raised *V* scar next to her belly button.

I knew without a doubt that she wouldn't be on her feet if the Vigilante behind her hadn't been holding her tightly against him. She didn't even look like she was fully conscious.

A fresh surge of anger hit me. The added adrenaline allowed me to lift the gun with my broken hand. I barely felt the pain as the man wrap his arm around Willow's exposed torso; keeping her upright.

I didn't know the Vigilante's name, but I'd seen him hanging around the singles plenty of times.

His greasy beard and thick dreadlocks were impossible to miss.

I aimed the gun at the man's face.

"Put the weapon down, Nolan Delany."

I merely stared at him; all of my rage simmering in my eyes.

"I'll kill Willow Rivers." He revealed the gun he was holding and rested it against Willow's waist. "Which would be a pity. I was hoping that Kain would allow me to keep her as a reward for finally finding you. *She's so pretty.*"

A shiver ran down my spine.

"I'll put my gun down after you let Willow go."

The Vigilante wheezed as he laughed; his wide eyes staring manically-

As though he were possessed by a deranged demon.

Willow stirred as the psychotic Vigilante continued laughing; his eyes boring into me.

I was tempted to just shoot him, but there was a chance I'd hit Willow.

"Blue Eyes?" Her weak voice was barely a whisper, but I was surprised that she was lucid. Let alone talking.

The Vigilante tightened his arm around her chest; pressing his face into her hair.

"Let. Her. Go."

The Vigilante wheezed again, as though he was going to have another laughing fit.

I found an opening. A small target directly between the insane man's eyes.

My finger tightened on the trigger and-

My entire arm wobbled with fatigue. I couldn't do it. I couldn't risk Willow's life.

"She feels nice in my arms. I have to enjoy it before the other singles join us."

I absolutely could not let that happen.

When the Vigilantes came charging down the tunnels, our room needed to be impregnable.

Willow opened her eyes. Sheer panic stared back at me.

The agony in her expression fueled my rage as one of her eyes fluttered. It was barely noticeable, but I recognized her signal.

I sighed in resignation; my heart thundering in my chest-

Willow rammed her elbow into the lunatic's gut. He grunted in pain and loosened his grip on her. She expected me to nail him in the forehead with a bullet, but my fingers weren't cooperating.

I swore as I finally got off a shot, but it was too late. My bullet hit the wall where the Vigilante's head had been mere seconds before.

The Vigilante rolled to the floor with Willow underneath him.

She screamed in agony as the man's full weight landed on her. Pinning her between his retched body and the concrete floor.

The gun fumbled out of my hands. Luckily, it didn't go off when it hit the floor. I wasn't about to push my luck by trying to pick it up again.

I never did like guns anyway.

I charged toward the Vigilante on unsteady feet.

I wasn't sure where I got the energy from. Maybe I was just running on pure adrenaline at this point.

My mind was almost blank as my survival instincts took over. I vaguely noticed the Vigilante wrapping his hands around Willow's throat.

I barely registered what was happening. That this piece of garbage was trying to strangle my best friend. All that mattered was the violent predator in front of me. The impending fight I knew I couldn't win.

I clumsily tackled the Vigilante off of Willow. He cursed viciously when we landed on the floor. I rolled away from him; trying in vain to sit up. My back and ribs throbbed, and for a moment I couldn't move.

A moment could change everything in a fight to the death.

The Vigilante grabbed me by the shirt.

The next thing I knew, I was being slammed into the wall. My head hit the concrete with a sickening crack. All the air rushed from my lungs as my vision blurred.

Willow screamed as the Vigilante pulled a knife out of the sheath on his hip.

A piercing pain in my side made me dizzy.

I instinctively grabbed the man's wrist; stopping him from plunging the knife deeper into my abdomen.

The pain was unreal. Unlike anything I'd ever experienced prior to this.

It was then that I realized-

I'd used my broken hand to stop the Vigilante from ending me with that knife. My other arm had somehow gotten pinned behind my back.

I grunted as the man tried to push the blade further into my flesh. My arm shook as I held his wrist with all my strength.

A primal scream escaped me as I pushed against the man's arm. A strength I didn't realize I possessed flared within in.

I felt the tip of the blade pull out of my body. Warm blood immediately surged from the gash, but I concentrated on holding the Vigilante's arm in place.

Willow appeared in front of me; hitting the man in the back of the head with a wooden club. The Vigilante cursed as the knife fell from his hand.

I released my hold on his wrist and slumped to the floor.

Exhausted. I was so horribly exhausted.

I couldn't take the time to recover though.

Willow failed to knock the man out, and he had turned to face her. Before she could swing the wooden club at his head again, he grabbed her wrist. He rammed his fist into her stomach.

Willow's eyes bulged; gagging from the force of the hit. The Vigilante roughly lifted her and threw her to the hard floor. He shifted to straddled her; releasing a maniacal chuckle that sent a chill down my spine.

I struggled to my feet; my vision blurred relentlessly. I tried to listen to what the Vigilante was saying as he pinned Willow's arms above her head. But I couldn't hear anything besides the blood pounding in my ears.

I reached my hand in front of the Vigilante's face and grabbed his beard. I yanked it towards me as I hard as I could.

The Vigilante shrieked in agony as his head snapped to the side.

Of course, I didn't have the strength to break his neck this way. But I couldn't help imagining how satisfying that would've been. Unfortunately, I had to settle for the chunk of facial hair that I managed to pull out of his face.

The Vigilante shoved me away. I stumbled backwards, unavoidably falling on my butt. I still had the chunk of beard in my fist, but I couldn't prise open my fingers to get rid of it.

The Vigilante swore as he advanced on me. Blood dripped from his chin; splattering on his unwashed t-shirt.

Serves him right for not shaving every once in a while.

To my shame, I flinched as the man moved to grab me.

I was in so much pain. I knew I couldn't handle much more of it. I was physically spent. Completely out of my mind with agony.

The Vigilante grabbed a fistful of my hair and-

He exhaled. His breath fogging as the temperature plummeted.

The Vigilante's grip on my hair slackened. His glossy eyes shifted around the room in confusion.

A violent shiver ripped through me as I struggled to turn my head toward Winter.

She somehow sat up on the bed. Her face was strikingly paler than it had been before. Her blue lips appeared hollow next to her sunken cheekbones.

A layer of frost covered the blanket and pillows. Cold radiated off of her in forceful waves-

All that vengeful power directed at the Vigilante that attacked us.

She raised her hand; revealing the icicles that stuck out of her fingertips and knuckles. Her blonde hair was streaked with pure white strands. Flecks of frost covered her cheeks in distinguished snowflake shapes that glistened from the cold surrounding her.

Winter screamed as a beam of frost burst from her hand. The Vigilante collapsed as it hit him directly in the face. Rendering him completely unconscious.

I was mildly surprised that he was still alive, and not a frozen ice statue. I had no doubt, that if Winter wasn't sick, the man would've died the second the frost beam hit him.

The temperature in the room went back to normal in an instant.

Winter slumped back onto the pillows in a dead faint.

I wanted to go to her, to make sure she was okay, but I knew I had to see to Willow first. The fact that Winter had used her powers was a good sign in and of itself.

Willow was bleeding. There was no telling what the Vigilante did to her when he'd had her pinned to the ground. I knew, from the stories she'd told me of her childhood, that being touched by a man was her worst nightmare-

Let alone being pinned down by one.

I studied Winter for a few more seconds. I watched her chest rise and fall as she stared sightlessly at the ceiling. Satisfied that she was okay for now, I turned towards Willow.

Her eyes were closed as she took deep breaths. Her shirt had been shredded and blood stained her skin.

I nearly gagged when I thought about what would've happened to her if I hadn't grabbed that psychopath's beard. She'd been tortured enough in her short life.

"Willow?"

I scooted closer to her. I slumped against the bed frame and rested my hand on Willow's shoulder.

Her eyes snapped open; flinching at my touch. She instantly relaxed when she saw that it was me.

Her brow furrowed as she glared up at me.

"No," she snapped. "I came here to help you, not the other way around, Blue Eyes."

"So, naturally, you brought the most disgusting human being on the planet with you." I mustered up a smirk. "Makes perfect sense."

"Shut up."

She pulled the remains of her shirt together to cover herself. Nothing sensitive was exposed, but Willow was always aware of her modesty.

"Are you okay?" I studied her closely. "Is anything broken?"

Willow hissed as she struggled to her feet. Her face paled, but she seemed to be steady.

"I might have a cracked rib. Mostly bruises and a few scrapes. He jumped me in the hallway right before I reached the door. I'm not sure how he knew about the secret scanner, but he forced me to open it. I figured we could take him out together, but apparently I was wrong."

She looked pointedly at Winter who was still staring at the ceiling.

I tried to get to my feet, but Willow put her hand on my shoulder to hold me down.

"What do you think you're doing? You were stabbed-"

"It's just a cut. I'm fine."

"- flogged, beaten, starved, and who knows what else. Just take it easy, yeah? I'll make sure nothing happens to you. Or Winter."

I sighed and slumped back against the bed.

Willow hurried to the unconscious Vigilante and grabbed his wrists.

"His skin feels like an ice cube."

I struggled to get to my feet again, but stopped when Willow pinned me with a stern glare.

"Don't. Move. Blue Eyes."

I rolled my eyes and forced myself to relax. Luckily, Winter's ice abilities made it so people stayed unconscious for long periods of time. Otherwise, I'd be worried that the Vigilante would wake up while Willow dragged him.

It wasn't easy to watch her work without helping her. I cursed myself for being weak, and distracted myself by checking my knife wound. Fortunately, it wasn't too deep. But there was no way that the Vigilante kept his knife clean.

I'd be battling another infection. I had dozens of infected wounds to deal with anyway. Why not add one more to my collection?

If I survived this bunker, it would be a miracle.

Willow finally got the Vigilante out of our room, and slid the door shut. The light above the door blinked once; indicating that the locks had engaged.

Willow wouldn't leave the same access code after what just happened. It would take Kain's techs a long time to get passed her firewalls that she, no doubt, would put in place.

"I'm gonna clean up and then take a look at you two."

Willow headed to the bathroom. When she disappeared behind the blanket, I forced myself to my feet. Without her glaring at me, it was easier to concentrate on what I needed to do.

I stumbled over to Winter while keeping pressure on my new wound. My swollen fingers were soon slick with warm blood, but I'd lost almost all feeling in my hands.

Winter was still staring at the ceiling. She hadn't moved since she'd collapsed on the pillows. The bedding was damp from the melted frost, but I wasn't concerned about that. It was when I touched her forehead that I knew her predicament had changed.

She was burning up. Her fever much higher than it had been before.

I tore the blanket off of her as fast as I could. I was getting blood on the bedding, but I no longer cared. Winter wouldn't survive long with a fever like that.

"Willow! Start a cold shower!"

"What's wrong?" Willow peeked out from behind the hanging blanket. She wore a fresh shirt and clean pants. It looked like she was in the process of washing her bloody hair in the sink.

It was lucky that she hadn't decided to jump in the shower.

"We need to get Winter's temperature down. She'll die if we don't do it now."

Willow hurried over to the bed and rested her hand on Winter's forehead. She glanced up at me in confusion.

"Yeah, she has a fever. But I don't think it's that bad."

"For her it is. Please, Willow-"

"Okay."

Without waiting for an explanation, Willow hurried back to the bathroom.

I closed my eyes; gathering what little strength I had left. I didn't know if I'd be able to lift her, but I had to try. I doubted Willow wanted any part of helping Winter after what had happened to Lexi, so I knew I had to do this.

I grunted as I lifted Winter off of the bed. She was wearing a tank top and jeans. I wasn't worried about the tank top, but the pants would have to go.

I really hoped that she'd forgive me for this later.

I got her into the bathroom, and Willow glanced up from where she knelt next to the shower. She started the water and let it run until the rusty water turned clear again. It had always been like that, but I didn't care.

It was better than washing in the creek.

Winter was already shivering by the time I set her down on the cold floor. Willow watched with a blank expression as I stripped off her jeans. It wasn't easy doing that, but I didn't think I'd be able to get her out of them if they were soaking wet.

"Winter, I'm putting you in the shower, okay. It's going to be cold, but it'll help you."

Winter's eyes were closed now. I wasn't sure if she was hearing anything I said, or was aware of what was going on. I hated doing this, but I couldn't live with myself if I didn't do everything possible to save her.

I moved to lift her again when Willow put a hand on my arm.

"Nolan, stop for a second."

I couldn't help but stare at her. She'd only ever called me *'Nolan'* when we were communicating in code in the dungeon.

"Why? Why do you care about her so much?"

I stared at Willow for a second longer before blinking in confusion. My mind went through all the possible code phrases that we came up with in the past, but I was drawing a blank. I was just so tired. So freaking tired.

"I'm not speaking in code. I'm not trying to confuse you, Blue Eyes. I'm just trying to understand. What is it that you see in her?"

My mind had to catch up for a moment as I pondered Willow's question.

"Winter brought me out of a very dark place when she came into my life. She insisted on spending every waking hour with me. I can't tell you how annoying it was. She was my shadow, and it drove me absolutely crazy for a while.

"Eventually, I realized that the only reason she annoyed me was because she was so *happy*. She had ample reason to hate life, but she didn't. She looked at everything as though it was her first time seeing it. She never complained when things got tough. She didn't let me push her away. And, trust me, I tried everything to get her to hate me. It wasn't long before I realized that I needed her in my life a lot more than she needed me."

I wasn't into sharing my feelings, but Willow needed to hear something good about Winter. She needed to understand that Winter wasn't just the girl that had been forced to killed her friend.

Willow nodded after my longwinded explanation.

"She saved you from the Vigilante that attacked us."

I nodded tiredly. "She saved *both* of us."

Willow shook her head.

"She didn't save me. She saved you. That alone is enough for me."

Willow took a deep breath and gently shifted Winter into the shower.

Winter gasped in shock. I took a hold of her hand in a feeble attempt to comfort her. She squeezed my fingers in a death grip, but I refused to let go despite how much it hurt.

"Is it the Sleeping Ache?"

"I'm pretty sure it is. I need to get her the cure, but-"

"I've got one dose in my pack. It won't be enough to cure her, since she seems to have a bad case of it. But it'll keep her alive until John can get here."

"Wait, what?"

Willow patted my arm and ducked behind the hanging blanket. She came back a few minutes later with a needle and syringe.

"I've gotta inject it in her leg."

Ignoring the spray of cold water, Willow inched forward with the needle.

Then, without warning, Winter let out a horrific scream.

Chapter 24: John

Escaping the bunker was easier than breaking in.

The Vigilantes were completely useless with their leader out of commission, which I intended to use to my advantage.

My plan wasn't to find George, since I knew I wouldn't be able to. He was Special Forces, and basically the king of hide-and-seek. Not to mention the fact that he probably had traps set up by now.

I really had no desire to experience being caught in one of those.

I found a place of my own to hide and pulled out my communicator. Luckily, George answered fairly quickly.

"Yeah, Boss."

I told him everything that happened since Willow and I entered the bunker. He listened without comment until I told him that I'd taken a round in the shoulder.

"You bleeding bad?"

"No, its just a graze." I glanced down at the bandage I was wrapping around the wound. "We've got three teenagers locked in a room in that bunker. We need to find a way to get them out."

"That's *if* Willow made it to the room." George grumbled over the communicator.

"We should give her more credit than that, George." I gritted my teeth as I tied off the bandage. "Have you found any Vigilantes in the forest?"

"Yeah, a few." George's tone sounded grim. "I had to take them out though. They seemed like the Feral Moron type. They didn't give me much choice."

"At this point, I don't really care what happens to them. They follow Kain blindly. I'm not sure if we'd be able to trust them after we take care of Kain anyway. It's almost like they're enthralled somehow."

"Been drinking that tempting Kool-aid." George sighed. "I've had to deal with a few cults before. It's never pretty."

"Yeah." It was challenging not to dwell on the cults I'd dealt with in the past as well.

"We'll get Nolan, Winter, and Willow. Then we'll take out Kain and get his stash of the cure. It's my understanding that, for those sick with the Sleeping Ache, they'll need more than one dose to cure them. I doubt that cooler Willow gave us will be enough with how many are sick in the community. I'm going to talk to Eliza and find out how things are going. Come and find me, yeah?"

"Sure thing, Boss. Watch your back."

I signed off and made sure the tracker on my tablet was activated for George to find me.

I called Eliza.

After a few rings, Shane's face popped up on my tablet.

His eyes were shaded with a bluish hue; making him look like he'd been punched, repeatedly, in the face. His cheeks were pale in contrast. Even his hair looked dull and stringy.

I had no doubt that, if I could see his entire body, he'd be skin and bones. The poor kid didn't have much weight to spare as it was.

He was overextending his powers.

"Shane, are you alright?"

"Hey, John." He croaked before clearing his throat. "Yeah. I'm fine. I was just sleeping. Eliza forced me to take a break."

"Good." I replied with a nod. "You need breaks. Food and rest are really important for you."

Shane's face paled slightly and he cleared his throat again.

"A few more kids died a couple hours ago." Shane's voice broke and his lips quivered. "I tried, John. But I couldn't-"

"Shane," I interrupted him. I knew he would go on and on about how badly he thought he'd failed. I didn't want to be harsh, but information was vital now. "Which ones?"

"Becky, Milo, and Trevor."

I blinked back tears.

We'd lost another orphan, and Fredrick lost both of his sons. I couldn't let myself worry about that now though.

"I thought they were doing okay, at first. But every time I tried to take their sickness, I started getting weaker. Now I can't help anyone. Tamara and Fredrick are both sick. They can't keep Alex, Tessa, Josh, and Ben anymore. So I'm staying with them for now. I tried to get them to let me take care of Lizzy too. But with Trevor and Milo gone- They don't want me anywhere near them now. They've asked me to stop coming to their cabin, but I can't exactly leave now. Not with having to take care of Tessa and the others."

I gritted my teeth and took a deep breath. Shane was more than just overtasked. He looked like he was sick himself, but that was probably because he'd overextended himself. Hopefully with some rest he'd be able to recover.

"Any other casualties that you know of?"

"A few elderly Scavengers have died, but I don't remember their names."

"Where's Eliza?"

If Shane was staying with the orphans, that meant he was probably in Tamara and Fredrick's living room.

And, if Eliza was there, that meant she was sick or was going to be.

"She's checking on Tamara, Fredrick, and Lizzy. Fredrick tried to tell her to leave them alone, but she's not listening."

"Have you seen Leif and James?" I asked after I managed to calm myself down enough to talk again. "They were supposed to bring you guys the cure. They have a small cooler full of it. They don't have enough to make everyone better, but it'll be enough to keep them alive."

Shane sighed and nodded.

"Yeah, John. They came. Eliza gave a dose to all the healthy Scavengers in the quarantine zone. Then she gave what was left to the sick, but it doesn't seem to be working. We need more of it."

Shane's eyes filled with tears.

"Tessa is so sick. I'm terrified that she'll be next. I can't lose another kid. I can't-"

"Shane," I interrupted him quickly before he could start spiraling. "I need you to listen to me, okay?"

He took a deep breath and nodded.

"I'm going to get you more doses of the cure." I kept my tone soothing, despite the anxiety in my gut. "Tessa is going to be fine. But what I need you to do- what *Tessa* needs you to do- is get some sleep. Maybe take the life force of a few trees. Get yourself back to normal. That's an order, Shane."

He nodded in agreement.

"I need to speak with Eliza. Don't get up to find her. Is she close enough for you to call for her?"

Shane nodded again and turned away from the screen. I was relieved to see that he didn't exert himself more than necessary. He called for Eliza, and her face appeared on the screen in front of me within seconds.

"John." Her eyes widened when she saw me on her screen. "There's blood all over you. Are you okay?"

I ignored her question and got straight to the root of my concerns.

"Did you give yourself a dose of the cure?"

Eliza nodded vigorously, and I sighed in relief.

"It was the first thing I did when Leif handed me the cooler. I tried to give some to Shane too, but he said that he didn't need it. I'm regretting that now. He doesn't seem to be doing well."

It was so good to see Eliza's face. I couldn't help but simply stare at the screen in my hands. It seemed like it had been weeks, rather than days, since I'd seen her. Touched her.

"How are you feeling?"

"I'm okay. Why are you covered in blood?"

I quickly explained the situation to her and her face paled slightly. Especially when she heard about Willow being Leif's long lost sister.

"Leif isn't going to be happy that you let his sister go off alone in the bunker, John."

I sighed; rubbing my eyes.

"I didn't have much of a choice. You know I wouldn't have done that if Nolan and Winter didn't need immediate help. I trust Willow and her abilities enough to get to them. To help them so that I can get rid of Kain."

Eliza pressed her lips together in concern as she studied me through the screen.

"I need you to promise me that you'll get out of there if things don't go your way. Even if you have to leave Kain alive and the cure behind. Get yourself out. No matter what."

I had just promised Shane that I would get the cure. I wasn't going to go back on that promise. No matter how much my wife needed me to if it came down to it.

"I'm going to get the cure," I told her evenly. "And we'll all get out alive. We will get this done. Have a little faith, Eliza."

She squeezed her eyes shut. A single tear dripped down her cheek.

"I'm just so damn tired, John. Tired of losing people. I can't lose you. I won't survive it."

I wished I was there with her, so I could hold her. I closed my eyes for a moment and took a shaky breath.

"You're not going to lose me. Nolan survived Kain. Winter is alive. We will all be together again soon. I know it."

Eliza blinked back the moisture in her eyes; nodding solemnly.

"I love you. You come back as soon as you can, alright?"

"I will." I smiled reassuringly. "I love you too. Get some rest."

Eliza nodded again and we said goodbye.

I blew out a shaky breath when the screen on my tablet went blank. There was a reason why I didn't keep in contact with Eliza while I was on missions. I worried so much about her, and it was hard to concentrate on the task at hand.

I forced myself to put Eliza, Shane, and the sick Scavengers out of my mind while I came up with a strategy to take out Kain.

It didn't take much longer for George to find me. I noticed his eyes flick to my bullet wound, but he didn't seem to be concerned.

Rightly so, since it wasn't much more than a gash. It burned like crazy, but other than that it wasn't a big deal.

"You got a plan, Boss?"

"Yeah, but it's got a major hole in it that might get us killed if I'm not right about something."

George raised an eyebrow. "What's that?"

"Ember." I ran a hand through my hair. "She's a wild card. I'm fairly certain that Kain is related to her somehow, but she seems to hate him. So far she's done all she can to thwart Kain's plans. She indicated that she wanted me and Kain to get over our differences. Take Amanda Lynch out together."

"Why do you think she's related to Kain?" George asked in confusion. "Far as I know, he doesn't have family."

"But Brian was his nephew," I pointed out. "Did you know about him?"

George shook his head, but didn't say anything else.

"Kain and Ember might not be related, but it's just the feeling I had when I saw them together. Kain was betrayed when Ember sided with Amanda Lynch originally. But even that seems like a gray area. I'm beginning to think that Ember has been forced by her mother to do some awful things. Now she wants to see her mother taken out. But Kain just sees Ember as a traitor."

George nodded, but still seemed confused.

"So, what does this have to do with us clearing the bunker?"

"We already know that Ember has rigged the place with explosives. So that tells me that she might want Kain dead too. If I'm wrong though, she might help Kain kill us when we confront him. She's extremely dangerous. I don't think we'll be able to take her out if she gets the chance to use her fire against us.

"What if this whole thing has been a setup? Maybe Ember made it look like she was rigging the bunker to throw us off track since they knew Willow was monitoring the footage."

George sat quietly for a moment as he processed what I was saying.

"Honestly, Boss, that sounds exactly like something Simon would do. Ember could be pulling our chain to drag us right into a trap. I could be wrong, but I'm thinking that we can't trust this fire girl."

I nodded in agreement, but I still felt like I was missing something. I hated it when I got gut feelings, but didn't really know what they meant. Something just wasn't right when it came to Ember. I needed to figure out what it was. In order to do that, we couldn't kill her. At least not yet.

"Okay." I blew out a frustrated breath. "Here's what we are going to do: we're going to go in there and quietly take out the infirmary. I don't want the injured people killed, but anyone else that resists us is fair game. Got me?"

George nodded in agreement, and I continued.

"We'll lock Kain and Cade into the dungeon, and figure out what we'll do with them later. As for the rest of the Vigilantes, we could give them a chance to surrender, or we'll take them out. I don't want any of them escaping, since they know where the bunker is. We can't have them running to Amanda Lynch, or getting caught by her Militia, with that kind of information."

George nodded again and gave me a slight smile.

"It's nothing like I would've planned, Boss. I like it."

I stared at him in confusion.

"Remember how I said that Simon knows me? Well, he'll be expecting me to take charge of the planning. He assumes that you'd delegate that to me since I've got Special Forces training. See, if I were in charge, we would've taken out the control room first. Make sure all the tech nerds were dead. I'd take control of the bunker's entire system before heading to the infirmary. But you just wanna go straight into the lion's den to grab Kain, and his buddy Cade, without any fanfare. I'm guessing Kain won't expect that. He'll have most of his Vigilantes protecting the control room."

I chuckled at George's longwinded explanation.

"Well, I figure if we cut off the head of the snake the body will eventually die."

"You figured right, Boss." George grinned earnestly. "Now let's do this thing and get our soldiers back, yeah?"

I nodded and let George pull me to my feet.

The entrance to the bunker was one of the most suspicious things I'd ever seen.

There were no guards and the door was wide open.

I couldn't hear any natural forest noises either, which only made me more paranoid. For all we knew, we could be surrounded by Vigilantes right now.

"I'm still not seeing any activity." George's voice whispered in my earpiece.

We were only about twelve feet away from each other, but we needed to keep as quiet as possible. I took another look through my binoculars.

"Yeah, me neither. It wasn't like this when Willow and I entered. When I escaped I shut the door behind me. There's no way this isn't a setup."

George grunted in agreement.

"Well, Boss, I got tear gas. I could get closer and toss it in the entrance. See what happens?"

I shook my head, but then remembered that he wouldn't see me.

"No. I don't want any excessive noise."

Before George could reply, the bushes rustled behind me.

I was laying on my belly in the brush, but I was on my knees with my gun in hand a split second later. I almost squeezed the trigger before I saw that it was Ember.

She was leaning against a thick tree. The shadows covered most of her, but I could tell that it was her from the moonlight illuminating her unruly dark hair.

"If you don't want excessive noise then why are you talking to yourself?" she asked dryly.

I didn't reply. I just kept my gun aimed at her chest. She didn't seem bothered by it, on the contrary, she seemed rather relieved.

"I'm glad you're not trusting me easily." Ember continued as though we were having a conversation. "It means that you're being smart."

I got to my feet without lowering the gun.

"Get on your knees and put your hands on your head."

"Crap," George whispered in my ear. "Sit tight, Boss. I'll be there in a sec."

I knew George wouldn't give away his position to Ember. She would never know that a trained sniper would have her in his sights while we talked.

That knowledge allowed me to keep my hands from shaking. The memory of the burns she'd given me whispered in the back of my mind.

Ember took a step away from the tree and into the moonlight. I nearly gaped in horror when she knelt before me, but I kept my composure.

Her face was covered in cuts and newly formed bruises. She was shivering as though she was cold. Blood soaked her arms and tank top. Her normally fierce blue eyes were dull and gray.

"You look like hell."

Ember chuckled humorlessly. "I feel even worse."

"You and I are gonna have a chat. If you lie to me, you're dead. Got it?"

Ember nodded as she put her hands on her head. It was obvious that the motion was painful for her. I wanted to know what happened, but I didn't need to get into that right now when there was more pressing issues.

"Why is the bunker open?"

"I didn't shut it when I made my escape. I'm not sure why the Vigilante's kept it open. They were right on my heels."

I ignored her attempt to steer the conversation in a different direction and kept on topic.

"Do you know if Willow made it to her room?"

Ember sighed. "I have no idea, John. I wasn't able to see where you and Willow went. I promised Nolan that I wouldn't blow the bunker like I wanted to, so I escaped instead. Hoping to find you."

That was interesting information, but I didn't know if it was fact or fiction. I really wished I had a portable lie detector right now. I really missed my detective gadgets that I used to have. Now, I had to rely on body language and facial expressions. So far, I was inclined to believe Ember. But I wasn't willing to trust her until I had more information.

"Is Kain in the infirmary?"

Ember blew out a breath and lowered her arms. I cocked my gun and took a step toward her threateningly. She grimaced and put her hands back on her head.

"Keep your hands there," I ordered sternly. "Now answer me."

"I told you I don't know anything," Ember said shakily. "I tried to get Kain to trust me, but he won't."

"Why would you want to do that?" I asked, letting her steer the conversation.

I was interested to see where this would go. Maybe it would give me more information about Ember as a person, since I was about ninety percent certain that she wasn't lying to me.

"Because he's my father," Ember bit out angrily.

The confirmation of their familial relationship stunned me, but I didn't lower my gun.

"What makes you think I'd believe that one, Ember?"

Her eyes clouded over and she let out a small sob. I had seen her act before when I'd first met her. She had tried to trick me into thinking that she was a street orphan, so I knew when she was lying.

She wasn't lying now.

The fact that she was crying made me lower my gun. I knew George would still have her in his sights until I told him to stand down. But for now, I wanted Ember to think that she was safe.

I couldn't help but consider the kind of childhood Ember endured. If the way Kain had choked her in front of me was any indication; it must've been horrible.

But I couldn't let those thoughts influence the decision I had to make regarding Ember right now. There were millions of people throughout history that had messed up childhoods. Most of them didn't become kidnappers and murderers because of it.

Ember was still a wild card as far as I was concerned.

"You're not going to believe anything I tell you." She wiped the tears from her cheeks. "And I don't blame you. I've done terrible things. But if you kept an open mind, and let me explain, then maybe you'd understand."

"Understand what?" I asked tersely.

"Why I did what I did."

"Nothing could ever make me understand that." I strapped my gun to my shoulder. "But it'd be nice if I knew the reason why you led a bunch of orphans to their deaths."

Ember visibly flinched; tears racing down her cheeks.

That's when I knew, without a doubt, that she wasn't playing me. No fifteen year old could act so convincingly unless they had anti personality disorder. Which I was pretty sure Ember didn't have.

"Dr. Darkwood reprogramed my brain. He didn't take my memories away, but he attempted to brainwash me. I was a very rebellious child. My mother always hated that about me. She wanted to control me. Dr. Darkwood wasn't able to completely make me compliant to Amanda's orders. I fought so hard against them. They had to constantly put me through these horrific treatments. It was almost like being hypnotized, but a thousand times worse.

"Amanda Lynch forced me to kidnap those kids. The only time I was able to fight against her orders, was when I met you and Winter. I knew who you both were. You guys gave me hope. Hope that, maybe, I'd be able to break away. That I'd be able to fight Amanda too. But when I realized you were talking about me in sign language-"

Ember shivered at the memory.

"Something in my brain snapped. I couldn't control my own body. I couldn't control the words that came from my mouth. I attacked you; nearly killed you. Amanda always wins. No matter how hard I try to fight her."

She took a shaky breath and wiped more tears from her eyes.

"After Shane killed Dr. Darkwood, the treatments stopped. I was able to escape with most of my sanity intact. Amanda Lynch has been trying to capture me for a few months now. I decided to turn to my father for help. Instead, I ended up in Brian's torture cage as penance for choosing Amanda over Kain. All I wanted was refuge with the Vigilantes. Imagine my surprise when I realized my father was just as evil as my psychotic mother."

Ember shifted from her knees and sat on her butt. She pulled her knees up to her chest and wrapped her arms around her legs. A breeze blew through the trees and ruffled her black hair.

She shivered violently.

"You might as well just shoot me now, John." Ember's teeth chattered as she spoke. "I'm going to die eventually. Nobody wants me. At least this way, it would be a quick death and I wouldn't die alone."

I merely stared at Ember with no outward emotion.

I couldn't show it to her right now with the situation we were in, but I felt horrible for her. I wanted to ask George what he thought about her story.

"Stand down."

Ember's eyes shot to mine in confusion.

"Are you thinking she's telling the truth, Boss?"

I held up two fingers, and George grunted in my ear.

"Can't say I don't believe her," he replied. "But I'm not completely certain yet. I'll just continue keeping an eye on her. Maybe she can help us get into the bunker."

I nodded twice in agreement as Ember continued to stare at me.

"I'm not going to shoot you. So don't ask me to do that again, understand? It pisses me off when kids ask me to do that."

Ember rolled her eyes and looked away from me.

There was that spunk that I was used to seeing from her. I decided to view that as a good sign.

"If you're telling me the truth, then you need to prove yourself to me." I kept my tone terse and firm, despite how my heart broke for her. "You're going to get me into that bunker, and help me put your father in a cage of his own."

Ember's eyelids drooped slightly, but she didn't shy away from the task I'd just given her. She squared her shoulders and jutted out her chin in determination.

"What is it you want me to do?"

For the first time since I'd met her, I gave her a genuine smile.

Chapter 25: Winter

I forced my jaw to relax as Dr. Darkwood inserted another needle into my arm.

I had clenched my teeth so much during this procedure that I was worried I'd chip a tooth. I'd done that once before and Dr. Darkwood had been angry that he had to fix my damaged teeth. The dental repair had been excruciating to endure-

I had no desire to go through that again.

Another needle poked into my leg this time, and I shuddered.

Another poke into my other leg. Another poke into my wrist. Another one in my upper arm.

It went on and on until finally the tears escaped my eyes. Dr. Darkwood didn't like seeing me cry either, but I just couldn't help it.

I knew what all of the needles meant-

I didn't know if I could endure another round in the tub.

I could hear the ice machine working as Dr. Darkwood filled the tub with countless chunks of solid ice. The water was already running, but I was determined to ignore it for as long as I could. There was no use in panicking before procedures. It just drained me of much needed energy.

Besides, it's not like Dr. Darkwood would ever stop what he was doing just because I was scared.

I had to be tough. I had to survive. I'd endured this long. I would endure this day too. If I couldn't fight back with my fists, then I would fight back with my resolve and determination to survive. Nothing Dr. Darkwood could do to me would kill me. I knew that because I'd already survived this long.

I'd already survived this long-

I jolted out of my spiraling thoughts as the bed moved under me. Dr. Darkwood quickly put the oxygen mask over my nose and mouth before I was lowered into the water.

I'd heard Dr. Darkwood talk about sensory deprivation tanks before. Then he'd explained that this wasn't exactly sensory deprivation. He still wanted me to feel one thing and one thing only: cold.

Freezing to death kind of cold.

When my bare skin hit the ice water, my whole body tensed for the agony. No matter how much I tried to relax, my body just wasn't having it. I strained against the straps that bound me to the bed as my face was submerged. I gasped in air from the oxygen mask, but it didn't feel like it was enough.

I was suffocating.

I was drowning in this frigid ice water.

But I wasn't really. I could take another breath just fine. Despite how panicked I was, I forced myself to count my breaths.

Inhale, one. Exhale, two. Inhale, three. Exhale, four.

I continued counting until my cold body finally went numb. I wasn't panicking anymore, but it was only because I couldn't feel anything now.

My mind drifted thoughtlessly when my body no longer had the energy to shiver. Maybe I would die this time. Maybe Dr. Darkwood would finally let me slip into death, so I could finally be free of this misery.

But, like always, something within me screamed to keep fighting. To keep going until there was no tomorrow. To show Dr. Darkwood that he would never beat me, no matter what he did to me. He could perform whatever experiments that he wanted on my body. He could take every precious memory that I had.

But he would never break my spirit.

The blindfold over my eyes started to really irritate me. I couldn't see anything. I couldn't feel anything anymore. Maybe this was what Dr. Darkwood meant by sensory deprivation.

Perhaps, I would eventually go insane, but for now I would rely on numbers to keep my mind occupied. It had helped me in the past and I knew it would help me now.

I counted backwards from three thousand. Repeating the process every time I got to zero.

Finally, Dr. Darkwood pulled me out of the tub. I had long since stopped shivering, but there was a dull ache in my limbs that wouldn't go away. I had a feeling it was from the countless needles that he inserted into my skin. I still didn't know what he was injecting me with, but I knew better than to let myself think about it too much.

The only thing that matter was counting.

But the numbers escaped me when I saw another needle coming at me. I didn't even remember Dr. Darkwood taking the blindfold off of me, but I saw that needle-

I shrieked in terror.

Dr. Darkwood jumped away from me, startled. He'd never done that before, but I didn't take the time to dwell on it.

I needed to get away from that needle! I had to get away! I already had too many needles in me and one more would kill me! I just knew it!

Then a man was there. I didn't know where the man came from, but he had no face.

No mouth. No eyes. No nose. No ears.

The faceless man didn't have any hair. Not even eyebrows.

I screamed in terror when he reached for me with mangled hands and broken fingers. There was no doubt in my mind that I was being attacked by a real life monster.

Whatever Dr. Darkwood had injected into me was, clearly, giving me an insane trip.

I tried to get out of the straps that kept me bound to the table, but my weak limbs ached. I whimpered when the faceless man touched me. Even though it didn't have a mouth, it still spoke to me in a soothing tone. I couldn't understand what the voice was saying, but the gentleness was disturbing.

Everything was disturbing here.

Dr. Darkwood smiled as the faceless man held me close to him. I still wasn't sure how I got free of the straps, but I tried to fight the faceless man off of me. I screamed, thrashing around fiercely.

The faceless man was too strong.

The soft voice kept trying to calm my terror, but I wouldn't let it! I was going to die the second Dr. Darkwood put that needle in my leg!

Suddenly, the needles in my body vanished.

Where did they go? Did the faceless man magically get rid of those too, like he did the straps that tied me to the gurney?

It didn't matter. I couldn't let Dr. Darkwood inject me again. I screamed as he inched closer, but the faceless man wouldn't let me move. The needle pierced my leg, and I shrieked in terrified defeat. I couldn't take another poke. I couldn't take anymore poison in my body.

Maybe I really would die here in this lab. In the arms of a faceless monster that held me close to him.

No, I wouldn't die-

All I had to do was continue counting.

"Three thousand, two thousand nine hundred and ninety-nine, two thousand nine hundred and ninety-eight, two thousand nine hundred and ninety-seven…"

The faceless man joined in counting down with me.

Then Dr. Darkwood joined in.

"Two thousand nine hundred and ninety-six, two thousand nine hundred and ninety-five-"

Chapter 26: Nolan

A flash of cold hit me a split second after Winter screamed.

I withdrew my hand from hers; frostbite rapidly covering my wounds.

Willow stumbled backwards, but I was too preoccupied with Winter's distress to truly process my friend's terror.

The temperature went back to normal just as quickly as the cold flash hit. I shuddered when Winter screamed again; tears leaking from her closed eyes.

Willow stared at me in horror when I scooted closer to Winter. She was shivering under the stream of cold water, but I ignored the frigid droplets that splattered on me. I couldn't feel much anyway.

I was in too much shock.

Winter ceased screaming, but her lips were moving soundlessly. Then she started mumbling incoherently.

I brought my ear as close as I could to her mouth without touching her.

"What's she saying?" Willow stood nearby with that same horrified look on her face.

I listened for a few more seconds; making sure I was actually hearing what I thought I was. I had hoped that I was wrong-

She was counting.

Winter was currently going through hell, and I didn't know what to do to help her.

I choked back the sob that tried to escape me.

"Two thousand nine hundred and eighty-seven, two thousand nine hundred and eighty-six, two thousand nine hundred and eighty-five-"

The numbers were more of a mumble, but I heard it as clear as day.

"She's counting backwards from three thousand. She's having a really bad flashback."

"Why is she counting? Does she have flashbacks often?"

I didn't want to talk about Winter's flashbacks at the moment, so I ignored Willow's question about that for now.

"She would count backwards from three thousand during some of the more gruesome experiments that Dr. Darkwood made her endure in his lab. I'm going to try to touch her now. If I can get her calmed down enough you're going to have to be quick with that-"

I nodded toward the needle so I didn't have to say it out loud.

Willow nodded in understanding, and I tried to pull off my shirt. She ended up helping me. Apparently, my hands were done doing anything useful for the day.

Once I was down to my boxers, I scooted closer to Winter. She was still counting, and stiff as a board sitting under the cold shower. Her cheeks were flushed, but the rest of her face was completely pale. Her breaths came rapidly, practically hyperventilating.

I had seen her in the thralls of a flashback before, but there was something different about this one. She was counting, for one thing, and she hadn't frozen anything near her with her ice. I was pretty sure that she tried, since my hands were frost burned, but the Sleeping Ache had made her powers incredibly weak.

The fact that she was counting scared the crap out of me. She had confided in me that she only did that when she was going through something she didn't think she would survive.

"Hey, Love." I didn't touch her yet. She could flash cold at any second. "It's Nolan. I'm here. I'm right here, and you're safe with me."

Winter went rigid again and she screamed. I felt Willow jerk behind me in surprise, but I remained as calm as I could.

"No one is going to hurt you. I'm trying to help you. My friend, Willow, is here. She's trying to help you too. You're safe with us. I promise."

It seemed like the more I talked, the more she screamed. Even though it was dangerous, I finally grabbed her shoulders and scooted behind her in the cold shower.

The water took my breath away, but I didn't care. I wrapped my arms around her chest; shivering violently.

Winter tried to fight me off, but I held her closer to me. I wrapped my legs around her; keeping her still so Willow could safely administer the cure. Luckily, she was able to be quick about it.

I glanced down at Winter's wrist and saw the IV needle was still there. I'd planned to keep it there in case Winter needed fluids and medicines later-

There was no way I was making her keep the needle in her wrist with what she was going through. She would have to get more doses of the cure, eventually. Hopefully, she'd be in a better frame of mind when that happened.

Winter's screaming morphed into hyperventilating once more.

I truly didn't know what to do.

This was the most horrific flashback she'd ever experienced; the Sleeping Ache messing with her mind. I'd learned in school of some plague victims that had severe hallucinations during the sickness. It usually meant they were close to death.

Tears filled my eyes as I prayed that the cure would give her more time. I couldn't lose her, especially not like this.

"I'm going to take that out." Willow pointed at the IV needle in Winter's wrist. "Maybe it'll help her snap out of it."

I wasn't surprised that Willow had noticed it was there. Hardly anything ever escaped her observance. Including the tears that fell from my eyes. I was hoping that the water from the shower would conceal them, but no such luck.

Willow wiped my eyes with a dry cloth and kissed my forehead reassuringly. Shock expanded in my chest, but Willow merely gave me a pat on the shoulder.

Slowly, she reached over to remove the needle. Winter tensed in my arms, but she didn't scream. Once the needle was removed, Winter began counting down from three thousand again.

I bent down and pressed my lips to the side of her head. Leaning in closer to her ear, I started counted with her.

I was surprised when Willow joined in. I glanced over at her and she gave me a small shrug. The concern in her eyes brought fresh tears to mine.

Tears fell as I continued counting. Even when Winter stopped counting, I kept at it until I got down to the low hundreds. My body was numb, even though Willow had turned off the cold water and wrapped us both in a blanket.

I finally stopped counting when I noticed that Winter's eyes were open.

She tensed slightly and groaned. She slumped further into my chest and rested the back of her head on my shoulder. She took a couple of breaths before trying to sit up again.

I tightened my arm around her waist; urging her to relax against me.

"It's okay, Love. Just rest, yeah?"

"Are we in a shower?"

"Uh huh." I rested my head against the cold tile. This was my favorite way to sit. It didn't put any added pressure on my back. It was extremely uncomfortable, but at least I could breath sitting like this.

"You scared me." I tightened my arms around her in emphasis.

"I had a flashback, didn't I?"

"I couldn't get you out of it. I didn't know what to do."

"I'm fine." She sounded so nonchalant. As though nothing could ever faze her. But I knew the truth.

"I need you to tell me about it."

I knew she didn't want to talk about it, but I needed to know the hell she just went through. I needed to have a better idea of what we were dealing with if she had another flashback.

"I don't remember."

"Bull crap," I whispered sternly. "Tell me."

She sighed in exhaustion, but I kept prodding her until she finally told me about the ice water tub. The countless needles that Dr. Darkwood stabbed her with. Then she told me about some faceless freak that kept trying to touch her.

"Did Dr. Darkwood actually have a faceless man?"

"I don't think so. I'm pretty sure I made that up. I think it was a flashback mixed with a nightmare."

Winter shivered, and I kissed the side of her head.

"I'm so sorry. I told Willow to give you a dose of the cure, and that sent you back there-"

"Not your fault, Nolan."

Willow pushed aside the blanket that gave the bathroom privacy. She looked a bit better than she had before. I assumed that she probably took a nap and ate something. Her hair was still disheveled and she looked stiff when she moved. But that was to be expected with the fight she'd had with that nasty Feral Moron.

"The cure won't be the only thing that saves you." Willow gave us both a stern glare. "You're both gonna die if you don't eat something. Blue Eyes, I'm pretty sure you'll bleed to death if you don't let me stitch you up."

I had almost forgotten about the gash from the Feral Moron's blade. I still hadn't cleaned it either.

Winter stiffened and turned to look at me.

"I knew you were injured, but I couldn't ask before." She studied my face intently. "How bad?"

I was about to reassure her that it wasn't that bad, but Willow interrupted me.

"Don't ask him that, Winter, he'll just lie to you." Willow snatched the blanket that she'd wrapped us in a while ago, exposing my bare torso.

I narrowed my eyes at her when Winter gasped.

"Glare all you want, Blue Eyes."

I would've sneered at her, but I was too tired.

Tears filled Winter's eyes as she stared at my bruised chest. She hadn't even gotten a look at the rest of my injuries yet, and she was already horrified.

But it would've been idiotic not to be honest with her about my condition.

"I was tortured pretty badly when Kain imprisoned me."

Her face paled further somehow, but I continued on before I lost my nerve.

"Do you know what flogging or whipping is?" She shook her head; her lips quivering. "Well, they did that to me. My back is covered with lacerations."

"Which are infected, by the way." Willow stepped behind me to get a better look.

Winter sway slightly and I held her a bit tighter.

"You're really not helping, Willow."

"Yeah, well someone's gotta get you angry, Blue Eyes." She smirked, but she could hide the worry in her eyes. "Otherwise, you'll be dead by morning."

Winter uttered a quiet sob before pressing her face into my bare chest. Willow finally seemed to notice how all of this was affecting her. She dropped the playful banter.

"I was just kidding, Winter. Blue Eyes is going to be fine."

"They thought you were dead," Winter whispered without acknowledging Willow. "Eliza cried for you everyday. John only cried two times, but I knew he was hurting just as much as Eliza was. I refused to believe that you were dead. I just knew, if anyone could survive, it would be you."

I was so stunned, I couldn't speak. I couldn't even move.

Eliza had cried for me every day? I couldn't imagine a strong woman like her crying over someone like me. And John-

No.

I couldn't even think about my brother.

"Shane kept telling me that you were still alive, but I knew that he didn't really believe that. I tried to find a way to get to you, but I failed."

I finally glanced down at her; urging her to look up at me. When she met my eyes, I held her gaze for a moment.

"We are together now. You didn't fail, Love."

Willow gathered her first aid supplies from the bathroom cabinet in an attempt to give us some privacy.

"Besides, I'm the one that failed. I was supposed to spy on Kain, but I ended up imprisoned. I would've been executed if Ember hadn't brought you into the bunker and stopped the proceedings."

Winter's eyes lit up at the mention of Ember.

"Did she really leave us that backpack full of food and medicine, or did I hallucinate that?"

I nodded, giving her a small smile.

"Maybe we misjudged her. Or maybe she just feels guilty for bringing you into this hellhole."

Willow walked toward us with the first aid kit slung to her shoulder, and stood in front of the shower.

"Alright you two, time to break up this reunion. Winter is probably going to crash again soon, and she needs to eat something first. Blue Eyes, you are in *serious* need of medical attention."

I grimaced at the thought of that. It would inevitably be agonizing, and I really needed a break from the constant pain.

"Don't you have some techie computer stuff that you gotta do?"

"Who do you think I am, Blue Eyes? I already took care of everything. I even have John on video right now. We can't talk to him, but he's on the security footage. You don't have to worry about Kain's people finding him. I put their cameras on a loop."

I stopped trying to listen to her when she delved into some more tech lingo that my tired brain didn't understand. I did, however, understand that John was here in the bunker.

"Is he okay?"

Willow nodded, a faint smile shadowing her lips.

"So far, yeah. He's got that fire girl, Ember, with him. So far she hasn't roasted him."

Willow refused to answer anymore of my questions until I got out of the shower. Winter managed to stand on her own two feet with Willow's help.

I, however, almost fainted when I stood. My vision went black and I nearly fell back into the shower. Luckily, Willow was quick and stopped me from cracking my skull on the tile floor.

"You're overdoing it," she whispered to me. "I seriously need you to rest."

I nodded at her in annoyance. I knew how much I needed to rest. I thought that's what I was doing in the shower with Winter.

In reality though, it's not like I could truly rest while Kain's Vigilantes were trying to kill us. It wouldn't surprise me if they were all standing outside the door. Just waiting for us to make a mistake so they could break in.

Willow managed to get me to the couch and made me lay on my stomach. It hurt, but I kept the pain to myself.

I watched Winter take a small sip of broth before I closed my eyes. Willow tried to convince me to eat too, but I only managed a few spoonfuls of the broth. She had to physically feed me since my hands had long since stopped moving.

I barely felt it when Willow stitched up the knife wound on my side. I'm pretty sure I fell asleep, but when she started in on my back, my eyes flew open at the burning pain.

Winter sat next to me while Willow cleaned the lacerations. She must've seen the pain in my eyes because she gently massaged my head with her soft fingers.

"You never said it back," Winter whispered in my ear. "But that's okay. I love you, Nolan."

I merely stared at her; completely speechless.

Without warning, Willow inserted a needle into my upper arm.

My eyelids closed instantly, and I lost all train of thought.

Chapter 27: John

"So, you're giving me free rein on the Vigilantes once we get in the bunker?" Ember shook her head in frustration. "Normally, I'd be fine with that, except Kain injected me with something. I don't know what it was, but I can't use my abilities. I'm trying not to freak out about it."

It wasn't difficult to discern that she'd been struggling to keep herself together.

Not being able to rely on her fire abilities would make things difficult though.

"Fine, then your job is to disarm all the explosives you set up down there. I'll stake out the infirmary. Then we'll make a plan to get Kain to the dungeon."

Ember sighed, folding her arms across her chest.

"Okay, but how do you know I'll do what you say?"

I raised my eyebrow at her.

"It's not like I've given you any reason to trust me, John. I certainly don't trust you."

I chuckled humorlessly. I had almost forgot how annoying rebellious teenage girls could be. Winter wasn't a normal teenager and Willow wasn't nearly as abrasive as Ember.

"Okay, you told me a lot of secrets about yourself." I grinned at her. "So I'll share one with you. Are you ready?"

Ember eyed me with suspicion.

"I've got a sniper friend in the woods. He's had you in his sight the entire time we've been talking." My grinned widened into something more feral. "I told him to stand down, but he's not revealing himself just yet. We aren't sure if we can trust you."

Ember gaped at me, and I gave her a wink.

George cursed in my ear, which turned into a creative string of profanity. I'm pretty sure by the time he was done he'd called me every derogatory name he could come up with.

"Hey, George," I cut him off mid rant. "I know you're pissed, but this stand off is getting us nowhere. I'm making a decision to trust her. I can only hope you'll do the same."

George sighed in annoyance, but ultimately agreed with me. Only because I'd given him no other choice.

"I'll tail you both. We need to get into the bunker soon. I'm starting to feel like a sitting duck out here."

Ember sighed and crossed her arms.

"I'll take care of the explosives. Just make sure that you don't get yourself caught. I'm not in the mood to do anymore rescuing today. Believe it or not, but stopping your brother's execution took a lot out of me."

I nodded in understanding. I briefly wondered how she knew about the execution in the first place, but I decided to leave it for later. Hopefully, there'd be time to question her further after we took out Kain.

"You good, George?"

"Sure thing, Boss." All the anger from before was replaced with his usual calmness.

"Alright, let's go."

Ember nodded and followed me through the woods toward the entrance to the bunker. We approached while staying in the shadows. Fortunately, Ember's clothing was just as dark as mine; blending us into our surroundings. There was no sign of movement except for the leaves blowing in the mild breeze.

"Sit-rep."

"I've still got eyes on you," George replied. "Nothing suspicious so far except the fire breather next to you."

I rolled my eyes, but otherwise didn't contribute to his unnecessary commentary.

"Four hostiles," George whispered suddenly. "Coming in quickly from the east. About twenty yards away. They're armed with rifles."

My jaw clenched. "Take them out."

"You got it, Boss."

I didn't hear the shots. George was using a professional sniper's rifle that could hit a target from over a mile away.

"Four hostiles down. You're safe to proceed."

"You'll be following us?" Adrenaline made my hands shake.

"Sure thing, Boss. I'll meet you at the infirmary as soon as I can."

Willow had the foresight to ensure we had maps of the bunker on our tablets. Hopefully she'd found Nolan to and was keeping an eye on things.

Once we were inside the tunnel, my gut sank. Something wasn't right-

The door automatically slammed shut behind us. I cursed under my breath and immediately tried to open the steel door. But the locking system shut down the moment the door had closed.

Ember stood close to me in the shadows of the tunnel. The dim lighting illuminated how pale she was. A small tremor ran through her, but I did my best to ignore her terror.

I had gotten her into this. I wouldn't let fear engulf me until we were safe.

"This isn't good, Boss." I blew out a breath of relief that my earbud was still working. "The second the door shut, Vigilantes started popping up from the bushes. There's four of them. Apparently, there were two teams out here that I missed."

I sighed in frustration, and relayed to Ember what George was reporting. Her face paled even more. The splatter of freckles on her nose and under her eyes became more prominent. Making her look much younger than she was.

"Get someplace safe. Try to contact Willow with the communicator."

"Then I won't be in contact with you, Boss," George replied, obviously concerned.

"I know, but I need you to find out what's going on with this door. Willow is our best bet to figure it out. Contact me after you get in touch with her."

"Sure thing, Boss. Signing off."

I switched my earbud to standby and gave Ember a cursory glance. She seemed to have a bit more color in her cheeks, but she still looked a bit shaky. When she noticed me studying her, she squared her shoulders and gave me a slight glare.

"I was going to have George shadow you while you disarmed the explosives, but obviously that's not going to happen now. I think we should stick together."

Ember rolled her eyes in annoyance. "It's gonna take at least three hours to disarm all of them."

"Seriously?" I stared at her incredulously. "How many explosives did you rig?"

Ember folded her arms and gave me a severe look.

"I really, *really,* don't like my dad." She sighed and ran a hand through her short hair in frustration. "But don't worry, they won't go off unless I do it myself. They're easy to disarm too. If someone comes across one of them they won't blow themselves up."

I wasn't so sure about that, but I didn't have any other choice but to trust her.

"We'll go to the infirmary first. Once we get Kain secured in the dungeon, we'll make our way around the bunker and disarm them together. Okay?"

Ember nodded and let me walk ahead of her.

The hallways were empty and completely dark. Appearances were most likely deceiving in this situation, so I gestured for Ember to keep a sharp eye out.

Kain had over one hundred Vigilantes in this bunker. So far, I hadn't seen very many of them. I couldn't help but wonder when we'd be ambushed. It was obvious that they knew we were here.

We travelled through the bunker; following the tablet in my hand. We'd almost made it to the middle of the compound when Ember silently tapped my shoulder. When I glanced back, her blue eyes widened and her jaw clenched.

That's when I heard the footsteps coming up behind us.

"Stay calm." I gave Ember a chin lift and she nodded in agreement.

"Halt!" A gruff voice echoed through the tunnel. There was no place to hide. We wouldn't find cover if a shootout happened.

I quickly turned off my tablet and stuffed it into my satchel. Ember stood as close to me as she could, but she managed to exude an impressive outward calmness.

We raised our hands above our heads.

"John Delany."

A hideous man with scars all over his face stood in front of us. He had a team of at least ten Vigilantes behind him. All of them with automatic assault rifles.

I *really* wished George had been able to get into the bunker.

"Kain expected you to return." The scarred man chuckled. "Can't say I thought you'd be that stupid. We've been following you since you entered the bunker."

I merely smiled at the brutish man.

"Congratulations. You got me."

He turned to the woman standing next to him. She looked to be in her mid thirties, but it was hard to tell in the darkness.

"Take the girl," the ugly man ordered. "I'd like it better if they were separated."

Ember stiffened next to me. I tried to give her a reassuring look, but she avoided my gaze. The woman stepped toward her and roughly grabbed her by the arm-

Ember's eyes flared with an orange gleam.

A flash of heat blazed through the tunnel. The Vigilante woman shrieked in pain and stumbled away; fingers and palm blistering.

I gasped as sweat broke out on my forehead. I barely managed to take a step away from the heat before it scorched me.

Ember raised her hands; pointing them at the Vigilantes as steam rose from the moist concrete. The ugly man and the others aimed their assault weapons.

"Run, John!" Ember shouted as a burst of flames erupted from her fingertips.

I didn't wait around for the flames to kill me.

I got as far away from Ember as I could; watching as her fire engulfed the Vigilantes. A few of them managed to get off a shot or two. I flinched when one of the bullets went wide and buried itself in the cement wall next to Ember's head.

Most of the Vigilante's were dead, or severely burned, within minutes. Ember stood in front of the pile of bodies, gasping heavily.

She glanced at me.

"You're burned. I tried to miss you. I'm sorry."

I glanced down at my camouflaged shirt as the smell of burnt flesh assaulted my nose. The buttons on my jacket were melted. Wisps of smoke drifted from my clothes. The fabric was frayed in a few areas; my skin completely blistered underneath.

I couldn't feel the pain. At least not yet.

Ember was staring at the bodies in front of her; completely indifferent. Her lack reaction made my blood run cold. I couldn't comprehend how a teenage girl could kill people with such a lack of emotion.

It was disturbing.

She flexed her fingers. "I'll take care of the explosives. I don't need your protection anymore."

All I could do was nod at her. I didn't like the idea of her going off on her own, but there really was no way for me to stop her.

"I'm going to do the same thing to any Vigilante I come across." She gestured to the smoking pile of bodies in front of her. "I'm not going to ask if they're on my side or not before I kill them."

I nodded again.

"Just make sure you don't hurt Willow if you come across her. I wouldn't have gotten this far without her."

Ember gave me a curt nod and turned away from me.

"Are you sure you want to go it alone?"

She hesitated and then turned to look at me.

"I don't ever want to see Kain again. You take care of him. I'll make sure this bunker is secure so you can bring the Scavengers here."

I was a little surprised that she assumed I wanted to bring the Scavengers to the underground bunker. I hadn't really thought much about that, and I couldn't afford to do it now.

I watched Ember walk away until she disappeared into the darkness.

I quickly pulled out the tablet and turned it back on. I was almost to the infirmary. If there were more Vigilantes hunting me, I doubted I'd be able to evade them on my own. But as long as I was taken to Kain, it didn't really matter.

All I had to do was get off one shot.

My muscles tensed as I got closer to the infirmary. The darkness and silence should've felt eery and unnatural, but I was actually grateful for it. It felt like more of a protection than a hindrance.

I got to the steel door of the infirmary and plugged my tablet into the wall. I typed in the codes that Willow had given me beforehand. The locking mechanism clicked and the door slid open.

I was expecting the infirmary to be dark too, but it wasn't.

A dim light illuminated the concrete walls. Beeping medical equipment echoed through the large room.

I quickly slid the door shut; keeping to the shadows with my gun in hand.

Just as I began to wonder where Kain was, voices echoed from the opposite end of the infirmary. Large curtains separated the rooms and I could see shadows of people in the dim lighting.

I took a deep breath and crept toward the voices.

"One more dose, sir," a man's wobbly voice sounded from behind the curtain. "The physical change will be immediate."

Even though I had no idea what the man was talking about, a chill ran up my spine.

"Do it," Kain ordered.

He didn't sound weak or injured like I would've expected him too. He sounded determined. Excited.

"But first, bring John Delany in here. He must bear witness."

Before I had time to react, two Vigilantes barreled into the room with pistols drawn. They looked like Kain's personal guards. But they didn't seem to be trained very well, considering how haphazardly they entered the room.

Using my handgun as a club, I knocked them both out pretty quickly. Two more Vigilantes came out from behind the curtain and charged me.

I hit the first one in the face with my handgun, but the other one landed a punch to my blistered chest. Pain exploded through me, and I saw stars. In that split second, the Vigilantes got the upper hand. Another one came out of nowhere and locked his arm around my neck in a strangling chokehold.

My gun slipped from my fingers.

I quickly slipped out of the hold, but the Vigilante in front of me pummeled my abdomen with surprisingly hard punches. I gasped for breath after the third or fourth hit, but managed to stomp kick the Vigilante. I didn't have a very good angle, since the man behind me kept trying to choke me, so the Vigilante only stumbled back a few steps.

I threw my head back; feeling a crunch as I made contact with the man's face. He cried out in agony when I bashed the back of my head into him a second time.

The man finally stopped trying to choke me from behind, but I didn't have time to check if I'd knocked him down or not.

The Vigilante in front of me aimed his handgun at my chest; a feral sneer on his face.

In that moment, time seemed to stand still.

He was too far away-

He pulled the trigger.

I was on the floor a split second later; gasping for breath. I didn't even feel the shot. My whole chest instantly went numb. My hand immediately moved to where I was hit and-

I pulled a dart out of my chest. My limbs went slack.

Drugged.

Nothing was going to stop Kain from having his way with me now.

The Vigilantes grabbed my wrists and dragged me into the medical room behind the curtain. Kain was sitting on a hospital bed;

connected to all sorts of tubes and wires. He stood up when I was dragged into the room, and I couldn't help but stare at him.

How was it possible that he was standing after what he'd been through?

"Congratulations, John Delany." Kain's psychotic smile split his face into a chillingly maniacal expression. "You're just in time to witness one of the greatest moments in the history of science."

I was thrust into a chair and strapped to it with leather cuffs.

It wasn't necessary. I couldn't really move anyway. The sedative they injected me with wasn't very strong, but it would take me a few minutes to get my bearings before I could plan my next move.

Kain was still talking, so I focus all my attention on what he was saying.

"As you know, Dr. Darkwood was truly brilliant in his experimentations. Especially in his successes with Subjects Thirty-One and Thirty-Three. Of course, Ember was also a success, even though he wasn't able to alter her brain like he did with Subject Thirty-One. Luckily, my own scientist was able to reconstruct Dr. Darkwood's formulas. He created a serum that'll change the genetic code of any individual that is receptive to it. Not everyone is compatible, but my genetic code is strong enough to accept the changes without killing me."

All I could do was stare at Kain; trying to wrap my mind around what I was seeing. He was hooked up to at least five different monitors. A bald, scrawny man stood next to him with the largest needle I'd ever seen. The syringe was filled with a clear liquid that was thicker than water.

I had no idea that Kain had a scientist in his back pocket. It shouldn't have surprised me as much as it did. He and Amanda Lynch were so similar, it was scary.

"Of course, I wouldn't have done this to myself without making sure it would work first. When I took samples of Nolan Delany's blood, I immediately noticed how strong his genetic code was. It was convenient to have such liberal access to him while he was my prisoner. The perfect lab rat for Dr. Mason's experiments."

I blinked a few times to clear the angry haze that blurred my vision. I clenched my fists as the last effects of the sedative disappeared.

Kain's words were just as effective as a bucket of ice water.

"It wasn't easy for Nolan- being my test subject for this serum. I had to bring his body to the brink of death quite a few times before coming up with the most desired formula. Mental, emotional, and physical torture was the key to our success.

"When Nolan fought back at his execution it was obvious that the serum was making him stronger. He shouldn't have been able to stand upright, let alone fight, after what we'd put his body through."

Kain flexed his arms and rolled his shoulders.

"Unfortunately, he killed Brian. I didn't anticipate that happening, but in the end the experiment was an enormous success. As you can see: my legs are already healed after merely one dose."

I worked my hands and wrists while Kain talked. I had no idea what the serum was capable of. I didn't want to be bound when Kain got his final dose.

"Are you ready, sir?" Dr. Mason pushed his glasses up the bridge of his nose.

Kain held his hands up toward the ceiling, and took a deep cleansing breath.

I glanced around the room to get my bearings while I worked to free myself. Cade and Krissy were in the room as well. Krissy was laying on a gurney with Cade sitting next to her.

Apparently, Kain didn't care to give them the healing serum. Or perhaps their genetic code wasn't compatible. I briefly wondered how screwed up Nolan was from the poison Kain pumped into him over the last month.

"I am ready," Kain whispered toward the ceiling, as though he was praying to the heavens.

He lowered his arms in a fluid-like motion before Dr. Mason inserted the large needle into his neck. I watched in horror as the serum disappeared from the syringe.

Kain let out a shriek of agony that morphed into a triumphant battlecry.

Chapter 28: Winter

Nolan's eyes rolled to the back of his head. Terror gripped me at the sight of the needle, but I stomped it down before I accidentally froze something.

"What did you give him?"

"It's a sedative. He needs his rest."

I grabbed the syringe from Willow before she could dispose of it.

I didn't trust this girl.

I knew Nolan did, but there was something off about her behavior. I wasn't good at spotting lies, but I was getting better at reading people the more I spent time with them.

This girl gave off the same vibe I got whenever I talked to Ember.

I stared at the label on the syringe and narrowed my eyes.

"It says 'genetic serum.'" I glared at Willow accusingly.

She let out a sigh and tried to take the syringe from me. I moved out of her way.

It was surprising how much energy I had now. I could practically feel the cure killing the Sleeping Ache that had been destroying my body for the past couple of days. I was still weak, but at least I could move.

Willow *could* take the syringe from me if she really wanted to, but she kept her distance from me. I obviously scared her.

"I'm not going to take the time to explain everything to you. But Blue Eyes was being poisoned with genetic altering serums for a month now. I just saved his life."

I merely stared at her; not attempting to hide my suspicion. She met my gaze, despite the terror that made her hands shake.

"He's my best friend. I wasn't about to let him die. No matter the cost."

I felt like something heavy was sitting on my chest. I couldn't have a panic attack now. I was strong enough that I could freeze the entire room by accident.

I knew a lot more than Willow thought I did. I knew exactly what genetic serum was. I had different variants of it pumped into me everyday for almost a year. Until Dr. Darkwood found a formula that would work to alter my genetic code-

I remembered *vividly* how painful it was to transform from human to abomination.

Willow had given Nolan a very large dose of the poison that turned me into what I was now.

I gasped for breath as the cold air rushed out of my body.

Willow stumbled away from me in horror, but I didn't let her get far.

She stuck Nolan with a needle without his consent. Forced poison into him.

She would pay for that.

Ultimately, I knew it couldn't be me that made her pay. That was up to Nolan to decide. If he ever woke up again.

Two large icicles had appeared in my hands, but I immediately dropped them to the floor. They shattered, and Willow stared at the chunks of ice as though they'd jump from the floor to attack her at any moment.

"You're going to tell me everything you know. Right now. Before he wakes up screaming."

Willow stared at me as though I'd gone insane.

"I doubt he'll scream. Nolan is tough. Besides, the serum should help with-"

"NO!" I shouted, unable to listen to her idiocy for a moment longer.

"It's going to feel like ice water and fire are running through his veins! He'll be convinced that he's going to die as each sensation wars against one another in his body! His DNA is going to evolve into something unnatural! His body will have to adapt to that! He's going to wake up disoriented and cold! He's going to have a hard time recognizing *where* he is, *who* he is, and *what* he is! I know Nolan is tough! You don't have to tell me that! But trust me-"

I shuddered, and knelt on the floor next to Nolan's head. I didn't dare touch him, though my fingers itched to.

"He's going to scream until his voice is raw."

Willow stared at me in shock. I, suddenly, realized I'd just told her more about my ordeal at the hands of Dr. Darkwood than I had anyone else.

I really was losing my mind.

"Tell me about the serum," I whispered, but the order was clear in my tone.

"I stole it from Kain's lab before I came to the room. I knew Blue Eyes needed it. I've had access to Dr. Mason's data ever since he started studying Dr. Darkwood's experiments. Kain wanted to alter himself so he could go up against Amanda Lynch's forces. We think she's creating an army of abominations to take over humanity."

Willow took a deep breath; folding her arms to ward off the cold that radiated from me. Her jaw chattered with each word she spoke.

"That's not exactly new information, Willow. What does this have to do with Nolan?"

I forced myself to gain control. I couldn't expect her to explain things clearly if she was freezing to death.

"Dr. Mason created serums from the information we stole from Dr. Darkwood's lab. I'm sure you remember that mission. Blue Eyes rescued you."

I nodded, indicating for her to continue.

"Kain ordered Cade and Krissy to give Blue Eyes doses of Dr. Mason's genetic serums. So far, they've all failed. Kain didn't want powers that came from nature like you, Subject Thirty-Three, and Ember Lynch have. He wanted to enhance his own physical strengths. In order to do that, he needed someone young, and equally as strong, to test the genetic serum on."

"And that person was Nolan."

Willow nodded.

"Kain wasn't going to give him the final dose he needed in order to make a complete change." A tear fell from her eye. "I overheard him talking to Dr. Mason about what would happen to Blue Eyes if he wasn't allowed to finish the doses."

She glanced at Nolan as he slept on the couch. I knew the peaceful scene wouldn't last long. I remembered how much I screamed when I woke up the day I'd changed.

I needed to prepare for the surge of power Nolan would feel too.

"His body would've slowly died. Everyday he would've gotten worse. He wouldn't be able to eat or drink anything. He'd eventually lose the ability to talk. All his senses would gradually stop working. Kain was just going to execute him to save him from an agonizing death. But when Blue Eyes fought back and killed Brian- Kain decided to let him suffer and die on his own."

Willow was still shivering, but the room was no longer cold. I didn't feel guilty for attacking her with a cold flash. She could've explained the situation to us before deciding to shove a very large needle into Nolan's arm.

I still wanted to throttle her for it, even if it might save him. There was still a chance he wouldn't wake up and die anyway.

I leaned against the couch that Nolan was laying on. He was breathing deeply, but his brow was furrowed as though he were in pain.

I glanced down at his hand that rested near his forehead. It was obviously broken; the skin swollen and bruised. His wrist was bloody with a rancid infection.

I grabbed alcohol out of the first aid bag and set to work cleaning his wrist. Willow finally calmed down enough to get near me again, and she busied herself with cleaning Nolan's other wounds.

His back was so awful. It took every ounce of concentration to keep myself from losing control.

There was a branding in the shape of a V on his shoulder blade. Unfortunately, that wasn't the most disturbing mark on his back. Almost every inch of skin was covered in long, red cuts that oozed bloody puss.

Seeing how badly Nolan was injured made me want to go find Kain and finish him off. But I was quickly losing the strength the cure had momentarily given me. By the time I was done wrapping Nolan's hand and wrist, I was breathing heavily from exertion.

I was so tired, I almost didn't notice Willow studying the tablet that was propped up on a table on the other side of the room.

I watched her pick up the communicator and talk to George. I'd heard John talk about George many times. I'd never met the man, but John trusted him.

I decided to let Willow take control of the situation, and closed my eyes. I rested my head against Nolan's and took comfort in just hearing him breathe.

"Winter, are you awake?"

I opened my eyes and nodded at Willow. She gave me a worried look before gesturing to her communicator.

"I think John is-"

Nolan's body twitched violently as though he was having a seizure; interrupting her.

I jumped to my feet and Willow rushed over to us. Before we could do anything to try to help him, his body stopped shaking.

He just laid there, perfectly still, as though he didn't have a seizure a split second ago-

A guttural scream exploded from his throat.

His eyes flew open as he thrashed around in agony. Willow and I grabbed his arms to try to hold him down.

Within a few seconds, we couldn't contend with his strength. He threw me off of him as though I were lighter than air; landing on my butt a few feet away.

Willow held on longer than I did, but she ended up being slammed into the wall behind the couch. She fell to the ground with an audible gasp.

Nolan didn't mean to hurt us. He just didn't have control of his body anymore. I watched in despair as he rolled from the couch to the concrete; screaming at the top of his lungs.

Willow rushed over to me; yanking me to my feet.

"We need to get away from him. His strength is enhanced."

I already knew that, but I didn't tell her so.

There was no way Nolan would've been able to throw us off of him in his current condition without unnatural strength. With the way his body moved when he thrashed around, I had a feeling that he was faster than normal too.

I watched, helplessly, as his screams turned to desperate whimpers. Gradually, he quieted down and just laid there on the floor. I wanted to go to him, but I knew that wouldn't be a good idea.

He'd never forgive himself if he accidentally hurt us.

After a few minutes, Nolan finally opened his eyes. They were still the same beautiful blue that I'd grown to love. He stared at me with that piercing gaze of his, and I had to blink back tears.

He didn't say anything for a long while. No one in the room moved since we were all in complete shock. The stunned stillness lasted until Willow cleared her throat.

"How do you feel, Blue Eyes?"

"I don't know."

His voice was painfully hoarse. I went to the rectangular box to get the water. His throat probably felt like he'd swallowed a bucket of sand. When I held a bottle of water out to Nolan, he took it and guzzled it down.

"What happened to me?" A tremor ran through him. He clenched his jaw, as though he was trying to stop his teeth from chattering.

"You've been injected with a variation of the genetic serum that Dr. Darkwood tested on me. According to Willow, Kain has been doing this to you for weeks now. She was able to get you the final genetic serum that you needed to survive what they did to you."

Nolan stared at Willow, incredulously.

"You knew what they were doing to me? You chose not to tell me?"

"Come on, Blue Eyes," she replied a bit defensively. "I didn't have time to explain anything to you."

Nolan leapt to his feet, so quickly, it startled everyone in the room. I stumbled away from him when he almost bumped into me. Willow remained in front of him with her back braced against the wall.

He hovered there for a moment, as though confused by what he'd just done. He glanced down at his hands and gently fisted them. I studied his face, and was surprised to see no pain in his expression. He was moving his broken hand without any trouble.

I couldn't help but think that was a bad sign.

"You should've given me a choice as to whether I wanted this or not, Willow."

"Yeah. Well, I didn't. I made the choice for you. I was worried you'd make the wrong one and let yourself die. If that makes me selfish, then so be it. *I already lost Lexie and Phoenix.* I wasn't going to let you go so easily."

"I wouldn't have died," Nolan replied, a lot more calmly than I thought he would.

"Yes, you would have." A profoundly agonizing look crossed Willow's features as she stared at the broken boy in front of her. "I had all the available information on my tablet, Blue Eyes. Everything pointed to you dying if you didn't complete the treatments. You can hate me if you want to, but at least you're alive."

He merely shook his head and turned away from her. I couldn't help but feel a pang of guilt for how I'd treated Willow earlier.

I treated her like an enemy when all she wanted was to save Nolan.

I shook my head as tears stung my eyes again. I swayed and blinked a few times. I needed to lie down before-

"Winter?" Nolan eyed me with concern. Nothing ever escaped his noticed, no matter what traumatic event he'd been forced to suffer through. "Are you okay?"

The ache in my muscles came rushing back with a vengeance, and I shuttered in pain. I thought I heard Nolan say my name again, but my brain wasn't keeping up with conversations anymore.

I was falling.

Chapter 29: Nolan

Waking up was rough.
Seriously rough.
Just realizing that Winter had gone through that agony on more than one occasion pissed me off.

I wasn't quite sure that I was still alive when I opened my eyes. But Winter was there; staring at me as though I had two heads.

I surged to my feet; wondering how I had the energy to stand. I couldn't feel the pain anymore. I could move my hands without any issue, but they didn't look any better than they were before Willow injected me.

I heard their conversation while I was mostly unconscious. But I still wasn't sure if I understood everything that had happened to me.

I gritted my teeth against the rage boiling inside me. I had this irrational urge to pound the concrete walls with my damaged fists. I wondered if it would hurt, or if I was no longer capable of feeling anything besides fury and hate.

Every physical sensation was gone. All that was left was this consuming rage. An unadulterated anger that focused itself on Willow. The one person in the room that I could hate for what had been done to me.

I forced myself to remain calm. I didn't want to go into a mindless fury and hurt Willow. I instinctively knew that I would never hurt Winter, but something had changed within me.

Willow is not your enemy. She's not your enemy.

The voice in my head sounded reasonable, so I was able to turn my back on Willow. At least for now.

When I focused on Winter, all of the anger dissipated in an instant.

She was so beautiful; despite her hollow eyes and sunken cheeks. Her eyes were bloodshot; her lips pursed as though she were in pain.

Not even the Sleeping Ache wreaking havoc on her could dampen the effect she had on me. I was so distracted by her beauty that I almost failed to notice her behavior.

She was utterly exhausted.

I said her name a few times, but she didn't respond. She swayed; her eyes rolling to the back of her head.

I thought I wasn't going to reach her fast enough when she dropped. Before I could fully process what I needed to do to help her—

She was in my arms.

The air rushed out of her lungs as though I'd crushed her. I instantly released my grip and dropped her on the bed. She moaned in her sleep.

"Oh crap."

It was fortunate that I didn't break Winter's bones. I stared at my hands again; fisting them once more.

No pain. No physical sensation at all.

"Blue Eyes." Willow was still bracing herself against the wall. I blinked a few times; trying to keep my anger at bay. "You have enhanced speed and strength. You need to be careful."

Her words slowly sank in, and I gritted my teeth. I still couldn't feel anything, but I wouldn't dwell on that now. Winter needed more cure, and I needed to find John and help him.

I didn't know why, but every instinct told me he was in danger.

"Oh no!" Willow's eyes grew wide as she stared at the table on the other side of the room. I studied her for a moment before turning my attention toward the table, and the tablet that was propped up on it.

John was in the infirmary with Kain, and a few other Vigilantes. I cursed as I watched the Viking go through the same transformation that I went through just minutes ago.

"Kain will have the same physical changes that you have." Willow winced when I glanced at her. I hated that she sounded so timid- so scared- of me. She'd noticed the murderous look I kept giving her every time I looked in her direction.

I *really* needed to control this anger before I did some irreversible damage.

"I've got to go. Stay here with Winter."

If Kain had enhanced strength, and speed, then John wouldn't be able to do anything to protect himself.

I made sure to keep my footing steady, so I wouldn't move too fast and run right into the door. I didn't know if I was strong enough to knock a steel door down, but I didn't want to experiment right now.

"Blue Eyes, wait!" I turned to see Willow still plastered against the wall. "Don't let Kain win."

I gave her a feral grin. She relaxed a little. I'd given her that particular smile countless times in the past.

"I'll see you later." I gestured to where Winter laid motionless on the bed. "Please, don't let her-"

"I've got meds for her. She'll still be here when you get back with the cure."

I nodded and opened the steel door. After making sure it was locked tight, I took off at a dead run through the tunnels.

And I was *very* fast.

It was hard to take a breath as I ran through the bunker. I had to concentrate on each inhale and exhale. I passed by a few people that stumbled away from me in shock.

Apparently, I wasn't running so fast that the Vigilantes couldn't see me.

The door to the infirmary appeared in front of me, and I managed to halt my momentum. I took a deep breath to steady myself before putting my hand to the scanner.

I grimaced when the alarm sounded.

They'd obviously made sure that my handprint would activate the alarm if I ever tried to get into one of the rooms.

I'm an idiot.

I yelled in desperation; punching the door with my broken hand. It didn't hurt at all, but I heard bone cracking and popping when my knuckles connected with the steel door. I knew it was a bad idea, but I kept punching dents into the door as fast as I could.

After both of my hands were too mangled to be of use, I started kicking the steel. Each hit left marks as though I'd used a sledge hammer. I couldn't take the time to marvel at how incredible that was, because I could hear John and Kain in the infirmary.

Even through the soundproof steel.

"After I break every bone in your body, John Delany, I will find Willow Rivers and kill her the same way. Then I'll-"

"If you're going to kill me you might as well get on with it."

I stopped listening and kicked at the door again.

John's hoarse screams rattled my brain as I gave the door one final kick. The steel finally gave way, and I forced it open with my bare hands. I was gasping for breath, completely exhausted, but I knew I couldn't stop now.

Kain had, no doubt, heard me breaking the door down even though the alarm hadn't stopped blaring.

As expected, Cade came from behind a curtain with a gun aimed right at me. I didn't give him a chance to pull the trigger as I raced toward him. He fell over the instant I pushed him.

His head cracked open when he hit the concrete floor. Blood pooled on the floor under his head; his eyes staring sightlessly at the ceiling.

Another Vigilante rushed toward me; swinging a baseball bat at my head. I dodged the blow in a blur of motion. The Vigilante could do nothing but gape at the vacant space left between us.

Instinct overtook me, and I pummeled the Vigilante to the ground. He let out an ear piercing scream before my fist connected with his face.

Bone shattered.

Blood burst from his nose, mouth, and eyeballs. As though a bomb had been set off in his brain.

I had to swallow down bile at the sight of what I'd just done to this man. Blood drenched my hands and arms within seconds. I shuddered with adrenaline; realizing that his blood was now smeared into my own wounds.

Apparently, I needed to be more careful when I fought people.

I stood up quickly, and faced four other Vigilantes that stood there watching me. They dropped their weapons instantly, and backed away from me. Raising their hands in desperate surrender.

A sweaty, rancid odor seeped from them; stinging my nose. Intuitively, I knew it was the smell of fear.

"I swear, Nolan Delany." One of them held up his hands in desperation. "We didn't do anything to your brother, John. We-"

I ignored the terrified Vigilantes; rushing toward the curtain that separated me from Kain and John. I didn't bother to slide it open as I gave it a hard tug. The curtain tore out of the ceiling and floated to the ground.

I smelled, rather than saw, Krissy hiding in the corner of the medical room. She was covered in the scent of blood, sweat, and fear. I wasn't sure what was wrong with her, but I pushed it to the back of my mind.

My feral gaze drifted to the Viking.

He stood in front of John's crippled form. It was obvious that Kain had been taking his time with him. Most likely testing out his new enhanced strength on my brother.

Rage surged through me at the sight of the blood on John's face. He was still breathing, but it sounded like a whistle when he exhaled.

Every breath I took was its own version of agony. The scent of fear, and pain, in the room was mixing with Kain's sweet odor of pleasure. My senses were all over the place, and it took me a precious second to get my bearings.

I narrowed my eyes at Kain; resisting the urge to look at John again. He had already taken too much from me. I wasn't about to let him take my brother too.

"You've come just in time, Nolan Delany."

I snarled at Kain's triumphant smile.

He raised his hand to deliver the final blow to the back of John's head.

Moving on pure adrenaline and instinct, I rushed the Viking. In a split second, I was standing between him and John. I didn't miss a beat as I shoved him in the chest with all of my enhanced strength.

Kain flew backwards, but stopped his momentum before he hit the wall behind him. I had hoped to throw him to the ground, but I wasn't strong enough to compete with his own enhanced strength.

The smell of adrenaline replaced the pleasure scent I'd previously detected on Kain.

I blinked a few times; trying to focus through the sensory distractions. The smells were getting stronger, and the sounds were getting louder. The constant beeps coming from the medical equipment sounded more like gunshots to me.

Kain grinned and let out a roar.

My hands automatically went to my ears. I still couldn't feel the physical pain of my injuries, but the loud noise hurt like hell. I tried not to stumble as I blinked the moisture from my eyes.

"You received the sensory enhancement that I'd been toying around with."

Kain gestured to the corner of the room where Dr. Mason stood. I had no idea how I'd missed seeing the doctor there. The oversight must've been a direct cause of the intense overload of changes that I was currently experiencing.

"We concluded that it would be a hindrance to Kain if I gave him the sensory enhancement that you are now experiencing. It will be advantageous to have the opportunity to dissect you. To see what kind of changes your physical form has gone through."

I stared at Dr. Mason; waited for him to come into focus. If I couldn't get my senses under control-

John and I were going to die. I was surprised that Kain hadn't taken this opportunity to beat the crap out of me yet.

"Tell me, Nolan Delany, is your eyesight enhanced as well? What about physical sensations? I assume you aren't feeling much physically, since you're still standing with your injuries. Are sounds and smells overwhelming?"

I glared at Dr. Mason in utter confusion.

Did he seriously want me to give him a rundown of the changes I was experiencing?

This guy was freaking crazy.

Without warning, I ran toward Kain again. I used my speed to deliver well placed punches to his solar plexus and groin. He blinked a few times in shock after I stopped pummeling him with my super strength and speed.

The reaction seemed delayed, but he cursed in pain and slumped to his knees. I grabbed a scalpel and imbedded it into his leg-

Blood squirted from the femoral artery.

Kain screamed in rage, and tried to staunch the blood flow. He'd bleed out within minutes if he didn't get medical attention soon. I just had to make sure that didn't happen. The only one that could potentially save him was standing just a few feet behind me.

I spun toward Dr. Mason, and grinned fiercely.

The doctor's face went completely white as he realized his life was about to end.

I threw the scalped at him with all the strength I had in me.

The little blade soared through the air, and shot straight through Dr. Mason's chest like a bullet. I threw it so hard that the bloody scalpel imbedded itself into the wall behind the psychotic doctor.

He stared at me in shock before soundlessly dropping to the floor. I could hear his heartbeat slow, and his breathing eventually stopped.

"NO!"

I whirled around in surprise. I was expecting to see blood everywhere, but there wasn't very much on the floor at all. Kain wasn't staunching the bleeding anymore. The wound had sealed itself shut.

Apparently, Kain had healing abilities too.

Figures.

He got to his feet without showing a hint of pain.

"Dr. Mason didn't get the chance to give me enhanced speed. It's not in the testing stage yet. I'd be very interested to learn how you ended up with it, Nolan Delany. Now my scientist is dead by your hand. You'll pay a steep price for killing him."

I quickly glanced around the medical room for a weapon. John's gun was laying in pieces on the floor next to him. All that I could find were scalpels and IV poles.

Kain tried to charge me, but I was too quick for him. I dodged his fists, and delivered a roundhouse kick to his face.

His nose shattered, and teeth flew out of his mouth. I couldn't help but smile when he screamed in frustration. Even though he healed quickly, it was obvious that he still felt the pain from my blows.

Good.

My vision went blurry for a second, and it was suddenly hard for me to breath.

I clenched my fists to throw another punch at Kain, but pain spiked through my broken hands and wrists. I gasped in agony, and let my hands hang loosely. The rest of my body exploded in pain before I could fully grasp what was going on with me.

My physical sensations came back with an intensity that nearly broke me. I crumpled to the floor; writhing in such agony I thought I would die.

In that moment, I truly wished for it.

I groaned as the first wave of physical pain subsided slightly, but I didn't have any time to recover.

Kain's boot connected with my stomach, and it felt like my guts exploded. Literally. I couldn't take a breath, and I thought I would throw up my innards.

"Dad, stop!"

I winced when my eardrums rang in protest at the desperate scream.

Every part of me ached with exhaustion.
Everything hurt.
Everything was just so *loud*.

"Ember, my dear. You've come back. How foolish of you."

Kain stepped around my crumpled form with heavy footfalls that vibrated through me. I was surprised that the concrete floor didn't crack beneath his boots.

I managed to roll over to get a glimpse of Ember. She was standing in the infirmary with flames up her arms, and orange glowing in her eyes.

Ember spared me a quick look of concern before concentrating on Kain again.

"I couldn't leave John to face you alone. Didn't know that Nolan was here, but that's okay. I have no problem saving him a second time. Or is this the third? I'm losing count these days."

I would've rolled my eyes if I was physically capable of it.

Kain cursed angrily; charging his daughter with his fists raised like a berserker.

Ember smirked and threw her flames at him with a beautiful gracefulness I'd never seen before. It was like I was watching in slow motion as she sent her brilliant flames across the infirmary. Her fire roared its intensity; melting everything in its path as it raced toward the Viking.

Kain screamed as he was engulfed by the orange and yellow fire. His clothes burned to ash, but any scorch mark that it left on Kain's skin healed instantly.

I tried to ignore the intense smell of burnt flesh as I thought of my next move. I managed to sit up, but I didn't think I'd be able to get to my feet anytime soon. The pain was subsiding, but I was having a hard time moving my limbs-

Something slid across the floor toward me. I glanced down and stared at a handgun. I quickly looked up at Krissy where she huddled on the floor in terror.

By scent alone, I discovered that she had been shot in the leg.

Kain's experiments had turned me into a freaking bloodhound.

Krissy gestured urgently to the gun, and I picked it up with great difficulty. I didn't think I'd be able to cock it, but I managed it with surprisingly quick speed. I took aim at Kain, but-

I had to wait for Ember to get out of the way before I could pull the trigger.

I watched in amazement as she threw flame after flame at her father. Each one engulfing him in the raging fires. They seemed to burn out quickly with minimal damage done.

I briefly wondered if I was fireproof too, or if Dr. Mason left that advantage specifically to Kain.

My brain sputtered at that thought, and I started shaking.

Everything was starting to catch up to me: The lack of food. The exhaustion. The physical and sensory changes. My injuries.

I needed to end this now before I went into severe shock.

The gun in my palm quivered as I tried to lift my arm to aim again.

Kain had somehow managed to get a hold of Ember's arm. The sound of her bone breaking was like an explosion. She shrieked in agony, but her father didn't loosen his powerful grip. He chuckled deeply in his throat before growling at her like an angry animal.

"You will pay for betraying me, Ember Lynch."

He wrapped his hand around her throat; ignoring the receding flames that cocooned her. She choked, but I didn't hear anything break this time. Thankfully.

"Nolan." John's voice was a breathless whisper, but I heard him loud and clear. "You got this. *You got this.*"

I nodded; mustering every ounce of strength I had left.

Hoping against hope that my aim was accurate despite my violent shaking-

I squeezed the trigger.

The gunshot was so loud, I cried out in pain. Blood trickled from my ears; soaking my fingers as I tried to cover them. For the longest moment, I didn't even know if I'd killed Kain or not.

Before I could pull myself together, I felt someone kneel down next to me. It was then that I realized I'd closed my eyes at some point. I forced them open; bracing for the impending assault.

But it wasn't Kain. This wasn't another attack.

I stared in disbelief at the fire girl. Even with smoke drifting from her charred clothing and her disheveled hair-

She was the most wonderful thing I'd ever seen.

"You killed him." Tears fell down her cheeks as she held her broken arm to her chest. "You killed my father."

The first thing that came to me was the need to apologize to her. To beg her to forgive me for being the one that had to do that. But, luckily, I bit my tongue before I started talking nonsense. I wasn't sorry for ridding this world of another monster, but-

This amazing woman didn't deserve any of this.

"You saved all of us."

Ember pressed her forehead to mine, and let out a shaky sigh. I didn't know if she was relieved, or if she was just numbly exhausted like I was.

The tightness in my chest loosened slightly, and I was finally able to fully exhale. In that moment, through all the pain and grief, I realized that I needed this.

We needed this.

We were merely resting. Our foreheads touching. Sharing calming breaths. But something ignited between us.

I knew that our tumultuous relationship had morphed into something else. Maybe it was solidarity, or maybe it was something more.

I wasn't entirely sure at this point.

I closed my eyes again at the comforting warmth that came from her. It was like she'd wrapped a blanket around me. But I wasn't a touchy guy, and my brother was mortally wounded.

"Please, help John."

Ember pulled away from me, and hurried to him. When she moved, I got a full view of Kain's large body crumpled on the floor of the infirmary. The smell of death hit me with full force, and I gagged. I willed myself not to throw up again.

I'd had enough of that to last me for a lifetime.

"Nolan." Krissy crawled her way over to me from the corner she was hunkered down in. "Where's Cade?"

I stared at her incredulously before struggling to my feet. Last I remembered, I shoved Cade to the concrete floor with an incredible amount of force. Hopefully, he was dead.

Cade could burn in hell alongside Kain for what they did to Phoenix.

As I stumbled toward John, the smell of his pain assaulted me. My stomach churned; bile racing up my throat.

"John, can you hear me?" Ember leaned over my brother's battered form. He hadn't moved the entire time I fought Kain.

I didn't hear if John replied or not. My vision went dark, and I lost my balance. Pain swept over me with such intensity that I was immediately rendered unconscious.

Chapter 30: John

I sat up before I was fully awake.

Breathing heavily, I forced my eyes open despite how painful it was. Kain snapped my spine. I wasn't sure how it was possible that I could move at all.

I forced myself to breathe evenly. Each inhale was absolute torture. Kain had beaten me so badly I was surprised I was still alive.

I stilled; attempting to get my bearings. I vaguely remembered Kain falling to the ground with a bullet in his brain. Everything after that was just a blur.

An IV was hooked up to my wrist. A few other monitors were connected to my fingers and chest.

"John?"

I turned my head with no small amount of effort. I had more than a few broken bones, alongside critical internal injuries. Kain's beating was the equivalent of being run down by a semi-truck.

So why was I conscious? Why was I hearing Eliza's voice?

"John, can you hear me?"

I blinked a few times until my vision came into focus. I drew in another steadying breath when I finally noticed her.

Eliza sat next to my hospital bed in a worn out chair. Shane slept in the corner behind her on a pile of pillows and blankets.

I must've been dreaming.

"John?" Eliza's tone was more urgent now. I finally exhaled, and glanced around the infirmary. My vision went in and out of focus.

"You need to lay back down." Eliza's fingers trembled when she pushed me back into the pillows.

"Eliza, how-" I paused and blinked again. Her face was so blurry, and my head wouldn't stop pounding. "How are you here?"

"Leif drove us to the bunker after George contacted him. He said you were locked in the bunker. He had a feeling that Shane would be needed. It took us a couple of days to get here."

Eliza's voice trembled as she ran her fingers through my hair.

"You were almost dead by the time we got to you. Luckily, George and Willow were able to keep you alive until we got here. Shane was able to heal you until you were stable. Then I made him take a break."

A million questions raced through my mind at once, but the most pressing was the one that came out of my mouth.

"Where's Nolan and Winter?"

"They're sharing the bed next to yours." Eliza gestured toward another hospital bed.

I gingerly turned my head so I could see them for myself. It wasn't that I didn't trust Eliza's word that they were safe. I just needed to see them. Especially my brother.

I vaguely remembered Nolan fighting Kain, but the images were nothing more than a blur in my memory.

He'd saved me. Again. He'd saved me.

I watched Nolan and Winter for a moment. Two brave souls that made it through a horrible journey to the other side.

The relief I felt at seeing them subsided when I studied them long enough.

Nolan was severely emaciated. Even his hair had thinned and dulled from the lack of nutrition. He looked like an actual corpse. Only the rise and fall of his shoulders as he breathed proved that he was still alive.

I had no idea how he managed to stand up to Kain. Let alone kill him.

Winter was a completely different story. She would've looked healthy if it wasn't for the IV she was hooked up to.

Nolan had his arm wrapped around her. His bandaged hand rested on her forearm. Directly above where the needle was. It wasn't hard to figure out that his embrace was the only reason she was able to sleep in the infirmary.

"Winter should be able to get out of here in the morning. I think the cure has worked. James took more of the cure back to the Community, so they should all be better soon too."

"What about Nolan?"

Eliza chuckled humorlessly.

"You're brother is the most stubborn person I've ever met. He wouldn't let Shane heal any of his injuries. He wouldn't let me help him either. He said you and Winter needed us more than he did."

I couldn't help but gape at her.

"It looks like a stiff breeze could blow him over."

"Yeah, well, looks can be deceiving," Nolan muttered without opening his eyes. "Glad you're doing okay, John. You had me worried."

I stared at my brother until his eyes opened. He scowled at me, and I couldn't help but smile. There was a time when I thought I'd never see that glare again.

I was so grateful to see it now.

"Why are you smiling?" Nolan asked with a raised eyebrow.

"You should let Eliza and Shane take care of you."

Nolan blew out a breath and shook his head.

"I'm different now, John. I can feel myself healing. It won't be long until I'm better."

I noticed that he didn't say '*I'm fine.*'

All that bravado that I was so used to seeing had been snuffed out of him. I could see it in his eyes. Maybe he was just tired, but I had a feeling that it was more than just that.

"Kain changed me. Luckily, he died before he could hurt anyone else. George even made sure that his body was cremated in case he was able to heal from a gunshot wound to the head."

Nolan talked in a whisper, but there was something off about his tone too. Being imprisoned, tortured, and experimented on had taken a lot out of him.

I held his gaze as he talked to me, but there wasn't the fierceness in his eyes that he'd always had before.

"Nolan, you're going to be okay. We're going to figure this out. I promise."

Finally, he rolled his eyes and smirked. That was another reaction I'd been desperate to see from him.

"Thanks for coming for me. I can't say that I really wanted you to, but I'm glad you did."

Emotion clogged my throat, and tears stung my eyes.

I should've tried to find Kain's bunker much sooner. Nolan suffered more than he should have. Now his genetic code was completely altered. He'd been tortured and poisoned.

I should've looked for him instead of assuming he was already gone.

Luckily, Eliza laid a hand on my arm before I could beg Nolan's forgiveness. I didn't deserve that from him.

"You better go back to sleep, John. Shane has more healing to do on you tomorrow. I doubt it's going to be pleasant for either of you."

I finally looked away from Nolan and glanced at Eliza. Her eyes were swimming with tears. I lifted my hand to wipe away a drop that escaped her eye. I rested my palm against her cheek as she leaned into my touch. She closed her eyes briefly; blinking the rest of the tears away.

"I'm so sorry you had to see me like that again."

She flinched and squeezed her eyes shut. I knew that seeing me mostly dead; not once, but twice, was too much for her to handle.

"I was supposed to get the cure and come back to you. I decided to infiltrate Kain's bunker instead."

Eliza sighed and leaned her forehead against mine.

"I don't like that you got hurt." Her breath tickled my face sweetly. "But I'm glad that you stopped Kain. Besides, I'm sure the women and children will love the underground bunker. Especially the plumbing and electricity."

I smiled and brushed my lips against hers gently. A pleasant sensation washed through me as she deepened the kiss. I was pretty sure that my entire mouth was bruised, but that didn't stop me from responding to Eliza with an urgent desperation.

I needed her next to me.

"There's room on this bed for two," I whispered when we finally broke our kiss.

Eliza raised her eyebrow and studied the hospital bed that I occupied. My feet practically dangled off the end, but I didn't care. I didn't want to sleep without her ever again.

"Sure there is; if the second person was an emaciated gnome."

I ignored her sarcasm, and gingerly scooted myself to the edge of the bed.

"You really shouldn't be moving, John."

I ignored her concern too. It hurt like crazy when I moved, but I didn't want her sleeping on the concrete floor. I patted the empty space on the bed, and Eliza sighed in defeat.

"Okay, but if you feel any unnecessary pain-"

"I'm fine," I lied.

Nolan chuckled from behind me.

If I wasn't in so much pain, I would've whirled around and stared at him. I couldn't remember the last time I'd heard my brother chuckle. It was extremely good to hear it. Especially considering everything he'd gone through.

Eliza checked my vitals once more, and crawled onto the bed. I draped my arm around her without putting too much strain on my joints. I finally felt like I could breathe again; holding her next to me. She tucked her head under my chin, and sighed in exhaustion.

It wasn't long until I felt like I was floating.

She had snuck something strong into my IV. I was okay with that though. I knew my recovery would take a while.

The drug induced sleep took me within seconds.

Chapter 31: Winter

A gentle hand shook me awake.

I knew that touch, but I couldn't place it with a name or a face. Was it my dad? No, he was dead. He couldn't be here. I didn't even know what he looked like.

"Time to get up, honey," the faceless man signed to me.

I should've been terrified, staring at a head with no face, but I felt oddly calm. I wasn't sure what it was about him, but I trusted him completely. I knew he loved me.

He loved me more than anything else in the world.

I sat up in bed urgently. I slept in again!

My heart pounded as I took a quick deep breath; glancing at the clock on my bedside table.

Seven-thirty.

The faceless man backed away from me; disappearing as though he were a ghost.

As though he'd never been there in the first place.

I flew out of bed and ran to the closet. I was wearing my summer pajamas; exposing a little bit of skin at my waist. I couldn't let dad see what I did the night before.

I was pretty sure he'd ground me for life.

I quickly changed into jeans and a sweater. Taking a deep breath, I went to the full length mirror that hung on the wall next to the door.

I smiled as I stared at my reflection.

My strawberry blonde hair was long. Almost brushing my hips. My green eyes flashed back at me mischievously. Freckles splattered across my nose and cheeks.

I couldn't help but scowl at them in disgust. I used to not care about my freckles, but recently I'd grown to hate them. I couldn't wait for the day my dad would allow me to wear make-up to conceal them.

Twelve was old enough to wear make-up, right? It's not like I'd be drawing anymore attention to myself. Using sign language to communicate already did that for me.

I glanced at the tablet that sat on the desk on the other side of the bedroom. I smiled at it, but I had no idea why I felt such a connection to the rectangular device. It gave me strange feelings though. A mixture of excitement and joy-

Along with a touch of regret.

I turned back to the mirror in front of me, and my smile widened. Yeah, dad would hate it, but we needed the connection. I had no idea what would happen in my future, or hers. We needed something memorable to tie us to each other. A symbol of our friendship and sisterhood.

I could always show it to dad later when I was a few years older.

I lifted my sweater and stared at the white bandaged that covered a small section of my stomach. I gently peeled it away; feeling the same flutter of excitement I had when I watched the artist prepare his needles.

The rose and flames contrasted against my porcelain skin beautifully. The swirls of orange and yellow flame surrounding the deep red rose almost made me want to cry. I'd never forget the day I finally got to see her in person. The day we became more than just half-sisters. We became best friends.

I would never forget her.
She would never forget me.

I sat up abruptly, and tried desperately not to scream.

My head pounded as I fought to control the ice that wanted to burst out of me.

I looked around the room; taking too long to realize I was in the same place I'd fallen asleep in.

Willow, Shane, and Leif were all sleeping in various places on the couch and floor. We'd all moved to Willow's room from the infirmary the night before.

Willow and Shane had insisted that Nolan sleep on the only bed in the room, since he was still recovering from his wounds. Of course, he refused to let me sleep anywhere without him-

Despite the fact that I could have a nightmare and freeze him to death in our sleep.

I pressed my hands to my temples when my headache intensified. I burst into tears as remnants of my dream slowly came to me.

Rose. Rose. Rose.

I barely registered Nolan's hand on my back, or how he kept trying to get me to look at him. He was talking, but I didn't really hear what he was saying. It sounded soothing, but it did nothing to ease my internal suffering.

I'd forgotten her.

I'd forgotten the one person that needed me the most in this world.

No wonder Ember hated me.

Tears dripped from my eyes, and Nolan kissed my forehead. His arms wrapped around me, and I involuntarily leaned into him. For the longest time, I couldn't speak.

I just sobbed as the only memory I had of my past kept assaulting me over and over again. I snuck out of my father's apartment to meet Ember. We rode the metro to the tattoo artist's office. I even remembered how painfully exciting it was to get inked with a design Ember and I created together.

Without thinking, I pulled away from Nolan and lifted my shirt. I stared in disbelief at the scarred flesh that used to be my tattoo. I choked back the fresh wave of sobs that I knew would break through eventually.

For now, I was just completely numb.

My tattoo was gone. Just like my memories.

"Love, can you please tell me?"

I glanced at him, and noticed that he was staring at my stomach in concern. I quickly pulled my shirt back down to cover the scars that were there.

"What happened?"

His hand rested on my stomach over where the scar was. Tears filled my eyes again, but I blinked them away. I didn't know where to begin. I had so many questions, and the one person that could answer them absolutely hated me.

I didn't even know if Ember was still in the bunker. I hadn't seen her since shortly after Kain was killed five days ago.

Why would I remember Ember, but not my father?

The tears came hard and fast again. I'd never cried like this before over my lost memories. But I'd never recovered a memory through a dream before either.

"Rose," I choked out between sobs.

"What?" Nolan studied me, worriedly.

"Rose." I gripped his arms with numb fingers, a lot harder than I meant to, but he didn't react to the pain at all. My nails dug into his skin as the panic hit me with full force. "My name was Rose."

I started shaking; my teeth chattering as though I was cold.

Shock. I'd experienced it enough to know when I was suffering from it.

Nolan's face gentled as he ran his hands up and down my arms, soothingly. Making the effort to soften his touch.

"Are you sure?" Unable to find my voice, I merely nodded. "How do you know?"

I took a shaky breath as he pulled me into his embrace. I buried my face into his shirt and closed my eyes. I took a moment to bask in his soft skin, and how his heart beat against me. He smelled of soap with a hint of perspiration.

Everything about him was completely soothing. There was no anger. No angst. It was just the two of us, and his comforting touch.

I told him everything that Ember said around the fire the night we escaped Brian and his Vigilantes. I told him about the tattoo on her wrist, and how I'd had a matching one on my stomach. I told him every detail of my dream.

My strawberry blonde hair, green eyes, and freckles. I told him about my bedroom, and the faceless man that I didn't know.

With each new revelation, Nolan's arms tightened around me. He didn't hurt me, but I couldn't move even if I wanted to.

His warmth was so comforting. It was the only reason I was able to put my memory into words.

When I stopped talking Nolan's lips brushed against my temple in a soft caress.

"Anything else you remembered?"

I shook my head; realizing that I'd soaked Nolan's shirt with my tears. He didn't seem to care though, so I didn't give it much thought.

"Why would I remember Ember and not my father?"

Nolan kissed my forehead; trying to lend me comfort.

"You probably remembered Ember because she told you about how she got her tattoo. Somewhere in your subconscious mind you must've been able to unlock that memory. Dr. Darkwood removed your tattoo in hopes that you'd never remember."

I knew that Nolan was right. The only reason I remembered Ember, my name, and the tattoo was because she told me about it. I would've never remembered it on my own.

The thought wasn't exactly comforting, so I pushed it to the back of my mind.

"I'll never remember my father. He's faceless in my memories."

Nolan pulled away from me and met my eyes. His blue irises were swimming with tears, but he didn't look away. He held my gaze and cleared his throat before he spoke.

"I wish there was something I could do to help you remember him. Maybe we could ask Ember-"

I quickly shook my head. There was no way I'd be asking Ember about anything.

"Okay, we don't have to ask her." Nolan's immediate agreement caught me off guard. He usually argued his point until he was blue in the face. "Only you can decide where we go from here concerning your memories."

I wiped my eyes with my sleeve and nodded. I didn't want anything to do with Ember at the moment. I wasn't sure if I could face her. I didn't think I could trust her. Not after everything that had happened.

"Are you going to be okay?" Nolan hadn't taken his eyes off of my face. His hand had gone back to my stomach where the tattoo used to be.

"I think so. Sorry, I soaked your shirt."

Nolan smirked and pulled his t-shirt over his head. He discarded it in the basket next to the bed, and shrugged nonchalantly.

I had to use my powers to stop myself from blushing.

Over the past couple of days, Nolan had gained a lot of muscle back. It was miraculous how quickly he recovered from his imprisonment.

We'd come to the determination that advanced healing was part of his abilities. He still had the horrific scars all over his back. He probably would always have them, but they were completely healed now.

He still had a hard time adjusting to his advanced hearing and sense of smell, but he'd told me that he'd get the hang of it eventually.

He could probably hear my heartbeat quicken and smell my embarrassment.

"I just thought of something," Nolan whispered, nonchalantly, as though he hadn't just torn his shirt off and made me blush like crazy. "You're probably older than we thought you were."

I stared at his chest for a second longer before meeting his fierce blue eyes.

"What?"

"Ember told you that her half sister was a year older than her. We know that Ember is fifteen. So that would make you sixteen. We're the same age."

He was right. Nolan just had a birthday recently. I didn't know when my birthday was, but I didn't think that was important. Especially considering all the other things I'd forgotten.

"We know your real name." Nolan smiled uncertainly. "Do you still want to go by 'Winter'? Or should we call you 'Rose'?"

All I could do was blink at him stupidly for a few seconds. I had no memory of anyone calling me *'Rose'* and something about it didn't feel right.

That was a name from another lifetime. One that I couldn't remember.

"Call me Winter. It's who I am."

Nolan's lips kicked up into a smile. "Yeah, it is."

I smiled back at him, and he leaned in closer to me. He didn't stop until his lips were practically on mine. With merely a breath of space between us, he paused.

I closed my eyes in anticipation.

He hadn't kissed me, *really kissed me*, since the day he rescued me from Dr. Darkwood's lab. It was one of my most cherished memories. One that I hoped I'd never forget.

"Can I kiss you?" My breath hitched at his words.

I responded by pressing my cold lips to his warmth.

Blood roared in my ears; my skin heating within seconds. I gasped for air as Nolan's hands went to my waist; holding me in a tight grip that was almost bruising. My fingers wandered to his hair as his lips moved over mine. His warmth entangled with my coolness. Stirring a desire inside of me that I'd never experienced before-

At least, not in my current memories, but I doubted that anyone had ever kissed me like this.

My hands fisted. I held his hair in my grip; loving the feel of his soft strands. His fingers flexed on my waist in response; sending a pleasant shiver through me.

Nolan groaned and forced himself to pull away. The kiss ended, but his taste and scent remained with me.

I didn't know if it was because we were both genetically enhanced now, but that kiss blew our first one out of the water.

I had to stop myself from leaning in and getting carried away. It helped that Nolan held me away from him, and I couldn't really move. His intense blue gaze bore into me, and I had to force myself not to blush again.

"I've been stubborn about this. I know it hurts you that I haven't told you how I feel. I'm so sorry about that. I just feel like '*I love you*' is too small a declaration for what I feel for you. I don't know how to put into words what I feel when I look at you. You are the best thing that has ever happened to me, Winter."

I stared at him in disbelief.

"We were strangers, and you went out of your way to help me when I was sick. You never gave up on me. Even when I was a complete jerk."

I smiled at that and snuggled into his chest.

"Yeah, well, you were just testing me."

Nolan stiffened slightly at that.

"How did you know?" He sounded hesitant-

As though I'd just revealed something about him that not even he realized before.

"Because I know *you*, Nolan." I pulled back so I could see his face. "You are emotionally guarded. You tried to see if you could push me away."

"It didn't work."

"No, it didn't. Because I liked you from the start."

Nolan's expression was intense as he leaned in closer. His lips brushed mine in a soft caress.

"I *loved* you from the start." His tone made my stomach flutter. "From the second I saw you, I knew you were someone special. Someone that I couldn't live without."

My eyes grew wide, and I couldn't help but stare at him.

"I tried to deny it for a long time." He just kept talking; unaware of what his words were doing to my insides. "I'm so sorry I left you for the Vigilantes, but I felt like it was something I had to do. But I promise. I promise that I will never leave you again. I'm yours, Love. Forever."

My eyes filled with fresh tears.

Nolan was promising himself to me. I didn't know what relationships were like before the natural disasters, but I did understand the concept of it.

To give love to each other freely. Unconditionally.

"And I'm yours, Nolan. I love you. I always will."

Nolan smiled at that and kissed me again. My mind reeled from the sensations of his strength and warmth clashing with my cold. I craved how the heat spread through my body from his touch.

I didn't know how much time had passed when he finally pulled away from me.

"We need to get back to sleep if we're going to be of any use to John tomorrow."

I sighed, but nodded in agreement.

Nolan jumped out of the bed so fast, I could barely register what he was doing. Mere seconds later, he was back in the bed with a new t-shirt on.

I stared at him for a moment, and finally blinked in surprise.

"That's gonna be something I'll have to get used to."

"Me too." Nolan stared down at his shirt as though he was trying to figure out where it came from. "I didn't mean to go that fast."

"Well, I'm sure super speed will have it's uses. I guess it'll be even more annoying when we're hiking in the woods now. If I couldn't keep up before-"

Nolan smiled and pulled me closer to him. I buried my head in the crook of his arm and closed my eyes.

"I love how annoying you are."

I nudged him in the stomach playfully, and he chuckled. The sound rumbled through me and I grinned. I didn't have to open my eyes to see how peaceful his face was. With the softness in his voice and the secure way he held me-

I didn't have to worry about him anymore.

I knew he was going to be okay.

Kain had lost. We were together. I didn't know what the future held for us. There would, no doubt, be more trials to face in the morning.

But for now, at this very moment, we were at peace.

About the Author

Mariah Dyer lives in Palmer, Alaska with her family, where she was born and raised. She's had a love of books since a young age, and has been telling stories for most of her life. As a homeschooling mother of five children, she is fortunate enough to spend her days with her absolute favorite people. She is also blest to be married to her childhood best friend. She and her husband enjoy talking about stories, playing games, and going on adventures together.

Made in the USA
Columbia, SC
28 February 2025

8c413a2b-cf2f-4526-96b6-cadbaee721bdR01